The SPIRIT
of the BORDER

The SPIRIT of the BORDER

ZANE GREY

PINNACLE BOOKS
KENSINGTON PUBLISHING CORP.
www.kensingtonbooks.com

PINNACLE BOOKS are published by

Kensington Publishing Corp.
119 West 40th Street
New York, NY 10018

All Kensington titles, imprints, and distributed lines are available at special quantity discounts for bulk purchases for sales promotions, premiums, fund-raising, educational, or institutional use. Special book excerpts or customized printings can also be created to fit specific needs. For details, write or phone the office of the Kensington special sales manager: Kensington Publishing Corp., 119 West 40th Street, New York, NY 10018, attn: Special Sales Department; phone: 1-800-221-2647.

PINNACLE BOOKS and the Pinnacle logo are Reg. U.S. Pat. & TM Off.

ISBN-13: 978-0-7860-2263-2
ISBN-10: 0-7860-2263-9

First printing: November 2010

10 9 8 7 6 5 4 3 2 1

Printed in the United States of America

Introduction

The author does not intend to apologize for what many readers may call the "brutality" of the story; but rather to explain that its wild spirit is true to the life of the Western border as it was known only a little more than one hundred years ago.

The writer is the fortunate possessor of historical material of undoubted truth and interest. It is the long-lost journal of Colonel Ebenezer Zane, one of the most prominent of the hunter-pioneers who labored in the settlement of the Western country.

The story of that tragic period deserves a higher place in historical literature than it has thus far been given, and this unquestionably because of a lack of authentic data regarding the conquering of the wilderness. Considering how many years the pioneers struggled on the border of this country, the history of their efforts is meager and obscure.

If the years at the close of the eighteenth and the beginning of the nineteenth century were full of stirring adventure on the part of the colonists along the Atlantic coast, how crowded must they have been for the almost forgotten pioneers who daringly invaded the trackless wilds! None there was to chronicle the fight of these sturdy travelers toward the setting sun. The story of their stormy lives, of their heroism, and of their sacrifice for the benefit of future generations is too little known.

It is to a better understanding of those days that the author has labored to draw from his ancestor's notes a new and striking portrayal of the frontier; one which shall paint the pioneer's fever of freedom, that powerful impulse which lured so many to unmarked graves; one which shall show his work, his love, the effect of the causes which rendered his life so hard, and surely one which does not forget the wronged Indian.

The frontier in 1777 produced white men so savage as to be men in name only. These outcasts and renegades lived among the savages, and during thirty years harassed the border, perpetrating all manner of fiendish cruelties upon the settlers. They were no less cruel to the redmen whom they ruled, and at the height of their bloody careers made futile the Moravian missionaries' long labors and destroyed the beautiful hamlet of the Christian Indians, called Gnaddenhutten, or Village of Peace.

And while the border produced such outlaws so did it produce hunters like Boone, the Zanes, the McCollochs, and Wetzel, the strange, silent man whose deeds are still whispered in the country where he once roamed in his insatiate pursuit of savages and renegades, and who was purely a product of the times. Civilization could not have brought forth a man like Wetzel. Great revolutions, great crises, great moments come, and produce the men to deal with them.

The border needed Wetzel. The settlers would have needed many more years in which to make permanent homes had it not been for him. He was never a pioneer; but always a hunter after Indians. When not on the track of the savage foe, he was in the settlement, with his keen eye and ear ever alert for signs of the enemy. To the superstitious Indians he was a shadow, a spirit of the border, which breathed menace from the dark forests. To the settlers he was the right arm of defense, a fitting leader for those few implacable and unerring frontiersmen who made the settlement of the West a possibility.

And if this story of one of his relentless pursuits shows the man as he truly was, loved by the pioneers, respected and feared by redmen, and hated by renegades; if it softens a little the ruthless name history accords him, the writer will have been repaid.

—Z.G.

Chapter
I

"Nell, I'm growing powerful fond of you."

"So you must be, Master Joe, if often telling makes it true."

The girl spoke simply, and with an absence of that roguishness which was characteristic of her. Playful words, arch smiles, and a touch of coquetry had seemed natural to Nell; but now her grave tone and her almost wistful glance disconcerted Joe.

During all the long journey over the mountains she had been cheerful and bright, while now, when they were about to part, perhaps never to meet again, she showed him the deeper and more earnest side of her character. It checked his boldness as nothing else had done. Suddenly there came to him the real meaning of a woman's love when she bestows it without reservation. Silenced by the thought that he had not understood her at all and the knowledge that he had been half in sport, he gazed out over the wild country before them.

The scene impressed its quietness upon the young couple and brought more forcibly to their minds the fact that they were at the gateway of the unknown West; that somewhere beyond this rude frontier settlement, out there in those unbroken forests stretching dark and silent before them, was to be their future home.

From the high bank where they stood the land sloped and narrowed gradually until it ended in a sharp point which marked the last bit of land between the Allegheny and Monongahela rivers. Here these swift streams merged and formed the broad Ohio. The newborn river, even here at its beginning proud and swelling as if already certain of its faraway grandeur, swept majestically round a wide curve and apparently lost itself in the forest foliage.

On the narrow point of land commanding a view of the rivers stood a long, low structure enclosed by a stockade fence, on the four corners of which were little box-shaped houses that bulged out as if trying to see what was going on beneath. The massive timbers used in the construction of this fort, the square, compact form, and the small, dark holes cut into the walls, gave the structure a threatening, impregnable aspect.

Below Nell and Joe, on the bank, were many log cabins. The yellow clay which filled the chinks between the logs gave these a peculiar striped appearance. There was life and bustle in the vicinity of these dwellings, in sharp contrast with the still grandeur of the neighboring forests. There were canvas-covered wagons around which curly-headed youngsters were playing. Several horses were grazing on the short grass, and six red and white oxen munched at the hay that had been thrown to them. The smoke of many fires curled upward, and near the blaze hovered ruddy-faced women who stirred the contents of steaming kettles. One man swung an axe with a vigorous sweep and the clean, sharp strokes rang on the air; another hammered stakes into the ground on which to hang a kettle. Before a large cabin a fur trader was exhibiting his wares to three Indians. A second redskin was carrying a pack of pelts from a canoe drawn up on the river-bank. A small group of persons stood near; some were indifferent, and others gazed curiously at the savages. Two children peeped from behind their mother's skirts as if half-curious, half-frightened.

From this scene, the significance of which had just dawned on him, Joe turned his eyes again to his companion. It was a sweet face he saw; one that was sedate, but had a promise of innumerable smiles. The blue eyes could not long hide flashes of merriment. The girl turned, and the two young people looked at each other. Her eyes softened with a woman's gentleness as they rested upon him, for, broad of shoulder, and lithe and strong as a deerstalker, he was good to look at.

"Listen," she said. "We have known each other only three weeks. Since you joined our wagon train, and have been so kind to me and so helpful to make that long, rough ride endurable, you have won my regard. I—I cannot say more, even if I would. You told me you ran away from your Virginian home to seek adventure on the frontier, and that you knew no one in all this wild country. You even said you could not, or would not, work at farming. Perhaps my sister and I are as unfitted as you for this life; but we must cling to our uncle because he is the only relative we have. He has come out to join the Moravians and to preach the gospel to these Indians. We shall share his life, and help him all we can. You have been telling me you—you cared for me, and now that we are about to part I—I don't know what to say to you—unless it is: Give up this intention of yours to seek adventure, and come with us. It seems to me you need not hunt for excitement here; it will come unsought."

"I wish I were Jim," said he, suddenly.

"Who is Jim?"

"My brother."

"Tell me of him."

"There's nothing much to tell. He and I are all that are left of our people, as you and Kate of yours. Jim's a preacher, and the best fellow—oh! I cared a lot for Jim."

"Then why did you leave him?"

"I was tired of Williamsburg—I quarreled with a fellow, and hurt him. Besides, I wanted to see the West; I'd like to hunt deer and bear and fight Indians. Oh, I'm not much good."

"Was Jim the only one you cared for?" asked Nell, smiling. She was surprised to find him grave.

"Yes, except my horse and dog, and I had to leave them behind," answered Joe, bowing his head a little.

"You'd like to be Jim because he's a preacher, and could help Uncle convert the Indians?"

"Yes, partly that, but mostly because—somehow—something different you've said or done has made me care for you in a different way, and I'd like to be worthy of you."

"I don't think I can believe it, when you say you are 'no good,' " she replied.

"Nell," he cried, and suddenly grasped her hand.

She wrenched herself free, and leaped away from him. Her face was bright now, and the promise of smiles was made good.

"Behave yourself, sir." She tossed her head with a familiar backward motion to throw the chestnut hair from her face, and looked at him with eyes veiled slightly under their lashes. "You will go with Kate and me?"

Before he could answer, a cry from someone on the plain below attracted their attention. They turned and saw another wagon train pulling into the settlement. The children were shouting and running alongside the weary oxen; men and women went forward expectantly.

"That must be the train Uncle expected. Let us go down," said Nell.

Joe did not answer but followed her down the path. When they gained a clump of willows near the cabins he bent forward and took her hand. She saw the reckless gleam in his eyes.

"Don't. They'll see," she whispered.

"If that's the only reason you have, I reckon I don't care," said Joe.

"What do you mean? I didn't say—I didn't tell—oh! let me go!" implored Nell.

She tried to release the hand Joe had grasped in his broad palm, but in vain; the more she struggled the firmer was his hold. A frown wrinkled her brow and her eyes sparkled with spirit. She saw the fur trader's wife looking out of the window, and remembered laughing and telling the good woman she did not like this young man; it was, perhaps, because she feared those sharp eyes that she resented his audacity. She opened her mouth to rebuke him; but no words came. Joe had bent his head and softly closed her lips with his own.

For a single instant during which Nell stood transfixed, as if with surprise, and looking up at Joe, she was dumb. Usually the girl was ready with sharp or saucy words and impulsive in her movements; but now the bewilderment of being kissed, particularly within view of the trader's wife, confused her. Then she heard voices, and as Joe turned away with a smile on his face, the unusual warmth in her heart was followed by an angry throbbing.

Joe's tall figure stood out distinctly as he leisurely strolled toward the incoming wagon train without looking backward. Flashing after him a glance that boded wordy trouble in the future, she ran into the cabin.

As she entered the door it seemed certain the grizzled

frontiersman sitting on the bench outside had grinned knowingly at her and winked as if to say he would keep her secret.
Mrs. Wentz, the fur trader's wife, was seated by the open
window which faced the fort; she was a large woman, strong
of feature, and with that calm placidity of expression common to people who have lived long in sparsely populated
districts. Nell glanced furtively at her and thought she de-
tected the shadow of a smile in the gray eyes.

"I saw you and your sweetheart kissing behind the willow," Mrs. Wentz said in a matter-of-fact voice. "I don't see
why you need hide to do it. We folks out here like to see the
young people sparkin'. Your young man is a fine-appearin'
chap. I felt certain you was sweethearts, for all you allowed
you'd known him only a few days. Lize Davis said she saw
he was sweet on you. I like his face. Jake, my man, says as
how he'll make a good husband for you, and he'll take to the
frontier like a duck does to water. I'm sorry you'll not tarry
here awhile. We don't see many lasses, especially any as
pretty as you, and you'll find it more quiet and lonesome the
farther West you get. Jake knows all about Fort Henry, and
Jeff Lynn, the hunter outside, he knows Eb and Jack Zane,
and Wetzel, and all those Fort Henry men. You'll be gettin'
married out there, won't you?"

"You are—quite wrong," said Nell, who all the while
Mrs. Wentz was speaking grew rosier and rosier. "We're not
anything—"

Then Nell hesitated and finally ceased speaking. She saw
that denials or explanations were futile; the simple woman
had seen the kiss and formed her own conclusions. During
the few days Nell had spent at Fort Pitt she had come to understand that the dwellers on the frontier took everything as
a matter of course. She had seen them manifest a certain
pleasure, but neither surprise, concern, nor any of the quick
impulses so common among other people. And this was an-

other lesson Nell took to heart. She realized that she was entering upon a life absolutely different from her former one, and the thought caused her to shrink from the ordeal. Yet all the suggestions regarding her future home; the stories told about Indians, renegades, and of the wild border life, fascinated her. These people who had settled in this wild region were simple, honest, and brave; they accepted what came as facts not to be questioned, and believed what looked true. Evidently the fur trader's wife and her female neighbors had settled in their minds the relation in which the girl stood to Joe.

This latter reflection heightened Nell's resentment toward her lover. She stood with her face turned away from Mrs. Wentz; the little frown deepened, and she nervously tapped her foot on the floor.

"Where is my sister?" she presently asked.

"She went to see the wagon train come in. Everybody's out there."

Nell deliberated a moment and then went into the open air. She saw a number of canvas-covered wagons drawn up in front of the cabins; the vehicles were dusty and the wheels encrusted with yellow mud. The grizzled frontiersman who had smiled at Nell stood leaning on his gun, talking to three men, whose travel-stained and worn homespun clothes suggested a long and toilsome journey. There was the bustle of excitement incident to the arrival of strangers; to the quick exchange of greetings, the unloading of wagons and unharnessing of horses and oxen.

Nell looked here and there for her sister. Finally she saw her standing near her uncle while he conversed with one of the teamsters. The girl did not approach them; but glanced quickly around in search of someone else. At length she saw Joe unloading goods from one of the wagons; his back was turned toward her, but she at once recognized the challenge conveyed by the broad shoulders. She saw no other person; gave heed to nothing save what was to her, righteous indignation.

Hearing her footsteps, the young man turned, and, glancing at her admiringly, said:

"Good evening, miss."

Nell had not expected such a matter-of-fact greeting from Joe. There was not the slightest trace of repentance in his calm face, and he placidly continued his labor.

"Aren't you sorry you—you treated me so?" burst out Nell.

His coolness was exasperating. Instead of contrition and apology she had expected, and which was her due, he evidently intended to tease her, as he had done so often.

The young man dropped a blanket and stared.

"I don't understand," he said gravely. "I never saw you before."

This was too much for quick-tempered Nell. She had had some vague idea of forgiving him, after he had sued sufficiently for pardon; but now, forgetting her good intentions in the belief that he was making sport of her when he should have pleaded for forgiveness, she swiftly raised her hand and slapped him smartly.

The red blood flamed to the young man's face; as he staggered backward with his hand to his cheek, she heard a smothered exclamation behind her, and then the quick joyous barking of a dog.

When Nell turned she was amazed to see Joe standing beside the wagon, while a big white dog was leaping upon him. Suddenly she felt faint. Bewildered, she looked from Joe to the man she had just struck; but could not say which was the man who professed to love her.

"Jim! So you followed me!" cried Joe, starting forward and flinging his arms around the other.

"Yes, Joe, and right glad I am to find you," answered the young man, while a peculiar expression of pleasure came over his face.

"It's good to see you again! And here's my old dog Mose! But how on earth did you know? Where did you strike my trail? What are you going to do out here on the frontier? Tell me all. What happened after I left——"

Then Joe saw Nell standing nearby, pale and distressed, and he felt something was amiss. He glanced quickly from her to his brother; she seemed to be dazed, and Jim looked grave.

"Nell, this is my brother Jim, the one I told you about. Jim, this is my friend, Miss Wells."

"I am happy to meet Miss Wells," said Jim, with a smile, "even though she did slap my face for nothing."

"Slapped you? What for?" Then the truth dawned on Joe, and he laughed until the tears came into his eyes. "She took you for me! Ha, ha, ha! Oh, this is great!"

Nell's face was now rosy red and moisture glistened in her eyes, but she tried bravely to stand her ground. Humiliation had taken the place of anger.

"I—I am sorry, Mr. Downs. I did take you for him. He— he has insulted me." Then she turned and ran into the cabin.

Chapter
II

Joe and Jim were singularly alike. They were nearly the same size, very tall, but so heavily built as to appear of medium height, while their gray eyes and, indeed, every feature of their clean-cut faces corresponded so exactly as to proclaim them brothers.

"Already up to your old tricks?" asked Jim, with his hand on Joe's shoulder, as they both watched Nell's flight.

"I'm really fond of her, Jim, and didn't mean to hurt her feelings. But tell me about yourself; what made you come West?"

"To teach the Indians, and I was, no doubt, strongly influenced by your being here."

"You're going to do as you ever have—make some sacrifice. You are always devoting yourself; if not to me, to some other. Now it's your life you're giving up. To try to convert the redskins and influence me for good is in both cases impossible. How often have I said there wasn't any good in me! My desire is to kill Indians, not preach to them, Jim. I'm glad to see you, but I wish you hadn't come. This wild frontier is no place for a preacher."

"I think it is," said Jim, quietly.

"What of Rose—the girl you were to marry?"

Joe glanced quickly at his brother. Jim's face paled slightly as he turned away.

"I'll speak once more of her, and then, never again," he answered. "You knew Rose better than I did. Once you tried to tell me she was too fond of admiration, and I rebuked you; but now I see that your wider experience of women had taught you things I could not then understand. She was untrue. When you left Williamsburg, apparently because you had gambled with Jewett and afterward fought him, I was not misled. You made the game of cards a pretence; you sought it simply as an opportunity to wreak your vengeance on him for his villainy toward me. Well, it's all over now. Though you cruelly beat and left him disfigured for life, he will live, and you are saved from murder, thank God! When I learned of your departure I yearned to follow. Then I met a preacher who spoke of having intended to go West with a Mr. Wells, of the Moravian Mission. I immediately said I would go in his place, and here I am. I'm fortunate in that I have found both him and you."

"I'm sorry I didn't kill Jewett; I certainly meant to. Anyway, there's some comfort in knowing I left my mark on him. He was a sneaking, cold-blooded fellow, with his white hair and pale face, and always fawning round the girls. I hated him, and gave it to him good." Joe spoke musingly and complacently as though it was a trivial thing to compass the killing of a man.

"Well, Jim, you're here now, and there's no help for it. We'll go along with this Moravian preacher and his nieces. If you haven't any great regrets for the past, why, all may be well yet. I can see that the border is the place for me. But now, Jim, for once in your life take a word of advice from me. We're out in the frontier, where every man looks after himself. Your being a minister won't protect you here where every man wears a knife and a tomahawk, and where most of them are desperadoes. Cut out that soft voice and most of your gentle ways, and be a little more like your brother. Be as kind as you like, and preach all you want to; but when some of these buckskin-legged frontiersmen try to walk all over you, as they will, take your own part in a way you have never taken it before. I had my lesson the first few days out with that wagon-train. It was a case of four fights; but I'm all right now."

"Joe, I won't run, if that's what you mean," answered Jim, with a laugh. "Yes, I understand that a new life begins here, and I am content. If I can find my work in it, and remain with you, I shall be happy."

"Ah! old Mose! I'm glad to see you," Joe cried to the big dog who came nosing round him. "You've brought this old fellow; did you bring the horses?"

"Look behind the wagon."

With the dog bounding before him, Joe did as he was directed, and there found two horses tethered side by side. Little wonder that his eyes gleamed with delight. One was jet-black; the other iron-gray; and in every line the clean-limbed animals showed the thoroughbred. The black threw up his slim head and whinnied, with affection clearly shining in his soft, dark eyes as he recognized his master.

"Lance, old fellow, how did I ever leave you?" murmured Joe, as he threw his arm over the arched neck. Mose stood by, looking up and wagging his tail in token of happiness at the reunion of the three old friends. There were tears in Joe's eyes when, with a last affectionate caress, he turned away from his pet.

"Come, Jim, I'll take you to Mr. Wells."

They started across the little square, while Mose went back under the wagon; but at a word from Joe he bounded after them, trotting contentedly at their heels. Halfway to the cabins a big, rawboned teamster, singing in a drunken voice, came staggering toward them. Evidently he had just left the group of people who had gathered near the Indians.

"I didn't expect to see drunkenness out here," said Jim, in a low tone.

"There's lots of it. I saw that fellow yesterday when he couldn't walk. Wentz told me he was a bad customer."

The teamster, his red face bathed in perspiration, and his sleeves rolled up, showing brown, knotty arms, lurched toward them. As they met he aimed a kick at the dog; but Mose leaped nimbly aside, avoiding the heavy boot. He did not growl nor show his teeth, but the great white head sank forward a little, and the lithe body crouched for a spring.

"Don't touch that dog; he'll tear your leg off!" Joe cried sharply.

"Say, pard, cum an' hev a drink," replied the teamster, with a friendly leer.

"I don't drink," answered Joe, curtly, and moved on.

The teamster growled something of which only the word "parson" was intelligible to the brothers. Joe stopped and looked back. His gray eyes seemed to contract; they did not flash, but shaded and lost their warmth. Jim saw the change, and knowing what it signified, took Joe's arm as he gently urged him away. The teamster's shrill voice could be heard until they entered the fur trader's cabin.

An old man with long, white hair flowing from beneath his wide-brimmed hat sat near the door holding one of Mrs. Wentz's children on his knee. His face was deep-lined and serious, but kindness shone from his mild blue eyes.

"Mr. Wells, this is my brother James. He is a preacher, and has come in place of the man you expected from Williamsburg."

The old minister arose and extended his hand, gazing

earnestly at the newcomer meanwhile. Evidently he approved of what he saw in his quick scrutiny of the other's face, for his lips were wreathed with a smile of welcome.

"Mr. Downs, I am glad to meet you, and to know you will go with me. I thank God I shall take into the wilderness one who is young enough to carry on the work when my days are done."

"I will make it my duty to help you in whatsoever way lies in my power," answered Jim, earnestly.

"We have a great work before us. I have heard many scoffers who claim that it is worse than folly to try to teach these fierce savages Christianity; but I know it can be done, and my heart is in the work. I have no fear; yet I would not conceal from you, young man, that the danger of going among these hostile Indians must be great."

"I will not hesitate because of that. My sympathy is with the redman. I have had an opportunity of studying Indian nature and believe the race inherently noble. He has been driven to make war, and I want to help him into other paths."

Joe left the two ministers talking earnestly and turned toward Mrs. Wentz. The fur trader's wife was glowing with pleasure. She held in her hand several rude trinkets and was explaining to her listener, a young woman, that the toys were for the children, having been brought all the way from Williamsburg.

"Kate, where's Nell?" Joe asked of the girl.

"She went on an errand for Mrs. Wentz."

Kate Wells was the opposite of her sister. Her motions were slow, easy and consistent with her large, full form. Her brown eyes and hair contrasted sharply with Nell's. The greatest difference in the sisters lay in that Nell's face was sparkling and full of the fire of her eager young life, while Kate's was calm, like the unruffled surface of a deep lake.

"That's Jim, my brother. We're going with you," said Joe.

"Are you? I'm glad," answered the girl, looking at the handsome, earnest face of the young minister.

"Your brother's like you for all the world," whispered Mrs. Wentz.

"He does look like you," said Kate, with her slow smile.

"Which means you think, or hope, that that is all," retorted Joe, laughingly. "Well, Kate, there the resemblance ends, thank God for Jim!"

He spoke in a sad, bitter tone which caused both women to look at him wonderingly. Joe had to them ever been full of surprises; never until then had they seen evidences of sadness in his face. A moment's silence ensued. Mrs. Wentz gazed lovingly at the children who were playing with the trinkets, while Kate mused over the young man's remark and began studying his half-averted face. She felt warmly drawn to him by the strange expression in the glance he had given his brother. The tenderness in his eyes did not harmonize with much of this wild and reckless boy's behavior. To Kate he had always seemed so bold, so cold, so different from other men, and yet here was proof that Master Joe loved his brother.

The murmured conversation of the two ministers was interrupted by a low cry from outside the cabin. A loud, coarse laugh followed, and then a husky voice:

"Hol' on, my purty lass."

Joe took two long strides, and was on the doorstep. He saw Nell struggling violently in the grasp of the half-drunken teamster.

"I'll jes' hev to kiss this lassie fer luck," he said in a tone of good humor.

At the same instant Joe saw three loungers laughing, and a fourth, the grizzled frontiersman, starting forward with a yell.

"Let me go!" cried Nell.

Just when the teamster had pulled her close to him and was bending his red, moist face to hers, two brown, sinewy hands grasped his neck with an angry clutch. Deprived thus of breath, his mouth opened, his tongue protruded; his eyes seemed starting from their sockets, and his arms beat the air. Then he was lifted and flung with a crash against the cabin wall. Falling, he lay in a heap on the grass, while the blood flowed from a cut on his temple.

"What's this?" cried a man, authoritatively. He had come swiftly up, and arrived at the scene where stood the grizzled frontiersman.

"It was purty handy, Wentz. I couldn't hev did better myself, and I was comin' for that purpose," said the frontiersman. "Leffler was tryin' to kiss the lass. He's been drunk fer two days. That little girl's sweetheart kin handle himself some, now you take my word on it."

"I'll agree Leff's bad when he's drinkin'," answered the fur trader, and to Joe he added, "he's liable to look you up when he comes around."

"Tell him if I am here when he gets sober, I'll kill him," Joe cried in a sharp voice. His gaze rested once more on the fallen teamster, and again an odd contraction of his eyes was noticeable. The glance was cutting, as if with the flash of cold gray steel. "Nell, I'm sorry I wasn't round sooner," he said, apologetically, as if it was owing to his neglect the affair had happened.

As they entered the cabin Nell stole a glance at him. This was the third time he had injured a man because of her. She had on several occasions seen that cold, steely glare in his eyes, and it had always frightened her. It was gone, however, before they were inside the building. He said something which she did not hear distinctly, and his calm voice allayed her excitement. She had been angry with him; but now she realized that her resentment had disappeared. He had spoken

so kindly after the outburst. Had he not shown that he considered himself her protector and lover? A strange emotion,
sweet and subtle as the taste of wine, thrilled her, while a
sense of fear because of his strength was mingled with her
pride in it. Any other girl would have been glad to have such
a champion; she would, too, hereafter, for he was a man of
whom to be proud.

"Look here, Nell, you haven't spoken to me," Joe cried
suddenly, seeming to understand that she had not even heard
what he said, so engrossed had she been with her reflections.
"Are you mad with me yet?" he continued. "Why, Nell, I'm
in—I love you!"

Evidently Joe thought such a fact a sufficient reason for
any act on his part. His tender tone conquered Nell, and she
turned to him with flushed cheeks and glad eyes.

"I wasn't angry at all," she whispered, and then, eluding
the arm he extended, she ran into the other room.

Chapter
III

Joe lounged in the doorway of the cabin, thoughtfully contemplating two quiet figures that were lying in the shade of a maple tree. One he recognized as the Indian with whom Jim had spent an earnest hour that morning; the red son of the woods was wrapped in slumber. He had placed under his head a many-hued homespun shirt which the young preacher had given him; but while asleep his head had rolled off this improvised pillow, and the bright garment lay free, attracting the eye. Certainly it had led to the train of thought which had found lodgment in Joe's fertile brain.

The other sleeper was a short, stout man whom Joe had seen several times before. This last fellow did not appear to be well-balanced in his mind, and was the butt of the settlers' jokes, while the children called him "Loorey." He, like the Indian, was sleeping off the effects of the previous night's dissipation.

During a few moments Joe regarded the recumbent figures with an expression on his face which told that he thought in them were great possibilities for sport. With one quick glance around he disappeared within the cabin, and when he showed himself at the door, surveying the village square with mirthful eyes, he held in his hand a small basket of Indian design. It was made of twisted grass, and simply contained several bits of soft, chalky stone such as the Indians used for painting, which collection Joe had discovered among the fur trader's wares.

He glanced around once more, and saw that all those in sight were busy with their work. He gave the short man a push, and chuckled when there was no response other than a lazy grunt. Joe took the Indian's gaudy shirt, and, lifting Loorey, slipped it around him, shoved the latter's arm through the sleeves, and buttoned it in front. He streaked the round face with red and white paint, and then, dexterously extracting the eagle plume from the Indian's headdress, stuck it in Loorey's thick shock of hair. It was all done in a moment, after which Joe replaced the basket and went down to the river.

Several times that morning he had visited the rude wharf where Jeff Lynn, the grizzled old frontiersman, busied himself with preparations for the raft journey down the Ohio.

Lynn had been employed to guide the missionary's party to Fort Henry, and as the brothers had acquainted him with their intention of accompanying the travelers, he had constructed a raft for them and their horses.

Joe laughed when he saw the dozen two-foot logs fastened together, upon which a rude shack had been erected for shelter. This slight protection from the sun and storm was all the brothers would have on their long journey.

Joe noted, however, that the larger raft had been prepared with some thought for the comfort of the girls. The floor of the little hut was raised so that the waves which broke over the logs could not reach it. Taking a peep into the structure, Joe was pleased to see that Nell and Kate would be comfortable, even during a storm. A buffalo robe and two red blankets gave to the interior a cosy, warm look. He observed that some of the girls' luggage was already onboard.

"When'll we be off?" he inquired.

"Sunup," answered Lynn, briefly.

"I'm glad of that. I like to be on the go in the early morning," said Joe, cheerfully.

"Most folks from over Eastways ain't in a hurry to tackle the river," replied Lynn, eyeing Joe sharply.

"It's a beautiful river, and I'd like to sail on it from here to where it ends, and then come back to go again," Joe replied, warmly.

"In a hurry to be a-goin'? I'll allow you'll see some slim red devils, with feathers in their hair, slippin' among the trees along the bank, and mebbe you'll hear the ping which's made when whistlin' lead hits. Perhaps you'll want to be back here by termorrer sundown."

"Not I," said Joe, with his short, cool laugh.

The old frontiersman slowly finished his task of coiling up a rope of wet cowhide, and then, producing a dirty pipe, he took a live ember from the fire and placed it on the bowl. He sucked slowly at the pipe stem, and soon puffed out a great cloud of smoke. Sitting on a log, he deliberately surveyed the robust shoulders and long, heavy limbs of the young man, with a keen appreciation of their symmetry and strength. Agility, endurance, and courage were more to a borderman than all else; a newcomer on the frontier was always "sized up" with reference to these "points" and respected in proportion to the measure in which he possessed them.

Old Jeff Lynn, riverman, hunter, frontiersman, puffed slowly at his pipe while he mused thus to himself: "Mebbe I'm wrong in takin' a likin' to this youngster so sudden. Mebbe it's because I'm fond of his sunny-haired lass, an' ag'in mebbe it's because I'm gettin' old an' likes young folks better'n I onct did. Anyway, I'm kinder thinkin', if this young feller gits worked out, say fer about twenty pounds less, he'll lick a whole raft-load of wildcats."

Joe walked to and fro on the logs, ascertained how the raft was put together, and took a pull on the long, clumsy steering oar. At length he seated himself beside Lynn. He was eager to ask questions; to know about the rafts, the river, the forest, the Indians—everything in connection with this wild life; but already he had learned that questioning these frontiersmen is a sure means of closing their lips.

"Ever handle the long rifle?" asked Lynn, after a silence.

"Yes," answered Joe, simply.

"Ever shoot anythin'?" the frontiersman questioned, when he had taken four or five puffs at his pipe.

"Squirrels."

"Good practice, shootin' squirrels," observed Jeff, after another silence, long enough to allow Joe to talk if he was so inclined. "Kin ye hit one—say, a hundred yards?"

"Yes, but not every time in the head," returned Joe. There was an apologetic tone in his answer.

Another interval followed in which neither spoke. Jeff was slowly pursuing his line of thought. After Joe's last remark he returned his pipe to his pocket and brought out a tobacco pouch. He tore off a large portion of the weed and thrust it into his mouth. Then he held out the little buckskin sack to Joe.

"Hev a chew," he said.

To offer tobacco to anyone was absolutely a borderman's guarantee of friendliness toward that person.

Jeff expectorated half a dozen times, each time coming a little nearer the stone he was aiming at, some five yards distant. Possibly this was the borderman's way of oiling up his conversational machinery. At all events, he commenced to talk.

"Yer brother's goin' to preach out here, ain't he? Preachin' is all right, I'll allow; but I'm kinder doubtful about preachin' to redskins. Howsumever, I've knowed Injuns who are good fellows, and there's no tellin'. What are ye goin' in fer—farmin'?"

"No, I wouldn't make a good farmer."

"Jest cum out kinder wild like, eh?" rejoined Jeff, knowingly.

"I wanted to come West because I was tired of tame life. I love the forest; I want to fish and hunt; and I think I'd like to—to see Indians."

"I kinder thought so," said the old frontiersman, nodding his head as though he perfectly understood Joe's case. "Well, lad, where you're goin' seein' Injuns ain't a matter of choice. You has to see 'em, and fight 'em, too. We've had bad times for years out here on the border, and I'm thinkin' wuss is comin'. Did ye ever hear the name Girty?"

"Yes; he's a renegade."

"He's a traitor, and Jim and George Girty, his brother, are p'isin rattlesnake Injuns. Simon Girty's bad enough; but Jim's the wust. He's now wusser'n a full-blooded Delaware. He's all the time on the lookout to capture white wimen to take to his Injun teepee. Simon Girty and his pals, McKee and Elliott, deserted from that thar fort right afore yer eyes. They're now livin' among the redskins down Fort Henry way, raisin' as much hell fer the settlers as they kin."

"Is Fort Henry near the Indian towns?" asked Joe.

"There's Delawares, Shawnees, and Hurons all along the Ohio below Fort Henry."

"Where is the Moravian Mission located?"

"Why, lad, the Village of Peace, as the Injuns call it, is right in the midst of that Injun country. I s'pect it's a matter of a hundred miles below and cross-country a little from Fort Henry."

"The fort must be an important point, is it not?"

"Wal, I guess so. It's the last place on the river," answered Lynn, with a grim smile. "There's only a stockade there, an' a handful of men. The Injuns hev swarmed down on it time and ag'in, but they hev never burned it. Only such men as Colonel Zane, his brother Jack, and Wetzel could hev kept that fort standin' all these bloody years. Eb Zane's got but a few men, yet he kin handle 'em some, an' with such scouts as Jack Zane and Wetzel, he allus knows what's goin' on among the Injuns."

"I've heard of Colonel Zane. He was an officer under Lord Dunmore. The hunters here speak often of Jack Zane and Wetzel. What are they?"

"Jack Zane is a hunter an' guide. I knowed him well a few years back. He's a quiet, mild chap; but a streak of chain-lightnin' when he's riled. Wetzel is an Injunkiller. Some people say as how he's crazy over scalp-huntin'; but I reckon that's not so. I've seen him a few times. He don't hang round the settlement 'cept when the Injuns are up, an' nobody sees him much. At home he sets round silent-like, an' then mebbe next mornin' he'll be gone, an' won't show up fer days or weeks. But all the frontier knows of his deeds. Fer instance, I've hearn of settlers gettin' up in the mornin' an' findin' a couple of dead and scalped Injuns right in front of their cabins. No one knowed who killed 'em, but everybody says 'Wetzel.' He's allus warnin' the settlers when they need to flee to the fort, and sure he's right every time, because when these men go back to their cabins they find nothin' but ashes. There couldn't be any farmin' done out there but fer Wetzel."

"What does he look like?" questioned Joe, much interested.

"Wetzel stands straight as the oak over thar. He'd hev to go sideways to git his shoulders in that door, but he's as light of foot an' fast as a deer. An' his eyes—why, lad, ye kin hardly look into 'em. If you ever see Wetzel you'll know him to onct."

"I want to see him," Joe spoke quickly, his eyes lighting with an eager flash. "He must be a great fighter."

"Is he? Lew Wetzel is the heftiest of 'em all, an' we hev some as kin fight out here. I was down the river a few years ago and joined a party to go out an' hunt up some redskins as had been reported. Wetzel was with us. We soon struck Injun sign, and then come on to a lot of the pesky varmints. We was all fer goin' home, because we had a small force. When we started to go we finds Wetzel sittin' calmlike on a log. We said: 'Ain't ye goin' home?' and he replied, 'I come out to find redskins, an' now as we've found 'em, I'm not goin' to run away.' An' we left him settin' thar. Oh, Wetzel is a fighter!"

"I hope I shall see him," said Joe once more, the warm light, which made him look so boyish, still glowing in his face.

"Mebbe ye'll git to; and sure ye'll see redskins, an' not tame ones, nuther."

At this moment the sound of excited voices near the cabins broke in upon the conversation. Joe saw several persons run toward the large cabin and disappear behind it. He smiled as he thought perhaps the commotion had been caused by the awakening of the Indian brave.

Rising to his feet, Joe went toward the cabin, and soon saw the cause of the excitement. A small crowd of men and women, all laughing and talking, surrounded the Indian brave and the little stout fellow. Joe heard someone groan, and then a deep, guttural voice:

"Paleface—big steal—ugh! Injun mad—heap mad—kill paleface."

After elbowing his way into the group, Joe saw the Indian holding Loorey with one hand, while he poked him in the ribs with the other. The captive's face was the picture of dismay: even the streaks of paint did not hide his look of fear and bewilderment. The poor, half-witted fellow was so badly frightened that he could only groan.

"Silvertip scalp paleface. Ugh!" growled the savage, giving Loorey another blow. This time he bent over in pain. The bystanders were divided in feeling; the men laughed, while the women murmured sympathetically.

"This's not a bit funny," muttered Joe, as he pushed his way nearly to the middle of the crowd. Then he stretched out a long arm that, bare and brawny, looked as though it might have been a blacksmith's, and grasped the Indian's sinewy wrist with a force that made him loosen his hold on Loorey instantly.

"I stole the shirt—fun—joke," said Joe. "Scalp me if you want to scalp anyone."

The Indian looked quickly at the powerful form before him. With a twist he slipped his arm from Joe's grasp.

"Big paleface heap fun—all squaw play," he said, scornfully. There was a menace in his somber eyes as he turned abruptly and left the group.

"I'm afraid you've made an enemy," said Jake Wentz to Joe. "An Indian never forgets an insult, and that's how he regarded your joke. Silvertip has been friendly here because he sells us his pelts. He's a Shawnee chief. There he goes through the willows!"

By this time Jim and Mr. Wells, Mrs. Wentz, and the girls had joined in the group. They all watched Silvertip get into his canoe and paddle away.

"A bad sign," said Wentz, and then, turning to Jeff Lynn, who joined the party at that moment, he briefly explained the circumstances.

"Never did like Silver. He's a crafty redskin, an' not to be trusted," replied Jeff.

"He has turned round and is looking back," Nell said quickly.

"So he has," observed the fur trader.

The Indian was now several hundred yards down the swift river, and for an instant had ceased paddling. The sun shone brightly on his eagle plumes. He remained motionless for a moment, and even at such a distance the dark, changeless face could be discerned. He lifted his hand and shook it menacingly.

"If ye don't hear from that redskin ag'in, Jeff Lynn don't know nothin'," calmly said the old frontiersman.

Chapter
IV

As the rafts drifted with the current the voyagers saw the settlers on the landing place diminish until they had faded from indistinct figures to mere black specks against the green background. Then came the last wave of a white scarf, faintly in the distance, and at length the dark outline of the fort was all that remained to their regretful gaze. Quickly that, too, disappeared behind the green hill, which, with its bold front, forces the river to take a wide turn.

The Ohio, winding in its course between high, wooded bluffs, rolled on and on into the wilderness.

Beautiful as was the ever-changing scenery, rugged, gray-faced cliffs on one side contrasting with green-clad hills on the other, there hovered over land and water something more striking than beauty. Above all hung a still atmosphere of calmness—of loneliness.

And this penetrating solitude marred somewhat the pleasure which might have been found in the picturesque scenery, and caused the voyagers, to whom this country was new, to take less interest in the gaily feathered birds and stealthy animals that were to be seen on the way. By the forms of wildlife along the banks of the river, this strange intruder on their peace was regarded with attention. The birds and beasts evinced little fear of the floating rafts. The sandhill crane, stalking along the shore, lifted his long neck as the unfamiliar thing came floating by, and then stood still and silent as a statue until the rafts disappeared from view. Blue herons feeding along the bars saw the unusual spectacle, and, uttering surprised "booms," they spread wide wings and lumbered away along the shore. The crows circled above the voyagers, cawing in not unfriendly excitement. Smaller birds alighted on the raised poles, and several—a robin, a catbird and a little brown wren—ventured with hesitating boldness to peck at the crumbs the girls threw to them. Deer waded knee deep in the shallow water, and, lifting their heads, instantly became motionless and absorbed. Occasionally a buffalo appeared on a level stretch of bank, and, tossing his huge head, seemed inclined to resent the coming of this stranger into his domain.

All day the rafts drifted steadily and swiftly down the river, presenting to the little party ever-varying pictures of densely wooded hills, of jutting, broken cliffs with scant evergreen growth; of long reaches of sandy bar that glistened golden in the sunlight, and over all the flight and call of wildfowl, the flitting of woodland songsters, and now and then the whistle and bellow of the horned watchers in the forest.

The intense blue of the vault above began to pale, and low down in the west a few fleecy clouds, gorgeously golden for a fleeting instant, then crimson-crowned for another, shaded and darkened as the setting sun sank behind the hills. Presently the red rays disappeared, a pink glow suffused the heavens, and at last, as gray twilight stole down over the hilltops, the crescent moon peeped above the wooded fringe of the western bluffs.

"Hard an' fast she is," sang out Jeff Lynn, as he fastened the rope to a tree at the head of a small island. "All off now, an' we'll hev supper. Thar's a fine spring under yon curly birch, an' I fetched along a leg of deer meat. Hungry, little 'un?"

He had worked hard all day steering the rafts, yet Nell had seen him smiling at her many times during the journey, and he had found time before the early start to arrange for her a comfortable seat. There was now a solicitude in the frontiersman's voice that touched her.

"I am famished," she replied, with her bright smile. "I am afraid I could eat a whole deer."

They all climbed the sandy slope and found themselves on the summit of an oval island, with a pretty glade in the middle surrounded by birches. Bill, the second raftsman, a stolid, silent man, at once swung his axe upon a log of driftwood. Mr. Wells and Jim walked to and fro under the birches, and Kate and Nell sat on the grass watching with great interest the old helmsman as he came up from the river, his brown hands and face shining from the scrubbing he had given them. Soon he had a fire cheerfully blazing, and after laying out the few utensils, he addressed himself to Joe:

"I'll tell ye right here, lad, good venison kin be spoiled by bad cuttin' and cookin'. You're slicin' it too thick. See—thar! Now salt good, an' keep outen the flame; on the red coals is best."

With a sharpened stick Jeff held the thin slices over the fire for a few moments. Then he laid them aside on some clean white-oak chips Bill's axe had provided. The simple meal of meat, bread, and afterward a drink of the cold spring water was keenly relished by the hungry voyagers. When it had been eaten, Jeff threw a log on his fire and remarked:

"Seein' as how we won't be in redskin territory fer awhile

yit, we kin hev a fire. I'll allow ye'll all be chilly and damp from river-mist afore long, so toast yerselves good."

"How far have we come today?" inquired Mr. Wells, his mind always intent on reaching the scene of his cherished undertaking.

" 'Bout thirty-odd miles, I reckon. Not much on a trip, thet's sartin, but we'll pick up termorrer. We've some quicker water, an' the rafts hev to go separate."

"How quiet!" exclaimed Kate, suddenly breaking the silence that followed the frontiersman's answer.

"Beautiful!" impetuously said Nell, looking up at Joe. A quick flash from his gray eyes answered her; he did not speak; indeed he had said little to her since the start, but his glance showed her how glad he was that she felt the sweetness and content of this wild land.

"I was never in a wilderness before," broke in the earnest voice of the young minister. "I feel an almost overpowering sense of loneliness. I want to get near you all, I feel lost. Yet it is grand, sublime!"

"Here is the promised land—the fruitful life—Nature as it was created by God," replied the old minister, impressively.

"Tell us a story," said Nell to the old frontiersman, as he once more joined the circle round the fire.

"So, little 'un, ye want a story?" queried Jeff, taking up a live coal and placing it in the bowl of his pipe. He took off his coonskin cap and carefully laid it aside. His weather-beaten face beamed in answer to the girl's request. He drew a long and audible pull at his black pipe, and sent forth slowly a cloud of white smoke. Deliberately poking the fire with a stick, as if stirring into life dead embers of the past, he sucked again at his pipe and emitted a great puff of smoke that completely enveloped the grizzled head. From out that white cloud came his drawling voice.

"Ye've seen thet big curly birch over thar—thet 'un as bends kind of sorrowful like. Wal, it used to stand straight an' proud. I've knowed thet tree all the years I've navigated this river, an' it seems natural like to me thet it now droops dyin', fer it shades the grave of as young, an' sweet, an' purty a lass as yerself, Miss Nell. Rivermen called this island George's Island, 'cause Washington onct camped here; but of late years the name's got changed, an' the men say suthin' like this: 'We'll try an' make Milly's birch afore sundown,' jest as Bill and me hev done today. Some years agone I was comin' up from Fort Henry an' had on board my slow old scow a lass named Milly—we never learned her other name. She come to me at the fort, an' tells as how her folks had been killed by Injuns, an' she wanted to git back to Pitt to meet her sweetheart. I was ag'in her comin' all along, an' fust off I said 'No.' But when I seen tears in her blue eyes, an' she puts her little hand on mine, I jest wilted, an' says to Jim Blair, 'She goes.' Wal, jest as might hev been expected—an' fact is I looked fer it—we wus tackled by redskins. Somehow, Jim Girty got wind of us hevin' a lass aboard, an' he ketched up with us jest below here. It's a bad place, called Shawnee Rock, an' I'll show it to ye termorrer. The renegade, with his red devils, attacked us thar, an' we had a fierce fight. Jim Blair, he was killed, an' we had a time gittin' away. Milly wus shot. She lived fer awhile, a couple of days, an' all the time was so patient, an' sweet, an' brave with thet renegade's bullet in her—fer he shot her, when he seen he couldn't capture her—thet thar wusn't a blame man of us who wouldn't hev died to grant her prayer, which wus that she could live to onct more see her lover."

There was a long silence, during which the old frontiersman sat gazing into the fire with sad eyes.

"We couldn't do nuthin', an' we buried her thar under thet birch, where she smiled her last sad, sweet smile an' died.

Ever since then the river has been eatin' away at this island. It's only half as big as it was onct, an' another flood will take away this sandbar, these few birches—an' Milly's grave."

The old frontiersman's story affected all his listeners. The elder minister bowed his head and prayed that no such fate might overtake his nieces. The young minister looked again, as he had many times that day, at Nell's winsome face. The girls cast grave glances at the drooping birch, and their bright tears glistened in the fire glow. Once more Joe's eyes glinted with that steely flash, and as he gazed out over the wide, darkening expanse of water his face grew cold and rigid.

"I'll allow I might hev told a more cheerful story, an' I'll do so next time; but I wanted ye all, particular the lasses, to know somethin' of the kind of country ye're goin' into. The frontier needs women; but jist yit it deals hard with them. An' Jim Girty, with more of his kind, ain't dead yit."

"Why don't someone kill him?" was Joe's sharp question.

"Easier said than done, lad. Jim Girty is a white traitor, but he's a cunnin' an' fierce redskin in his ways an' life. He knows the woods as a crow does, an' keeps outer sight 'cept when he's least expected. Then ag'in, he's got Simon Girty, his brother, an' almost the whole redskin tribe behind him. Injuns stick close to a white man that has turned ag'inst his own people, an' Jim Girty hadn't ever been ketched. How-sumever, I heard last trip thet he'd been tryin' some of his tricks round Fort Henry, an' thet Wetzel is on his trail. Wal, if it's so thet Lew Wetzel is arter him, I wouldn't give a pinch o' powder fer the white-redskin's chances of a long life."

No one spoke, and Jeff, after knocking the ashes from his pipe, went down to the raft, returning shortly afterward with his blanket. This he laid down and rolled himself in. Presently from under his coonskin cap came the words:

"Wal, I've turned in, an' I advise ye all to do the same."

All save Joe and Nell acted on Jeff's suggestion. For a long time the young couple sat close together on the bank, gazing at the moonlight on the river.

The night was perfect. A cool wind fanned the dying embers of the fire and softly stirred the leaves. Earlier in the evening a single frog had voiced his protest against the loneliness; but now his dismal croak was no longer heard. A snipe, belated in his feeding, ran along the sandy shore uttering his *tweet-tweet,* and his little cry, breaking in so softly on the silence, seemed only to make more deeply felt the great, vast stillness of the night.

Joe's arm was around Nell. She had demurred at first, but he gave no heed to her slight resistance, and finally her head rested against his shoulder. There was no need of words.

Joe had a pleasurable sense of her nearness, and there was a delight in the fragrance of her hair as it waved against his cheek; but just then love was not uppermost in his mind. All day he had been silent under the force of an emotion which he could not analyze. Some power, some feeling in which the thought of Nell had no share, was drawing him with irresistible strength. Nell had just begun to surrender to him in the sweetness of her passion; and yet even with that knowledge knocking reproachfully at his heart, he could not help being absorbed in the shimmering water, in the dark reflection of the trees, the gloom and shadow of the forest.

Presently he felt her form relax in his arms; then her soft, regular breathing told him she had fallen asleep, and he laughed low to himself. How she would pout on the morrow when he teased her about it! Then, realizing that she was tired with her long day's journey, he reproached himself for keeping her from the needed rest, and instantly decided to carry her to the raft. Yet such was the novelty of the situation that he yielded to its charm and did not go at once. The moonlight found bright threads in her wavy hair; it shone caressingly on her quiet face, and tried to steal under the downcast lashes.

Joe made a movement to rise with her, when she muttered indistinctly as if speaking to someone. He remembered then she had once told him that she talked in her sleep, and how greatly it annoyed her. He might hear something more with which to tease her; so he listened.

"Yes—Uncle—I will go—Kate, we must—go . . ."

Another interval of silence, then more murmurings. He distinguished his own name, and presently she called clearly, as if answering some inward questioner.

"I—love him—yes—I love Joe—he has mastered me. Yet I wish he were—like Jim—Jim who looked at me—so—with his deep eyes—and I . . ."

Joe lifted her as if she were a baby, and carrying her down to the raft, gently laid her by her sleeping sister.

The innocent words which he should not have heard were like a blow. What she would never have acknowledged in her waking hours had been revealed in her dreams. He recalled the glance of Jim's eyes as it had rested on Nell many times that day, and now these things were most significant.

He found at the end of the island a great, mossy stone. On this he climbed, and sat where the moonlight streamed, upon him. Gradually that cold bitterness died out from his face, as it passed from his heart, and once more he became engrossed in the silver sheen on the water, the lapping of the waves on the pebbly beach, and in that speaking, mysterious silence of the woods.

When the first faint rays of red streaked over the eastern hilltops, and the river mist arose from the water in a vapory cloud, Jeff Lynn rolled out his blanket, stretched his long limbs, and gave a hearty call to the morning. His cheerful welcome awakened all the voyagers except Joe, who had spent the night in watching and the early morning in fishing.

"Wal, I'll be darned," ejaculated Jeff as he saw Joe. "Up afore me, an' ketched a string of fish."

"What are they?" asked Joe, holding up several bronze-backed fish.

"Bass—black bass, an' thet big feller is a lammin' hefty 'un. How'd ye ketch 'em?"

"I fished for them."

"Wal, so it 'pears," growled Jeff, once more reluctantly yielding to his admiration for the lad. "How'd ye wake up so early?"

"I stayed up all night. I saw three deer swim from the mainland, but nothing else came around."

"Try yer hand at cleanin' 'em fer breakfast," continued Jeff, beginning to busy himself with preparations for that meal. "Wal, wal, if he ain't surprisin'! He'll do somethin' out here on the frontier, sure as I'm a born sinner," he muttered to himself, wagging his head in his quaint manner.

Breakfast over, Jeff transferred the horses to the smaller raft, which he had cut loose from his own, and giving a few directions to Bill, started downstream with Mr. Wells and the girls.

The rafts remained close enough together for a while, but as the current quickened and was more skilfully taken advantage of by Jeff, the larger raft gained considerable headway, gradually widening the gap between the two.

All day they drifted. From time to time Joe and Jim waved their hands to the girls; but the greater portion of their attention was given to quieting the horses. Mose, Joe's big white dog, retired in disgust to the hut, where he watched and dozed by turns. He did not fancy this kind of voyaging. Bill strained his sturdy arms all day on the steering oar.

About the middle of the afternoon Joe observed that the

hills grew more rugged and precipitous, and the river ran faster. He kept a constant lookout for the wall of rock which marked the point of danger. When the sun had disappeared behind the hills, he saw ahead a gray rock protruding from the green foliage. It was ponderous, overhanging, and seemed to frown down on the river. This was Shawnee Rock. Joe looked long at the cliff, and wondered if there was now an Indian scout hidden behind the pines that skirted the edge. Prominent on the top of the bluff a large, dead tree projected its hoary twisted branches.

Bill evidently saw the landmark, for he stopped in his monotonous walk to and fro across the raft, and pushing his oar amidships he looked ahead for the other raft. The figure of the tall frontiersman could be plainly seen as he labored at the helm.

The raft disappeared round a bend, and as it did so Joe saw a white scarf waved by Nell.

Bill worked the clumsy craft over toward the right shore where the current was more rapid. He pushed with all his strength, and when the oar reached its widest sweep, he lifted it and ran back across the raft for another push. Joe scanned the river ahead. He saw no rapids; only rougher water whirling over some rocks. They were where the channel narrowed and ran close to the right-hand bank. Under a willow-flanked lodge was a sandbar. To Joe there seemed nothing hazardous in drifting through this pass.

"Bad place ahead," said Bill, observing Joe's survey of the river.

"It doesn't look so," replied Joe.

"A raft ain't a boat. We could pole a boat. You has to hev water to float logs, an' the river's run out considerable. I'm only afeerd fer the hosses. If we hit or drag, they might plunge around a bit."

When the raft passed into the head of the bend it struck

the rocks several times, but finally gained the channel safely, and everything seemed propitious for an easy passage.

But, greatly to Bill's surprise, the wide craft was caught directly in the channel, and swung round so that the steering oar pointed toward the opposite shore. The water roared a foot deep over the logs.

"Hold hard on the hosses!" yelled Bill. "Somethin's wrong. I never seen a snag here."

The straining mass of logs, insecurely fastened together, rolled and then pitched loose again, but the short delay had been fatal to the steering apparatus.

Joe would have found keen enjoyment in the situation, had it not been for his horse, Lance. The thoroughbred was difficult to hold. As Bill was making strenuous efforts to get in a lucky stroke of the oar, he failed to see a long length of grapevine floating like a brown snake on the water below. In the excitement they heeded not the barking of Mose. Nor did they see the grapevine straighten and become taut just as they drifted upon it; but they felt the raft strike and hold on some submerged object. It creaked and groaned and the foamy water surged, gurgling, between the logs.

Jim's mare snorted with terror, and rearing high, pulled her halter loose and plunged into the river. But Jim still held her, at risk of being drawn overboard.

"Let go! She'll drag you in!" yelled Joe, grasping him with his free hand. Lance trembled violently and strained at the rope, which his master held with a strong grip.

"Crack!"

The stinging report of a rifle rang out above the splashing of the water.

Without a cry, Bill's grasp on the oar loosened; he fell over it limply, his head striking the almost submerged log. A dark-red fluid colored the water; then his body slipped over the oar and into the river, where it sank.

"My God! Shot!" cried Jim, in horrified tones.

He saw a puff of white smoke rising above the willows. Then the branches parted, revealing the dark forms of several Indian warriors. From the rifle in the foremost savage's hand a slight veil of smoke rose. With the leap of a panther the redskin sprang from the strip of sand to the raft.

"Hold, Jim! Drop that axe! We're caught!" cried Joe.

"It's that Indian from the fort!" gasped Jim.

The stalwart warrior was indeed Silvertip. But how changed! Stripped of the blanket he had worn at the settlement, now standing naked but for his buckskin breechcloth, with his perfectly proportioned form disclosed in all its sinewy beauty, and on his swarthy, evil face an expression of savage scorn, he surely looked a warrior and a chief.

He drew his tomahawk and flashed a dark glance at Joe. For a moment he steadily regarded the young man; but if he expected to see fear in the latter's face he was mistaken, for the look was returned coolly.

"Paleface steal shirt," he said in his deep voice. "Fool paleface play—Silvertip no forget."

Chapter
V

Silvertip turned to his braves, and giving a brief command, sprang from the raft. The warriors closed in around the brothers; two grasping each by the arms, and the remaining Indian taking care of the horse. The captives were then led ashore, where Silvertip awaited them.

When the horse was clear of the raft, which task necessitated considerable labor on the part of the Indians, the chief seized the grapevine, which was now plainly in sight, and severed it with one blow of his tomahawk. The raft dashed forward with a lurch and drifted downstream.

In the clear water Joe could see the cunning trap which had caused the death of Bill, and ensured the captivity of himself and his brother. The crafty savages had trimmed a six-inch sapling and anchored it under the water. They weighted the heavy end, leaving the other pointing upstream. To this last had been tied the grapevine. When the drifting raft reached the sapling, the Indians concealed in the willows pulled hard on the improvised rope; the end of the sapling stuck up like a hook, and the raft was caught and held. The killing of the helmsman showed the Indians' foresight; even had the raft drifted on downstream the brothers would have been helpless on a craft they could not manage. After all, Joe thought, he had not been so far wrong when he half fancied that an Indian lay behind Shawnee Rock, and he marveled at this clever trick which had so easily effected their capture.

But he had little time to look around at the scene of action. There was a moment only in which to survey the river to learn if the unfortunate raftsman's body had appeared. It was not to be seen. The river ran swiftly and hid all evidence of the tragedy under its smooth surface. When the brave who had gone back to the raft for the goods joined his companion the two hurried Joe up the bank after the others.

Once upon level ground Joe saw before him an open forest. On the border of this the Indians stopped long enough to bind the prisoners' wrists with thongs of deerhide. While two of the braves performed this office, Silvertip leaned against a tree and took no notice of the brothers. When they were thus securely tied one of their captors addressed the chief, who at once led the way westward through the forest. The savages followed in single file, with Joe and Jim in the middle of the line. The last Indian tried to mount Lance; but the thoroughbred would have none of him, and after several efforts the savage was compelled to desist. Mose trotted reluctantly along behind the horse.

Although the chief preserved a dignified mien, his braves were disposed to be cheerful. They were in high glee over their feat of capturing the palefaces, and kept up an incessant jabbering. One Indian, who walked directly behind Joe, continually prodded him with the stock of a rifle; and whenever Joe turned, the brawny redskin grinned as he grunted, "Ugh!" Joe observed that this huge savage had a broad face of rather a lighter shade of red than his companions. Perhaps he intended those rifle prods in friendliness, for although they certainly amused him, he would allow no one else to touch Joe; but it would have been more pleasing had he shown his friendship in a gentle manner. This Indian carried Joe's pack, much to his own delight, especially as his companions evinced an envious curiosity. The big fellow would not, however, allow them to touch it.

"He's a cheerful brute," remarked Joe to Jim.

"Ugh!" grunted the big Indian, jamming Joe with his rifle-stock.

Joe took heed of the warning and spoke no more. He gave all his attention to the course over which he was being taken. Here was his first opportunity to learn something of Indians and their woodcraft. It occurred to him that his captors would not have been so pleased and careless had they not believed themselves safe from pursuit, and he concluded they were leisurely conducting him toward one of the Indian towns. He watched the supple figure before him, wondering at the quick step, light as the fall of a leaf, and tried to walk as softly. He found, however, that where the Indian readily avoided the sticks and brush, he was unable to move without snapping twigs. Now and then he would look up and study the lay of the land ahead; and as he came nearer to certain rocks and trees he scrutinized them closely, in order to remember their shape and general appearance. He believed he was blazing out in his mind this woodland trail, so that should fortune favor him and he contrive to escape, he would be able to find his way back to the river. Also, he was enjoying the wild scenery.

This forest would have appeared beautiful, even to one indifferent to such charms, and Joe was far from that. Every movement he felt steal stronger over him a subtle influence which he could not define. Half unconsciously he tried to analyze it, but it baffled him. He could no more explain what fascinated him than he could understand what caused the melancholy quiet which hung over the glades and hollows. He had pictured a real forest so differently from this. Here was a long lane paved with springy moss and fenced by bright-green sassafras; there a secluded dale, dotted with pale-blue blossoms, over which the giant cottonwoods leaned their heads, jealously guarding the delicate flowers from the sun. Beech trees, growing close in clanny groups, spread their straight limbs gracefully; the white birches gleamed like silver wherever a stray sunbeam stole through the foliage, and the oaks, monarchs of the forest, rose over all, dark, rugged, and kingly.

Joe soon understood why the party traveled through such open forest. The chief, seeming hardly to deviate from his direct course, kept clear of broken ground, matted thickets, and tangled windfalls. Joe got a glimpse of dark ravines and heard the music of tumbling waters; he saw gray cliffs grown over with vines and full of holes and crevices; steep ridges, covered with dense patches of briar and hazel, rising in the way. Yet the Shawnee always found an easy path.

The sun went down behind the foliage in the west, and shadows appeared low in the glens; then the trees faded into an indistinct mass; a purple shade settled down over the forest, and night brought the party to a halt.

The Indians selected a sheltered spot under the lee of a knoll, at the base of which ran a little brook. Here in this enclosed space were the remains of a campfire. Evidently the Indians had halted there that same day, for the logs still smoldered. While one brave fanned the embers, another took from a neighboring branch a haunch of deer meat. A blaze was soon coaxed from the dull coals, more fuel was added, and presently a cheerful fire shone on the circle of dusky forms.

It was a picture which Joe had seen in many a boyish dream; now that he was a part of it he did not dwell on the hopelessness of the situation, nor on the hostile chief whose enmity he had incurred. Almost, it seemed, he was glad of this chance to watch the Indians and listen to them. He had been kept apart from Jim, and it appeared to Joe that their captors treated his brother with a contempt which they did not show him. Silvertip had, no doubt, informed them that Jim had been on his way to teach the Indians of the white man's God.

Jim sat with drooping head; his face was sad, and evidently he took the most disheartening view of his capture. When he had eaten the slice of venison given to him he lay down with his back to the fire.

Silvertip, in these surroundings, showed his real character. He had appeared friendly in the settlement; but now he was the relentless savage, a son of the wilds, free as an eagle. His dignity as a chief kept him aloof from his braves. He had taken no notice of the prisoners since the capture. He remained silent, steadily regarding the fire with his somber eyes. At length, glancing at the big Indian, he motioned toward the prisoners, and with a single word stretched himself on the leaves.

Joe noted the same changelessness of expression in the other dark faces as he had seen in Silvertip's. It struck him forcibly. When they spoke in their soft, guttural tones, or burst into a low, not unmusical laughter, or sat gazing stolidly into the fire, their faces seemed always the same, inscrutable, like the depths of the forest now hidden in the night. One thing Joe felt rather than saw—these savages were fierce and untamable. He was sorry for Jim, because, as he believed, it would be as easy to teach the panther gentleness toward his prey as to instill into one of these wild creatures a belief in Christ.

The braves manifested keen pleasure in anticipation as to what they would get out of the pack, which the Indian now opened. Time and again the big brave placed his broad hand on the shoulder of a comrade Indian and pushed him backward.

Finally the pack was opened. It contained a few articles of wearing apparel, a pair of boots, and a pipe and pouch of tobacco. The big Indian kept the latter articles, grunting with satisfaction, and threw the boots and clothes to the others. Immediately there was a scramble. One brave, after a struggle with another, got possession of both boots. He at once slipped off his moccasins and drew on the white man's foot covering. He strutted around in them a few moments, but his proud manner soon changed to disgust.

Cowhide had none of the soft, yielding qualities of buckskin and hurt the Indian's feet. Sitting down, he pulled one off, not without difficulty, for the boots were wet; but he could not remove the other. He hesitated a moment, being aware of the subdued merriment of his comrades, and then held up his foot to the nearest one. This chanced to be the big Indian, who evidently had a keen sense of humor. Taking hold of the boot with both hands, he dragged the luckless brave entirely around the campfire. The fun, however, was not to be all one-sided. The big Indian gave a more strenuous pull, and the boot came off suddenly. Unprepared for this, he lost his balance and fell down the bank almost into the creek. He held on to the boot, nevertheless, and getting up, threw it into the fire.

The braves quieted down after that, and soon lapsed into slumber, leaving the big fellow, to whom the chief had addressed his brief command, acting as guard. Observing Joe watching him as he puffed on his new pipe, he grinned and spoke in broken English that was intelligible, and much of a surprise to the young man.

"Paleface—tobac'—heap good."

Then, seeing that Joe made no effort to follow his

brother's initiative, for Jim was fast asleep, he pointed to the recumbent figures and spoke again.

"Ugh! Paleface sleep—Injun wigwams—near setting sun."

On the following morning Joe was awakened by the pain in his legs, which had been bound all night. He was glad when the bonds were cut and the party took up its westward march.

The Indians, though somewhat quieter, displayed the same carelessness: they did not hurry, nor use particular caution, but selected the most open paths through the forest. They even halted while one of their number crept up on a herd of browsing deer. About noon the leader stopped to drink from a spring; his braves followed suit and permitted the white prisoners to quench their thirst.

When they were about to start again the single note of a bird far away in the woods sounded clearly on the quiet air. Joe would not have given heed to it had he been less attentive. He instantly associated this peculiar bird-note with the sudden stiffening of Silvertip's body and his attitude of intense listening. Low exclamations came from the braves as they bent to catch the lightest sound. Presently, above the murmur of the gentle fall of water over the stones, rose that musical note once more. It was made by a bird, Joe thought, and yet, judged by the actions of the Indians, how potent with meaning beyond that of the simple melody of the woodland songster! He turned, half expecting to see somewhere in the treetops the bird which had wrought so sudden a change in his captors. As he did so from close at hand came the same call, now louder, but identical with the one that had deceived him. It was an answering signal, and had been given by Silvertip.

It flashed into Joe's mind that other savages were in the forest; they had run across the Shawnees' trail, and were thus communicating with them. Soon dark figures could be discerned against the patches of green thicket; they came nearer and nearer, and now entered the open glade where Silvertip stood with his warriors.

Joe counted twelve, and noted that they differed from his captors. He had only time to see that this difference consisted in the headdress and in the color and quantity of paint on their bodies, when his gaze was attracted and riveted to the foremost figures.

The first was that of a very tall and stately chief, toward whom Silvertip now advanced with every show of respect. In this Indian's commanding stature, in his reddish-bronze face, stern and powerful, there were readable the characteristics of a king. In his deep-set eyes, gleaming from under a ponderous brow, in his mastifflike jaw; in every feature of his haughty face were visible all the high intelligence, the consciousness of past valor, and the power and authority that denote a great chieftain.

The second figure was equally striking for the remarkable contrast it afforded to the chief's. Despite the gaudy ornaments, the paint, the fringed and beaded buckskin leggings—all the Indian accoutrements and garments which bedecked this person—he would have been known anywhere as a white man. His skin was burned to a dark bronze, but it had not the red tinge which characterizes the Indian. This white man had, indeed, a strange physiognomy. The forehead was narrow and sloped backward from the brow, denoting animal instincts. The eyes were close together, yellowish-brown in color, and had a peculiar vibrating movement, as though they were hung on a pivot, like a compass needle. The nose was long and hooked, and the mouth set in a thin, cruel line. There was in the man's aspect an extraordinary combination of ignorance, vanity, cunning, and ferocity.

While the two chiefs held a short consultation, this savage-appearing white man addressed the brothers.

"Who're you, an' where you goin'?" he asked gruffly, confronting Jim.

"My name is Downs. I am a preacher, and was on my way to the Moravian Mission to preach to the Indians. You are a white man; will you help us?"

If Jim expected the information would please his interrogator, he was mistaken.

"So you're one of 'em? Yes, I'll do suthin' fer you when I git back from this hunt. I'll cut your heart out, chop it up, an' feed it to the buzzards," he said fiercely, concluding his threat by striking Jim a cruel blow on the head.

Joe paled deathly white at this cowardly action, and his eyes, as they met the gaze of the ruffian, contracted with their characteristic steely glow, as if some powerful force within the depths of his being were at white heat and only this pale flash came to the surface.

"You ain't a preacher?" questioned the man, meeting something in Joe's glance that had been absent from Jim's.

Joe made no answer, and regarded his questioner steadily.

"Ever see me afore? Ever hear of Jim Girty?" he asked boastfully.

"Before you spoke I knew you were Girty," answered Joe quietly.

"How d'you know? Ain't you afeared?"

"Of what?"

"Me—me?"

Joe laughed in the renegade's face.

"How'd you know me?" growled Girty. "I'll see thet you hev cause to remember me after this."

"I figured there was only one so-called white man in these woods who is coward enough to strike a man whose hands are tied."

"Boy, ye're too free with your tongue. I'll shet off your

wind." Girty's hand was raised, but it never reached Joe's neck.

The big Indian had an hour or more previous cut Joe's bonds, but he still retained the thong which was left attached to Joe's left wrist. This allowed the young man free use of his right arm, which, badly swollen or not, he brought into quick action.

When the renegade reached toward him Joe knocked up the hand, and, instead of striking, he grasped the hooked nose with all the powerful grip of his fingers. Girty uttered a frightful curse; he writhed with pain, but could not free himself from the viselike clutch. He drew his tomahawk and with a scream aimed a vicious blow at Joe. He missed his aim, however, for Silvertip had intervened and turned the course of the keen hatchet. But the weapon struck Joe a glancing blow, inflicting a painful, though not dangerous, wound.

The renegade's nose was skinned and bleeding profusely. He was frantic with fury and tried to get at Joe, but Silvertip remained in front of his captive until some of the braves led Girty into the forest, where the tall chief had already disappeared.

The nose-pulling incident added to the gaiety of the Shawnees, who evidently were pleased with Girty's discomfiture. They jabbered among themselves and nodded approvingly at Joe, until a few words spoken by Silvertip produced a sudden change.

What the words were Joe could not understand, but to him they sounded like French. He smiled at the absurdity of imagining he had heard a savage speak a foreign language. At any rate, whatever had been said was trenchant with meaning. The Indians changed from cheerful to grave; they picked up their weapons and looked keenly on every side;

the big Indian at once retied Joe, and then all crowded round the chief.

"Did you hear what Silvertip said, and did you notice the effect it had?" whispered Jim, taking advantage of the moment.

"It sounded like French, but of course it wasn't," replied Joe.

"It was French. *'Le Vent de la Mort'* "

"By Jove, that's it. What does it mean?" asked Joe, who was not a scholar.

"The Wind of Death."

"That's English, but I can't apply it here. Can you?"

"No doubt it is some Indian omen."

The hurried consultation over, Silvertip tied Joe's horse and dog to the trees, and once more led the way; this time he avoided the open forest and kept on low ground. For a long time he traveled in the bed of the brook, wading when the water was shallow and always stepping where there was the least possibility of leaving a footprint. Not a word was spoken. If either of the brothers made the lightest splash in the water, or tumbled a stone into the brook, the Indian behind rapped him on the head with a tomahawk handle.

At certain places, indicated by the care which Silvertip exercised in walking, the Indian in front of the captives turned and pointed where they were to step. They were hiding the trail. Silvertip hurried them over the stony places; went more slowly through the water, and picked his way carefully over the soft ground it became necessary to cross. At times he stopped, remaining motionless many seconds.

This vigilance continued all the afternoon. The sun sank; twilight spread its gray mantle, and soon black night enveloped the forest. The Indians halted, but made no fire; they sat close together on a stony ridge, silent and watchful.

Joe pondered deeply over this behavior. Did the Shawnees fear pursuit? What had that Indian chief told Silvertip? To Joe it seemed that they acted as if believing foes were on all sides. Though they hid their tracks, it was, apparently, not the fear of pursuit alone which made them cautious.

Joe reviewed the afternoon's march and dwelt upon the possible meaning of the catlike steps, the careful brushing aside of branches, the roving eyes, suspicious and gloomy, the eager watchfulness of the advance as well as to the rear, and always the strained effort to listen, all of which gave him the impression of some grave, unseen danger.

And now as he lay on the hard ground, nearly exhausted by the long march and suffering from the throbbing wound, his courage lessened somewhat, and he shivered with dread. The quiet and gloom of the forest; these fierce, wild creatures, free in the heart of their own wilderness yet menaced by a foe, and that strange French phrase which kept recurring in his mind—all had the effect of conjuring up giant shadows in Joe's fanciful mind. During all his life, until this moment, he had never feared anything; now he was afraid of the darkness. The spectral trees spread long arms overhead, and phantom forms stalked abroad; somewhere out in that dense gloom stirred this mysterious foe—the "Wind of Death."

Nevertheless, he finally slept. In the dull gray light of early morning the Indians once more took up the line of march toward the west. They marched all that day, and at dusk halted to eat and rest. Silvertip and another Indian stood watch.

Some time before morning Joe suddenly awoke. The night was dark, yet it was lighter than when he had fallen asleep. A pale crescent moon shone dimly through the murky clouds. There was neither movement of the air nor the chirp of an insect. Absolute silence prevailed.

Joe saw the Indian guard leaning against a tree, asleep. Silvertip was gone. The captive raised his head and looked around for the chief. There were only four Indians left, three on the ground and one against the tree.

He saw something shining near him. He looked more closely, and made out the object to be an eagle plume Silvertip had worn in his headdress. It lay on the ground near the tree. Joe made some slight noise which awakened the guard. The Indian never moved a muscle; but his eyes roved everywhere. He, too, noticed the absence of the chief.

At this moment from out of the depths of the woods came a swelling sigh, like the moan of the night wind. It rose and died away, leaving the silence apparently all the deeper.

A shudder ran over Joe's frame. Fascinated, he watched the guard. The Indian uttered a low gasp; his eyes started and glared wildly; he rose very slowly to his full height and stood waiting, listening. The dark hand which held the tomahawk trembled so that little glints of moonlight glanced from the bright steel.

From far back in the forest deeps came that same low moaning:

"Um-m-mm-woo-o-o-o!"

It rose from a faint murmur and swelled to a deep moan, soft but clear, and ended in a wail like that of a lost soul.

The break it made in that dead silence was awful. Joe's blood seemed to have curdled and frozen; a cold sweat oozed from his skin, and it was as if a clammy hand clutched at his heart. He tried to persuade himself that the fear displayed by the savage was only superstition, and that that moan was but the sigh of the night wind.

The Indian sentinel stood as if paralyzed an instant after that weird cry, and then, swift as a flash, and as noiseless, he was gone into the gloomy forest. He had fled without awakening his companions.

Once more the moaning cry arose and swelled mournfully on the still night air. It was close at hand!

"The Wind of Death," whispered Joe.

He was shaken and unnerved by the events of the past two days and dazed from his wound. His strength deserted him, and he lost consciousness.

Chapter
VI

One evening, several days previous to the capture of the brothers, a solitary hunter stopped before a deserted log cabin which stood on the bank of a stream fifty miles or more inland from the Ohio River. It was rapidly growing dark; a fine, drizzling rain had set in, and a rising wind gave promise of a stormy night.

Although the hunter seemed familiar with his surroundings, he moved cautiously, and hesitated as if debating whether he should seek the protection of this lonely hut, or remain all night under dripping trees. Feeling of his hunting frock, he found that it was damp and slippery. This fact evidently decided him in favor of the cabin, for he stooped his tall figure and went in. It was pitch dark inside; but having been there before, the absence of a light did not trouble him. He readily found the ladder leading to the loft, ascended it, and lay down to sleep.

During the night a noise awakened him. For a moment he heard nothing except the fall of the rain. Then came the hum of voices, followed by the soft tread of moccasined feet. He knew there was an Indian town ten miles across the country, and believed some warriors, belated on a hunting trip, had sought the cabin for shelter.

The hunter lay perfectly quiet, awaiting developments. If the Indians had flint and steel, and struck a light, he was almost certain to be discovered. He listened to their low conversation, and understood from the language that they were Delawares.

A moment later he heard the rustling of leaves and twigs, accompanied by the metallic click of steel against some hard substance. The noise was repeated, and then followed by a hissing sound, which he knew to be the burning of powder on a piece of dry wood, after which rays of light filtered through cracks of the unstable floor of the loft.

The man placed his eye to one of these crevices, and counted eleven Indians, all young braves, with the exception of the chief. The Indians had been hunting; they had haunches of deer and buffalo tongues, together with several packs of hides. Some of them busied themselves drying their weapons; others sat down listlessly, plainly showing their weariness, and two worked over the smouldering fire. The damp leaves and twigs burned faintly, yet there was light enough to cause the hunter fear that he might be discovered. He believed he had not much to worry about from the young braves, but the hawkeyed chief was dangerous.

And he was right. Presently the stalwart chief heard, or saw, a drop of water fall from the loft. It came from the hunter's wet coat. Almost anyone save an Indian scout would have fancied this came from the roof. As the chief's gaze roamed everywhere over the interior of the cabin his expression was plainly distrustful. His eye searched the wet clay floor, but hardly could have discovered anything there, because the hunter's moccasined tracks had been obliterated by the footprints of the Indians. The chief's suspicions seemed to be allayed.

But in truth this chief, with the wonderful sagacity natural to Indians, had observed matters which totally escaped the eyes of the young braves, and, like a wily old fox, he waited to see which cub would prove the keenest. Not one of them, however, noted anything unusual. They sat around the fire, ate their meat and parched corn, and chatted volubly.

The chief arose and, walking to the ladder, ran his hand along one of the rungs.

"Ugh!" he exclaimed.

Instantly he was surrounded by ten eager, bright-eyed braves. He extended his open palm; it was smeared with wet clay like that under his feet. Simultaneously with their muttered exclamations the braves grasped their weapons. They knew there was a foe above them. It was a paleface, for an Indian would have revealed himself.

The hunter, seeing he was discovered, acted with the unerring judgment and lightninglike rapidity of one long accustomed to perilous situations. Drawing his tomahawk and noiselessly stepping to the hole in the loft, he leaped into the midst of the astounded Indians.

Rising from the floor like the rebound of a rubber ball, his long arm with the glittering hatchet made a wide sweep, and the young braves scattered like frightened sheep.

He made a dash for the door and, incredible as it may seem, his movements were so quick he would have escaped from their very midst without a scratch but for one unforeseen circumstance. The clay floor was wet and slippery; his feet were hardly in motion before they slipped from under him and he fell headlong.

With loud yells of triumph the band jumped upon him. There was a convulsive, heaving motion of the struggling mass, one frightful cry of agony, and then hoarse commands. Three of the braves ran to their packs from which they took cords of buckskin. So exceedingly powerful was the hunter that six Indians were required to hold him while the others tied his hands and feet. Then, with grunts and chuckles of satisfaction, they threw him into a corner of the cabin.

Two of the braves had been hurt in the brief struggle, one having a badly wrenched shoulder and the other a broken arm. So much for the hunter's power in that single moment of action.

The loft was searched and found to be empty. Then the excitement died away, and the braves settled themselves down for the night. The injured ones bore their hurts with characteristic stoicism; if they did not sleep, both remained quiet and not a sigh escaped them.

The wind changed during the night, the storm abated, and when daylight came the sky was cloudless. The first rays of the sun shone in the open door, lighting up the interior of the cabin.

A sleepy Indian who had acted as guard stretched his limbs and yawned. He looked for the prisoner and saw him sitting up in the corner. One arm was free and the other nearly so. He had almost untied the thongs which bound him; a few moments more and he would have been free.

"Ugh!" exclaimed the young brave, awakening his chief and pointing to the hunter.

The chief glanced at his prisoner; then looked more closely, and with one spring was on his feet, a drawn tomahawk in his hand. A short, shrill yell issued from his lips. Roused by that clarion call, the young braves jumped up, trembling in eager excitement. The chief's summons had been the sharp war cry of the Delawares.

He manifested as intense emotion as could possibly have been betrayed by a matured, experienced chieftain, and pointing to the hunter, he spoke a single word.

* * *

At noonday the Indians entered the fields of corn which marked the outskirts of the Delaware encampment.

"Kol-loo—kol-loo—kol-loo."

The long signal, heralding the return of the party with important news, pealed throughout the quiet valley; and scarcely had the echoes died away when from the village came answering shouts.

Once beyond the aisles of waving corn the hunter saw over the shoulders of his captors the home of the redmen. A grassy plain, sloping gradually from the woody hill to a winding stream, was brightly beautiful with chestnut trees and long, well-formed lines of lodges. Many-hued blankets hung fluttering in the sun, and rising lazily were curling columns of blue smoke. The scene was picturesque and reposeful; the vivid hues suggesting the Indian's love of color and ornament; the absence of life and stir, his languorous habit of sleeping away the hot noonday hours.

The loud whoops, however, changed the quiet encampment into a scene of animation. Children ran from the wigwams, maidens and braves dashed here and there, squaws awakened from their slumber, and many a doughty warrior rose from his rest in the shade. French fur traders stared curiously from their lodges, and renegades hurriedly left their blankets, roused to instant action by the well-known summons.

The hunter, led down the lane toward the approaching crowd, presented a calm and fearless demeanor. When the Indians surrounded him one prolonged, furious yell rent the air, and then followed an extraordinary demonstration of fierce delight. The young braves' staccato yell, the maidens' scream, the old squaws' screech, and the deep war cry of the warriors intermingled in a fearful discordance.

Often had this hunter heard the name which the Indians called him; he had been there before, a prisoner; he had run the gauntlet down the lane; he had been bound to a stake in front of the lodge where his captors were now leading him. He knew the chief, Wingenund, sachem of the Delawares. Since that time, now five years ago, when Wingenund had tortured him, they had been bitterest foes.

If the hunter heard the hoarse cries, or the words hissed into his ears; if he saw the fiery glances of hatred, and sudden giving way to ungovernable rage, unusual to the Indian nature; if he felt in their fierce exultation the hopelessness of succor or mercy, he gave not the slightest sign.

"Atelang! Atelang! Atelang!" rang out the strange Indian name.

The French savages, like real savages, ran along with the procession, their feathers waving, their paint shining, their faces expressive of as much excitement as the Indians' as they cried aloud in their native tongue:

"Le Vent de la Mort! Le Vent de la Mort! Le Vent de la Mort!"

The hunter, while yet some paces distance, saw the lofty figure of the chieftain standing in front of his principal men. Well he knew them all. There were the crafty Pipe, and his savage comrade, the Half King; there was Shingiss, who wore on his forehead a scar—the mark of the hunter's bullet; there were Kotoxen, the Lynx, and Misseppa, the Source, and Winstonah, the War-cloud, chiefs of sagacity and renown. Three renegades completed the circle; and these three traitors represented a power which had for ten years left an awful, bloody trail over the country. Simon Girty, the so-called White Indian, with his keen, authoritative face turned expectantly; Elliott, the Tory deserter, from Fort Pitt, a wiry, spiderlike little man; and last, the gaunt and gaudily arrayed form of the demon of the frontier—Jim Girty.

The procession halted before this group, and two brawny braves pushed the hunter forward. Simon Girty's face betrayed satisfaction; Elliott's shifty eyes snapped, and the dark, repulsive face of the other Girty exhibited an exultant joy. These desperadoes had feared this hunter.

Wingenund, with a majestic wave of his arms, silenced the yelling horde of frenzied savages and stepped before the captive.

The deadly foes were once again face-to-face. The chieftain's lofty figure and dark, sleek head, now bare of plumes, towered over the other Indians, but he was not obliged to lower his gaze in order to look straight into the hunter's eyes.

Verily this hunter merited the respect which shone in the great chieftain's glance. Like a mountain ash he stood, straight and strong, his magnificent frame tapering wedge-like from his broad shoulders. The bulging line of his thick neck, the deep chest, the knotty contour of his bared forearm, and the full curves of his legs—all denoted a wonderful muscular development.

The power expressed in this man's body seemed intensified in his features. His face was white and cold, his jaw squared and set; his coal-black eyes glittered with almost a superhuman fire. And his hair, darker than the wing of a crow, fell far below his shoulders; matted and tangled as it was, still it hung to his waist, and had it been combed out, must have reached his knees.

One long moment Wingenund stood facing his foe, and then over the multitude and through the valley rolled his sonorous voice:

"Deathwind dies at dawn!"

The hunter was tied to a tree and left in view of the Indian populace. The children ran fearfully by; the braves gazed long at the great foe of their race; the warriors passed in gloomy silence. The savages' tricks of torture, all their dia-

bolical ingenuity of inflicting pain were suppressed, awaiting the hour of sunrise when this hated Long Knife was to
die.

Only one person offered an insult to the prisoner; he was
a man of his own color. Jim Girty stopped before him, his
yellowish eyes lighted by a tigerish glare, his lips curled in a
snarl, and from between them issuing the odor of the fur
traders' vile rum.

"You'll soon be feed fer the buzzards," he croaked, in his
hoarse voice. He had so often strewed the plains with human
flesh for the carrion birds that the thought had a deep fascination for him. "D'ye hear, scalp-hunter? Feed for buzzards!" He deliberately spat in the hunter's face. "D'ye
hear?" he repeated.

There was no answer save that which glittered in the
hunter's eye. But the renegade could not read it because he
did not meet that flaming glance. Wild horses could not have
dragged him to face this man had he been free. Even now a
chill crept over Girty. For a moment he was enthralled by a
mysterious fear, half paralyzed by a foreshadowing of what
would be this hunter's vengeance. Then he shook off his
craven fear. He was free; the hunter's doom was sure. His
sharp face was again wreathed in a savage leer, and he spat
once more on the prisoner.

His fierce impetuosity took him a step too far. The
hunter's arms and waist were fastened, but his feet were free.
His powerful leg was raised suddenly; his foot struck Girty
in the pit of the stomach. The renegade dropped limp and
gasping. The braves carried him away, his gaudy feathers
trailing, his long arms hanging inertly, and his face distorted
with agony.

The maidens of the tribe, however, showed for the prisoner an interest that had in it something of veiled sympathy.
Indian girls were always fascinated by white men. Many

records of Indian maidens' kindness, of love, of heroism for white prisoners brighten the dark pages of frontier history. These girls walked past the hunter, averting their eyes when within his range of vision, but stealing many a sidelong glance at his impressive face and noble proportions. One of them, particularly, attracted the hunter's eye.

This was because, as she came by with her companions, while they all turned away, she looked at him with her soft, dark eyes. She was a young girl, whose delicate beauty bloomed fresh and sweet as that of a wild rose. Her costume, fringed, beaded, and exquisitely wrought with fanciful designs, betrayed her rank—she was Wingenund's daughter. The hunter had seen her when she was a child, and he recognized her now. He knew that the beauty of Aola, of Whispering Winds Among the Leaves, had been sung from the Ohio to the Great Lakes.

Often she passed him that afternoon. At sunset, as the braves untied him and led him away, he once more caught the full, intense gaze of her lovely eyes.

That night as he lay securely bound in the corner of a lodge, and the long hours wore slowly away, he strained at his stout bonds, and in his mind revolved different plans of escape. It was not in this man's nature to despair; while he had life he would fight. From time to time he expanded his muscles, striving to loosen the wet buckskin thongs.

The dark hours slowly passed, no sound coming to him save the distant bark of a dog and the monotonous tread of his guard; a dim grayness pervaded the lodge. Dawn was close at hand—his hour was nearly come.

Suddenly his hearing, trained to a most acute sensibility, caught a faint sound, almost inaudible. It came from without, on the other side of the lodge. There it was again, a slight tearing sound, such as is caused by a knife when it cuts through soft material.

Someone was slitting the wall of the lodge.

The hunter rolled noiselessly over and over until he lay against the skins. In the dim grayness he saw a bright blade moving carefully upward through the deer-hide. Then a long knife was pushed into the opening; a small, brown hand grasped the hilt. Another little hand followed and felt the wall and floor, reaching out with groping fingers.

The hunter rolled again so that his back was against the wall and his wrists in front of the opening. He felt the little hand on his arm; then it slipped down to his wrists. The contact of cold steel sent a tremor of joy through his heart. The pressure of his bonds relaxed, ceased; his arms were free. He turned to find the long-bladed knife on the ground. The little hands were gone.

In a twinkling he rose unbound, armed, desperate. In another second an Indian warrior lay upon the ground in his death throes, while a fleeing form vanished in the gray morning mist.

Chapter
VII

Joe felt the heavy lethargy rise from him like the removal of a blanket; his eyes became clear, and he saw the trees and the forest gloom; slowly he realized his actual position.

He was a prisoner, lying helpless among his sleeping captors. Silvertip and the guard had fled into the woods, frightened by the appalling moan which they believed sounded their death knell. And Joe believed he might have fled himself had he been free. What could have caused that sound? He fought off the numbing chill that once again began to creep over him. He was wide awake now; his head was clear, and he resolved to retain his senses. He told himself there could be nothing supernatural in that wind, or wail, or whatever it was, which had risen murmuring from out the forest depths.

Yet, despite his reasoning, Joe could not allay his fears. That thrilling cry haunted him. The frantic flight of an Indian brave—nay, of a cunning, experienced chief—was not to be lightly considered. The savages were at home in these untracked wilds. Trained from infancy to scent danger and to fight when they had an equal chance, they surely would not run without good cause.

Joe knew that something moved under those dark trees. He had no idea what. It might be the fretting night wind, or a stealthy, prowling, soft-footed beast, or a savage alien to these wild Indians, and wilder than they by far. The chirp of a bird awoke the stillness. Night had given way to morning. Welcoming the light that was chasing away the gloom, Joe raised his head with a deep sigh of relief. As he did so he saw a bush move; then a shadow seemed to sink into the ground. He had seen an object lighter than the trees, darker than the gray background. Again that strange sense of the nearness of *something* thrilled him.

Moments passed—to him long as hours. He saw a tall fern waver and tremble. A rabbit, or perhaps a snake, had brushed it. Other ferns moved, their tops agitated, perhaps, by a faint breeze. No; that wavering line came straight toward him; it could not be the wind; it marked the course of a creeping, noiseless thing. It must be a panther crawling nearer and nearer.

Joe opened his lips to awaken his captors, but could not speak; it was as if his heart had stopped beating. Twenty feet away the ferns were parted to disclose a white, gleaming face, with eyes that seemingly glittered. Brawny shoulders were upraised, and then a tall, powerful man stood revealed. Lightly he stepped over the leaves into the little glade. He bent over the sleeping Indians. Once, twice, three times a long blade swung high. One brave shuddered, another gave a sobbing gasp, and the third moved two fingers—thus they passed from life to death.

"Wetzel!" cried Joe.

"I reckon so," said the deliverer, his deep, calm voice contrasting strangely with what might have been expected from his aspect. Then, seeing Joe's head covered with blood, he continued: "Able to get up?"

"I'm not hurt," answered Joe, rising when his bonds had been cut.

"Brothers, I reckon?" Wetzel said, bending over Jim.

"Yes, we're brothers. Wake up, Jim, wake up! We're saved!"

"What? Who's that?" cried Jim, sitting up and staring at Wetzel.

"This man has saved our lives! See, Jim, the Indians are dead! And, Jim, it's Wetzel, the hunter. You remember, Jeff Lynn said I'd know him if I ever saw him, and—"

"What happened to Jeff?" inquired Wetzel, interrupting. He had turned from Jim's grateful face.

"Jeff was on the first raft, and for all we know he is now safe at Fort Henry. Our steersman was shot, and we were captured."

"Has the Shawnee anythin' ag'inst you boys?"

"Why, yes, I guess so. I played a joke on him—took his shirt and put it on another fellow."

"Might jes' as well kick an' Injun. What has he ag'in you?"

"I don't know. Perhaps he did not like my talk to him," answered Jim. "I am a preacher, and have come west to teach the gospel to the Indians."

"They're good Injuns now," said Wetzel, pointing to the prostrate figures.

"How did you find us?" eagerly asked Joe.

"Run acrost yer trail two days back."

"And you've been following us?"

The hunter nodded.

"Did you see anything of another band of Indians? A tall chief and Jim Girty were among them."

"They've been arter me fer two days. I was followin' you when Silvertip got wind of Girty an' his Delawares. The big chief was Wingenund. I seen you pull Girty's nose. Arter the Delawares went I turned loose yer dog an' horse an' lit out on yer trail."

"Where are the Delawares now?"

"I reckon they're nosin' my back trail. We must be gittin'. Silvertip'll soon hev a lot of Injuns here."

Joe intended to ask the hunter about what had frightened the Indians, but despite his eager desire for information, he refrained from doing so.

"Girty nigh did fer you," remarked Wetzel, examining Joe's wound. "He's in a bad humor. He got kicked a few days back, and then hed the skin pulled offen his nose. Somebody'll hev to suffer. Wal, you fellers grab yer rifles, an' we'll be startin' fer the fort."

Joe shuddered as he leaned over one of the dusky forms to detach powder and bullet horn. He had never seen a dead Indian, and the tense face, the sightless, vacant eyes made him shrink. He shuddered again when he saw the hunter scalp his victims. He shuddered a third time when he saw Wetzel pick up Silvertip's beautiful white eagle plume, dabble it in a pool of blood, and stick it in the bark of a tree. Bereft of its graceful beauty, drooping with its gory burden, the long feather was a deadly message. It had been Silvertip's pride; it was now a challenge, a menace to the Shawnee chief.

"Come," said Wetzel, leading the way into the forest.

Shortly after daylight on the second day following the release of the Downs brothers the hunter brushed through a thicket of alder and said:

"That's Fort Henry."

The boys were on the summit of a mountain from which the land sloped in a long incline of rolling ridges and gentle valleys like a green, billowy sea, until it rose again abruptly into a peak higher still than the one upon which they stood. The broad Ohio, glistening in the sun, lay at the base of the mountain.

Upon the bluff overlooking the river, and under the brow of the mountain, lay the frontier fort. In the clear atmosphere it stood out in bold relief. A small, low structure surrounded by a high stockade fence was all, and yet it did not seem unworthy of its fame. Those watchful, forbidding loopholes, the blackened walls and timbers, told the history of ten long, bloody years. The whole effect was one of menace, as if the fort sent out a defiance to the wilderness, and meant to protect the few dozen log cabins clustered on the hillside.

"How will we ever get across that big river?" asked Jim, practically.

"Wade—swim," answered the hunter, laconically, and began the descent of the ridge. An hour's rapid walking brought the three to the river. Depositing his rifle in a clump of willows and directing the boys to do the same with their guns, the hunter splashed into the water. His companions followed him into the shallow water and waded a hundred yards, which brought them near the island that they now perceived hid the fort. The hunter swam the remaining distance, and, climbing the bank, looked back for the boys. They were close behind him. Then he strode across the island, perhaps a quarter of a mile wide.

"We've a long swim here," said Wetzel, waving his hand toward the main channel of the river. "Good fer it?" he inquired of Joe, since Jim had not received any injuries during the short captivity and consequently showed more endurance.

"Good for anything," answered Joe, with that coolness Wetzel had been quick to observe in him.

The hunter cast a sharp glance at the lad's haggard face, his bruised temple, and his hair matted with blood. In that look he read Joe thoroughly. Had the young man known the result of that scrutiny, he would have been pleased as well as puzzled, for the hunter had said to himself: "A brave lad an' the border fever's on him."

"Swim close to me," said Wetzel, and he plunged into the river. The task was accomplished without accident.

"See the big cabin, thar, on the hillside? Thar's Colonel Zane in the door," said Wetzel.

As they neared the building several men joined the one who had been pointed out as the colonel. It was evident the boys were the subject of their conversation. Presently Colonel Zane left the group and came toward them. The brothers saw a handsome, stalwart man, in the prime of life.

"Well, Lew, what luck?" he said to Wetzel.

"Not much. I treed five Injuns, an' two got away," answered the hunter as he walked toward the fort.

"Lads, welcome to Fort Henry," said Colonel Zane, a smile lighting his dark face. "The others of your party arrived safely. They certainly will be overjoyed to see you."

"Colonel Zane, I had a letter from my uncle to you," replied Jim; "but the Indians took that and everything else we had with us."

"Never mind the letter. I knew your uncle, and your father, too. Come into the house and change those wet clothes. And you, my lad, have got an ugly knock on the head. Who gave you that?"

"Jim Girty."

"What?" exclaimed the colonel.

"Jim Girty did that. He was with a party of Delawares who ran across us. They were searching for Wetzel."

"Girty and the Delawares! The devil's to pay now. And you say hunting Wetzel? I must learn more about it. It looks bad. But tell me, how did Girty come to strike you?"

"I pulled his nose."

"You did? Good! Good!" cried Colonel Zane, heartily. "By George, that's great! Tell me—but wait until you are more comfortable. Your packs came safely on Jeff's raft, and you will find them inside."

As Joe followed the colonel he heard one of the other men say:

"Like as two peas in a pod."

Farther on he saw an Indian standing a little apart from the others. Hearing Joe's slight exclamation of surprise, he turned, disclosing a fine, manly countenance, characterized by calm dignity. The Indian read the boy's thought.

"Ugh! Me friend," he said in English.

"That's my Shawnee guide, Tomepomehala. He's a good fellow, although Jonathan and Wetzel declare the only good Indian is a dead one. Come right in here. There are your packs, and you'll find water outside the door."

Thus saying, Colonel Zane led the brothers into a small room, brought out their packs, and left them. He came back presently with a couple of soft towels.

"Now you lads fix up a bit; then come out and meet my family and tell us all about your adventure. By that time dinner will be ready."

"Geminy! Don't that towel remind you of home?" said Joe, when the colonel had gone. "From the looks of things, Colonel Zane means to have comfort here in the wilderness. He struck me as being a fine man."

The boys were indeed glad to change the few articles of clothing the Indians had left them, and when they were shaved and dressed they presented an entirely different appearance. Once more they were twin brothers, in costume and feature. Joe contrived, by brushing his hair down on his forehead, to conceal the discolored bump.

"I think I saw a charming girl," observed Joe.

"Suppose you did—what then?" asked Jim, severely.

"Why—nothing—see here, mayn't I admire a pretty girl if I want?"

"No, you may not. Joe, will nothing ever cure you? I should think the thought of Miss Well's—"

"Look here, Jim; she don't care—at least, it's very little she cares. And I'm—I'm not worthy of her."

"Turn around here and face me," said the young minister sharply.

Joe turned and looked in his brother's eyes.

"Have you trifled with her, as you have with so many others? Tell me. I know you don't lie."

"No."

"Then what do you mean?"

"Nothing much, Jim, except I'm really not worthy of her. I'm no good, you know, and she ought to get a fellow like—like you."

"Absurd! You ought to be ashamed of yourself."

"Never mind me. See here; don't you admire her?"

"Why—why, yes," stammered Jim, flushing a dark guilty red at the direct question. "Who could help admiring her?"

"That's what I thought. And I know she admires you for qualities which I lack. Nell's like a tender vine just beginning to creep around and cling to something strong. She cares for me; but her love is like the vine. It may hurt her a little to tear that love away, but it won't kill her; and in the end it will be best for her. You need a good wife. What could I do with a woman? Go in and win her, Jim."

"Joe, you're sacrificing yourself again for me," cried Jim, white to the lips. "It's wrong to yourself and wrong to her. I tell you—"

"Enough!" Joe's voice cut in cold and sharp. "Usually you influence me; but sometimes you can't. I say this: Nell will drift into your arms as surely as the leaf falls. It will not hurt her—it will be best for her. Remember, she is yours for the winning."

"You do not say whether that will hurt you," whispered Jim.

"Come—we'll find Colonel Zane," said Joe, opening the door.

They went out in the hallway which opened into the yard as well as the larger room through which the colonel had first conducted them. As Jim, who was in advance, passed into this apartment a trim figure entered from the yard. It was Nell, and she ran directly against him. Her face was flushed, her eyes were beaming with gladness, and she seemed the incarnation of girlish joy.

"Oh, Joe," was all she whispered. But the happiness and welcome in that whisper could never have been better expressed in longer speech. Then slightly, ever so slightly, she tilted her sweet face up to his.

It all happened with the quickness of thought. In a single instant Jim saw the radiant face, the outstretched hands, and heard the glad whisper. He knew that she had again mistaken him for Joe; but for his life he could not draw back his head. He had kissed her, and even as his lips thrilled with her tremulous caress he flushed with the shame of his deceit.

"You're mistaken again—I'm Jim," he whispered.

For a moment they stood staring into each other's eyes, slowly awakening to what had really happened, slowly conscious of a sweet, alluring power. Then Colonel Zane's cheery voice rang in their ears.

"Ah, here's Nellie and your brother! Now, lads, tell me which is which!"

"That's Jim, and I'm Joe," answered the latter. He appeared not to notice his brother, and his greeting to Nell was natural and hearty. For the moment she drew the attention of the others from them.

Joe found himself listening to the congratulations of a number of people. Among the many names he remembered were those of Mrs. Zane, Silas Zane, and Major McColloch. Then he found himself gazing at the most beautiful girl he had ever seen in his life.

"My only sister, Mrs. Alfred Clarke—once Betty Zane, and the heroine of Fort Henry," said Colonel Zane proudly, with his arm around the slender, dark-eyed girl.

"I would brave the Indians and the wilderness again for this pleasure," replied Joe gallantly, as he bowed low over the little hand she cordially extended.

"Bess, is dinner ready?" inquired Colonel Zane of his comely wife. She nodded her head, and the colonel led the way into the adjoining room. "I know you boys must be hungry as bears."

During the meal Colonel Zane questioned his guests about their journey, and as to the treatment they had received at the hands of the Indians. He smiled at the young minister's earnestness in regard to the conversion of the redmen, and he laughed outright when Joe said he guessed he came to the frontier because it was too slow at home.

"I am sure your desire for excitement will soon be satisfied, if indeed it is not so already," remarked the colonel. "But as to the realization of your brother's hopes I am not so sanguine. Undoubtedly the Moravian missionaries have accomplished wonders with the Indians. Not long ago I visited the Village of Peace—the Indian name for the mission—and was struck by the friendliness and industry which prevailed there. Truly it *was* a village of peace. Yet it is almost too early to be certain of permanent success of this work. The

Indian's nature is one hard to understand. He is naturally roving and restless, which, however, may be owing to his habit of moving from place to place in search of good hunting grounds. I believe—though I must confess I haven't seen any pioneers who share my belief—that the savage has a beautiful side to his character. I know of many noble deeds done by them, and I believe, if they are honestly dealt with, they will return good for good. There are bad ones, of course; but the French traders, and men like the Girtys, have caused most of this long war. Jonathan and Wetzel tell me the Shawnees and Chippewas have taken the warpath again. Then the fact that the Girtys are with the Delawares is reason for alarm. We have been comparatively quiet here of late. Did you boys learn to what tribe your captors belong? Did Wetzel say?"

"He did not; he spoke little, but I will say he was exceedingly active," answered Joe, with a smile.

"To have seen Wetzel fight Indians is something you are not likely to forget," said Colonel Zane grimly. "Now, tell me, how did those Indians wear their scalplock?"

"Their heads were shaved closely, with the exception of a little place on top. The remaining hair was twisted into a tuft, tied tightly, and into this had been thrust a couple of painted pins. When Wetzel scalped the Indians the pins fell out. I picked one up, and found it to be bone."

"You will make a woodsman, that's certain," replied Colonel Zane. "The Indians were Shawnees on the warpath. Well, we will not borrow trouble, for when it comes in the shape of redskins it usually comes quickly. Mr. Wells seemed anxious to resume the journey down the river; but I shall try to persuade him to remain with us awhile. Indeed, I am sorry I cannot keep you all here at Fort Henry, and more especially the girls. On the border we need young people, and while I do not want to frighten the women, I fear there will be more than Indians fighting for them."

"I hope not; but we have come prepared for anything," said Kate, with a quiet smile. "Our home was with Uncle, and when he announced his intention of going west we decided our duty was to go with him."

"You were right, and I hope you will find a happy home," rejoined Colonel Zane. "If life among the Indians proves to be too hard, we shall welcome you here. Betty, show the girls your pets and Indian trinkets. I am going to take the boys to Silas' cabin to see Mr. Wells, and then show them over the fort."

As they went out Joe saw the Indian guide standing in exactly the same position as when they entered the building.

"Can't that Indian move?" he asked curiously.

"He can cover one hundred miles in a day, when he wants to," replied Colonel Zane. "He is resting now. An Indian will often stand or sit in one position for many hours."

"He's a fine-looking chap," remarked Joe, and then to himself: "but I don't like him. I guess I'm prejudiced."

"You'll learn to like Tome, as we call him."

"Colonel Zane, I want a light for my pipe. I haven't had a smoke since the day we were captured. That blamed redskin took my tobacco. It's lucky I had some in my other pack. I'd like to meet him again; also Silvertip and that brute Girty."

"My lad, don't make such wishes," said Colonel Zane, earnestly. "You were indeed fortunate to escape, and I can well understand your feelings. There is nothing I should like better than to see Girty over the sights of my rifle; but I never hunt after danger, and to look for Girty is to court death."

"But Wetzel—"

"Ah, my lad, I know Wetzel goes alone in the woods; but then, he is different from other men. Before you leave I will tell you all about him."

Colonel Zane went around the corner of the cabin and returned with a live coal on a chip of wood, which Joe placed in the bowl of his pipe, and because of the strong breeze stepped close to the cabin wall. Being a keen observer, he noticed many small, round holes in the logs. They were so near together that the timbers had an odd, speckled appearance, and there was hardly a place where he could have put his thumb without covering a hole. At first he thought they were made by a worm or bird peculiar to that region; but finally he concluded that they were bullet holes. He thrust his knife blade into one, and out rolled a leaden ball.

"I'd like to have been here when these were made," he said.

"Well, at the time I wished I was back on the Potomac," replied Colonel Zane.

They found the old missionary on the doorstep of the adjacent cabin. He appeared discouraged when Colonel Zane interrogated him, and said that he was impatient because of the delay.

"Mr. Wells, is it not possible that you underrate the danger of your enterprise?"

"I fear naught but the Lord," answered the old man.

"Do you not fear for those with you?" went on the colonel earnestly. "I am heart and soul with you in your work, but want to impress upon you that the time is not propitious. It is a long journey to the village, and the way is beset with dangers of which you have no idea. Will you not remain here with me for a few weeks, or, at least, until my scouts report?"

"I thank you; but go I will."

"Then let me entreat you to remain here for a few days, so that I may send my brother Jonathan and Wetzel with you. If any can guide you safely to the Village of Peace it will be they."

At this moment Joe saw two men approaching from the fort, and recognized one of them as Wetzel. He doubted not that the other was Lord Dunmore's famous guide and hunter, Jonathan Zane. In features he resembled the colonel, and was as tall as Wetzel, although not so muscular or wide of chest.

Joe felt the same thrill he had experienced while watching the frontiersmen at Fort Pitt. Wetzel and Jonathan spoke a word to Colonel Zane and then stepped aside. The hunters stood lithe and erect, with the easy, graceful poise of Indians.

"We'll take two canoes, day after tomorrow," said Jonathan, decisively, to Colonel Zane. "Have you a rifle for Wetzel? The Delawares got his."

Colonel Zane pondered over the question; rifles were not scarce at the fort, but a weapon that Wetzel would use was hard to find.

"The hunter may have my rifle," said the old missionary. "I have no use for a weapon with which to destroy God's creatures. My brother was a frontiersman; he left this rifle to me. I remember hearing him say once that if a man knew exactly the weight of lead and powder needed, it would shoot absolutely true."

He went into the cabin, and presently came out with a long object wrapped in linsey cloths. Unwinding the coverings, he brought to view a rifle, the proportions of which caused Jonathan's eyes to glisten, and brought an exclamation from Colonel Zane. Wetzel balanced the gun in his hands. It was fully six feet long; the barrel was large, and the dark steel finely polished; the stock was black walnut, ornamented with silver trimmings. Using Jonathan's powder flask and bullet pouch, Wetzel proceeded to load the weapon. He poured out a quantity of powder in the palm of his hand, performing the action quickly and dexterously, but was so slow while measuring it that Joe wondered if he were counting the grains. Next he selected a bullet out of a dozen which Jonathan held toward him. He examined it carefully and tried it in the muzzle of the rifle. Evidently it did not please him, for he took another. Finally he scraped a bullet with his knife, and placing it in the center of a small linsey rag, deftly forced it down. He adjusted the flint, dropped a few grains of powder in the pan, and then looked around for a mark at which to shoot.

Joe observed that the hunters and Colonel Zane were as serious regarding the work as if at that moment some important issue depended upon the accuracy of the rifle.

"There, Lew; there's a good shot. It's pretty far, even for you, when you don't know the gun," said Colonel Zane, pointing toward the river.

Joe saw the end of a log, about the size of a man's head, sticking out of the water, perhaps a hundred and fifty yards distant. He thought to hit it would be a fine shot; but was amazed when he heard Colonel Zane say to several men who had joined the group that Wetzel intended to shoot at a turtle on the log. By straining his eyes Joe succeeded in distinguishing a small lump, which he concluded was the turtle.

Wetzel took a step forward; the long, black rifle was raised with a stately sweep. The instant it reached a level a thread of flame burst forth, followed by a peculiarly clear, ringing report.

"Did he hit?" asked Colonel Zane, eagerly as a boy.

"I allow he did," answered Jonathan.

"I'll go and see," said Joe. He ran down the bank, along the beach, and stepped on the log. He saw a turtle about the size of an ordinary saucer. Picking it up, he saw a bullet hole in the shell near the middle. The bullet had gone through the turtle, and it was quite dead. Joe carried it to the waiting group.

"I allowed so," declared Jonathan.

Wetzel examined the turtle, and turning to the old missionary, said:

"Your brother spoke the truth, an' I thank you fer the rifle."

Chapter
VIII

"So you want to know all about Wetzel?" inquired Colonel Zane of Joe, when, having left Jim and Mr. Wells, they returned to the cabin.

"I am immensely interested in him," replied Joe.

"Well, I don't think there's anything singular in that. I know Wetzel better, perhaps, than any man living; but have seldom talked about him. He doesn't like it. He is by birth a Virginian; I should say, forty years old. We were boys together, and I am a little beyond that age. He was like any of the lads, except that he excelled us all in strength and agility. When he was nearly eighteen years old a band of Indians—Delawares, I think—crossed the border on a marauding expedition far into Virginia. They burned the old Wetzel homestead and murdered the father, mother, two sisters, and a baby brother. The terrible shock nearly killed Lewis, who for a time was very ill. When he recovered he went in search of his brothers, Martin and John Wetzel, who were hunting, and brought them back to their desolated home. Over the ashes of the home and the graves of the loved ones the broth-

ers swore sleepless and eternal vengeance. The elder brothers have been devoted all these twenty years and more to the
killing of Indians; but Lewis has been the great foe of the
redman. You have already seen an example of his deeds, and
will hear of more. His name is a household word on the border. Scores of times he has saved, actually saved, this fort
and settlement. His knowledge of savage ways surpasses by
far Boone's, Major McColloch's, Jonathan's, or any of the
hunters'."

"Then hunting Indians is his sole occupation?"

"He lives for that purpose alone. He is very seldom in the
settlement. Sometimes he stays here a few days, especially if
he is needed; but usually he roams the forests."

"What did Jeff Lynn mean when he said that some people
think Wetzel is crazy?"

"There are many who think the man mad; but I do not.
When the passion for Indian hunting comes upon him he is
fierce, almost frenzied, yet perfectly sane. While here he is
quiet, seldom speaks except when spoken to, and is taciturn
with strangers. He often comes to my cabin and sits beside
the fire for hours. I think he finds pleasure in the conversation and laughter of friends. He is fond of the children, and
would do anything for my sister Betty."

"His life must be lonely and sad," remarked Joe.

"The life of any borderman is that; but Wetzel's is particularly so."

"What is he called by the Indians?"

"They call him *Atelang,* or, in English, Deathwind."

"By George! That's what Silvertip said in French—'*Le
Vent de la Mort.*' "

"Yes; you have it right. A French fur trader gave Wetzel
that name years ago, and it has clung to him. The Indians say

the Deathwind blows through the forest whenever Wetzel stalks on their trail."

"Colonel Zane, don't you think me superstitious," whispered Joe, leaning toward the colonel, "but I heard the wind blow through the forest."

"What!" exclaimed Colonel Zane. He saw that Joe was in earnest, for the remembrance of the moan had more than once paled his cheek and caused beads of perspiration to collect on his brow.

Joe related the circumstances of that night, and at the end of his narrative Colonel Zane sat silent and thoughtful.

"You don't really think it was Wetzel who moaned?" he asked, at length.

"No, I don't," replied Joe quickly; "but, Colonel Zane, I heard the moan as plainly as I can hear your voice. I heard it twice. Now, what was it?"

"Jonathan said the same thing to me once. He had been out hunting with Wetzel; they separated, and during the night Jonathan heard the wind. The next day he ran across a dead Indian. He believes Wetzel makes the noise, and so do the hunters; but I think it is simply the moan of the night wind through the trees. I have heard it at times, when my very blood ran cold."

"I tried to think it was the wind soughing through the pines, but am afraid I didn't succeed very well. Anyhow, I knew Wetzel instantly, just as Jeff Lynn said I would. He killed those Indians in an instant, and he must have an iron arm."

"Wetzel excels in strength and speed any man, red or white, on the frontier. He can run away from Jonathan, who is as swift as an Indian. He's stronger than any of the other men. I remember one day old Hugh Bennet's wagon wheels stuck in a bog down by the creek. Hugh tried, as several others did, to move the wheels; but they couldn't be made to budge. Along came Wetzel, pushed away the men, and lifted the wagon unaided. It would take hours to tell you about him. In brief, among all the border scouts and hunters Wetzel stands alone. No wonder the Indians fear him. He is as swift as an eagle, strong as mountain ash, keen as a fox, and absolutely tireless and implacable."

"How long have you been here, Colonel Zane?"

"More than twelve years, and it has been one long fight."

"I'm afraid I'm too late for the fun," said Joe, with his quiet laugh.

"Not by about twelve more years," answered Colonel Zane, studying the expression on Joe's face. "When I came out here years ago I had the same adventurous spirit which I see in you. It has been considerably quelled, however. I have seen many a daring young fellow get the border fever, and with it his death. Let me advise you to learn the ways of the hunters; to watch someone skilled in woodcraft. Perhaps Wetzel himself will take you in hand. I don't mind saying that he spoke of you to me in a tone I never heard Lew use before."

"He did?" questioned Joe, eagerly, flushing with pleasure. "Do you think he'd take me out? Dare I ask him?"

"Don't be impatient. Perhaps I can arrange it. Come over here now to Metzar's place. I want to make you acquainted with him. These boys have all been cutting timber; they've just come in for dinner. Be easy and quiet with them; then you'll get on."

Colonel Zane introduced Joe to five sturdy boys and left him in their company. Joe sat down on a log outside a cabin and leisurely surveyed the young men. They all looked about the same: strong without being heavy, light-haired and bronzed-faced. In their turn they carefully judged Joe. A newcomer from the East was always regarded with some doubt. If they expected to hear Joe talk much they were mistaken. He appeared good-natured, but not too friendly.

"Fine weather we're havin'," said Dick Metzar.

"Fine," agreed Joe, laconically.

"Like frontier life?"

"Sure."

A silence ensued after this breaking of the ice. The boys were awaiting their turn at a little wooden bench upon which stood a bucket of water and a basin.

"Hear ye got ketched by some Shawnees?" remarked another youth, as he rolled up his shirtsleeves. They all looked at Joe now. It was not improbable their estimate of him would be greatly influenced by the way he answered this question.

"Yes; was captive for three days."

"Did ye knock any redskins over?" The question was artfully put to draw Joe out. Above all things, the bordermen detested boastfulness; tried on Joe the ruse failed signally.

"I was scared speechless most of the time," answered Joe, with his pleasant smile.

"By gosh, I don't blame ye!" burst out Will Metzar. "I hed that experience onct, an' onct's enough."

The boys laughed and looked in a more friendly manner at Joe. Though he said he had been frightened, his cool and careless manner belied his words. In Joe's low voice and clear, gray eye there was something potent and magnetic, which subtly influenced those with whom he came in contact.

While his new friends were at dinner Joe strolled over to where Colonel Zane sat on the doorstep of his home.

"How did you get on with the boys?" inquired the colonel.

"All right, I hope. Say, Colonel Zane, I'd like to talk to your Indian guide."

Colonel Zane spoke a few words in the Indian language to the guide, who left his post and came over to them. The colonel then had a short conversation with him, at the conclusion of which he pointed toward Joe.

"How do—shake," said Tome, extending his hand.

Joe smiled, and returned the friendly hand pressure.

"Shawnee—ketch'um?" asked the Indian, in his fairly intelligible English.

Joe nodded his head, while Colonel Zane spoke once more in Shawnee, explaining the cause of Silvertip's enmity.

"Shawnee—chief—one—bad—Injun," replied Tome, seriously. "Silver—mad—thunder-mad. Ketchtum paleface—scalp'um sure."

After giving this warning the chief returned to his former position near the corner of the cabin.

"He can talk in English fairly well, much better than the Shawnee brave who talked with me the other day," observed Joe.

"Some of the Indians speak the language almost fluently," said Colonel Zane. "You could hardly have distinguished Logan's speech from a white man's. Cornplanter uses good English, as also does my brother's wife, a Wyandot girl."

"Did your brother marry an Indian?" and Joe plainly showed his surprise.

"Indeed he did, and a most beautiful girl she is. I'll tell you Isaac's story sometime. He was a captive among the Wyandots for ten years. The chief's daughter, Myeerah, loved him, kept him from being tortured, and finally saved him from the stake."

"Well, that floors me," said Joe; "yet I don't see why it should. I'm just surprised. Where is your brother now?"

"He lives with the tribe. He and Myeerah are working hard for peace. We are now on more friendly terms with the great Wyandots, or Hurons, as we call them, than ever before."

"Who is the big man coming from the fort?" asked Joe, suddenly observing a stalwart frontiersman approaching.

"Major Sam McColloch. You have met him. He's the man who jumped his horse from yonder bluff."

"Jonathan and he have the same look, the same swing," observed Joe, as he ran his eye over the major. His faded buckskin costume, beaded, fringed, and laced, was similar to that of the colonel's brother. Powder flask and bullet pouch were made from cow horns and slung around his neck on deerhide strings. The hunting coat was unlaced, exposing, under the long, fringed borders, a tunic of the same well-tanned, but finer and softer, material. As he walked, the flaps of his coat fell back, showing a belt containing two knives, sheathed in heavy buckskin, and a bright tomahawk. He carried a long rifle in the hollow of his arm.

"These hunters have the same kind of buckskin suits," continued Joe; "still, it doesn't seem to me the clothes make the resemblance to each other. The way these men stand, walk, and act is what strikes me particularly, as in the case of Wetzel."

"I know what you mean. The flashing eye, the erect poise of expectation, and the springy step—those, my lad, come from a life spent in the woods. Well, it's a grand way to live."

"Colonel, my horse is laid up," said Major McColloch, coming to the steps. He bowed pleasantly to Joe.

"So you are going to Short Creek? You can have one of my horses, but first come inside and we'll talk over your expedition."

The afternoon passed uneventfully for Joe. His brother and Mr. Wells were absorbed in plans for their future work, and Nell and Kate were resting; therefore he was forced to find such amusement or occupation as was possible in or near the stockade.

Chapter
IX

Joe went to bed that night with a promise to himself to rise early next morning, for he had been invited to take part in a "raising," which term meant that a new cabin was to be erected, and such task was ever an event in the lives of the settlers.

The following morning Joe rose early, dressing himself in a complete buckskin suit, for which he had exchanged his good garments of cloth. Never before had he felt so comfortable. He wanted to hop, skip, and jump. The soft, undressed buckskin was as warm and smooth as silk plush; the weight so light, the moccasins so well-fitting and springy, that he had to put himself under considerable restraint to keep from capering about like a frolicsome colt.

The possession of this buckskin outfit, and the rifle and accoutrements which went with the bargain, marked the last stage in Joe's surrender to the border fever. The silent, shaded glens, the mystery of the woods, the breath of this wild, free life claimed him from this moment entirely and forever.

He met the others, however, with a serene face, showing

no trace of the emotion which welled up strongly from his heart. Nell glanced shyly at him; Kate playfully voiced her admiration; Jim met him with a brotherly ridicule which bespoke his affection as well as his amusement; but Colonel Zane, having once yielded to the same burning, riotous craving for freedom which now stirred in the boy's heart, understood, and felt warmly drawn toward the lad. He said nothing, though as he watched Joe his eyes were grave and kind. In his long frontier life, where many a day measured the life and fire of ordinary years, he had seen lad after lad go down before this forest fever. It was well, he thought, because the freedom of the soil depended on these wild, light-footed boys; yet it always made him sad. How many youths, his brother among them, lay under the fragrant pine needle carpet of the forest, in their last earthly sleep!

The "raising" brought out all the settlement—the women to look on and gossip, while the children played; the men to bend their backs in the moving of the heavy timbers. They celebrated the erection of a new cabin as a noteworthy event. As a social function it had a prominent place in the settlers' short list of pleasures.

Joe watched the proceeding with the same pleasure and surprise he had felt in everything pertaining to border life.

To him this log-raising appeared the hardest kind of labor. Yet it was plain these hardy men, these low-voiced women, and merry children regarded the work as something far more significant than the mere building of a cabin. After a while he understood the meaning of the scene. A kindred spirit, the spirit of the pioneer, drew them all into one large family. This was another cabin; another home; another advance toward the conquering of the wilderness, for which these brave men and women were giving their lives. In the bright-eyed children's glee, when they clapped their little hands at the mounting logs, Joe saw the progress, the march of civilization.

"Well, I'm sorry you're to leave us tonight," remarked Colonel Zane to Joe, as the young man came over to where he, his wife, and sister watched the work. "Jonathan said all was ready for your departure at sundown."

"Do we travel by night?"

"Indeed, yes, my lad. There are Indians everywhere on the river. I think, however, with Jack and Lew handling the paddles, you will slip by safely. The plan is to keep along the south shore all night; then cross over at a place called Girty's Point, where you are to remain in hiding during daylight. From there you paddle up Yellow Creek; then portage across country to the head of the Tuscarawas. Another night's journey will then bring you to the Village of Peace."

Jim and Mr. Wells, with his nieces, joined the party now, and all stood watching as the last logs were put in place.

"Colonel Zane, my first log-raising is an education to me," said the young minster, in his earnest manner.

"This scene is so full of life. I never saw such goodwill among laboring men. Look at that brawny-armed giant standing on the topmost log. How he whistles as he swings his ax! Mr. Wells, does it not impress you?"

"The pioneers must be brothers because of their isolation and peril; to be brothers means to love one another; to love one another is to love God. What you see in this fraternity is God. And I want to see this same beautiful feeling among the Indians."

"I have seen it," said Colonel Zane, to the old missionary. "When I came out here alone twelve years ago the Indians were peaceable. If the pioneers had paid for land, as I paid Cornplanter, there would never have been a border war. But no; the settlers must grasp every acre they could. Then the

Indians rebelled; then the Girtys and their allies spread discontent, and now the border is a bloody warpath."

"Have the Jesuit missionaries accomplished anything with these war tribes?" inquired Jim.

"No; their work has been chiefly among the Indians near Detroit and northward. The Hurons, Delawares, Shawnees, and other western tribes have been demoralized by the French traders' rum and incited to fierce hatred by Girty and his renegades. Your work at Gnaddenhutten must be among these hostile tribes, and it is surely a hazardous undertaking."

"My life is God's," murmured the old minister. No fear could assail his steadfast faith.

"Jim, it strikes me you'd be more likely to impress these Indians Colonel Zane spoke of if you'd get a suit like mine and wear a knife and tomahawk," interposed Joe, cheerfully. "Then, if you couldn't convert, you could scalp them."

"Well, well, let us hope for the best," said Colonel Zane, when the laughter had subsided. "We'll go over to dinner now. Come, all of you. Jonathan, bring Wetzel. Betty, make him come, if you can."

As the party slowly wended its way toward the colonel's cabin Jim and Nell found themselves side by side. They had not exchanged a word since the evening previous, when Jim had kissed her. Unable to look at each other now, and finding speech difficult, they walked in embarrassed silence.

"Doesn't Joe look splendid in his hunting suit?" asked Jim, presently.

"I hadn't noticed. Yes; he looks well," replied Nell, carelessly. She was too indifferent to be natural.

"Are you angry with him?"

"Certainly not."

Jim was always simple and frank in his relations with women. He had none of his brother's fluency of speech, with neither confidence, boldness, nor understanding of the intricate mazes of a woman's moods.

"But—you are angry with—me?" he whispered.

Nell flushed to her temples, yet she did not raise her eyes nor reply.

"It was a terrible thing for me to do," went on Jim, hesitatingly. "I don't know why I took advantage—of—of your mistaking me for Joe. If you only hadn't held up your mouth. No—I don't mean that—of course you didn't. But—well, I couldn't help it. I'm guilty. I have thought of little else. Some wonderful feeling has possessed me ever since— since—"

"What has Joe been saying about me?" demanded Nell, her eyes burning like opals.

"Why, hardly anything," answered Jim, haltingly. "I took him to task about—about what I considered might be wrong to you. Joe has never been very careful of young ladies' feelings, and I thought—well, it was none of my business. He said he honestly cared for you, that you had taught him how unworthy he was of a good woman. But he's wrong there. Joe is wild and reckless, yet his heart is a well of gold. He is a diamond in the rough. Just now he is possessed by wild notions of hunting Indians and roaming through these forests; but he'll come round all right. I wish I could tell you how much he has done for me, how much I love him, how I know him! He can be made worthy of any woman. He will outgrow this fiery, daring spirit, and then—won't you help him?"

"I will, if he will let me," softly whispered Nell, irresistibly drawn by the strong, earnest love thrilling in his voice.

Chapter
X

Once more out under the blue-black vault of heaven, with its myriads of twinkling stars, the voyagers resumed their westward journey. Whispered farewells of new but sincere friends lingered in their ears. Now the great looming bulk of the fort above them faded into the obscure darkness, leaving a feeling as if a protector had gone—perhaps forever. Admonished to absolute silence by the stern guides, who seemed indeed to have embarked upon a dark and deadly mission, the voyagers lay back in the canoes and thought and listened. The water eddied with soft gurgles in the wake of the racing canoes; but that musical sound was all they heard. The paddles might have been shadows, for all the splash they made; they cut the water swiftly and noiselessly. Onward the frail barks glided into black space, side by side, close under the overhanging willows. Long moments passed into long hours, as the guides paddled tirelessly as if their sinews were cords of steel.

With gray dawn came the careful landing of the canoes, a cold breakfast eaten under cover of a willow thicket, and the beginning of a long day while they were lying hidden from the keen eyes of Indian scouts, waiting for the friendly mantle of night.

The hours dragged until once more the canoes were launched, this time not on the broad Ohio, but on a stream that mirrored no shining stars as it flowed still and somber under the dense foliage.

The voyagers spoke not, nor whispered, nor scarcely moved, so menacing had become the slow, listening caution of Wetzel and Zane. Snapping of twigs somewhere in the inscrutable darkness delayed them for long moments. Any moment the air might resound with the horrible Indian war whoop. Every second was heavy with fear. How marvelous that these scouts, penetrating the wilderness of gloom, glided on surely, silently, safely! Instinct, or the eyes of the lynx, guided their course. But another dark night wore on to the tardy dawn, and each of its fearful hours numbered miles past and gone.

The sun was rising in ruddy glory when Wetzel ran his canoe into the bank just ahead of a sharp bend in the stream.

"Do we get out here?" asked Jim, seeing Jonathan turn his canoe toward Wetzel's.

"The village lies yonder, around the bend," answered the guide. "Wetzel cannot go there, so I'll take you all in my canoe."

"There's no room; I'll wait," replied Joe, quietly. Jim noted his look—a strange, steady glance it was—and then saw him fix his eyes upon Nell, watching her until the canoe passed around the green-bordered bend in the stream.

Unmistakable signs of an Indian town were now evident. Dozens of graceful birchen canoes lay upon the well-cleared banks; a log bridge spanned the stream; above the slight ridge of rising ground could be seen the poles of Indian teepees.

As the canoe grated upon the sandy beach a little Indian

boy, who was playing in the shallow water, raised his head and smiled.

"That's an Indian boy," whispered Kate.

"The dear little fellow!" exclaimed Nell.

The boy came running up to them, when they were landed, with pleasure and confidence shining in his dusky eyes. Save for tiny buckskin breeches, he was naked, and his shiny skin gleamed gold-bronze in the sunlight. He was a singularly handsome child.

"Me—Benny," he lisped in English, holding up his little hand to Nell.

The action was as loving and trusting as any that could have been manifested by a white child. Jonathan Zane stared with a curious light in his dark eyes; Mr. Wells and Jim looked as though they doubted the evidence of their own sight. Here, even in an Indian boy, was incontestable proof that the savage nature could be tamed and civilized.

With a tender exclamation Nell bent over the child and kissed him.

Jonathan Zane swung his canoe upstream for the purpose of bringing Joe. The trim little bark slipped out of sight round the bend. Presently its gray curved nose peeped from behind the willows; then the canoe swept into view again. There was only one person in it, and that the guide.

"Where is my brother?" asked Jim, in amazement.

"Gone," answered Zane, quietly.

"Gone! What do you mean? Gone? Perhaps you have missed the spot where you left him."

"They're both gone."

Nell and Jim gazed at each other with slowly whitening faces.

"Come, I'll take you up to the village," said Zane, getting out of his canoe. All noticed that he was careful to take his weapons with him.

"Can't you tell us what it means—this disappearance?" asked Jim, his voice low and anxious.

"They're gone, canoe and all. I knew Wetzel was going, but I didn't calkilate on the lad. Mebbe he followed Wetzel, mebbe he didn't," answered the taciturn guide, and he spoke no more.

In his keen expectation and wonder as to what the village would be like, Jim momentarily forgot his brother's disappearance, and when he arrived at the top of the bank he surveyed the scene with eagerness. What he saw was more imposing than the Village of Peace which he had conjured up in his imagination. Confronting him was a level plain, in the center of which stood a wide, low structure surrounded by log cabins, and these in turn encircled by Indian teepees. A number of large trees, mostly full-foliaged maples, shaded the clearing. The settlement swarmed with Indians. A few shrill halloos uttered by the first observers of the newcomers brought braves, maidens, and children trooping toward the party with friendly curiosity.

Jonathan Zane stepped before a cabin adjoining the large structure and called in at the open door. A short, stoop-shouldered white man, clad in faded linsey, appeared on the threshold. His serious, lined face had the unmistakable benevolent aspect peculiar to most teachers of the gospel.

"Mr. Zeisberger, I've fetched a party from Fort Henry," said Zane, indicating those he had guided. Then, without another word, never turning his dark face to the right or left, he hurried down the lane through the throng of Indians.

Jim remembered, as he saw the guide vanish over the bank of the creek, that he had heard Colonel Zane say that Jonathan, as well as Wetzel, hated the sight of an Indian. No doubt long years of war and bloodshed had rendered these two great hunters callous. To them there could be no discrimination—an Indian was an Indian.

"Mr. Wells, welcome to the Village of Peace!" exclaimed Mr. Zeisberger, wringing the old missionary's hand. "The years have not been so long but that I remember you."

"Happy, indeed, am I to get here, after all these dark, dangerous journeys," returned Mr. Wells. "I have brought my nieces, Nell and Kate, who were children when you left Williamsburg, and this young man, James Downs, a minister of God, and earnest in his hope for our work."

"A glorious work it is! Welcome, young ladies, to our peaceful village. And, young man, I greet you with heartfelt thankfulness. We need young men. Come in, all of you, and share my cabin. I'll have your luggage brought up. I have lived in this hut alone. With some little labor, and the magic touch women bring to the making of a home, we can be most comfortable here."

Mr. Zeisberger gave his own room to the girls, assuring them with a smile that it was the most luxurious in the village. The apartment contained a chair, a table, and a bed of Indian blankets and buffalo robes. A few pegs driven in the chinks between the logs completed the furnishings. Sparse as were the comforts, they appealed warmly to the girls, who, weary from their voyage, lay down to rest.

"I am not fatigued," said Mr. Wells, to his old friend. "I want to hear all about your work, what you have done, and what you hope to do."

"We have met with wonderful success, far beyond our wildest dreams," responded Mr. Zeisberger. "Certainly we have been blessed of God."

Then the missionary began a long, detailed account of the Moravian Mission's efforts among the western tribes. The work lay chiefly among the Delawares, a noble nation of redmen, intelligent, and wonderfully susceptible to the teaching of the gospel. Among the eastern Delawares, living on the other side of the Allegheny Mountains, the missionaries had succeeded in converting many; and it was chiefly through the western exploration of Frederick Post that his Church decided the Indians of the west could as well be taught to lead Christian lives. The first attempt to convert the western redmen took place upon the upper Allegheny, where many Indians, including Allemewi, a blind Delaware chief, accepted the faith. The mission decided, however, it would be best to move farther west, where the Delawares had migrated and were more numerous.

In April, 1770, more than ten years before, sixteen canoes, filled with converted Indians and missionaries, drifted down the Allegheny to Fort Pitt; thence down the Ohio to the Big Beaver; up that stream, and far into the Ohio wilderness.

Upon a tributary of the Muskingong, called the Tuscarawas, a settlement was founded. Near and far the news was circulated. Redmen from all tribes came flocking to the new colony. Chiefs and warriors, squaws and maidens, were attracted by the new doctrine of the converted Indians. They were astonished at the missionaries' teachings. Many doubted, some were converted, all listened. Great excitement prevailed when old Glickhican, one of the wisest chiefs of the Turtle tribe of the Delawares, became a convert to the palefaces' religion.

The interest widened, and in a few years a beautiful, prosperous town arose, which was called Village of Peace. The Indians of the warlike tribes bestowed the appropriate name. The vast forests were rich in every variety of game; the deep, swift streams were teeming with fish. Meat and grain in abundance, buckskin for clothing, and soft furs for winter garments were to be had for little labor. At first only a few wigwams were erected. Soon a large log structure was thrown up and used as a church. Then followed a school, a mill, and a workshop. The verdant fields were cultivated and surrounded by rail fences. Horses and cattle grazed with the timid deer on the grassy plains.

The Village of Peace blossomed as a rose. The reports of the love and happiness existing in this converted community spread from mouth to mouth, from town to town, with the result that inquisitive savages journeyed from all points to see this haven. Peaceful and hostile Indians were alike amazed at the change in their brethren. The good fellowship and industry of the converts had a widespread and wonderful influence. More, perhaps, than any other thing, the great fields of waving corn, the hills covered with horses and cattle, those evidences of abundance, impressed the visitors with the well-being of the Christians. Bands of traveling Indians, whether friendly or otherwise, were treated with hospitality, and never sent away empty-handed. They were asked to partake of the abundance and solicited to come again.

A feature by no means insignificant in the popularity of the village was the church bell. The Indians loved music, and this bell charmed them. On still nights the savages in distant towns could hear at dusk the deep-toned, mellow notes of the bell summoning the worshipers to the evening service. Its ringing clang, so strange, so sweet, so solemn, breaking the vast dead wilderness quiet, haunted the savage ear as though it were a call from a woodland god.

"You have arrived most opportunely," continued Mr. Zeisberger. "Mr. Edwards and Mr. Young are working to establish other missionary posts. Heckewelder is here now in the interest of this branching out."

"How long will it take me to learn the Delaware language?" inquired Jim.

"Not long. You do not, however, need to speak the Indian tongue, for we have excellent interpreters."

"We heard much at Fort Pitt and Fort Henry about the

danger, as well as uselessness, of our venture," Jim continued. "The frontiersmen declared that every rod of the way was beset with savage foes, and that, even in the unlikely event of our arriving safely at the Village of Peace, we would then be hemmed in by fierce, vengeful tribes."

"Hostile savages abound here, of course; but we do not fear them. We invite them. Our work is to convert the wicked, to teach them to lead good, useful lives. We will succeed."

Jim could not help warming to the minister for his unswervable faith, his earnest belief that the work of God could not fail; nevertheless, while he felt no fear and intended to put all his heart in the work, he remembered with disquietude Colonel Zane's warnings. He thought of the wonderful precaution and eternal vigilance of Jonathan and Wetzel—men of all men who most understood Indian craft and cunning. It might well be possible that these good missionaries, wrapped up in saving the souls of these children of the forest, so full of God's teachings as to have little mind for aught else, had no knowledge of the Indian nature beyond what the narrow scope of their work invited. If what these frontiersmen asserted was true, then the ministers' zeal had struck them blind.

Jim had a growing idea of the way in which the savages could be best taught. He resolved to go slowly; to study the redmen's natures; not to preach one word of the gospel to them until he had mastered their language and could convey to their simple minds the real truth. He would make Christianity as clear to them as were the deer trails on the moss and leaves of the forest.

"Ah, here you are. I hope you have rested well," said Mr. Zeisberger, when at the conclusion of this long recital Nell and Kate came into the room.

"Thank you, we feel much better," answered Kate. The girls

certainly looked refreshed. The substitution of clean gowns
for their former travel-stained garments made a change that
called forth the minister's surprise and admiration.

"My! My! Won't Edwards and Young beg me to keep
them here now!" he exclaimed, his pleased eyes resting on
Nell's piquant beauty and Kate's noble proportions and rich
coloring. "Come; I will show you over the Village of Peace."

"Are all these Indians Christians?" asked Jim.

"No, indeed. These Indians you see here, and out yonder
under the shade, though they are friendly, are not Christians.
Our converts employ themselves in the fields or shops.
Come; take a peep in here. This is where we preach in the
evenings and during inclement weather. On pleasant days we
use the maple grove yonder."

Jim and the others looked in at the door of the large log
structure. They saw an immense room, the floor covered
with benches, and a raised platform at one end. A few windows let in the light. Spacious and barnlike was this apartment; but, undoubtedly, seen through the beaming eyes of
the missionary, it was a grand amphitheater for worship. The
hard-packed clay floor was velvet carpet; the crude seats soft
as eiderdown; the platform with its white oak cross an altar
of marble and gold.

"This is one of our shops," said Mr. Zeisberger, leading
them to a cabin. "Here we make brooms, harness for the
horses, farming implements—everything useful that we can.
We have a forge here. Behold an Indian blacksmith!"

The interior of the large cabin presented a scene of
bustling activity. Twenty or more Indians bent their backs in
earnest employment. In one corner a savage stood holding a
piece of red-hot iron on an anvil, while a brawny brave
wielded a sledgehammer. The sparks flew; the anvil rang. In
another corner a circle of braves sat around a pile of dried
grass and flags. They were twisting and fashioning these ma-

terials into baskets. At a bench three Indian carpenters were pounding and swaying. Young braves ran back and forth, carrying pails, rough-hewn boards, and blocks of wood.

Instantly struck by two things, Jim voiced his curiosity:

"Why do these Indians all wear long hair, smooth and shiny, without adornment?"

"They are Christians. They wear neither headdress, war-bonnet, nor scalplock," replied Mr. Zeisberger, with unconscious pride.

"I did not expect to see a blacksmith's anvil out here in the wilderness. Where did you procure these tools?"

"We have been years getting them here. Some came by way of the Ohio River; others overland from Detroit. That anvil has a history. It was lost once, and lay for years in the woods, until some Indians found it again. It is called the Ringing Stone, and Indians come from miles around to see and hear it."

The missionary pointed out wide fields of corn, now growing yellow, and hillsides dotted with browsing cattle, droves of sturdy-limbed horses, and pens of fat, grunting pigs—all of which attested to the growing prosperity of the Village of Peace.

On the way back to the cabin, while the others listened to and questioned Mr. Zeisberger, Jim was silent and thoughtful, for his thoughts reverted to his brother.

Later, as he walked with Nell by the golden-fringed stream, he spoke of Joe.

"Joe wanted so much to hunt with Wetzel. He will come back; surely he will return to us when he has satisfied his wild craving for adventure. Do you not think so?"

There was an eagerness that was almost pleading in Jim's voice. What he so much hoped for—that no harm had befallen Joe, and that he would return—he doubted. He needed the encouragement of his hope.

"Never," answered Nell, solemnly.

"Oh, why—why do you say that?"

"I saw him look at you—a strange, intent glance. He gazed long at me as we separated. Oh! I can feel his eyes. No; he will never come back."

"Nell, Nell, you do not mean he went away deliberately—because, oh! I cannot say it."

"For no reason, except that the wilderness called him more than love for you or—me."

"No, no," returned Jim, his face white. "You do not understand. He really loved you—I know it. He loved me, too. Ah, how well! He has gone because—I can't tell you."

"Oh, Jim, I hope—he loved—me," sobbed Nell, bursting into tears. "His coldness—his neglect—those last few days—hurt me—so. If he cared—as you say—I won't be—so—miserable."

"We are both right—you when you say he will never return, and I when I say he loved us both," said Jim sadly, as the bitter certainty forced itself into his mind.

As she sobbed softly, and he gazed with set, stern face into the darkening forest, the deep, mellow notes of the church bell pealed out. So thrilled, so startled were they by this melody wondrously breaking the twilight stillness, that they gazed mutely at each other. Then they remembered. It was the missionary's bell summoning the Christian Indians to the evening service.

Chapter
XI

The sultry, drowsy, summer days passed with no untoward event to mar their slumbering tranquility. Life for the new-comers to the Village of Peace brought a content, the like of which they had never dreamed of. Mr. Wells at once began active work among the Indians, preaching every day to them through an interpreter; Nell and Kate, in hours apart from household duties, busied themselves brightening their new abode, and Jim entered upon the task of acquainting himself with the modes and habits of the redmen. Truly, the young people might have found perfect happiness in this new and novel life, if only Joe had returned. His disappearance and sub-sequent absence furnished a theme for many talks and many a quiet hour of dreamy sadness. The fascination of his per-sonality had been so impelling that long after it was with-drawn a charm lingered around everything which reminded them of him; a subtle and sweet memory, with perverse and half-bitter persistence, returned hauntingly. No trace of Joe had been seen by any of the friendly Indian runners. He was gone into the mazes of deep-shadowed forests, where to hunt for him would be like striving to trail the flight of a swallow. Two of those he had left behind always remembered him, and in their thoughts followed him in his wanderings.

Jim settled down to his study of Indians with single-heartedness of purpose. He spent part of every morning with the interpreters, with whose assistance he rapidly acquired the Delaware language. He went freely among the Indians, endeavoring to win their goodwill. There were always fifty to a hundred visiting Indians at the village; sometimes, when the missionaries had advertised a special meeting, there were assembled in the shady maple grove as many as five hundred savages. Jim had, therefore, golden opportunities to practice his offices of friendliness.

Fortunately for him, he at once succeeded in establishing himself in the good graces of Glickhican, the converted Delaware chief. The wise old Indian was of inestimable value to Jim. Early in their acquaintance he evinced an earnest regard for the young minister, and talked with him for hours.

From Glickhican Jim learned the real nature of the redmen. The Indian's love of freedom and honor, his hatred of subjection and deceit, as explained by the good old man, recalled to Jim Colonel Zane's estimate of the savage character. Surely, as the colonel had said, the Indians had reason for their hatred of the pioneers. Truly, they were a blighted race.

Seldom had the rights of the redmen been thought of. The settler pushed onward, plodding, as it were, behind his plow with a rifle. He regarded the Indian as little better than a beast; he was easier to kill than to tame. How little the settler knew the proud independence, the wisdom, the stainless chastity of honor, which belonged so truly to many Indian chiefs!

The redmen were driven like hounded deer into the untrodden wilds. From freemen of the forest, from owners of the great boundless plains, they passed to stern, enduring fugitives on their own lands. Small wonder that they became cruel where once they had been gentle! Stratagem and cunning, the night assault, the daylight ambush took the place of their onetime open warfare. Their chivalrous courage, that sublime inheritance from ancestors who had never known the paleface foe, degenerated into a savage ferocity.

Interesting as was this history to Jim, he cared more for Glickhican's rich portrayal of the redmen's domestic life, for the beautiful poetry of his tradition and legends. He heard with delight the exquisite fanciful Indian lore. From these romantic legends, beautiful poems, and marvelous myths he hoped to get ideas of the Indian's religion. Sweet and simple as children's dreams were these quaint tales—tales of how the woodland fairies dwelt in fern-carpeted dells; how at sunrise they came out to kiss open the flowers; how the forest walks were spirit-haunted paths; how the leaves whispered poetry to the winds; how the rocks harbored Indian gods and masters who watched over their chosen ones.

Glickhican wound up his long discourse by declaring he had never lied in the whole course of his seventy years, he had never stolen, never betrayed, never murdered, never killed, save in self-defense. Gazing at the chief's fine features, now calm, yet showing traces of past storms, Jim believed he spoke the truth.

When the young minister came, however, to study the hostile Indians who flocked to the village, any conclusive delineation of character, or any satisfactory analysis of their mental state in regard to the paleface religion, eluded him. Their passive, silent, sphinxlike secretiveness was baffling. Glickhican had taught him how to propitiate the friendly braves, and with these he was successful. Little he learned, however, from the unfriendly ones. When making gifts to these redmen he could never be certain that his offerings were appreciated. The jewels and gold he had brought west with him went to the French traders, who in exchange gave him trinkets, baubles, bracelets, and weapons. Jim made hundreds of presents. Boldly going up to befeathered and befringed chieftains, he offered them knives, hatchets, or strings of silvery beads. Sometimes his kindly offerings were repelled with a haughty stare; at other times they would be accepted coldly, suspiciously, as if the gifts brought some unknown obligation.

For a white man it was a never-to-be-forgotten experience to see eight or ten of these grim, slowly stepping forest kings, arrayed in all the rich splendor of their costume, stalking among the teepees of the Village of Peace. Somehow, such a procession always made Jim shiver. The singing, praying, and preaching they heard unmoved. No emotion was visible on their bronzed faces; nothing changed their unalterable mien. Had they not moved, or gazed with burning eyes, they would have been statues. When these chieftains looked at the converted Indians, some of whom were braves of their nations, the contempt in their glances betrayed that they now regarded these Christian Indians as belonging to an alien race.

Among the chiefs Glickhican pointed out to Jim were Wingenund, the Delaware; Tellane, the Half King; Shingiss and Kotoxen—all of the Wolf tribe of the Delawares.

Glickhican was careful to explain that the Delaware nation had been divided into the Wolf and Turtle tribes; the former warlike people, and the latter peaceable. Few of the Wolf tribe had gone over to the new faith, and those who had were scorned. Wingenund, the great power of the Delawares—indeed, the greatest of all the western tribes—maintained a neutral attitude toward the Village of Peace. But it was well known that his right-hand war chiefs, Pipe and Wishtonah, remained coldly opposed.

Jim turned all he had learned over and over in his mind,

trying to construct part of it to fit into a sermon that would be different from any the Indians had ever heard. He did not want to preach far over their heads. If possible, he desired to keep to their ideals—for he deemed them more beautiful than his own—and to conduct his teaching along the simple lines of their belief, so that when he stimulated and developed their minds he could pass from what they knew to the unknown Christianity of the white man.

His first address to the Indians was made one day during the indisposition of Mr. Wells—who had been overworking himself—and the absence of the other missionaries. He did not consider himself at all ready for preaching, and confined his efforts to a simple, earnest talk, a recital of the thoughts he had assimilated while living here among the Indians.

Amazement would not have described the state of his feelings when he learned that he had made a powerful impression. The converts were loud in his praise; the unbelievers silent and thoughtful. In spite of himself, long before he had been prepared, he was launched on his teaching. Every day he was called upon to speak; every day one savage, at least, was convinced; every day the throng of interested Indians was augmented. The elder missionaries were quite overcome with joy; they pressed him day after day to speak, until at length he alone preached during the afternoon service.

The news flew apace; the Village of Peace entertained more redmen than ever before. Day after day the faith gained a stronger foothold. A kind of religious trance affected some of the converted Indians, and this greatly influenced the doubting ones. Many of them half believed the Great Manitou had come.

Heckewelder, the acknowledged leader of the western Moravian Mission, visited the village at this time, and, struck by the young missionary's success, arranged a three days' religious festival. Indian runners were employed to carry invitations to all the tribes. The Wyandots in the west, the Shawnees in the south, and the Delawares in the north were especially requested to come. No deception was practiced to lure the distant savages to the Village of Peace. They were asked to come, partake of the feasts, and listen to the white man's teaching.

Chapter
XII

From dawn until noon on Sunday bands of Indians arrived at the Village of Peace. Hundreds of canoes glided down the swift stream and bumped their prows into the pebbly beach. Groups of mounted warriors rode out of the forests into the clearing; squaws with pappooses, maidens carrying wicker baskets, and children playing with rude toys came trooping along the bridle paths.

Gifts were presented during the morning, after which the visitors were feasted. In the afternoon all assembled in the grove to hear the preaching.

The maple grove wherein the service was to be conducted might have been intended by Nature for just such a purpose as it now fulfilled. These trees were large, spreading, and situated far apart. Mossy stones and the thick carpet of grass afforded seats for the congregation.

Heckewelder—a tall, spare, and kindly appearing man—directed the arranging of the congregation. He placed the converted Indians just behind the knoll upon which the presiding minister was to stand. In a half circle facing the knoll he seated the chieftains and important personages of the various tribes. He then made a short address in the Indian language, speaking of the work of the mission, what wonders it had accomplished, what more good work it hoped to do, and concluded by introducing the young missionary.

While Heckewelder spoke, Jim, who stood just behind, employed the few moments in running his eyes over the multitude. The sight which met his gaze was one he thought he would never forget. An involuntary word escaped him.

"Magnificent!" he exclaimed.

The shady glade had been transformed into a theater, from which gazed a thousand dark, still faces. A thousand eagles plumes waved, and ten thousand bright-hued feathers quivered in the soft breeze. The fantastically dressed scalps presented a contrast to the smooth, unadorned heads of the converted redmen. These proud plumes and defiant feathers told the difference between savage and Christian.

In front of the knoll sat fifty chiefs, attentive and dignified. Representatives of every tribe as far west as the Scioto River were numbered in that circle. There were chiefs renowned for war, for cunning, for valor, for wisdom. Their stately presence gave the meeting tenfold importance. Could these chiefs be interested, moved, the whole western world of Indians might be civilized.

Hepote, a Maumee chief, of whom it was said he had never listened to words of the paleface, had the central position in this circle. On his right and left, respectively, sat Shaushoto and Pipe, implacable foes of all white men. The latter's aspect did not belie his reputation. His copper-colored, repulsive visage compelled fear; it breathed vindictiveness and malignity. A singular action of his was that he always, in what must have been his arrogant vanity, turned his profile to those who watched him, and it was a remarkable one; it sloped in an oblique line from the top of his fore-head to his protruding chin, resembling somewhat the carved bowl of his pipe, which was of flint and a famed in-heritance from his ancestors. From it he took his name. One solitary eagle plume, its tip stained vermilion, stuck from his scalplock. It slanted backward on a line with his profile.

Among all these chiefs, striking as they were, the figure of Wingenund, the Delaware, stood out alone.

His position was at the extreme left of the circle, where he leaned against a maple. A long, black mantle, trimmed with spotless white, enveloped him. One bronzed arm, circled by a heavy bracelet of gold, held the mantle close about his lofty form. His headdress, which trailed to the ground, was exceed-ingly beautiful. The eagle plumes were of uniform length and pure white, except the black-pointed tips.

At his feet sat his daughter, Whispering Winds. Her maid-ens were gathered round her. She raised her soft, black eyes, shining with a wondrous light of surprise and expectation, to the young missionary's face.

Beyond the circle the Indians were massed together, even beyond the limits of the glade. Under the trees on every side sat warriors astride their steeds; some lounged on the green turf; many reclined in the branches of low-spreading maples.

As Jim looked out over the sea of faces he started in sur-prise. The sudden glance of fiery eyes had impelled his gaze. He recognized Silvertip, the Shawnee chief. The Indian sat motionless on a powerful black horse. Jim started again, for the horse was Joe's thoroughbred, Lance. But Jim had no further time to think of Joe's enemy, for Heckewelder stepped back.

Jim took the vacated seat, and, with a far-reaching, reso-nant voice, began his discourse to the Indians.

"Chieftains, warriors, maidens, children of the forest, listen, and your ears shall hear no lie. I am come from where the sun rises to tell you of the Great Spirit of the white man.

"Many, many moons ago, as many as blades of grass grow on yonder plain, the Great Spirit of whom I shall speak created the world. He made the sparkling lakes and swift rivers, the boundless plains and tangled forests, over which He caused the sun to shine and the rain to fall. He gave life to the kingly elk, the graceful deer, the rolling bison, the bear, the fox—all the beasts and birds and fishes. But He was not content; for nothing He made was perfect in His sight. He created the white man in His own image, and from this first man's rib He created his mate—a woman. He turned them free in a beautiful forest.

"Life was fair in the beautiful forest. The sun shone always, the birds sang, the waters flowed with music, the flowers cast sweet fragrance on the air. In this forest, where fruit bloomed always, was one tree, the Tree of Life, the apple of which they must not eat. In all this beautiful forest of abundance this apple alone was forbidden them.

"Now evil was born with woman. A serpent tempted her to eat of the apple of Life, and she tempted the man to eat. For their sin the Great Spirit commanded the serpent to crawl forever on his belly, and He drove them from the beautiful forest. The punishment for their sin was to be visited on their children, always, until the end of time. The two went afar into the dark forests to learn to live as best they might. From them all tribes descended. The world is wide. A warrior might run all his days and not reach the setting sun, where tribes of yellowskins live. He might travel half his days toward the southwind, where tribes of blackskins abound. People of all colors inhabited the world. They lived in hatred toward one another. They shed each other's blood; they stole each other's lands, gold; and women. They sinned.

"Many moons ago the Great Spirit sorrowed to see His chosen tribe, the palefaces, living in ignorance and sin. He sent His only Son to redeem them, and said if they would listen and believe, and teach the other tribes, He would forgive their sin and welcome them to the beautiful forest.

"That was moons and moons ago, when the paleface killed his brother for gold and lands, and beat his women slaves to make them plant his corn. The Son of the Great Spirit lifted the cloud from the palefaces' eyes, and they saw and learned. So pleased was the Great Spirit that He made the palefaces wiser and wiser, and masters of the world. He bid them go afar to teach the ignorant tribes.

"To teach you is why the young paleface journeyed from the rising sun. He wants no lands or power. He has given all that he had. He walks among you without gun or knife. He can gain nothing but the happiness of opening the redmen's eyes.

"The Great Spirit of whom I teach and the Great Manitou, your idol, are the same; the happy hunting ground of the Indian and the beautiful forest of the paleface are the same; the paleface and the redman are the same. There is but one Great Spirit, that is God; but one eternal home, that is heaven; but one human being, that is man.

"The Indian knows the habits of the beaver; he can follow the paths of the forests; he can guide his canoe through the foaming rapids; he is honest, he is brave, he is great; but he is not wise. His wisdom is clouded with the original sin. He lives in idleness; he paints his face; he makes his squaw labor for him, instead of laboring for her; he kills his brothers. He worships the trees and rocks. If he were wise he would not make gods of the swift arrow and bounding canoe; of the flowering ash and the flaming flint. For these things have not life. In his dreams he sees his arrow speed to the running deer. In his dreams he sees his canoes shoot over the crest of shining waves; and in his mind he gives them life, when his eyes are opened he will see they have no spirit. The spirit is in his own heart. It guides the arrow to the running deer, and steers the canoe over the swirling current. The spirit makes him find the untrodden paths, and do brave deeds, and love his children and his honor. It makes him meet his foe face-to-face, and if he is to die it gives him strength to die—a man. The spirit is what makes him different from the arrow, the canoe, the mountain, and all the birds and beasts. For it is born of the Great Spirit, the creator of all. Him you must worship.

"Redmen, this worship is understanding your spirit and teaching it to do good deeds. It is called Christianity. Christianity is love. If you will love the Great Spirit you will love your wives, your children, your brothers, your friends, your foes—you will love the palefaces. No more will you idle in winter and wage wars in summer. You will wear your knife and tomahawk only when you hunt for meat. You will be kind, gentle, loving, virtuous—you will have grown wise. When your days are done you will meet all your loved ones in the beautiful forest. There, where the flowers bloom, the fruits ripen always, where the pleasant water glides and the summer winds whisper sweetly, there peace will dwell forever.

"Comrades, be wise, think earnestly. Forget the wicked paleface; for there are many wicked palefaces. They sell the serpent firewater; they lie and steal and kill. These palefaces' eyes are still clouded. If they do not open they will never see the beautiful forest. You have much to forgive, but those who forgive please the Great Spirit; you must give yourselves to love, but those who love are loved; you must work, but those who work are happy.

"Behold the Village of Peace! Once it contained few; now there are many. Where once the dark forest shaded the land, see the cabins, the farms, the horses, the cattle! Field on field of waving, golden grain shine there under your eyes. The earth has blossomed abundance. Idling and fighting made not these rich harvests. Belief made love; love made wise eyes; wise eyes saw, and lo! there came plenty.

"The proof of love is happiness. These Christian Indians are happy. They are at peace with the redman and the pale-face. They till the fields and work in the shops. In days to come cabins and farms and fields of corn will be theirs. They will bring up their children, not to hide in the forest to slay, but to walk hand in hand with the palefaces as equals.

"Oh, open your ears! God speaks to you; peace awaits you! Cast the bitterness from your hearts; it is the serpent poison. While you hate, God shuts His eyes. You are great on the trail, in the council, in war; now be great in forgiveness. Forgive the palefaces who have robbed you of your lands. Then will come peace. If you do not forgive, the war will go on; you will lose lands and homes, to find unmarked graves under the forest leaves. Revenge is sweet; but it is not wise. The price of revenge is blood and life. Root it out of your hearts. Love these Christian Indians; love the missionaries as they love you; love all living creatures. Your days are but few; therefore, cease the strife. Let us say, 'Brothers, that is God's word, His law; that is love; that is Christianity!' If you will say from your heart, brother, you are a Christian.

"Brothers, the paleface teacher beseeches you. Think not of this long, bloody war, of your dishonored dead, of your si-lenced wigwams, of your nameless graves, of your homeless children. Think of the future. One word from you will make peace over all this broad land. The paleface must honor a Christian. He can steal no Christian's land. All the palefaces, as many as the stars of the great white path, dare not invade the Village of Peace. For God smiles here. Listen to His words: 'Come unto me all ye that are weary and heavy laden, and I will give you rest.' "

Over the multitude brooded an impressive, solemn silence. Then an aged Delaware chief rose, with a mien of profound thought, and slowly paced before the circle of chiefs. Presently he stopped, turned to the awaiting Indians, and spoke:

"Netawatwees is almost persuaded to be a Christian." He resumed his seat.

Another interval of penetrating quiet ensued. At length a venerable-looking chieftain got up:

"White Eyes hears the rumbling thunder in his ears. The smoke blows from his eyes. White Eyes is the oldest chief of the Lenni-Lenape. His days are many; they are full; they draw near the evening of his life; he rejoices that wisdom is come before his sun is set.

"White Eyes believes the young White Father. The ways of the Great Spirit are many as the fluttering leaves; they are strange and secret as the flight of a loon; White Eyes believes the redman's happy hunting grounds need not be forgotten to love the palefaces' God. As a young brave pants and puzzles over his first trail, so the grown warrior feels in his understanding of his God. He gropes blindly through dark ravines.

"White Eyes speaks few words today, for he is learning wisdom; he bids his people hearken to the voice of the White Father. War is wrong; peace is best. Love is the way to peace. The paleface advances one step nearer his God. He labors for his home; he keeps the peace; he asks but little; he frees his women. That is well. White Eyes has spoken."

The old chief slowly advanced toward the Christian Indians. He laid aside his knife and tomahawk, and then his eagle plumes and warbonnet. Bareheaded, he seated himself among the converted redmen. They began chanting in low, murmuring tones.

Amid the breathless silence that followed this act of such great significance, Wingenund advanced toward the knoll with slow, stately step. His dark eye swept the glade with lightning scorn; his glance alone revealed the passion that swayed him.

"Wingenund's ears are keen; they have heard a feather fall in the storm; now they hear a soft-voiced thrush. Wingenund thunders to his people, to his friends, to the chiefs of other tribes: *'Do not bury the hatchet!'* The young White Father's tongue runs smooth like the gliding brook; it sings as the thrush calls its mate. Listen; but wait, wait! Let time prove his beautiful tale; let the moons go by over the Village of Peace.

"Wingenund does not flaunt his wisdom. He has grown old among his warriors; he loves them; he fears for them. The dream of the palefaces' beautiful forest glimmers as the rainbow glows over the laughing falls of the river. The dream of the paleface is too beautiful to come true. In the days of long ago, when Wingenund's forefathers heard not the paleface's axe, they lived in love and happiness such as the young White Father dreams may come again. They waged no wars. A white dove sat in every wigwam. The lands were theirs and they were rich. The paleface came with his leaden death, his burning firewater, his ringing axe, and the glory of the redmen faded forever.

"Wingenund seeks not to inflame his braves to anger. He is sick of blood-spilling—not from fear; for Wingenund cannot feel fear. But he asks his people to wait. Remember, the gifts of the paleface ever contained a poisoned arrow. Wingenund's heart is sore. The day of the redman is gone. His sun is setting. Wingenund feels already the gray shades of evening."

He stopped for one long moment as if to gather breath for his final charge to his listeners. Then with a magnificent gesture he thundered:

"Is the Delaware a fool? When Wingenund can cross unarmed to the Big Water he shall change his mind. When Deathwind ceases to blow his bloody trail over the fallen leaves Wingenund will believe."

Chapter
XIII

As the summer waned, each succeeding day, with its melancholy calm, its changing lights and shades, its cool, damp evening winds, growing more and more suggestive of autumn, the little colony of white people in the Village of Peace led busy, eventful lives.

Upwards of fifty Indians, several of them important chiefs, had become converted since the young missionary began preaching. Heckewelder declared that this was a wonderful showing, and if it could be kept up would result in gaining a hold on the Indian tribes which might not be shaken. Heckewelder had succeeded in interesting the savages west of the Village of Peace to the extent of permitting him to establish missionary posts in two other localities— one near Goshhocking, a Delaware town; and one on the Muskingong, the principal river running through central Ohio. He had, with his helpers, Young and Edwards, journeyed from time to time to these points, preaching, making gifts, and soliciting help from chiefs.

The most interesting feature, perhaps, of the varied life of the missionary party was a rivalry between Young and Edwards for the elder Miss Wells. Usually Nell's attractiveness appealed more to men than Kate's; however, in this instance, although the sober teachers of the gospel admired Nell's winsome beauty, they fell in love with Kate. The missionaries were both under forty, and good, honest men, devoted to the work which had engrossed them for years. Although they were ardent lovers, certainly they were not picturesque. Two homelier men could hardly have been found. Moreover, the sacrifice of their lives to missionary work had taken them far from the companionship of women of their own race, so that they lacked the ease of manner which women would like to see in men. Young and Edwards were awkward, almost uncouth. Embarrassment would not have done justice to their state of feeling while basking in the sunshine of Kate's quiet smile. They were happy, foolish, and speechless.

If Kate shared in the merriment of the others—Heckewelder could not conceal his, and Nell did not try very hard to hide hers—she never allowed a suspicion of it to escape. She kept the easy, even tenor of her life, always kind and gracious in her quaint way, and precisely the same to both her lovers. No doubt she well knew that each possessed, under all his rough exterior, a heart of gold.

One day the genial Heckewelder lost, or pretended to lose, his patience.

"Say, you worthy gentlemen are becoming ornamental instead of useful. All this changing of coals, trimming of mustaches, and eloquent sighing doesn't seem to have affected the young lady. I've a notion to send you both to Maumee town, one hundred miles away. This young lady is charming, I admit, but if she is to keep on seriously hindering the work of the Moravian Mission I must object. As for that matter, I might try conclusions myself. I'm as young as either of you, and, I flatter myself, much handsomer. You'll have a dangerous rival presently. Settle it! You can't both have her; settle it!"

This outburst from their usually kind leader placed the earnest but awkward gentlemen in a terrible plight.

On the afternoon following the crisis Heckewelder took Mr. Wells to one of the Indian shops, and Jim and Nell went canoeing. Young and Edwards, after conferring for one long, trying hour, determined on settling the question.

Young was a pale, slight man, very homely except when he smiled. His smile not only broke up the plainness of his face, but seemed to chase away a serious shadow, allowing his kindly, gentle spirit to shine through. He was nervous and had a timid manner. Edwards was his opposite, being a man of robust frame, with a heavy face, and a manner that would have suggested self-confidence in another man.

They were true and tried friends.

"Dave, I couldn't ask her," said Young, trembling at the very thought. "Besides, there's no hope for me, I know it. That's why I'm afraid, why I don't want to ask her. What'd such a glorious creature see in a poor, puny little thing like me?"

"George, you're not over-handsome," admitted Dave, shaking his head. "But you can never tell about women. Sometimes they like even little, insignificant fellows. Don't be too scared about asking her. Besides, it will make it easier for me. You might tell her—about me—you know, sort of feel her out, so I'd—"

Dave's voice failed him here; but he had said enough, and that was most discouraging to poor George. Dave was so busy screwing up his courage that he forgot all about his friend.

"No; I couldn't," gasped George, falling into a chair. He was ghastly pale. "I couldn't ask her to accept me, let alone do another man's wooing. She thinks more of you. She'll accept you."

"You really think so?" whispered Dave, nervously.

"I know she will. You're such a fine, big figure of a man. She'll take you, and I'll be glad. This fever and fretting has about finished me. When she's yours I'll not be so bad. I'll be happy in your happiness. But, Dave, you'll let me see her occasionally, won't you? Go! Hurry—get it over!"

"Yes; we must have it over," replied Dave, getting up with a brave effort. Truly, if he carried that determined front to his lady love he would look like a masterful lover. But when he got to the door he did not at all resemble a conqueror.

"You're sure she—cares for me?" asked Dave, for the hundredth time. This time, as always, his friend was faithful and convincing.

"I know she does. Go—hurry. I tell you I can't stand this any longer," cried George, pushing Dave out of the door.

"You won't go—first?" whispered Dave, clinging to the door.

"I won't go at all. I couldn't ask her—I don't want her— go! Get out!"

Dave started reluctantly toward the adjoining cabin, from the open window of which came the song of the young woman who was responsible for all this trouble. George flung himself on his bed. What a relief to feel it was all over! He lay there with eyes shut for hours, as it seemed. After a time Dave came in. George leaped to his feet and saw his friend stumbling over a chair. Somehow, Dave did not look as usual. He seemed changed, or shrunken, and his face wore a discomfited, miserable expression.

"Well?" cried George, sharply. Even to his highly excited imagination this did not seem the proper condition for a victorious lover.

"She refused—refused me," faltered Dave. "She was very sweet and kind; said something about being my sister—I don't remember just what—but she wouldn't have me."

"What did you say to her?" whispered George, a paralyzing hope almost rendering him speechless.

"I—I told her everything I could think of," replied Dave, despondently; "even what you said."

"What I said? Dave, what did you tell her I said?"

"Why, you know—about she cared for me—that you were sure of it, and that you didn't want her—"

"*Jackass!*" roared George, rising out of his meekness like a lion from slumber.

"Didn't you—say so?" inquired Dave, weakly.

"*No! No! No! Idiot!*"

As one possessed, George rushed out of the cabin, and a moment later stood disheveled and frantic before Kate.

"Did that fool say I didn't love you?" he demanded.

Kate looked up, startled; but as an understanding of George's wild aspect and wilder words dawned upon her, she resumed her usual calm demeanor. Looking again to see if this passionate young man was indeed George, she turned her face as she said:

"If you mean Mr. Edwards, yes; I believe he did say as much. Indeed, from his manner he seemed to have monopolized all the love near the Village of Peace."

"But it's not true. I *do* love you. I love you to distraction. I have loved you ever since I first saw you. I told Dave that. Heckewelder knows it; even the Indians know it," cried George, protesting vehemently against the disparaging allusion to his affections. He did not realize he was making a most impassioned declaration of love. When he was quite out of breath he sat down and wiped his moist brow.

A pink bloom tinged Kate's cheeks, and her eyes glowed with a happy light; but George never saw these womanly evidences of pleasure.

"Of course I know you don't care for me—"

"Did Mr. Edwards tell you so?" asked Kate, glancing up quickly.

"Why, yes, he has often said he thought that. Indeed, he always seemed to regard himself as the fortunate object of your affections. I always believed he was."

"But it wasn't true."

"What?"

"It's not true."

"What's not true?"

"Oh—about my—not caring."

"Kate!" cried George, quite overcome with rapture. He fell over two chairs getting to her; but he succeeded, and fell on his knees to kiss her hand.

"Foolish boy! It has been you all the time," whispered Kate, with her quiet smile.

"Look here, Downs; come to the door. See there," said Heckewelder to Jim.

Somewhat surprised at Heckewelder's grave tone, Jim got up from the supper table and looked out of the door. He saw two tall Indians pacing to and fro under the maples. It was still early twilight, and light enough to see clearly. One Indian was almost naked; the lithe, graceful symmetry of his dark figure standing out in sharp contrast to the gaunt, gaudily costumed form of the other.

"Silvertip! Girty!" exclaimed Jim, in a low voice.

"Girty I knew, of course; but I was not sure the other was the Shawnee who captured you and your brother," replied Heckewelder, drawing Jim into another room.

"What do they mean by loitering around the village?" inquired Jim, apprehensively. Whenever he heard Girty's name mentioned, or even thought of him, he remembered with a shudder the renegade's allusion to the buzzards. Jim never saw one of these carrion birds soaring overhead but his thoughts instantly reverted to the frontier ruffian and his horrible craving.

"I don't know," answered Heckewelder. "Girty has been here several times of late. I saw him conferring with Pipe at Goshhocking. I hope there's no deviltry afoot. Pipe is a relentless enemy of all Christians, and Girty is a fiend, a hyena. I think, perhaps, it will be well for you and the girls to stay indoors while Girty and Silvertip are in the village."

That evening the entire missionary party were gathered in Mr. Wells' room. Heckewelder told stories of Indian life; Nell sang several songs, and Kate told of many amusing things said and done by the little Indian boys in her class at the school. Thus the evening passed pleasantly for all.

"So next Wednesday I am to perform the great ceremony," remarked Heckewelder, laying his hand kindly on Young's knee. "We'll celebrate the first white wedding in the Village of Peace."

Young looked shyly down at his boots; Edwards crossed one leg over the other and coughed loudly to hide his embarrassment. Kate wore, as usual, her pensive smile; Nell's eyes twinkled, and she was about to speak when Heckwelder's quizzical glance in her direction made her lips mute.

"I hope I'll have another wedding on my hands soon," he said, placidly.

This ordinary remark had an extraordinary effect. Nell turned with burning cheeks and looked out of the window. Jim frowned fiercely and bit his lips. Edwards began to laugh, and even Mr. Wells' serious face lapsed into a smile.

"I mean I've picked out a nice little Delaware squaw for Dave," said Heckewelder, seeing his badinage had somehow gone amiss.

"Oh-h!" suddenly cried Nell, in shuddering tones.

They all gazed at her in amazement. Every vestige of color

had receded from her face, leaving it marblelike. Her eyes
were fixed in startled horror. Suddenly she relaxed her grasp
on the windowsill and fell back limp and senseless.

Heckewelder ran to the door to look out, while the others
bent over the unconscious girl, endeavoring to revive her.
Presently a fluttering breath and a quivering of her dark
lashes noted a return of suspended life. Then her beautiful
eyes opened wide to gaze with wonder and fear into the
grave faces bent so anxiously over her.

"Nell, dearest, you are safe. What was it? What frightened you so?" said Kate, tenderly.

"Oh, it was fearful!" gasped Nell, sitting up. She clung to
her sister with one hand, while the other grasped Jim's
sleeve.

"I was looking out into the dark, when suddenly I beheld
a face, a terrible face!" cried Nell. Those who watched her
marveled at the shrinking, awful fear in her eyes. "It was
right by the window. I could have touched it. Such a greedy,
wolfish face, with a long, hooked nose! The eyes, oh! the
eyes! I'll never forget them. They made me sick; they paralyzed me. It wasn't an Indian's face. It belonged to that white
man, that awful white man! I never saw him before; but I
knew him."

"Girty!" said Heckewelder, who had come in with his
quiet step. "He looked in at the window. Calm yourself, Nellie. The renegade has gone."

The incident worried them all at the time, and made Nell
nervous for several days; but as Girty had disappeared, and
nothing more was heard of him, gradually they forgot.
Kate's wedding day dawned with all the little party well and
happy. Early in the afternoon Jim and Nell, accompanied by
Kate and her lover, started out into the woods just beyond
the clearing for the purpose of gathering wildflowers to dec-
orate the cabin.

"We are both thinking of—him," Jim said, after he and Nell had walked some little way in silence.

"Yes," answered Nell, simply.

"I hope—I pray Joe comes back, but if he doesn't—Nell—won't you care a little for me?"

He received no answer. But Nell turned her face away.

"We both loved him. If he's gone forever our very love for him should bring us together. I know—I know he would have wished that."

"Jim, don't speak of love to me now," she whispered. Then she turned to the others. "Come quickly; here are great clusters of wild clematis and goldenrod. How lovely! Let us gather a quantity."

The young men had almost buried the girls under huge masses of the beautiful flowers when the soft tread of moccasined feet caused them all to turn in surprise. Six savages stood waist-deep in the bushes, where they had lain concealed. Fierce, painted visages scowled from behind leveled rifles.

"Don't yell!" cried a hoarse voice in English. Following the voice came a snapping of twigs, and then two other figures came into view. They were Girty and Silvertip.

"Don't yell, er I'll leave you layin' here fer the buzzards," said the renegade. He stepped forward and grasped Young, at the same time speaking in the Indian language and pointing to a nearby tree. Strange to relate, the renegade apparently wanted no bloodshed. While one of the savages began to tie Young to the tree, Girty turned his gaze on the girls. His little, yellow eyes glinted; he stroked his chin with a bony hand, and his dark, repulsive face was wreathed in a terrible, meaning smile.

"I've been layin' fer you," he croaked, eyeing Nell.

"Ye're the purtiest lass, 'ceptin' mebbe Bet Zane, I ever seed on the border. I got cheated outen her, but I've got you;

arter I feed yer Injun preacher to ther buzzards mebbe ye'll larn to love me."

Nell gazed one instant into the monster's face. Her terror-stricken eyes were piteous to behold. She tried to speak; but her voice failed. Then, like a stricken bird, she fell on the grass.

Chapter
XIV

Not many miles from the Village of Peace rose an irregular chain of hills, the first faint indication of the Appalachian mountain system; these ridges were thickly wooded with white oak, poplar, and hickory, among which a sentinel pine reared here and there its evergreen head. There were clefts in the hills, passes lined by gray-stoned cliffs, below which ran clear brooks, tumbling over rocks in a hurry to meet their majestic father, the Ohio.

One of these valleys, so narrow that the sun seldom brightened the merry brook, made a deep cut in the rocks. The head of this valley tapered until the walls nearly met; it seemed to lose itself in the shade of fern-faced cliffs, shadowed as they were by fir trees leaning over the brink as though to search for secrets of the ravine. So deep and dark and cool was this sequestered nook that here late summer had not dislodged early spring. Everywhere was a soft, fresh, bright green. The old gray cliffs were festooned with ferns, lichens, and moss. Under a great, shelving rock, damp and stained by the copper-colored water dripping down its side, was a dewy dell into which the sunshine had never peeped. Here the swift book tarried lovingly, making a wide turn under the cliff, as though loath to leave this quiet nook, and then leaped once more to enthusiasm in its murmuring flight.

Life abounded in this wild, beautiful, almost inaccessible spot. Little brown and yellow birds flitted among the trees; thrushes ran along the leaf-strewn ground; orioles sang their melancholy notes; robins and flickers darted beneath the spreading branches. Squirrels scurried over the leaves like little whirlwinds and leaped daringly from the swinging branches or barked noisily from woody perches. Rabbits hopped inquisitively here and there while nibbling at the tender shoots of sassafras and laurel.

Along this flower-skirted stream a tall young man, carrying a rifle, cautiously stepped, peering into the branches overhead. A gray flash shot along a limb of a white oak; then the bushy tail of a squirrel flitted into a well-protected notch, from whence, no doubt, a keen little eye watched the hunter's every movement.

The rifle was raised; then lowered. The hunter walked around the tree. Presently up in the tree top, snug under a knotty limb, he espied a little ball of gray fur. Grasping a branch of underbrush, he shook it vigorously. The thrashing sound worried the gray squirrel, for he slipped from his retreat and stuck his nose over the limb. *Crack!* With a scratching and tearing of bark the squirrel loosened his hold and then fell, alighting with a thump. As the hunter picked up his quarry a streak of sunshine glinting through the treetop brightened his face.

The hunter was Joe.

He was satisfied now, for after stowing the squirrel in the pocket of his hunting coat he shouldered his rifle and went back up the ravine. Presently a dull roar sounded above the babble of the brook. It grew louder as he threaded his way carefully over the stones. Spots of white foam flecked the brook. Passing under the gray, stained cliff, Joe turned around a rocky corner, and came to an abrupt end of the ravine. A waterfall marked the spot where the brook entered. The water was brown as it took the leap, light green when it thinned out; and below, as it dashed on the stones, it became a beautiful, sheeny white.

Upon a flat rock, so near the cascade that spray flew over him, sat another hunter. The roaring falls drowned all other sounds, yet the man roused from his dreamy contemplation of the waterfall when Joe rounded the corner.

"I heerd four shots," he said, as Joe came up.

"Yes; I got a squirrel for every shot."

Wetzel led the way along a narrow foot trail which gradually wound toward the top of the ravine. This path emerged presently, some distance above the falls, on the brink of the bluff. It ran along the edge of the precipice a few yards, then took a course back into densely wooded thicket. Just before stepping out on the open cliff Wetzel paused and peered keenly on all sides. There was no living thing to be seen; the silence was the deep, unbroken calm of the wilderness.

Wetzel stepped to the bluff and looked over. The stony wall opposite was only thirty feet away, and somewhat lower. From Wetzel's action it appeared as if he intended to leap the fissure. In truth, many a band of Indians pursuing the hunter into this rocky fastness had come out on the bluff, and, marveling at what they thought Wetzel's prowess, believed he had made a wonderful leap, thus eluding them. But he had never attempted that leap, first, because he knew it was well-nigh impossible, and, second, there had never been any necessity for such risk.

Anyone leaning over this cliff would have observed, perhaps ten feet below, a narrow ledge projecting from the face of the rock. He would have imagined if he were to drop on that ledge there would be no way to get off, and he would be in a worse predicament.

Without a moment's hesitation Wetzel swung himself over the ledge. Joe followed suit. At one end of this lower ledge grew a hardy shrub of the ironwood species, and above it a scrub pine leaned horizontally out over the ravine. Laying his rifle down, Wetzel grasped a strong root and cautiously slid over the side. When all of his body had disappeared, with the exception of his sinewy fingers, they loosened their hold on the root, grasped the rifle, and dragged it down out of sight. Quietly, with similar caution, Joe took hold of the same root, let himself down, and when at full length swung himself in under the ledge. His feet found a pocket in the cliff. Letting go of the root, he took his rifle, and in another second was safe.

Of all Wetzel's retreats—for he had many—he considered this one the safest. The cavern under the ledge he had discovered by accident. One day, being hotly pursued by Shawnees, he had been headed off on this cliff, and had let himself down on the ledge, intending to drop from it to the tops of the trees below. Taking advantage of every little aid, he swung over by means of the shrub, and was in the act of leaping when he saw that the cliff shelved under the ledge, while within reach of his feet was the entrance to a cavern. He found the cave to be small, with an opening at the back into a split in the rock. Evidently the place had been entered from the rear by bears, who used the hole for winter sleeping quarters. By crawling on his hands and knees, Wetzel found the rear opening. Thus he had established a hiding place where it was almost impossible to locate him. He provisioned his retreat, which he always entered by the cliff and left by the rear.

An evidence of Wetzel's strange nature, and of his love for this wild home, manifested itself when he bound Joe to secrecy. It was unlikely, even if the young man ever did get safely out of the wilderness, that any stories he might relate would reveal the hunter's favorite rendezvous. But Wetzel seriously demanded this secrecy, as earnestly as if the forest were full of Indians and white men, all prowling in search of his burrow.

Joe was in the seventh heaven of his delight, and took to the free life as a wild gosling takes to the water. No place had ever appealed to him as did this dark, silent hole far up on the side of a steep cliff. His interest in Wetzel soon passed into a great admiration, and from that deepened to love.

This afternoon, when they were satisfied that all was well within their refuge, Joe laid aside his rifle, and, whistling softly, began to prepare supper. The back part of the cave permitted him to stand erect and was large enough for comparative comfort. There was a neat little stone fireplace, and several cooking utensils and gourds. From time to time Wetzel had brought these things. A pile of wood and a bundle of pinecones lay in the corner. Haunches of dried beef, bear, and buffalo meat hung from pegs; a bag of parched corn, another of dried apples lay on a rocky shelf. Nearby hung a powder horn filled with salt and pepper. In the cleft back of the cave was a spring of clear, cold water.

The wants of woodsmen are few and simple. Joe and Wetzel, with appetites whetted by their stirring outdoor life, relished the frugal fare as they could never have enjoyed a feast. As the shadows of evening entered the cave, they lighted their pipes to partake of the hunger's sweetest solace, a quiet smoke.

Strange as it may appear, this lonely, stern Indian hunter and the reckless, impulsive boy were admirably suited for companionship. Wetzel had taken a liking to the young man when he led the brothers to Fort Henry. Subsequent events strengthened his liking, and now, many days after, Joe having followed him into the forest, a strong attachment had been insensibly forged between them.

Wetzel understood Joe's burning desire to roam the forests, but he half expected the lad would soon grow tired of this roving life. But exactly the opposite symptoms were displayed. The hunter had intended to take his comrade on a hunting trip, and to return with him, after that was over, to Fort Henry. They had now been in the woods for weeks, and every day in some way had Joe showed his mettle. Wetzel finally admitted him into the secrets of his most cherished hiding place. He did not want to hurt the lad's feelings by taking him back to the settlement; he could not send him back. So the days wore on swiftly; full of heart-satisfying incident and life, with man and boy growing closer in an intimacy that was as warm as it was unusual.

Two reasons might account for this: First, there is no sane human being who is not better off for companionship. An exile would find something of happiness in one who shared his misery. And, second, Joe was a most acceptable comrade, even for a slayer of Indians. Wedded as Wetzel was to the forest trails, to his lonely life, to the Nemesis pursuit he had followed for eighteen long years, he was still a white man, kind and gentle in his quiet hours, and because of this, though he knew it not, still capable of affection. He had never known youth; his manhood had been one pitiless warfare against his sworn foes; but once in all those years had his sore, cold heart warmed; and that was toward a woman who was not for him. His life had held only one purpose—a bloody one. Yet the man had a heart, and he could not prevent it from responding to another. In his simple ignorance he rebelled against this affection for anything other than his forest homes. Man is weak against hate; what can he avail against love? The dark caverns of Wetzel's great heart opened, admitting to their gloomy depths this stranger. So now a new love was born in that cheerless heart, where for so long a lonely inmate, the ghost of old love, had dwelt in chill seclusion.

The feeling of comradeship which Wetzel had for Joe was something altogether new in the hunter's life. True, he had hunted with Jonathan Zane and accompanied expeditions where he was forced to sleep with another scout; but a companion, not to say friend, he had never known. Joe was a boy, wilder than an eagle, yet he was a man. He was happy and enthusiastic, still his good spirits never jarred on the hunter; they were restrained. He never asked questions, as would seem the case in any eager lad; he waited until he was spoken to. He was apt; he never forgot anything; he had the eye of a born woodsman, and lastly, perhaps what went far with Wetzel, he was as strong and supple as a young lynx, and absolutely fearless.

On this evening Wetzel and Joe followed their usual custom; they smoked a while before lying down to sleep. Tonight the hunter was even more silent than usual, and the lad, tired out with his day's tramp, lay down on a bed of fragrant boughs.

Wetzel sat there in the gathering gloom while he puffed slowly on his pipe. The evening was very quiet; the birds had ceased their twittering; the wind had died away; it was too early for the bay of a wolf, the wail of a panther, or hoot of an owl; there was simply perfect silence.

The lad's deep, even breathing caught Wetzel's ear, and he

found himself meditating, as he had often of late, on this new something that had crept into his life. For Joe loved him; he could not fail to see that. The lad had preferred to roam with the lonely Indian hunter through the forests, to encounter the perils and hardships of a wild life, rather than accept the smile of fortune and of love. Wetzel knew that Colonel Zane had taken a liking to the boy, and had offered him work and a home; and, also, the hunter remembered the warm light he had seen in Nell's hazel eyes. Musing thus, the man felt stir in his heart an emotion so long absent that it was unfamiliar. The Avenger forgot, for a moment, his brooding plans. He felt strangely softened. When he laid his head on the rude pillow it was with some sense of gladness that, although he had always desired a lonely life, and wanted to pass it in the fulfillment of his vow, his loneliness was now shared by a lad who loved him.

Joe was awakened by the merry chirp of a chipmunk that every morning ran along the seamy side of the opposite wall of the gorge. Getting up, he went to the back of the cave, where he found Wetzel combing out his long hair. The lad thrust his hands into the cold pool and bathed his face. The water was icy cold and sent an invigorating thrill through him. Then he laughed as he took a rude comb Wetzel handed to him.

"My scalp is nothing to make an Indian very covetous, is it?" said he, eyeing in admiration the magnificent black hair that fell over the hunter's shoulders.

"It'll grow," answered Wetzel.

Joe did not wonder at the care Wetzel took of his hair, nor did he misunderstand the hunter's simple pride. Wetzel was very careful of his rifle, he was neat and clean about his person, he brushed his buckskin costume, he polished his knife and tomahawk; but his hair received more attention than all else. It required much care. When combed out it reached fully to his knees. Joe had seen him, after he returned from a long hunt, work patiently for an hour with his wooden comb, and not stop until every little burr was gone, or tangle smoothed out. Then he would comb it again in the morning—this of course, when time permitted—and twist and tie it up so as to offer small resistance to his slipping through the underbrush. Joe knew the hunter's simplicity was such that if he cut off his hair it would seem he feared the Indians—for that streaming black hair the Indians had long coveted and sworn to take. It would make any brave a famous chief, and was the theme of many a savage war tale.

After breakfast Wetzel said to Joe:

"You stay here, an' I'll look round some; mebbe I'll come back soon, and we'll go out an' kill a buffalo. Injuns sometimes foller up a buffalo trail, and I want to be sure none of the varlets are chasin' that herd we saw today."

Wetzel left the cave by the rear. It took him fifteen minutes to crawl to the end of the tortuous, stony passage. Lifting the stone which closed up the aperture, he looked out and listened. Then, rising, he replaced the stone, and passed down the wooded hillside.

It was a beautiful morning; the dew glistened on the green leaves, the sun shone bright and warm, the birds warbled in the trees. The hunter's moccasins pressed so gently on the moss and leaves that they made no more sound than the soft foot of a panther. His trained ear was alert to catch any unfamiliar noise; his keen eyes sought first the remoter open glades and glens, then bent their gaze on the mossy bluff beneath his feet. Fox squirrels dashed from before him into bushy retreats; grouse whirred away into the thickets; startled deer whistled, and loped off with their white flags upraised. Wetzel knew from the action of these denizens of the woods that he was the only creature, not native to these haunts, who had disturbed them this morning. Otherwise the deer would not have been grazing, but lying low in some close thicket; fox squirrels seldom or never were disturbed by a hunter twice in one day, for after being frightened these little animals, wilder and shyer than gray squirrels, remained hidden for hours, and grouse that have been flushed a little while before, always get up unusually quick, and fly very far before alighting.

Wetzel circled back over the hill, took a long survey from a rock eminence, and then reconnoitered the lowland for several miles. He located the herd of buffalo, and satisfying himself there were no Indians near—for the bison were grazing quietly—he returned to the cave. A soft whistle into the back door of the rocky home told Joe that the hunter was waiting.

"Coast clear?" whispered the lad, thrusting his head out of the entrance. His gray eyes gleamed brightly, showing his eager spirit.

The hunter nodded, and, throwing his rifle in the hollow of his arm, proceeded down the hill. Joe followed closely, endeavoring, as Wetzel had trained him, to make each step precisely in the hunter's footprint. The lad had soon learned to step nimbly and softly as a cat. When halfway down the hill Wetzel paused.

"See anythin'?" he whispered.

Joe glanced on all sides. Many mistakes had taught him to be cautious. He had learned from experience that for every woodland creature he saw, there were ten watching his every move. Just now he could not see even a little red squirrel. Everywhere were sturdy hickory and oak trees, thickets and hazelnuts, slender ash saplings, and, in the open glades, patches of sumac. Rotting trees lay on the ground, while ferns nodded long, slender heads over the fallen monarchs.

Joe could make out nothing but the colors of the woods, the gray of the tree trunks, and, in the openings through the forest green, the dead purple haze of forests farther on. He smiled, and, shaking his head at the hunter, by his action admitted failure.

"Try again. Dead ahead," whispered Wetzel.

Joe bent a direct gaze on the clump of sassafras one hundred feet ahead. He searched the open places, the shadows—even the branches. Then he turned his eyes slowly to the right. Whatever was discernible to human vision he studied intently. Suddenly his eye became fixed on a small object protruding from behind a beech tree. It was pointed, and in color darker than the gray bark of the beech. It had been a very easy matter to pass over this little thing; but now that the lad saw it, he knew to what it belonged.

"That's a buck's ear," he replied.

Hardly had he finished speaking when Wetzel intentionally snapped a twig. There was a crash and commotion in the thicket; branches moved and small saplings waved; then out into the open glade bounded a large buck with a whistle of alarm. Throwing his rifle to a level, Joe was trying to cover the bounding deer when the hunter struck up his piece.

"Lad, don't kill fer the sake of killin'," he said, quietly. "We have plenty of venison. We'll go arter a buffalo. I hev a hankerin' fer a good rump steak."

Half an hour later, the hunters emerged from the forest into a wide plain of waving grass. It was a kind of oval valley, encircled by hills, and had been at one time, perhaps, covered with water. Joe saw a herd of large animals browsing, like cattle, in a meadow. His heart beat high, for until that moment the only buffalo he had seen were the few which stood on the riverbanks as the raft passed down the Ohio. He would surely get a shot at one of these huge fellows.

Wetzel bade Joe do exactly as he did, whereupon he dropped on his hands and knees and began to crawl through the long grass. This was easy for the hunter, but very hard for the lad to accomplish. Still, he managed to keep his comrade in sight, which was a matter for congratulation, because the man crawled as fast as he walked. At length, after what to Joe seemed a very long time, the hunter paused.

"Are we near enough?" whispered Joe, breathlessly.

"Nope. We're just circlin' on 'em. The wind's not right, an' I'm afeered they'll get our scent."

Wetzel rose carefully and peeped over the top of the grass; then, dropping on all fours, he resumed the advance.

He paused again, presently and waited for Joe to come up.

"See here, young feller, remember, never hurry unless the bizness calls fer speed, an' then act like lightnin'."

Thus admonishing the eager lad, Wetzel continued to crawl. It was easy for him. Joe wondered how those wide shoulders got between the weeds and grasses without breaking, or, at least, shaking them. But so it was.

"Flat now," whispered Wetzel, putting his broad hand on Joe's back and pressing him down. "Now's yer time fer good practice. Trail yer rifle over yer back—if yer careful it won't slide off—an' reach out far with one arm an' dig yer fingers in deep. Then pull yerself forrard."

Wetzel slipped through the grass like a huge buckskin snake. His long, lithe body wormed its way among the reeds. But for Joe, even with the advantage of having the hunter's trail to follow, it was difficult work. The dry reeds broke under him, and the stalks of saw grass shook. He worked persistently at it, learning all the while, and improving with every rod. He was surprised to hear a swish, followed by a dull blow on the ground. Raising his head, he looked forward. He saw the hunter wipe his tomahawk on the grass.

"Snake," whispered Wetzel.

Joe saw a huge blacksnake squirming in the grass. Its head had been severed. He caught glimpses of other snakes gliding away, and glossy round moles darting into their holes. A gray rabbit started off with a leap.

"We're near enough," whispered Wetzel, stopping behind a bush. He rose and surveyed the plain; then motioned Joe to look.

Joe raised himself on his knees. As his gaze reached the level of the grassy plain his heart leaped. Not fifty yards away was a great, shaggy, black buffalo. He was the king of the herd; but ill at ease, for he pawed the grass and shook his huge head. Near him were several cows and a half-grown calf. Beyond was the main herd, extending as far as Joe could see—a great sea of black humps! The lad breathed hard as he took in the grand sight.

"Pick out the little feller—the reddish-brown one—an' plug him behind the shoulder. Shoot close now, fer if ye miss, mebbe I can't hit one, because I'm not used to shootin' at sich small marks."

Wetzel's rare smile lighted up his dark face. Probably he could have shot a fly off the horn of the bull, if one of the big flies or bees, plainly visible as they swirled around the huge head, had alighted there.

Joe slowly raised his rifle. He had covered the calf, and was about to pull the trigger, when, with a sagacity far beyond his experience as hunter, he whispered to Wetzel:

"If I fire, they may run toward us."

"Nope; they'll run away," answered Wetzel, thinking the lad was as keen as an Indian.

Joe quickly covered the calf again, and pulled the trigger. Bellowing loud, the big bull dashed off. The herd swung around toward the west, and soon were galloping off with a lumbering roar. The shaggy humps bobbed up and down like short, angry waves on a storm-blackened sea.

Upon going forward, Wetzel and Joe found the calf lying dead in the grass.

"You might hev did better'n that," remarked the hunter, as he saw where the bullet had struck. "You went a little too fer back, but mebbe that was 'cause the calf stepped as you shot."

Chapter
XV

So the days passed swiftly, dreamily, each one bringing Joe a keener delight. In a single month he was as good a woodsman as many pioneers who had passed years on the border, for he had the advantage of a teacher whose woodcraft was incomparable. Besides, he was naturally quick in learning, and with all his interest centered upon forest lore, it was no wonder he assimilated much of Wetzel's knowledge. He was ever willing to undertake anything whereby he might learn. Often when they were miles away in the dense forest, far from their cave, he asked Wetzel to let him try to lead the way back to camp. And he never failed once, though many times he got off a straight course, thereby missing the easy traveling.

Joe did wonderfully well, but he lacked, as nearly all white men do, the subtler, intuitive forest instinct, which makes the Indian as much at home in the woods as in his teepee. Wetzel had this developed to a high degree. It was born in him. Years of training, years of passionate, unrelenting search for Indians, had given him a knowledge of the wilds that was incomprehensible to white men and appalling to his red foes.

Joe saw how Wetzel used this ability, but what it really was baffled him. He realized that words were not adequate to explain fully this great art. Its possession required a marvelously keen vision, an eye perfectly familiar with every creature, tree, rock, shrub, and thing belonging in the forest; an eye so quick in sight as to detect instantly the slightest change in nature, or anything unnatural to that environment. The hearing must be delicate, like that of a deer, and the finer it is, the keener will be the woodsman. Lastly, there is the feeling that prompts the old hunter to say: "No game today." It is something in him that speaks when, as he sees a nighthawk circling low near the ground, he says: "A storm tomorrow." It is what makes an Indian at home in any wilderness. The clouds may hide the guiding star; the northing may be lost; there may be no moss on the trees, or difference in their bark; the ridges may be flat or lost altogether, and there may be no watercourses; yet the Indian brave always goes for his teepee, straight as a crow flies. It was this voice which rightly bade Wetzel, when he was baffled by an Indian's trail fading among the rocks, to cross, or circle, or advance in the direction taken by his wily foe.

Joe had practiced trailing deer and other hoofed game until he was true as a hound. Then he began to perfect himself in the art of following a human being through the forest. Except a few old Indian trails, which the rain had half obliterated, he had no tracks to discover save Wetzel's, and these were as hard to find as the airy course of a grosbeak. On soft ground or marshy grass, which Wetzel avoided where he could, he left a faint trail, but on a hard surface, for all the traces he left, he might as well not have gone over the ground at all.

Joe's persistence stood him in good stead; he hung on, and the more he failed, the harder he tried. Often he would slip out of the cave after Wetzel had gone, and try to find which way he had taken. In brief, the lad became a fine marksman, a good hunter, and a close, persevering student of the wilderness. He loved the woods, and all they contained. He learned the habits of the wild creatures. Each deer, each squirrel, each grouse that he killed, taught him some lesson.

He was always up with the lark to watch the sun rise red and grand over the eastern hills, and chase away the white mist from the valleys. Even if he was not hunting, or roaming the woods, if it was necessary for him to lie low in camp awaiting Wetzel's return, he was always content. Many hours he idled away lying on his back, with the west wind blowing softly over him, his eye on the distant hills, where the cloud shadows swept across with slow, majesic movement, like huge ships at sea.

If Wetzel and Joe were far distant from the cave, as was often the case, they made camp in the open woods, and it was here that Joe's contentment was fullest. Twilight shades stealing down over the campfire; the cheery glow of red embers; the crackling of dry stocks; the sweet smell of wood smoke, all had for the lad a subtle, potent charm.

The hunter would broil a venison steak, or a partridge, on the coals. Then they would light their pipes and smoke while twilight deepened. The oppressive stillness of the early evening hour always brought to the younger man a sensation of awe. At first he attributed this to the fact that he was new to this life; however, as the days passed and the emotion remained, nay, grew stronger, he concluded it was imparted by this close communion with nature. Deep, solemn, tranquil, the gloaming hour brought him no ordinary fullness of joy and clearness of perception.

"Do you ever feel this stillness?" he asked Wetzel one evening, as they sat near their flickering fire.

The hunter puffed his pipe and like an Indian seemed to let the question take deep root.

"I've scalped redskins every hour of the day, 'ceptin' twilight," he replied.

Joe wondered no longer whether the hunter was too hardened to feel this beautiful tranquility. That hour which wooed Wetzel from his implacable pursuit was indeed a bewitching one.

There was never a time, when Joe lay alone in camp waiting for Wetzel, that he did not hope the hunter would return with information of Indians. The man never talked about the savages, and if he spoke at all it was to tell of some incident of his day's travel. One evening he came back with a large, black fox that he had killed.

"What beautiful, glossy fur!" said Joe. "I never saw a black fox before."

"I've been layin' fer this feller some time," replied Wetzel, as he began his first evening task, that of combing his hair. "Jest back here in a clump of cottonweeds there's a holler log full of leaves. Happen' to see a blacksnake sneakin' round, I thought mebbe he was up to somethin', so I investigated, an' found a nest full of young rabbits. I killed the snake, an' arter that took an interest in 'em. Every time I passed I'd look in at the bunnies, an' each time I seen signs that some tarnal varmint had been prowlin' round. One day I missed a bunny, an' next day another; so on until only one was left, a peart white and gray little scamp. Somethin' was stealin' of 'em, and it made me mad. So yistidday an' today I watched, an' finally I plugged this black thief. Yes, he's got a glossy coat; but he's a bad un for all his fine looks. These black foxes are bigger, stronger an' cunniner than red ones. In every litter you'll find a dark one, the black sheep of the family. Because he grows so much faster, an' steals all the food from the others, the mother jest takes him by the nape of the neck an' chucks him out in the world to shift fer himself. An' it's a good thing."

The next day Wetzel told Joe that they would go across country to seek new game fields. Accordingly the two set out and tramped industriously until evening. They came upon a country no less beautiful than the one they had left, though the picturesque cliffs and rugged hills had given way to a rolling land, the luxuriance of which was explained by the abundant springs and streams. Forests and fields were thickly interspersed with bubbling springs, narrow and deep streams and here and there a small lake with a running outlet.

Wetzel had said little concerning this region, but that little was enough to rouse all Joe's eagerness, for it was to the effect that they were now in a country much traversed by Indians, especially runners and hunting parties traveling from north to south. The hunter explained that through the center of this tract ran a buffalo road; that the buffalo always picked out the straightest, lowest, and dryest path from one range to another, and the Indians followed these first pathfinders.

Joe and Wetzel made camp on the bank of a stream that night, and as the lad watched the hunter build a hidden campfire, he peered furtively around, half expecting to see dark forms scurrying through the forest. Wetzel was extremely cautious. He stripped pieces of bark from fallen trees and built a little hut over his firewood. He rubbed some powder on a piece of punk, and then with flint and steel dropped two or three sparks on the inflammable substance. Soon he had a blaze. He arranged the covering so that not a ray of light escaped. When the flames had subsided and the wood had burned down to a glowing bed of red, he threw aside the bark and broiled the strips of venison they had brought with them.

They rested on a bed of boughs which they had cut and arranged alongside a huge log. For hours Joe lay awake; he could not sleep. He listened to the breeze rustling the leaves, and shivered at the thought of the sighing wind he had once heard moan through the forest. Presently he turned over. The slight noise instantly awakened Wetzel, who lifted his dark face while he listened intently. He spoke one word: "Sleep," and lay back again on the leaves. Joe forced himself to be quiet, relaxed all his muscles, and soon slumbered.

On the morrow Wetzel went out to look over the hunting prospects. About noon he returned. Joe was surprised to find some slight change in the hunter. He could not tell what it was.

"I seen Injun sign," said Wetzel. "There's no tellin' how soon we may run agin the sneaks. We can't hunt here. Like as not there's Hurons and Delawares skulkin' round. I think I'd better take you back to the village."

"It's all on my account you say that," said Joe.

"Sure," Wetzel replied.

"If you were alone what would you do?"

"I calkilate I'd hunt fer some redskinned game."

The supreme moment had come. Joe's heart beat hard. He could not miss this opportunity; he must stay with the hunter. He looked closely at Wetzel.

"I won't go back to the village," he said.

The hunter stood in his favorite position, leaning on his long rifle, and made no response.

"I won't go," continued Joe, earnestly. "Let me stay with you. If at any time I hamper you, or cannot keep the pace, then leave me to shift for myself; but don't make me go until I weaken. Let me stay."

Fire and fearlessness spoke in Joe's every word, and his gray eyes contracted with their peculiar steely flash. Plain it was that, while he might fail to keep pace with Wetzel he did not fear this dangerous country, and, if it must be, would face it alone.

Wetzel extended his broad hand and gave his comrade's a viselike squeeze. To allow the lad to remain with him was more than he would have done for any other person in the world. Far better to keep the lad under his protection while it was possible, for Joe was taking that war trail which had for every hunter, somewhere along its bloody course, a bullet, a knife, or a tomahawk. Wetzel knew that Joe was conscious of this inevitable conclusion, for it showed in his white face and in the resolve in his big, gray eyes.

So there, in the shade of a towering oak, the Indian killer admitted the boy into his friendship and into a life which would no longer be play, but eventful, stirring, hazardous.

"Wal, lad, stay," he said, with that rare smile which brightened his dark face like a ray of stray sunshine. "We'll hang round these diggin's a few days. First off, we'll take in the lay of the land. You go downstream a ways an' scout round some, while I go up, an' then circle down. Move slow, now, an' don't miss nothin'."

Joe followed the stream a mile or more. He kept close in the shade of willows, and never walked across an open glade without first waiting and watching. He listened to all sounds; but none were unfamiliar. He closely examined the sand along the stream and the moss and leaves under the trees. When he had been separated from Wetzel several hours and concluded he would slowly return to camp, he ran across a well-beaten path winding through the forest. This was, perhaps, one of the bridle trails Wetzel had referred to. He bent over the worn grass with keen scrutiny.

Crack!

The loud report of a heavily charged rifle rang out. Joe felt the zip of a bullet as it fanned his cheek. With an agile leap he gained the shelter of a tree, from behind which he peeped to see who had shot at him. He was just in time to detect the dark form of an Indian dart behind the foliage a hundred yards down the path. Joe expected to see other Indians, and to hear more shots, but he was mistaken. Evidently the savage was alone, for the tree Joe had taken refuge behind was scarcely large enough to screen his body, which disadvantage the other Indians would have been quick to note.

Joe closely watched the place where his assailant had disappeared, and presently saw a dark hand, then a naked elbow and finally the ramrod of a rifle. The savage was reloading. Soon a rifle barrel protruded from behind the tree. With his heart beating like a triphammer, and the skin tightening on his face, Joe screened his body as best he might. The tree was small, but it served as a partial protection. Rapidly he revolved in his mind plans to outwit the enemy. The Indian was behind a large oak with a low limb over which he could fire without exposing his own person to danger.

"Bang!" The Indian's rifle bellowed; the bullet crumbled the bark close to Joe's face. The lad yelled loudly, staggered to his knees, and then fell into the path, where he lay quiet.

The redskin gave an exultant shout. Seeing that the fallen figure remained quite motionless, he stepped forward, drawing his knife as he came. He was a young brave, quick and eager in his movements, and came nimbly up the path to gain his coveted trophy, the paleface's scalp.

Suddenly Joe sat up, raised his rifle quickly as thought, and fired point-blank at the Indian.

But he missed.

The redskin stopped aghast when he saw the lad thus seemingly come back to life. Then, realizing that Joe's aim had been futile, he bounded forward, brandishing his knife, and uttering infuriated yells.

Joe rose to his feet with rifle swung high above his head.

When the savage was within twenty feet, so near that his dark face, swollen with fierce passion, could be plainly discerned, a peculiar whistling noise sounded over Joe's shoulder. It was accompanied, rather than followed, by a clear, ringing rifle shot.

The Indian stopped as if he had encountered a heavy shock from a tree or stone barring his way. Clutching at his breast, he uttered a weird cry and sank slowly on the grass.

Joe ran forward to bend over the prostrate figure. The Indian, a slender, handsome young brave, had been shot through the breast. He held his hand tightly over the wound, while bright red blood trickled between his fingers, flowed down his side and stained the grass.

The brave looked steadily up at Joe. Shot as he was, dying as he knew himself to be, there was no yielding in the dark eyes—only an unquenchable hatred. Then the eyes glazed; the fingers ceased twitching.

Joe was bending over a dead Indian.

It flashed into his mind, of course, that Wetzel had come up in time to save his life, but he did not dwell on the thought; he shrank from this violent death of a human being. But it was from the aspect of the dead, not from remorse for the deed. His heart beat fast, his fingers trembled, yet he felt only a strange coldness in all his being. The savage had tried to kill him, perhaps, even now, had it not been for the hunter's unerring aim, would have been gloating over a bloody scalp.

Joe felt, rather than heard, the approach of someone, and he turned to see Wetzel coming down the path.

"He's a lone Shawnee runner," said the hunter, gazing down at the dead Indian. "He was tryin' to win his eagle plumes. I seen you both from the hillside."

"You did!" exclaimed Joe. Then he laughed. "It was lucky for me. I tried the dodge you taught me, but in my eagerness I missed."

"Wal, you hadn't no call fer hurry. You worked the trick clever, but you missed him when there was plenty of time. I had to shoot over your shoulder, or I'd hev plugged him sooner."

"Where were you?" asked Joe.

"Up there by that bit of sumac!" and Wetzel pointed to an open ridge on a hillside not less than one hundred and fifty yards distant.

Joe wondered which of the two bullets, the death-seeking one fired by the savage or the life-saving missile from Wetzel's fatal weapon, had passed nearest to him.

"Come," said the hunter, after he had scalped the Indian.

"What's to be done with this savage?" inquired Joe as Wetzel started up the path.

"Let him lay."

They returned to camp without further incident. While the hunter busied himself reinforcing their temporary shelter—for the clouds looked threatening—Joe cut up some buffalo meat, and then went down to the brook for a gourd of water. He came hurriedly back to where Wetzel was working, and spoke in a voice which he vainly endeavored to hold steady:

"Come quickly. I have seen something which may mean a good deal."

He led the way down to the brookside.

"Look!" Joe said, pointing at the water.

Here the stream was about two feet deep, perhaps twenty wide, and had just a noticeable current. Shortly before, it had been as clear as a bright summer sky; it was now tinged with yellow clouds that slowly floated downstream, each one enlarging and becoming fainter as the clear water permeated and stained. Grains of sand glided along with the current, little pieces of bark floated on the surface, and minnows darted to and fro nibbling at these drifting particles.

"Deer wouldn't roil the water like that. What does it mean?" asked Joe.

"Injuns, an' not fer away."

Wetzel returned to the shelter and tore it down. Then he bent the branch of a beech tree low over the place. He pulled down another branch over the remains of the campfire. These precautions made the spot less striking. Wetzel knew that an Indian scout never glances casually; his roving eyes survey the forest, perhaps quickly, but thoroughly. An unnatural position of bush or log always leads to an examination.

This done, the hunter grasped Joe's hand and led him up the knoll. Making his way behind a well-screened tree, which had been uprooted, he selected a position where, hidden themselves, they could see the creek.

Hardly had Wetzel admonished Joe to lie perfectly still, when from a short distance up the stream came the sound of splashing water; but nothing could be seen above the open glade, as in that direction willows lined the creek in dense thickets. The noise grew more audible.

Suddenly Joe felt a muscular contraction pass over the powerful frame lying close beside him. It was a convulsive thrill such as passes through a tiger when he is about to spring upon his quarry. So subtle and strong was its meaning, so clearly did it convey to the lad what was coming, that he felt it himself; save that in his case it was a cold, chill shudder.

Breathless suspense followed. Then into the open space along the creek glided a tall Indian warrior. He was knee deep in the water, where he waded with slow, cautious steps. His garish, befrilled costume seemed familiar to Joe. He carried a rifle at a low trail, and passed slowly ahead with evident distrust. The lad believed he recognized that head, with its tangled black hair, and when he saw the swarthy, villainous countenance turned full toward him, he exclaimed:

"Girty! By—"

Wetzel's powerful arm forced him so hard against the log that he could not complete the exclamation; but he could still see. Girty had not heard that stifled cry, for he continued his slow wading, and presently his tall, gaudily decorated form passed out of sight.

Another savage appeared in the open space, and then another. Close between them walked a white man, with hands bound behind him. The prisoner and guards disappeared downstream among the willows.

The splashing continued—grew even louder than before. A warrior came into view, then another, and another. They walked close together. Two more followed. They were wading by the side of a raft made of several logs, upon which were two prostrate figures that closely resembled human beings.

Joe was so intent upon the lithe forms of the Indians that he barely got a glimpse of their floating prize, whatever it might have been. Bringing up the rear was an athletic warrior, whose broad shoulders, sinewy arms, and shaved, polished head Joe remembered well. It was the Shawnee chief, Silvertip.

When he, too, passed out of sight in the curve of willows, Joe found himself trembling. He turned eagerly to Wetzel; but instantly recoiled.

. Terrible, indeed, had been the hunter's transformation. All calmness of facial expression was gone; he was now stern, somber. An intense emotion was visible in his white face; his eyes seemed reduced to two dark shining points, and they emitted so fierce, so piercing a flash, so deadly a light, that Joe could not bear their glittering gaze.

"Three white captives, two of 'em women," muttered the hunter, as if weighing in his mind the importance of this fact.

"Were those women on the raft?" questioned Joe, and as Wetzel nodded, he continued. "A white man and two women, six warriors, Silvertip, and that renegade, Jim Girty!"

Wetzel deigned not to answer Joe's passionate outburst, but maintained silence and his rigid posture. Joe glanced once more at the stern face.

"Considering we'd go after Girty and his redskins if they were alone, we're pretty likely to go quicker now that they've got white women prisoners, eh?" and Joe laughed fiercely between his teeth.

The lad's heart expanded, while along every nerve tingled an exquisite thrill of excitement. He had yearned for wild, border life. Here he was in it, with the hunter whose name alone was to the savages a symbol for all that was terrible.

Wetzel evidently decided quickly on what was to be done, for in few words he directed Joe to cut up so much of the buffalo meat as they could stow in their pockets. Then bidding the lad to follow, he turned into the woods, walking rapidly, and stopping now and then for a brief instant. Soon they emerged from the forest into more open country. They faced a wide plain skirted on the right by a long, winding strip of bright green willows which marked the course of the stream. On the edge of this plain Wetzel broke into a run. He kept this pace for a distance of a hundred yards, then stopped to listen intently as he glanced sharply on all sides, after which he was off again.

Halfway across this plain Joe's wind began to fail, and his breathing became labored; but he kept close to the hunter's heels. Once he looked back to see a great wise expanse of waving grass. They had covered perhaps four miles at a rapid pace, and were nearing the other side of the plain. The lad felt as if his head was about to burst; a sharp pain seized upon his side; a bloodred film obscured his sight. He kept doggedly on, and when utterly exhausted fell to the ground.

When, a few minutes later, having recovered his breath, he got up, they had crossed the plain and were in a grove of beeches. Directly in front of him ran a swift stream, which was divided at the rocky head of what appeared to be a wooded island. There was only a slight ripple and fall of the water, and, after a second glance, it was evident that the point of land was not an island, but a portion of the mainland which divided the stream. The branches took almost opposite courses.

Joe wondered if they had headed off the Indians. Certainly they had run fast enough. He was wet with perspiration. He glanced at Wetzel, who was standing near. The man's broad breast rose and fell a little faster; that was the only evidence of exertion. The lad had a painful feeling that he could never keep pace with the hunter if this five-mile run was a sample of the speed he would be forced to maintain.

"They've got ahead of us, but which crick did they take?" queried Wetzel, as though debating the question with himself.

"How do you know they've passed?"

"We circled," answered Wetzel, as he shook his head and pointed into the bushes. Joe stepped over and looked into the thicket. He found a quantity of dead leaves, sticks, and litter thrown aside, exposing to light a long, hollowed place on the ground. It was what would be seen after rolling over a log that had lain for a long time. Little furrows in the ground, holes, mounds, and curious winding passages showed where grubs and crickets had made their homes. The frightened insects were now running round wildly.

"What was here? A log?"

"A twenty-foot canoe was hid under thet stuff. The Injuns has taken one of these streams."

"How can we tell which one?"

"Mebbe we can't; but we'll try. Grab up a few of them bugs, go below thet rocky point, an' crawl close to the bank so you can jest peep over. Be keerful not to show the tip of your head, an' don't knock nothin' off'n the bank into the water. Watch fer trout. Look everywhere, an' drop in a bug now and then. I'll do the same fer the other stream. Then we'll come back here an' talk over what the fish has to say about the Injuns."

Joe walked downstream a few paces, and, dropping on his knees, crawled carefully to the edge of the bank. He slightly parted the grass so he could peep through, and found himself directly over a pool with a narrow shoal running out from the opposite bank. The water was so clear he could see the pebbly bottom in all parts, except a dark hole near the bend in the shore close by. He did not see a living thing in the water, not a crawfish, turtle, nor even a frog. He peered round closely, then flipped in one of the bugs he had brought along. A shiny yellow fish flared up from the depths of the deep hole and disappeared with the cricket; but it was a bass or a pike, not a trout. Wetzel had said there were a few trout living near the cool springs of these streams. The lad tried again to coax one to the surface. This time the more fortunate cricket swam and hopped across the stream to safety.

When Joe's eyes were thoroughly accustomed to the clear

water, with its deceiving lights and shades, he saw a fish lying snug under the side of a stone. The lad thought he recognized the snub-nose, the hooked, wolfish jaw, but he could not get sufficient of a view to classify him. He crawled to a more advantageous position farther downstream, and then he peered again through the weeds. Yes, sure enough, he had espied a trout. He well knew those spotted silver sides, that broad, square tail. Such a monster! In his admiration for the fellow, and his wish for a hook and line to try conclusions with him, Joe momentarily forgot his object. Remembering, he tossed out a big, fat cricket, which alighted on the water just above the fish. The trout never moved, nor even blinked. The lad tried again, with no better success. The fish would not rise. Thereupon Joe returned to the point where he had left Wetzel.

"I couldn't see nothin' over there," said the hunter, who was waiting. "Did you see any?"

"One, and a big fellow."

"Did he see you?"

"No."

"Did he rise to a bug?"

"No, he didn't; but then maybe he wasn't hungry," answered Joe, who could not understand what Wetzel was driving at.

"Tell me exactly what he did."

"That's just the trouble; he didn't do anything," replied Joe, thoughtfully. "He just lay, stifflike, under a stone. He never batted an eye. But his side fins quivered like an aspen leaf."

"Them side fins tell us the story. Girty an' his redskins hev took this branch," said Wetzel, positively. "The other leads to the Huron towns. Girty's got a place near the Delaware camp somewheres. I've tried to find it a good many times. He's took more'n one white lass there, an' nobody ever seen her agin."

"Fiend! To think of a white woman, maybe a girl like Nell Wells, at the mercy of those red devils!"

"Young feller, don't go wrong. I'll allow Injuns is bad enough; but I never hearn tell of one abusin' a white woman, as mayhap you mean. Injuns marry white women sometimes; kill an' scalp 'em often, but that's all. It's men of our own color, renegades like this Girty, as do worse'n murder."

Here was the amazing circumstance of Lewis Wetzel, the acknowledged unsatiable foe of all redmen, speaking a good word for his enemies. Joe was so astonished he did not attempt to answer.

"Here's where they got in the canoe. One more look, an' then we're off," said Wetzel. He strode up and down the sandy beach, examined the willows, and scrutinized the sand. Suddenly he bent over and picked up an object from the water. His sharp eyes had caught the glint of something white, which, upon being examined, proved to be a small ivory or bone buckle with a piece broken out. He showed it to Joe.

"By heavens! Wetzel, that's a buckle off Nell Wells' shoe. I've seen it too many times to mistake it."

"I was afraid Girty hed your friends, the sisters, an' mebbe your brother, too. Jack Zane said the renegade was hangin' round the village, an' that couldn't be fer no good."

"Come on. Let's kill the fiend!" cried Joe, white to the lips.

"I calkilate they're about a mile downstream, makin' camp fer the night. I know the place. There's a fine spring, an' look! D'ye see them crows flyin' round the big oak with the bleached top? Hear them cawin'? You might think they was chasin' a hawk, or kingbirds were arter 'em, but thet fuss the're makin' is because they see Injuns."

"Well?" asked Joe, impatiently.

"It'll be moonlight a while arter midnight. We'll lay low an' wait, an' then—"

The sharp click of his teeth, like the snap of a steel trap, completed the sentence. Joe said no more, but followed the hunter into the woods. Stopping near a fallen tree Wetzel raked up a bundle of leaves and spread them on the ground. Then he cut a few spreading branches from a beech and leaned them against a log. Bidding the lad crawl in before him, he took one last look around and then made his way under the shelter.

It was yet daylight, which seemed a strange time to creep into this little nook; but, Joe thought, it was not to sleep, only to wait, wait, wait for the long hours to pass. He was amazed once more, because, by the time twilight had given place to darkness, Wetzel was asleep. The lad said then to himself that he would never again be surprised at the hunter. He assumed once and for all that Wetzel was capable of anything. Yet how could he lose himself in slumber? Feeling, as he must, over the capture of the girls; eager to draw a bead on the black-hearted renegade; hating Indians with all his soul and strength and lying there but a few hours before what he knew would be a bloody battle, Wetzel calmly went to sleep. Knowing the hunter to be as bloodthirsty as a tiger, Joe had expected he would rush to a combat with his foes, but, no, this man with his keen sagacity, knew when to creep upon his enemy; he bided that time, and, while he waited, slept.

Joe could not close his eyes in slumber. Through the interstices in the branches he saw the stars come out one by one, the darkness deepened, and the dim outline of tall trees over the dark hill came out sharply. The moments dragged. Each one an hour. He heard a whip-poor-will call, lonely and dismal; then an owl hoot monotonously. A stealthy-footed animal ran along the log, sniffed at the boughs, and then scurried away over the dry leaves. By and by the dead silence of night fell over all. Still Joe lay there wide awake, listening—his heart on fire. He was about to rescue Nell; to kill the hawk-nosed renegade; to fight Silvertip to the death.

The hours passed, but not Joe's passionate eagerness. When at last he saw the crescent moon gleam silver-white over the black hilltop he knew the time was nigh, and over him ran thrill on thrill.

Chapter
XVI

When the waning moon rose high enough to shed a pale light over forest and field, two dark figures, moving silently from the shade of the trees, crossed the moonlit patches of ground, out to the open plain where low on the grass hung silver mists.

A timber wolf, gray and gaunt, came loping along with lowered nose. A new scent brought the animal to a standstill. His nose went up, his fiery eyes scanned the plain. Two men had invaded his domain, and with a short, dismal bark, he dashed away.

Like specters, gliding swiftly with noiseless tread, the two vanished. The long grass had swallowed them.

Deserted once again seemed the plain. It became unutterably lonely. No stir, no sound, no life; nothing but a wide expanse bathed in sad, gray light.

The moon shone steadily; the silver radiance mellowed, the stars paled before this brighter glory.

Slowly the night hours wore away.

On the other side of the plain, near where the adjoining forest loomed darkling, the tall grass parted to disclose a black

form. Was it only a deceiving shade cast by a leafy branch—
only a shadow? Slowly it sank, and was lost. Once more the
gray, unwavering line of silver-crested grass tufts was unbroken.

Only the night breeze, wandering caressingly over the
grass, might have told of two dark forms gliding, gliding,
gliding so softly, so surely, so surely toward the forest. Only
the moon and the pale stars had eyes to see these creeping
figures.

Like avengers they moved, on a mission to slay and to
save!

On over the dark line where plain merged into forest they
crawled. No whispering, no hesitating; but a silent, slow,
certain progress showed their purpose. In single file they
slipped over the moss, the leader clearing the path. Inch by
inch they advanced. Tedious was this slow movement, difficult and painful this journey which must end in lightninglike
speed. They rustled no leaf, nor snapped a twig, nor shook a
fern, but passed onward slowly, like the approach of Death.
The seconds passed as minutes; minutes as hours; an entire
hour was spent in advancing twenty feet!

At last the top of the knoll was reached. The Avenger
placed his hand on his follower's shoulder. The strong pressure was meant to remind, to warn, to reassure. Then, like a
huge snake, the first glided away.

He who was left behind raised his head to look into the
open place, called the glade of the Beautiful Spring. An oval
space lay before him, exceedingly lovely in the moonlight; a
spring, as if a pearl, gemmed the center. An Indian guard
stood statuelike against a stone. Other savages lay in a row,
their polished heads shining. One slumbering form was bedecked with feathers and frills. Near him lay an Indian blanket, from the border of which peeped two faces, gleaming
white and sad in the pitying moonlight.

The watcher quivered at the sight of those pale faces; but
he must wait while long moments passed. He must wait for
the Avenger to creep up, silently kill the guard, and release
the prisoners without awakening the savages. If that plan
failed, he was to rush into the glade, and in the excitement
make off with one of the captives.

He lay there waiting, listening, wrought up to the intens-
est pitch of fierce passion. Every nerve was alert, every ten-
don strung, and every muscle strained ready for the leap.

Only the faint rustling of leaves, the low swish of swaying
branches, the soft murmur of falling water, and over all the
sigh of the night wind, proved to him that this picture was
not an evil dream. His gaze sought the quiet figures, lingered
hopefully on the captives, menacingly on the sleeping savages, and glowered over the gaudily arrayed form. His glance
sought the upright guard, as he stood a dark blot against the
gray stone. He saw the Indian's plume, a single feather waving silver-white. Then it became riveted on the bubbling, re-
fulgent spring. The pool was round, perhaps five feet across,
and shone like a burnished shield. It mirrored the moon, the
twinkling stars, the specter trees.

An unaccountable horror suddenly swept over the watching man. His hair stood straight up; a sensation as of cold
stole chilling over him. Whether it was the climax of this long
night's excitement or anticipation of the bloody struggle soon
to come, he knew not. Did this boiling spring, shimmering in
the silver moon rays, hold in its murky depths a secret? Did
these lonesome, shadowing trees, with their sad, drooping
branches, harbor a mystery? If a future tragedy was to be enacted here in this quiet glade, could the murmuring water or
leaves whisper its portent? No; they were only silent, only
unintelligible with nature's mystery.

The waiting man cursed himself for a craven coward; he
fought back the benumbing sense; he steeled his heart. Was

this his vaunted willingness to share the Avenger's danger? His strong spirit rose up in arms; once more he was brave and fierce.

He fastened a piercing gaze on the plumed guard. The Indian's lounging posture against the rock was the same as it had been before, yet now it seemed to have a kind of strained attention. The savage's head was poised, like that of a listening deer. The wary Indian scented danger.

A faint moan breathed low above the sound of gently splashing water somewhere beyond the glade.

"Woo-o-oo."

The guard's figure stiffened and became rigidly erect; his blanket slowly slid to his feet.

"Ah-oo-o," sighed the soft breeze in the tree tops.

Louder then, with a deep wail, a moan arose out of the dark gray shadows, swelled thrilling on the still air, and died away mournfully.

"Um-m-mmwoo-o-o-o!"

The sentinel's form melted into the shade. He was gone like a phantom.

Another Indian rose quietly and glanced furtively around the glade. He bent over a comrade and shook him. Instantly the second Indian was on his feet. Scarcely had he gained a standing posture when an object, bounding like a dark ball, shot out of the thicket and hurled both warriors to the earth. A moonbeam glinted upon something bright. It flashed again on a swift, sweeping circle. A short, choking yell aroused the other savages. Up they sprang, alarmed, confused.

The shadow form darted among them. It moved with inconceivable rapidity; it became a monster. Terrible was the convulsive conflict. Dull blows, the click of steel, angry shouts, agonized yells, and thrashing, wrestling sounds mingled together and half drowned by an awful roar like that of a mad bull. The strife ceased as suddenly as it had begun.

Warriors lay still on the grass; others writhed in agony. For an instant a fleeting shadow crossed the open lane leading out of the glade; then it vanished.

Three savages had sprung toward their rifles. A blinding flash, a loud report burst from the thicket overhead. The foremost savage sank lifelessly. The others were intercepted by a giant shadow with brandished rifle. The watcher on the knoll had entered the glade. He stood before the stacked rifles and swung his heavy gun. Crash! An Indian went down before that sweep, but rose again. The savages backed away from this threatening figure, and circled around it.

The noise of the other conflict ceased. More savages joined the three who glided to and fro before their desperate foe. They closed in upon him, only to be beaten back. One savage threw a glittering knife, another hurled a stone, a third flung his tomahawk, which struck fire from the swinging rifle.

He held them at bay. While they had no firearms he was master of the situation. With every sweep of his arms he brought the long rifle down and knocked a flint from the firelock of an enemy's weapon. Soon the Indians' guns were useless. Slowly then he began to edge away from the stone, toward the opening where he had seen the fleeing form vanish.

His intention was to make a dash for life, for he had heard a noise behind the rock and remembered the guard.

He saw the savages glance behind him, and anticipated danger from that direction, but he must not turn. A second there might be fatal. He backed defiantly along the rock until he gained its outer edge. But too late! The Indians glided before him, now behind him; he was surrounded. He turned around and around, with the ever-circling rifle whirling in the faces of the baffled foe.

Once opposite the lane leading from the glade he

changed his tactics and plunged with fierce impetuosity into the midst of the painted throng. Then began a fearful conflict. The Indians fell before the sweep of his powerful arms but grappled with him from the ground. He literally plowed his way through the struggling mass, warding off a hundred vicious blows. Savage after savage he flung off, until at last he had a clear path before him. Freedom lay beyond that shiny path. Into it he bounded.

As he left the glade the plumed guard stepped from behind a tree near the entrance of the path, and cast his tomahawk.

A white, glittering flash, it flew after the fleeing runner, its aim was true.

Suddenly the moonlight path darkened in the runner's sight; he saw a million flashing stars; a terrible pain assailed him; he sank slowly, slowly down; then all was darkness.

Chapter
XVII

Joe awoke as from a fearsome nightmare. Returning consciousness brought a vague idea that he had been dreaming of clashing weapons, of yelling savages, of a conflict in which he had been clutched by sinewy fingers. An acute pain pulsed through his temples; a bloody mist glazed his eyes; a sore pressure cramped his arms and legs. Surely he dreamed this distress, as well as the fight. The red film cleared from his eyes. His wandering gaze showed the stern reality.

The bright sun, making the dewdrops glisten on the leaves, lighted up a tragedy. Near him lay an Indian whose vacant, sightless eyes were fixed in death. Beyond lay four more savages, the peculiar, inert position of whose limbs, the formlessness, as it were, as if they had been thrown from a great height and never moved again, attested that here, too, life had been extinguished. Joe took only one detail—the cloven skull of the nearest—when he turned away sickened. He remembered it all now. The advance, the rush, the fight— all returned. He saw again Wetzel's shadowy form darting like a demon into the whirl of conflict; he heard again that hoarse, booming roar with which the Avenger accompanied his blows. Joe's gaze swept the glade, but found no trace of the hunter.

He saw Silvertip and another Indian bathing a wound on Girty's head. The renegade groaned and writhed in pain. Near him lay Kate, with white face and closed eyes. She was unconscious or dead. Jim sat crouched under a tree to which he was tied.

"Joe, are you badly hurt?" asked the latter, in deep solicitude.

"No, I guess not; I don't know," answered Joe. "Is poor Kate dead?"

"No, she has fainted."

"Where is Nell?"

"Gone," replied Jim, lowering his voice, and glancing at the Indians. They were too busy trying to bandage Girty's head to pay any attention to their prisoners. "That whirlwind was Wetzel, wasn't it?"

"Yes; how'd you know?"

"l was awake last night. I had an oppressive feeling, perhaps a presentiment. Anyway, I couldn't sleep. I heard that wind blow through the forest and thought my blood would freeze. The moan is the same as the night wind, the same soft sigh, only louder and somehow pregnant with superhuman power. To speak of it in broad daylight one seems superstitious, but to hear it in the darkness of this lonely forest, it is fearful! I hope I am not a coward; I certainly know I was deathly frightened. No wonder I was scared! Look at these dead Indians, all killed in a moment. I heard the moan; I saw Silvertip disappear and the other two savages rise. Then something huge dropped from the rock; a bright object seemed to circle round the savages; they uttered one short yell, and sank to rise no more. Somehow at once I suspected that this shadowy form, with its lightninglike movements, its glittering hatchet, was Wetzel. When he plunged into the midst of

the other savages I distinctly recognized him, and saw that
he had a bundle, possibly his coat, wrapped round his left
arm, and his right hand held the glittering tomahawk. I saw
him strike that big Indian there, the one lying with split
skull. His wonderful daring and quickness seemed to make
the savages turn at random. He broke through the circle,
swung Nell under his arm, slashed at my bonds as he passed
by, and then was gone as he had come. Not until after you
were struck, and Silvertip came up to me, was I aware my
bonds were cut. Wetzel's hatchet had severed them; it even
cut my side, which was bleeding. I was free to help, to fight,
and I did not know it. Fool that I am!"

"l made an awful mess of my part of the rescue," groaned
Joe. "I wonder if the savages know it was Wetzel."

"Do they? Well, I rather think so. Did you not hear them
scream that French name? As far as I am able to judge, only
two Indians were killed instantly. The others died during the
night. I had to sit there, tied and helpless, listening as they
groaned and called the name of their slayer, even in their
death throes. Deathwind! They have named him well."

"I guess he nearly killed Girty."

"Evidently, but surely the evil one protects the renegade."

"Jim Girty's doomed," whispered Joe, earnestly. "He's as
good as dead already. I've lived with Wetzel, and know him.
He told me Girty had murdered a settler, a feeble old man,
who lived near Fort Henry with his son. The hunter swore to
kill the renegade; but mind you, he did not tell me that. I saw
it in his eyes. It wouldn't surprise me to see him jump out of
these bushes any moment. I'm looking for it. If he knows
there are only three left, he'll be after them like a hound on a
trail. Girty must hurry. Where's he taking you?"

"To the Delaware town."

"I don't suppose the chiefs will let any harm befall you;

but Kate and I would be better off dead. If we can only delay the march, Wetzel will surely return."

"Hush! Girty's up."

The renegade staggered to an upright position, and leaned on the Shawnee's arm. Evidently he had not been seriously injured, only stunned. Covered with blood from a swollen, gashed lump on his temple, he certainly presented a savage appearance.

"Where's the yellow-haired lass?" he demanded, pushing away Silvertip's friendly arm. He glared around the glade. The Shawnee addressed him briefly, whereupon he raged to and fro under the tree, cursing with foam-flecked lips, and actually howling with baffled rage. His fury was so great that he became suddenly weak, and was compelled to sit down.

"She's safe, you villainous renegade!" cried Joe.

"Hush, Joe! Do not anger him. It can do no good," interposed Jim.

"Why not? We couldn't be worse off," answered Joe.

"I'll git her, I'll git her agin," panted Girty. "I'll keep her, an' she'll love me."

The spectacle of this perverted wretch speaking as if he had been cheated out of love was so remarkable, so pitiful, so monstrous, that for a moment Joe was dumfounded.

"Bah! You white-livered murderer!" Joe hissed. He well knew it was not wise to give way to his passion; but he could not help it. This beast in human guise, whining for love, maddened him. "Any white woman on earth would die a thousand deaths and burn for a million years afterward rather than love you!"

"I'll see you killed at the stake, beggin' for mercy, an' be feed fer buzzards," croaked the renegade.

"Then kill me now, or you may slip up in one of your cherished buzzard-feasts," cried Joe, with glinting eye and taunting voice. "Then go sneaking back to your hole like a hyena, and stay there. Wetzel is on your trail! He missed you last night; but it was because of the girl. He's after you, Girty; he'll get you one of these days, and when he does— My God!—"

Nothing could be more revolting than that swarthy, evil face turned pale with fear. Girty's visage was a ghastly, livid white. So earnest, so intense was Joe's voice, that it seemed to all as if Wetzel was about to dart into the glade, with his avenging tomahawk uplifted to wreak an awful vengeance on the abductor. The renegade's white, craven heart contained no such thing as courage. If he ever fought it was like a wolf, backed by numbers. The resemblance ceased here, for even a cornered wolf will show his teeth, and Girty, driven to bay, would have cringed and cowered. Even now at the mention of Wetzel's enmity he trembled.

"I'll shet yer wind," he cried, catching up his tomahawk and making for Joe.

Silvertip intervened and prevented the assault. He led Girty back to his seat and spoke low, evidently trying to soothe the renegade's feelings.

"Silvertip, give me a tomahawk, and let me fight him," implored Joe.

"Paleface brave—like Injun chief. Paleface Shawnee's prisoner—no speak more," answered Silvertip, with respect in his voice.

"Oh, where's Nellie?"

A grief-stricken whisper caught Jim's ear. He turned to see Kate's wide, questioning eyes fixed upon him.

"Nell was rescued."

"Thank God!" murmured the girl.

"Come along," shouted Girty, in his harsh voice, as, grasping Kate's arm, he pulled the girl violently to her feet.

Then, picking up his rifle, he led her into the forest. Silvertip followed with Joe, while the remaining Indian guarded Jim.

The great council lodge of the Delawares rang with savage and fiery eloquence. Wingenund paced slowly before the orators. Wise as he was, he wanted advice before deciding what was to be done with the missionary. The brothers had been taken to the chief, who immediately called council. The Indians sat in a half circle around the lodge. The prisoners, with hands bound, guarded by two brawny braves, stood in one corner gazing with curiosity and apprehension at this formidable array. Jim knew some of the braves, but the majority of those who spoke bitterly against the palefaces had never frequented the Village of Peace. Nearly all were of the Wolf tribe of Delawares. Jim whispered to Joe, interpreting that part of the speeches bearing upon the disposal to be made of them. Two white men, dressed in Indian garb, held prominent positions before Wingenund. The boys saw a resemblance between one of these men and Jim Girty, and accordingly concluded he was the famous renegade, or so-called White Indian, Simon Girty. The other man was probably Elliott, the Tory, with whom Girty had deserted from Fort Pitt. Jim Girty was not present. Upon nearing the encampment he had taken his captive and disappeared in a ravine.

Shingiss, seldom in favor of drastic measures with prisoners, eloquently urged initiating the brothers into the tribe. Several other chiefs were favorably inclined, though not so positive as Shingiss. Kotoxen was for the death penalty; the implacable Pipe for nothing less than burning at the stake. Not one was for returning the missionary to his Christian Indians. Girty and Elliott, though requested to speak, maintained an ominous silence.

Wingenund strode with thoughtful mien before his council. He had heard all his wise chiefs and his fiery warriors. Supreme was his power. Freedom or death for the captives awaited the wave of his hand. His impassive face gave not the slightest inkling of what to expect. Therefore the prisoners were forced to stand there with throbbing hearts while the chieftain waited the customary dignified interval before addressing the council.

"Wingenund has heard the Delaware wise men and warriors. The White Indian opens not his lips; his silence broods evil for the palefaces. Pipe wants the blood of the white men; the Shawnee chief demands the stake. Wingenund says free the white father who harms no Indian. Wingenund hears no evil in the music of his voice. The white father's brother should die. Kill the companion of Deathwind!"

A plaintive murmur, remarkable when coming from an assembly of stern-browed chiefs, ran round the circle at the mention of the dread appellation.

"The white father is free," continued Wingenund. "Let one of my runners conduct him to the Village of Peace."

A brave entered and touched Jim on the shoulder.

Jim shook his head and pointed to Joe. The runner touched Joe.

"No, no. I am not the missionary," cried Joe, staring aghast at his brother. "Jim, have you lost your senses?"

Jim sadly shook his head, and turning to Wingenund made known in a broken Indian dialect that his brother was the missionary, and would sacrifice himself, taking this opportunity to practice the Christianity he had taught.

"The white father is brave, but he is known," broke in Wingenund's deep voice, while he pointed to the door of the lodge. "Let him go back to his Christian Indians."

The Indian runner cut Joe's bonds and once more attempted to lead him from the lodge. Rage and misery shone in the lad's face. He pushed the runner aside. He exhausted himself trying to explain, to think of Indian words enough to show he was not the missionary. He even implored Girty to speak for him. When the renegade sat there stolidly silent Joe's rage burst out.

"Curse you all for a lot of ignorant redskins. I am not a missionary. I am Deathwind's friend. I killed a Delaware. I was the companion of *La Vent de la Mort*!"

Joe's passionate vehemence, and the truth that spoke from his flashing eyes compelled the respect, if not the absolute belief, of the Indians. The savages slowly shook their heads. They beheld the spectacle of two brothers, one a friend, the other an enemy of all Indians, each willing to go to the stake, to suffer an awful agony, for love of the other. Chivalrous deeds always stir an Indian's heart. It was like a redman to die for his brother. The indifference, the contempt for death, won their admiration.

"Let the white father stand forth," sternly called Wingenund.

A hundred somber eyes turned on the prisoners. Except that one wore a buckskin coat, the other a linsey one, there was no difference. The strong figures were the same, the white faces alike, the stern resolve in the gray eyes identical—they were twin brothers.

Wingenund once more paced before his silent chiefs. To deal rightly with this situation perplexed him. To kill both palefaces did not suit him. Suddenly he thought of a way to decide.

"Let Wingenund's daughter come," he ordered.

A slight, girlish figure entered. It was Whispering Winds. Her beautiful face glowed while she listened to her father.

"Wingenund's daughter has her mother's eyes, that were

beautiful as a doe's, keen as a hawk's, far-seeing as an eagle's. Let the Delaware maiden show her blood. Let her point out the white father."

Shyly but unhesitatingly Whispering Winds laid her hand on Jim's arm.

"Missionary, begone!" came the chieftain's command. "Thank Wingenund's daughter for your life, not the God of your Christians!"

He waved his hand to the runner. The brave grasped Jim's arm.

"Good-bye, Joe," brokenly said Jim.

"Old fellow, good-bye," came the answer.

They took one last, long look into each other's eyes. Jim's glance betrayed his fear—he would never see his brother again. The light in Joe's eyes was the old steely flash, the indomitable spirit—while there was life there was hope.

"Let the Shawnee chief paint his prisoner black," commanded Wingenund.

When the missionary left the lodge with the runner, Whispering Winds had smiled, for she had saved him whom she loved to hear speak; but the dread command that followed paled her cheek. Black paint meant hideous death. She saw this man so like the white father. Her piteous gaze tried to turn from that white face; but the cold, steely eyes fascinated her.

She had saved one only to be the other's doom!

She had always been drawn toward white men. Many prisoners had she rescued. She had even befriended her nation's bitter foe, Deathwind. She had listened to the young missionary with rapture; she had been his savior. And now when she looked into the eyes of this young giant, whose fate had rested on her all unwitting words, she resolved to save him.

She had been a shy, shrinking creature, fearing to lift her

eyes to a paleface's, but now they were raised clear and steadfast.

As she stepped toward the captive and took his hand, her whole person radiated with conscious pride in her power. It was the knowledge that still she could save. When she kissed his hand and knelt before him, she expressed a tender humility.

She had claimed the unquestionable right of an Indian maiden; she asked what no Indian dared refuse a chief's daughter; she took the paleface for her husband.

Her action was followed by an impressive silence. She remained kneeling. Wingenund resumed his slow march to and fro. Silvertip retired to his corner with gloomy face. The others bowed their heads as if the maiden's decree was irrevocable.

Once more the chieftain's sonorous command rang out. An old Indian, wrinkled and worn, weird of aspect, fanciful of attire, entered the lodge and waved his wampum wand. He mumbled strange words, and departed chanting a love song.

Whispering Winds arose, a soft, radiant smile playing over her face, and, still holding Joe's hand, she led him out of the lodge, through long rows of silent Indians, down a lane bordered by teepees, he following like one in a dream.

He expected to awaken at any minute to see the stars shining through the leaves. Yet he felt the warm, soft pressure of a little hand. Surely this slender, graceful figure was real.

She bade him enter a lodge of imposing proportions. Still silent, in amazement and gratitude, he obeyed.

The maiden turned to Joe. Though traces of pride still lingered, all her fire had vanished. Her bosom rose with each quick-panting breath; her lips quivered, she trembled like a trapped doe.

But at last the fluttering lashes rose. Joe saw two velvety eyes dark with timid fear, yet veiling in their lustrous depths an unuttered hope and love.

"Whispering Winds—save—paleface," she said, in a voice low and tremulous. "Fear—Father. Fear—tell—Wingenund— she—Christian."

Indian summer, that enchanted time, unfolded its golden, dreamy haze over the Delaware village. The forests blazed with autumn fire, the meadows bloomed in rich luxuriance. All day low down in the valleys hung a purple smoke which changed, as the cool evening shades crept out of the woodland, into a cloud of white mist. All day the asters along the brooks lifted golden-brown faces to the sun as if to catch the waning warmth of his smile. All day the plains and forests lay in melancholy repose. The sad swish of the west wind over the tall grass told that he was slowly dying away before the enemy, the north wind. The sound of dropping nuts was heard under the motionless trees.

For Joe the days were days of enchantment. His wild heart had found its mate. A willing captive he was now. All his fancy for other women, all his memories faded into love for his Indian bride.

Whispering Winds charmed the eye, mind, and heart. Every day her beauty seemed renewed. She was as apt to learn as she was quick to turn her black-crowned head, but her supreme beauty was her loving, innocent soul. Untainted as the clearest spring, it mirrored the purity and simplicity of her life. Indian she might be, one of a race whose morals and manners were alien to those of the man she loved, yet she would have added honor to the proudest name.

When Whispering Winds raised her dark eyes they

showed radiant as a lone star; when she spoke low her voice made music.

"Beloved," she whispered one day to him, "teach the Indian maiden more love for you, and truth, and God. Whispering Winds yearns to go to the Christians, but she fears her stern father. Wingenund would burn the Village of Peace. The Indian tribes tremble before the thunder of his wrath. Be patient, my chief. Time changes the leaves, so it will the anger of the warriors. Whispering Winds will set you free and be free herself to go far with you toward the rising sun, where dwell your people. Her love will be an eternal spring where blossoms bloom ever anew and fresh, and sweet. She will love your people, and raise Christian children, and sit ever in the door of your home praying for the west wind to blow. Or, if my chief wills, we shall live the Indian life, free as two eagles on their lonely crag."

Although Joe gave himself up completely to his love for his bride, he did not forget that Kate was in the power of the renegade, and that he must rescue her. Knowing Girty had the unfortunate girl somewhere near the Delaware encampment, he resolved to find the place. Plans of all kinds he revolved in his mind. The best one he believed lay through Whispering Winds. First to find the whereabouts of Girty; kill him if possible, or at least free Kate, and then get away with her and his Indian bride. Sanguine as he invariably was, he could not but realize the peril of this undertaking. If Whispering Winds betrayed her people, it meant death to her as well as to him. He would far rather spend the remaining days of his life in the Indian village than doom the maiden whose love had saved him. Yet he thought he might succeed in getting away with her, and planned to that end. His natural spirit, daring, reckless, had gained while he was associated with Wetzel.

Meanwhile he mingled freely with the Indians, and here, as elsewhere, his winning personality, combined with his athletic prowess, soon made him well liked. He was even on friendly terms with Pipe. The swarthy war chief liked Joe because, despite the animosity he had aroused in some former lovers of Whispering Winds, he actually played jokes on them. In fact, Joe's pranks raised many a storm, but the young braves who had been suitors for Wingenund's lovely daughter feared the muscular paleface and the tribe's ridicule more; so he continued his trickery unmolested. Joe's idea was to lead the savages to believe he was thoroughly happy in his new life, and so he was, but it suited him better to be free. He succeeded in misleading the savages. At first he was closely watched, then the vigilance relaxed and finally ceased.

This last circumstance was owing, no doubt, to a ferment of excitement that had suddenly possessed the Delawares. Council after council was held in the big lodge. The encampment was visited by runner after runner. Some important crisis was pending.

Joe could not learn what it all meant, and the fact that Whispering Winds suddenly lost her gladsome spirit and became sad caused him further anxiety. When he asked her the reason for her unhappiness, she was silent. Moreover, he was surprised to learn, when he questioned her upon the subject of their fleeing together, that she was eager to go immediately. While all this mystery puzzled Joe, it did not make any difference to him or to his plans. It rather favored the latter. He understood that the presence of Simon Girty and Elliott, with several other renegades unknown to him, was significant of unrest among the Indians. These presagers of evil were accustomed to go from village to village, exciting the savages to acts of war. Peace meant the downfall and death of these men. They were busy all day and far into the night. Often Joe heard Girty's hoarse voice lifted in the council lodge. Pipe thundered incessantly for war. But Joe could not learn against whom. Elliott's suave, oily oratory exhorted the Indians to vengeance. But Joe could not guess upon whom. He was, however, destined to learn.

The third day of the councils a horseman stopped before Whispering Winds' lodge and called her. Stepping to the door, Joe saw a white man, whose dark, keen, handsome face seemed familiar. Yet Joe knew he had never seen this stalwart man.

"A word with you," said the stranger. His tone was curt, authoritative, as that of a man used to power.

"As many as you would like. Who are you?"

"I am Isaac Zane. Are you Wetzel's companion, or the renegade Deering?"

"I am not a renegade any more than you are. I was rescued by the Indian girl, who took me as her husband," said Joe coldly. He was surprised, and did not know what to make of Zane's manner.

"Good! I'm glad to meet you," instantly replied Zane, his tone and expression changing. He extended his hand to Joe. "I wanted to be sure. I never saw the renegade Deering. He is here now. I am on my way to the Wyandot town. I have been to Fort Henry, where my brother told me of you and the missionaries. When I arrived here I heard your story from Simon Girty. If you can, you must get away from here. If I dared I'd take you to the Huron village, but it's impossible. Go, while you have a chance."

"Zane, I thank you. I've suspected something was wrong. What is it?"

"Couldn't be worse," whispered Zane, glancing around to see if they were overheard. "Girty and Elliott, backed by this Deering, are growing jealous of the influence of Christianity on the Indians. They are plotting against the Village of Peace. Tarhe, the Huron chief, has been approached, and asked to join in a concerted movement against religion. Seemingly it is not so much the missionaries as the converted Indians that the renegades are fuming over. They know if the Christian savages are killed, the strength of the missionaries' hold will be forever broken. Pipe is wild for blood. These renegades are slowly poisoning the minds of the few chiefs who are favorably disposed. The outlook is bad! bad!"

"What can I do?"

"Cut out for yourself. Get away, if you can, with a gun. Take the creek below, follow the current down to the Ohio, and then make east for Fort Henry.

"But I want to rescue the white girl Jim Girty has concealed here somewhere."

"Impossible! Don't attempt it unless you want to throw your life away. Buzzard Jim, as we call Girty, is a butcher; he has probably murdered the girl."

"I won't leave without trying. And there's my wife, the Indian girl who saved me. Zane, she's a Christian. She wants to go with me. I can't leave her."

"I am warning you, that's all. If I were you I'd never leave without a try to find the white girl, and I'd never forsake my Indian bride. I've been through the same thing. You must be a good woodsman, or Wetzel wouldn't have let you stay with him. Pick out a favorable time and make the attempt. I suggest you make your Indian girl show you where Girty is. She knows, but is afraid to tell you, for she fears Girty. Get your dog and horse from the Shawnees. That's a fine horse. He can carry you both to safety. Take him away from Silvertip."

"How?"

"Go right up and demand your horse and dog. Most of these Delawares are honest, for all their blood-shedding and cruelty. With them might is right. The Delawares won't try to get your horse for you; but they'll stick to you when you assert your rights. They don't like the Shawnee, anyhow. If

Silvertip refuses to give you the horse, grab him before he can draw a weapon, and beat him good. You're big enough to do it. The Delawares will be tickled to see you pound him. He's thick with Girty, that's why he lays round here. Take my word, it's the best way. Do it openly, and no one will interfere."

"By Heavens, Zane, I'll give him a drubbing. I owe him one, and am itching to get hold of him."

"I must go now. I shall send a Wyandot runner to your brother at the village. They shall be warned. Good-bye. Good luck. May we meet again."

Joe watched Zane ride swiftly down the lane and disappear in the shrubbery. Whispering Winds came to the door of the lodge. She looked anxiously at him. He went within, drawing her along with him, and quickly informed her that he had learned the cause of the councils, that he had resolved to get away, and she must find out Girty's hiding place. Whispering Winds threw herself into his arms declaring with an energy and passion unusual to her, that she would risk anything for him. She informed Joe that she knew the direction from which Girty always returned to the village. No doubt she could find his retreat. With a cunning that showed her Indian nature, she suggested a plan which Joe at once saw was excellent. After Joe got his horse, she would ride around the village, then off into the woods, where she could leave the horse and return to say he had run away from her. As was their custom during afternoons, they would walk leisurely along the brook, and, trusting to the excitement created by the councils, get away unobserved. Find the horse, if possible rescue the prisoner, and then travel east with all speed.

Joe left the lodge at once to begin the working out of the plan. Luck favored him at the outset, for he met Silvertip before the council lodge. The Shawnee was leading Lance and the dog followed at his heels. The spirit of Mose had been broken. Poor dog, Joe thought; he had been beaten until he was afraid to wag his tail at his old master. Joe's resentment blazed into fury, but he kept cool outwardly.

Right before a crowd of Indians waiting for the council to begin, Joe planted himself in front of the Shawnee, barring his way.

"Silvertip has the paleface's horse and dog," said Joe, in a loud voice.

The chief stared haughtily while the other Indians sauntered nearer. They all knew how the Shawnee had got the animals, and now awaited the outcome of the white man's challenge.

"Paleface—heap—liar," growled the Indian. His dark eyes glowed craftily, while his hand dropped, apparently in careless habit, to the haft of his tomahawk.

Joe swung his long arm; his big fist caught the Shawnee on the jaw, sending him to the ground. Uttering a frightful yell, Silvertip drew his weapon and attempted to rise, but the moment's delay in seizing the hatchet was fatal to his design. Joe was upon him with tigerlike suddenness. One kick sent the tomahawk spinning, another landed the Shawnee again on the ground. Blind with rage, Silvertip leaped up, and without a weapon rushed at his antagonist; but the Indian was not a boxer, and he failed to get his hands on Joe. Shifty and elusive, the lad dodged around the struggling savage. One, two, three hard blows staggered Silvertip, and a fourth, delivered with the force of Joe's powerful arm, caught the Indian when he was off his balance, and felled him, battered and bloody, on the grass. The surrounding Indians looked down at the vanquished Shawnee, expressing their approval in characteristic grunts.

With Lance prancing proudly and Mose leaping lovingly beside him, Joe walked back to his lodge. Whispering Winds

sprang to meet him with joyful face. She had feared the outcome of trouble with the Shawnee, but no queen ever bestowed upon returning victorious lord a loftier look of pride,
a sweeter glance of love, then the Indian maiden bent upon
her lover.

Whispering Winds informed Joe that an important council was to be held that afternoon. It would be wise for them
to make the attempt to get away immediately after the con-
vening of the chiefs. Accordingly she got upon Lance and
rode him up and down the village lane, much to the pleasure
of the watching Indians. She scattered the idle crowds on the
grass plots, she dashed through the side streets, and let
everyone in the encampment see her clinging to the black
stallion. Then she rode him out along the creek. Accustomed
to her imperious will, the Indians thought nothing unusual.
When she returned an hour later, with flying hair and disheveled costume, no one paid particular attention to her.

That afternoon Joe and his bride were the favored of fortune. With Mose running before them, they got clear of the
encampment and into the woods. Once in the forest Whispering Winds rapidly led the way east. When they climbed to
the top of a rocky ridge she pointed down into a thicket before her, saying that somewhere in this dense hollow was
Girty's hut. Joe hesitated about taking Mose. He wanted the
dog, but in case he had to run it was necessary Whispering
Winds should find his trail, and for this he left the dog with
her.

He started down the ridge, and had not gone a hundred
paces when over some gray boulders he saw the thatched
roof of a hut. So wild and secluded was the spot that he
would never have discovered the cabin from any other point
than this, which he had been so fortunate as to find.

His study and practice under Wetzel now stood him in
good stead. He picked out the best path over the rough

stones and through the brambles, always keeping under-cover. He stepped as carefully as if the hunter was behind him. Soon he reached level ground. A dense laurel thicket hid the cabin, but he knew the direction in which it lay. Throwing himself flat on the ground, he wormed his way through the thicket, carefully, yet swiftly, because he knew there was no time to lose. Finally the rear of the cabin stood in front of him.

It was made of logs, rudely hewn, and as rudely thrown together. In several places clay had fallen from chunks between the timbers, leaving small holes. Like a snake, Joe slipped close to the hut. Raising his head, he looked through one of the cracks.

Instantly he shrank back into the grass, shivering with horror. He almost choked in his attempt to prevent an outcry.

Chapter
XVIII

The sight which Joe had seen horrified him, for several moments, into helpless inaction. He lay breathing heavily, im-
potent, in an awful rage. As he remained there stunned by
the shock, he gazed up through the open space in the leaves,
trying to still his fury, to realize the situation, to make no
hasty move. The soft blue of the sky, the fleecy clouds drifting eastward, the fluttering leaves, and the twittering birds—
all assured him he was wide awake. He had found Girty's
den where so many white women had been hidden, to see
friends and home no more. He had seen the renegade sleeping, calmly sleeping like any other man. How could the
wretch sleep? He had seen Kate. It had been the sight of her
that had paralyzed him. To make a certainty of his fears, he
again raised himself to peep into the hole. As he did so a
faint cry came from within.

Girty lay on a buffalo robe near a barred door. Beyond
him sat Kate, huddled in one corner of the cabin. A long
buckskin thong was knotted round her waist, and tied to a
log. Her hair was matted and tangled, and on her face and

arms were many discolored bruises. Worse still, in her plaintive moaning, in the meaningless movement of her head, in
her vacant expression, was proof that her mind had gone.
She was mad. Even as an agonizing pity came over Joe, to be
followed by the surging fire of rage, blazing up in his breast,
he could not but thank God that she was mad! It was merciful that Kate was no longer conscious of her suffering.

Like leaves in a storm wavered Joe's hands as he clenched
them until the nails brought blood. "Be calm, be cool," whispered his monitor, Wetzel, ever with him in spirit. But God!
Could he be cool? Bounding with lion spring he hurled his
heavy frame against the door.

Crash! The door was burst from its fastenings.

Girty leaped up with a startled yell, drawing his knife as he
rose. It had not time to descend before Joe's second spring,
more fierce even than the other, carried him directly on top
of the renegade. As the two went down Joe caught the villain's wrist with a grip that literally cracked the bones. The
knife fell and rolled away from the struggling men. For an
instant they tumbled about on the floor, clasped in a crushing
embrace. The renegade was strong, supple, slippery as an
eel. Twice he wriggled from his foe. Gnashing his teeth, he
fought like a hyena. He was fighting for life—life, which is
never so dear as to a coward and a murderer. Doom glared
from Joe's big eyes, and scream after scream issued from the
renegade's white lips.

Terrible was this struggle, but brief. Joe seemingly had
the strength of ten men. Twice he pulled Girty down as a
wolf drags a deer. He dashed him against the wall, throwing
him nearer and nearer the knife. Once within reach of the
blade Joe struck the renegade a severe blow on the temple
and the villain's wrestling became weaker. Planting his heavy
knee on Girty's breast, Joe reached for the knife and swung it
high. Exultantly he cried, mad with lust for the brute's blood.

But the slight delay saved Girty's life.

The knife was knocked from Joe's hand, and he leaped erect to find himself confronted by Silvertip. The chief held a tomahawk with which he struck the weapon from the young man's grasp, and, to judge from his burning eyes and malignant smile, he meant to brain the now defenseless paleface.

In a single fleeting instant Joe saw that Girty was helpless for the moment, that Silvertip was confident of his revenge, and that the situation called for Wetzel's characteristic advice, "act like lightnin'."

Swifter than the thought was the leap he made past Silvertip. It carried him to a wooden bar which lay on the floor. Escape was easy, for the door was before him and the Shawnee behind, but Joe did not flee! He seized the bar and rushed at the Indian. Then began a duel in which the savage's quickness and cunning matched the white man's strength and fury. Silvertip dodged the vicious swings Joe aimed at him; he parried many blows, any one of which would have crushed his skull. Nimble as a cat, he avoided every rush, while his dark eyes watched for an opening. He fought wholly on the defensive, craftily reserving his strength until his opponent should tire.

At last, catching the bar on his hatchet, he broke the force of the blow, and then, with agile movement, dropped to the ground and grappled Joe's legs. Long before this he had drawn his knife, and now he used it, plunging the blade into the young man's side.

Cunning and successful as was the savage's ruse, it failed signally, for to get hold of the Shawnee was all Joe wanted. Feeling the sharp pain as they fell together, he reached his hand behind him and caught Silvertip's wrist. Exerting all his power, he wrenched the Indian's arm so that it was not only dislocated, but the bone cracked.

Silvertip saw his fatal mistake, but he uttered no sound. Crippled though he was, he yet made a supreme effort, struggling desperately, to whirl or writhe away from Joe; but it was as if he had been in the hands of a giant. The lad handled him with remorseless and resistless fury. Suddenly he grasped the knife, which Silvertip had been unable to hold with his crippled hand, and thrust it deeply into the Indian's side.

All Silvertip's muscles relaxed as if a strong tension had been removed. Slowly his legs straightened, his arms dropped, and from his side gushed a dark flow. A shadow crept over his face, not dark nor white, but just a shadow. His eyes lost their hate; they no longer saw the foe, they looked beyond with gloomy question, and then were fixed cold in death. Silvertip died as he had lived—a chief.

Joe glared round for Girty. He was gone, having slipped away during the fight. The lad turned to release the poor prisoner, when he started back with a cry of fear. Kate lay bathed in a pool of blood—dead. The renegade, fearing she might be rescued, had murdered her, and then fled from the cabin.

Almost blinded by horror, and staggering with weakness, Joe turned to leave the cabin. Realizing that he was seriously, perhaps dangerously, wounded he wisely thought he must not leave the place without weapons. He had marked the pegs where the renegade's rifle hung, and had been careful to keep between that and his enemies. He took down the gun and horns, which were attached to it, and, with one last shuddering glance at poor Kate, left the place.

He was conscious of a strange lightness in his head, but he suffered no pain. His garments were dripping with blood. He did not know how much of it was his, or the Indian's. Instinct rather than sight was his guide. He grew weaker and weaker, his head began to whirl, yet he kept on, knowing that life and freedom were his if he found Whispering Winds. He gained the top of the ridge; his eyes were blurred, his strength gone. He called aloud, and then plunged forward on his face. He heard dimly, as though the sound were afar off, the whine of a dog. He felt something soft and wet on his face. Then consciousness left him.

When he regained his senses he was lying on a bed of ferns under a projecting rock. He heard the gurgle of running water mingling with the song of birds. Near him lay Mose, and beyond rose a wall of green thicket. Neither Whispering Winds nor his horse was visible.

He felt a dreamy lassitude. He was tired, but had no pain. Finding he could move without difficulty, he concluded his weakness was more from loss of blood than a dangerous wound. He put his hand on the place where he had been stabbed, and felt a soft, warm compress such as might have been made by a bunch of wet leaves. Someone had unlaced his hunting shirt—for he saw the strings were not as he usually tied them—and had dressed the wound. Joe decided, after some deliberation, that Whispering Winds had found him, made him as comfortable as possible, and, leaving Mose on guard, had gone out to hunt for food, or perhaps back to the Indian encampment. The rifle and horn he had taken from Girty's hut, together with Silvertip's knife, lay beside him.

As Joe lay there hoping for Whispering Winds' return, his reflections were not pleasant. Fortunate, indeed, he was to be alive; but he had no hope he could continue to be favored of fortune. Odds were now against his escape. Girty would have the Delawares on his trail like a pack of hungry wolves. He could not understand the absence of Whispering Winds.

She would have died sooner than desert him. Girty had, perhaps, captured her, and was now scouring the woods for him.

"I'll get him next time, or he'll get me," muttered Joe, in bitter wrath. He could never forgive himself for his failure to kill the renegade.

The recollection of how nearly he had forever ended Girty's brutal career brought before Joe's mind the scene of the fight. He saw again Buzzard Jim's face, revolting, unlike anything human. There stretched Silvertip's dark figure, lying still and stark, and there was Kate's white form in its winding, crimson wreath of blood. Hauntingly her face returned, sad, stern in its cold rigidity.

"Poor girl, better for her to be dead," he murmured. "Not long will she be unavenged!"

His thoughts drifted to the future. He had no fear of starvation, for Mose could catch a rabbit or woodchuck at any time. When the strips of meat he had hidden in his coat were gone, he could start a fire and roast more. What concerned him most was pursuit. His trail from the cabin had been a bloody one, which would render it easily followed. He dared not risk exertion until he had given his wound time to heal. Then, if he did escape from Girty and the Delawares, his future was not bright. His experiences of the last few days had not only been sobering, but brought home to him this real border life. With all his fire and daring he knew he was no fool. He had eagerly embraced a career which, at the present stage of his training, was beyond his scope—not that he did not know how to act in sudden crisis, but because he had not had the necessary practice to quickly and surely use his knowledge.

Bitter, indeed, was his self-scorn when he recalled that of the several critical positions he had been in since his aquaintance with Wetzel, he had failed in all but one. The exception was the killing of Silvertip. Here his fury had made him fight as Wetzel fought with only his everyday incentive. He realized that the border was no place for any save the boldest and most experienced hunters—men who had become inured to hardship, callous as to death, keen as Indians. Fear was not in Joe nor lack of confidence; but he had good sense, and realized he would have done a wiser thing had he stayed at Fort Henry. Colonel Zane was right. The Indians were tigers, the renegades vultures, the vast untrammeled forests and plains their covert. Ten years of war had rendered this wilderness a place where those few white men who had survived were hardened to the spilling of blood, stern even in those few quiet hours which peril allowed them, strong in their sacrifice of all for future generations.

A low growl from Mose broke into Joe's reflections. The dog had raised his nose from his paws and sniffed suspiciously at the air. The lad heard a slight rustling outside, and in another moment was overjoyed at seeing Whispering Winds. She came swiftly, with a lithe, graceful motion, and, flying to him like a rush of wind, knelt beside him. She kissed him and murmured words of endearment.

"Winds, were have you been?" he asked her, in the mixed English and Indian dialect in which they conversed.

She told him the dog had led her to him two evenings before. He was insensible. She had bathed and bandaged his wound, and remained with him all that night. The next day, finding he was ill and delirious, she decided to risk returning to the village. If any questions arose, she could say he had left her. Then she would find a way to get back to him, bringing healing herbs for his wound and a soothing drink. As it turned out Girty had returned to the camp. He was battered and bruised, and in a white heat of passion. Going at once to Wingenund, the renegade openly accused Whispering Winds of aiding her paleface lover to escape. Wingenund called his daughter before him, and questioned her. She confessed all to her father.

"Why is the daughter of Wingenund a traitor to her race?" demanded the chief.

"Whispering Winds is a Christian."

Wingenund received this intelligence as a blow. He dismissed Girty and sent his braves from his lodge, facing his daughter alone. Gloomy and stern, he paced before her.

"Wingenund's blood might change, but would never betray. Wingenund is the Delaware chief," he said. "Go. Darken no more the door of Wingenund's wigwam. Let the flower of the Delawares fade in alien pastures. Go. Whispering Winds is free!"

Tears shone brightly in the Indian girl's eyes while she told Joe her story. She loved her father, and she would see him no more.

"Winds is free," she whispered. "When strength returns to her master she can follow him to the white villages. Winds will live her life for him."

"Then we have no one to fear?" asked Joe.

"No redman, now that the Shawnee chief is dead."

"Will Girty follow us? He is a coward; he will fear to come alone."

"The white savage is a snake in the grass."

Two long days followed, during which the lovers lay quietly in hiding. On the morning of the third day Joe felt that he might risk the start for the Village of Peace. Whispering Winds led the horse below the stone upon which the invalid stood, thus enabling him to mount. Then she got on behind him.

The sun was just gilding the horizon when they rode out of the woods into a wide plain. No living thing could be seen. Along the edge of the forest the ground was level, and the horse traveled easily. Several times during the morning Joe dismounted beside a pile of stones or a fallen tree. The miles were traversed without serious inconvenience to the invalid, except that he grew tired. Toward the middle of the afternoon, when they had ridden perhaps twenty-five or thirty miles, they crossed a swift, narrow brook. The water was a beautiful clear brown. Joe made a note of this, as it was an unusual circumstance. Nearly all the streams, when not flooded, were green in color. He remembered that during his wanderings with Wetzel they had found one stream of this brown, copper-colored water. The lad knew he must take a roundabout way to the village so that he might avoid Indian runners or scouts, and he hoped this stream would prove to be the one he had once camped upon.

As they were riding toward a gentle swell or knoll covered with trees and shrubbery, Whispering Winds felt something warm on her hand, and, looking, was horrified to find it covered with blood. Joe's wound had opened. She told him they must dismount here and remain until he was stronger. The invalid himself thought this conclusion was wise. They would be practically safe now, since they must be out of the Indian path, and many miles from the encampment. Accordingly he got off the horse and sat down on a log, while Whispering Winds searched for a suitable place in which to erect a temporary shelter.

Joe's wandering gaze was arrested by a tree with a huge knotty formation near the ground. It was like many trees, but this peculiarity was not what struck Joe. He had seen it before. He never forgot anything in the woods that had once attracted his attention. He looked around on all sides. Just behind him was an opening in the clump of trees. Within this was a perpendicular stone covered with moss and lichens;

above it a beech tree spread long, graceful branches. He thrilled with the remembrance these familiar marks brought. This was Beautiful Spring, the place where Wetzel rescued Nell, where he had killed the Indians in that night attack Joe would never forget.

Chapter
XIX

One evening a week or more after the disappearance of Jim and the girls, George Young and David Edwards, the missionaries, sat on the cabin steps, gazing disconsolately upon the forest scenery. Hard as had been the ten years of their labor among the Indians, nothing had shaken them as the loss of their young friends.

"Dave, I tell you your theory about seeing them again is absurd," asserted George. "I'll never forget that wretch, Girty, as he spoke to Nell. Why, she just wilted like a flower blasted by fire. I can't understand why he let me go, and kept Jim, unless the Shawnee had something to do with it. I never wished until now that I was a hunter. I'd go after Girty. You've heard as well as I of his many atrocities. I'd rather have seen Kate and Nell dead than have them fall into his power. I'd rather have killed them myself!"

Young had aged perceptibly in these last few days. The blue veins showed at his temples; his face had become thinner and paler, his eyes had a look of pain. The former expression of patience, which had sat so well on him, was gone.

"George, I can't account for my fancies or feelings, else, perhaps, I'd be easier in mind," answered Dave. His face, too, showed the ravages of grief. "I've had strange thoughts lately, and dreams such as I never had before. Perhaps it's this trouble which has made me so nervous. I don't seem able to pull myself together. I can neither preach nor work."

"Neither can I! This trouble has hit you as hard as it has me. But, Dave, we've still our duty. To endure, to endure—that is our life. Because a beam of sunshine brightened, for a brief time, the gray of our lives, and then faded away, we must not shirk nor grow sour and discontented."

"But how cruel is this border life!"

"Nature itself is brutal."

"Yes, I know, and we have elected to spend our lives here in the midst of this ceaseless strife, to fare poorly, to have no pleasure, never to feel the comfort of a woman's smiles, nor the joy of a child's caress, all because out in the woods are ten or twenty or a hundred savages we may convert."

"That is why, and it is enough. It is hard to give up the women you love to a black-souled renegade, but that is not my thought. What kills me is the horror for her—for her."

"I, too, suffer with that thought; more than that, I am morbid and depressed. I feel as if some calamity awaited us here. I have never been superstitious, nor have I had presentiments, but of late there are strange fears in my mind."

At this juncture Mr. Wells and Heckewelder came out of the adjoining cabin.

"I had word from a trustworthy runner today. Girty and his captives have not been seen in the Delaware towns," said Heckewelder.

"It is most unlikely that he will take them to the towns," replied Edwards. "What do you make of his capturing Jim?"

"For Pipe, perhaps. The Delaware Wolf is snapping his

teeth. Pipe is particularly opposed to Christianity, and—
what's that?"

A low whistle from the bushes near the creek bank attracted the attention of all. The younger men got up to inves-
tigate, but Heckewelder detained them.

"Wait," he added. "There is no telling what that signal
may mean."

They waited with breathless interest. Presently the whistle was repeated, and an instant later the tall figure of a man
stepped from behind a thicket. He was a white man, but not
recognizable at that distance, even if a friend. The stranger
waved his hand as if asking them to be cautious, and come to
him.

They went toward the thicket, and when within a few
paces of the man Mr. Wells exclaimed:

"It's the man who guided my party to the village. It is
Wetzel!"

The other missionaries had never seen the hunter, though,
of course, they were familiar with his name, and looked at
him with great curiosity. The hunter's buckskin garments
were wet, torn, and covered with burrs. Dark spots, evidently
bloodstains, showed on his hunting shirt.

"Wetzel?" interrogated Heckewelder.

The hunter nodded, and took a step behind the bush. Bending over he lifted something from the ground. It was a girl. It
was Nell! She was very white—but alive. A faint, glad smile
lighted up her features.

Not a word was spoken. With an expression of tender
compassion Mr. Wells received her into his arms. The four
missionaries turned fearful, questioning eyes upon the
hunter, but they could not speak.

"She's well, an' unharmed," said Wetzel, reading their
thoughts, "only worn out. I've carried her these ten miles."

"God bless you, Wetzel!" exclaimed the old missionary. "Nellie, Nellie, can you speak?"

"Uncle dear—I'm—all right," came the faint answer.

"Kate? What—of her?" whispered George Young with lips as dry as corn husks.

"I did my best," said the hunter with a simple dignity. Nothing but the agonized appeal in the young man's eyes could have made Wetzel speak of his achievement.

"Tell us," broke in Heckewelder, seeing that fear had stricken George dumb.

"We trailed 'em, an' got away with the golden-haired lass. The last I saw of Joe he was braced up agin a rock fightin' like a wildcat. I tried to cut Jim loose as I was goin' by. I s'pect the wost fer the brothers an' the other lass."

"Can we do nothing?" asked Mr. Wells.

"Nothin'!"

"Wetzel, has the capturing of James Downs any significance to you?" inquired Heckewelder.

"I reckon so."

"What?"

"Pipe an' his white-redskin allies are agin Christianity."

"Do you think we are in danger?"

"I reckon so."

"What do you advise?"

"Pack up a few of your traps, take the lass, an' come with me. I'll see you back in Fort Henry."

Heckewelder nervously walked up to the tree and back again. Young and Edwards looked blankly at one another. They both remembered Edwards' presentiment. Mr. Wells uttered an angry exclamation.

"You ask us to fail in our duty? No, never! To go back to the white settlements and acknowledge we were afraid to continue teaching the Gospel to the Indians! You cannot understand Christianity if you advise that. You have no religion. You are a killer of Indians."

A shadow that might have been one of pain flitted over the hunter's face.

"No, I ain't a Christian, an' I am a killer of Injuns," said Wetzel, and his deep voice had a strange tremor. "I don't know nothin' much 'cept the woods an' fields, an' if there's a God fer me He's out thar under the trees an' grass. Mr. Wells, you're the first man as ever called me a coward, an' I overlook it because of your callin'. I advised you to go back to Fort Henry, because if you don't go now the chances are against your ever goin'. Christianity or no Christianity, such men as you hev no bisness in these woods."

"I thank you for your advice, and bless you for your rescue of this child; but I cannot leave my work, nor can I understand why all this good work we have done should be called useless. We have converted Indians, saved their souls. Is that not being of some use, of some good here?"

"It's accordin' to how you look at it. Now I know the bark of an oak is different accordin' to the side we see it from. I'll allow, hatin' Injuns as I do, is no reason you oughtn't to try an' convert 'em. But you're bringin' on a war. These Injuns won't allow this Village of Peace here with its big fields of corn, an' shops an' workin' redskins. It's agin their nature. You're only sacrificin' your Christian Injuns."

"What do you mean?" asked Mr. Wells, startled by Wetzel's words.

"Enough. I'm ready to guide you to Fort Henry."

"I'll never go."

Wetzel looked at the other men. No one would have doubted him. No one could have failed to see he knew that some terrible danger hovered over the Village of Peace.

"I believe you, Wetzel, but I cannot go," said Heckewelder, with white face.

"I will stay," said George, steadily.

"And I," said Dave.

Wetzel nodded and had turned to depart when George grasped his arm. The young missionary's face was drawn and haggard; he fixed an intense gaze upon the hunter.

"Wetzel, listen;" his voice was low and shaken with deep feeling. "I am a teacher of God's word, and I am as earnest in that purpose as you are in your life work. I shall die here; I shall fill an unmarked grave; but I shall have done the best I could. This is the life destiny has marked out for me, and I will live it as best I may; but in this moment, preacher as I am, I would give all I have or hope to have, all the little good I may have done, all my life, to be such a man as you. For I would avenge the woman I loved. To torture, to kill Girty! I am only a poor, weak fellow who would be lost a mile from this village, and if not, would fall before the youngest brave. But you with your glorious strength, your incomparable woodcraft, you are the man to kill Girty. Rid the frontier of this fiend. Kill him! Wetzel, kill him. I beseech you for the sake of some sweet girl who even now may be on her way to this terrible country, and who may fall into Girty's power—for her sake, Wetzel, kill him. Trail him like a bloodhound, and when you find him remember my broken heart, remember Nell, remember, oh, God! remember poor Kate!"

Young's voice broke into dry sobs. He had completely exhausted himself, so that he was forced to lean against the tree for support.

Wetzel spoke never a word. He stretched out his long, brawny arm and gripped the young missionary's shoulder. His fingers clasped hard. Simple, without words as the action was, it could not have been more potent. And then, as he stood, the softer look faded slowly from his face. A ripple seemed to run over his features, which froze, as it subsided, into a cold, stone rigidity.

His arms dropped; he stepped past the tree, and, bounding lightly as a deer, cleared the creek and disappeared in the bushes.

Mr. Wells carried Nell to his cabin where she lay for hours with wan face and listless languor. She swallowed the nourishing drink an old Indian nurse forced between her teeth; she even smiled weakly when the missionaries spoke to her; but she said nothing nor seemed to rally from her terrible shock. A dark shadow lay always before her eyes. At times she remained gazing straight before her, conscious of nothing present, living over again her frightful experience. Again she seemed sunk in dull apathy.

"Dave, we're going to lose Nell. She's fading slowly," said George, one evening, several days after the girl's return. "Wetzel said she was unharmed, yet she seems to have received a hurt more fatal than a physical one. It's her mind—her mind. If we cannot brighten her up to make her forget, she'll die."

"We've done all within our power. If she could only be brought out of this trance! She lies there all day long with those staring eyes. I can't look into them. They are the eyes of a child who has seen murder."

"We must try in some way to get her out of this stupor, and I have an idea. Have you noticed that Mr. Wells has failed very much in the last few weeks?"

"Indeed I have, and I'm afraid he's breaking down. He has grown so thin, eats very little, and doesn't sleep. He is old, you know, and, despite his zeal, this border life is telling on him."

"Dave, I believe he knows it. Poor, earnest old man! He never says a word about himself, yet he must know he is going downhill. Well, we all begin, sooner or later, that descent which ends in the grave. I believe we might stir Nellie by telling her Mr. Wells' health is breaking."

"Let us try."

A hurried knock on the door interrupted their conversation.

"Come in," said Edwards.

The door opened to admit a man, who entered eagerly.

"Jim! Jim!" exclaimed both missionaries, throwing themselves upon the newcomer.

It was, indeed, Jim, but no answering smile lighted his worn, distressed face while he wrung his friends' hands.

"You're not hurt?" asked Dave.

"No, I'm uninjured."

"Tell us all. Did you escape? Did you see your brother? Did you know Wetzel rescued Nell?"

"Wingenund set me free in spite of many demands for my death. He kept Joe a prisoner and intends to kill him, for the lad was Wetzel's companion. I saw the hunter come into the glade where we camped, break through the line of fighting Indians, and carry Nell off."

"Kate?" faltered Young, with ashen face.

"George, I wish to God I could tell you she is dead," answered Jim, nervously pacing the room. "But she was well when I last saw her. She endured the hard journey better than either Nell or I. Girty did not carry her into the encampment, as Silvertip did Joe and me, but the renegade left us on the outskirts of the Delaware town. There was a rocky ravine with dense undergrowth when he disappeared with his captive. I suppose he has his den somewhere in that ravine."

George sank down and buried his face in his arms; neither movement nor sound betokened consciousness.

"Has Wetzel come in with Nell? Joe said he had a cave where he might have taken her in case of illness or accident."

"Yes, he brought her back," answered Edwards, slowly.

"I want to see her," said Jim, his haggard face expressing a keen anxiety. "She's not wounded? hurt? ill?"

"No nothing like that. It's a shock which she can't get over, can't forget."

"I must see her," cried Jim, moving toward the door.

"Don't go," replied Dave, detaining him. "Wait. We must see what's best to be done. Wait till Heckewelder comes. He'll be here soon. Nell thinks you're dead, and the surprise might be bad for her."

Heckewelder came in at that moment, and shook hands warmly with Jim.

"The Delaware runner told me you were here. I am overjoyed that Wingenund freed you," said the missionary. "It is a most favorable sign. I have heard rumors from Goshocking and Sandusky that have worried me. This good news more than offsets the bad. I am sorry about your brother. Are you well?"

"Well, but miserable. I want to see Nell. Dave tells me she is not exactly ill, but something is wrong with her. Perhaps I ought not to see her just yet."

"It'll be exactly the tonic for her," replied Heckewelder. "She'll be surprised out of herself. She is morbid, apathetic, and, try as we may, we can't interest her. Come at once."

Heckewelder had taken Jim's arm and started for the door when he caught sight of Young, sitting bowed and motionless. Turning to Jim he whispered:

"Kate?"

"Girty did not take her into the encampment," answered Jim, in a low voice. "I hoped he would, because the Indians are kind, but he didn't. He took her to his den."

Just then Young raised his face. The despair in it would have melted a heart of stone. It had become the face of an old man.

"If only you'd told me she had died," he said to Jim, "I'd have been man enough to stand it, but—this—this kills me—I can't breathe!"

He staggered into the adjoining room, where he flung himself upon a bed.

"It's hard, and he won't be able to stand up under it, for he's not strong," whispered Jim.

Heckewelder was a mild, pious man, in whom no one would ever expect strong passion; but now depths were stirred within his heart that had ever been tranquil. He became livid, and his face was distorted with rage.

"It's bad enough to have these renegades plotting and working against our religion; to have them sow discontent, spread lies, make the Indians think we have axes to grind, to plant the only obstacle in our path—all this is bad; but to doom an innocent white woman to worse than death! What can I call it?"

"What can we do?" asked Jim.

"Do? That's the worst of it. We can do nothing, nothing. We dare not move."

"Is there no hope of getting Kate back?"

"Hope? None. That villain is surrounded by his savages. He'll lie low now for a while. I've heard of such deeds many a time, but it never before came so close home. Kate Wells was a pure, loving Christian woman. She'll live an hour, a day, a week, perhaps, in that snake's clutches, and then she'll die. Thank God!"

"Wetzel has gone on Girty's trail. I know that from his manner when he left us," said Edwards.

"Wetzel may avenge her, but he can never save her. It's too late. Hello—"

The exclamation was called forth by the appearance of Young, who entered with a rifle in his hands.

"George, where are you going with that gun?" asked Edwards, grasping his friend by the arm.

"I'm going after her," answered George, wildly. He tottered as he spoke but wrenched himself free from Dave.

"Come, George, listen, listen to reason," interposed Heckewelder, laying hold of Young. "You are frantic with grief now. So are all of us. But calm yourself. Why, man, you're a preacher, not a hunter. You'd be lost, you'd starve in the woods before getting halfway to the Indian town. This is terrible enough; don't make it worse by throwing your life away. Think of us, your friends; think of your Indian pupils who rely so much on you. Think of the Village of Peace. We can pray, but we can't prevent these border crimes. With civilization, with the spread of Christianity, they will pass away. Bear up under this blow for the sake of your work. Remember we alone can check such barbarity. But we must not fight. We must sacrifice all that men hold dear, for the sake of the future."

He took the rifle away from George, and led him back into the little, dark room. Closing the door he turned to Jim and Dave.

"He's in a bad way, and we must carefully watch him for a few days."

"Think of George starting out to kill Girty!" exclaimed Dave. "I never fired a gun, but yet I'd go too."

"So would we all, if we did as our hearts dictate," retorted Heckewelder, turning fiercely upon Dave as if stung. "Man, we have a village full of Christians to look after. What would become of them? I tell you we've all we can do here to outwit these border ruffians. Simon Girty is plotting our ruin. I heard it today from the Delaware runner who is my friend. He is jealous of our influence, when all we desire is to save these poor Indians. And Jim, Girty has killed our happiness. Can we ever recover from the misery brought upon us by poor Kate's fate?"

The missionary raised his hand as if to exhort some power above.

"Curse the Girtys!" he exclaimed in a sudden burst of uncontrollable passion. "Having conquered all other obstacles, must we fail because of wicked men of our own race? Oh, curse them!"

"Come," he said, presently, in a voice which trembled with the effort he made to be calm. "We'll go in to Nellie."

The three men entered Mr. Wells' cabin. The old missionary, with bowed head and hands clasped behind his back, was pacing to and fro. He greeted Jim with glad surprise.

"We want Nellie to see him," whispered Heckewelder. "We think the surprise will do her good."

"I trust it may," said Mr. Wells.

"Leave it to me."

They followed Heckewelder into an adjoining room. A torch flickered over the rude mantel shelf, lighting up the room with fitful flare. It was a warm night, and the soft breeze coming in the window alternately paled and brightened the flame.

Jim saw Nell lying on the bed. Her eyes were closed, and her long, dark lashes seemed black against the marble paleness of her skin.

"Stand behind me," whispered Heckewelder to Jim.

"Nellie," he called softly, but only a faint flickering of her lashes answered him.

"Nellie, Nellie," repeated Heckewelder, his deep, strong voice thrilling.

Her eyes opened. They gazed at Mr. Wells on one side, at Edwards standing at the foot of her bed, at Heckewelder leaning over her, but there was no recognition or interest in her look.

"Nellie, can you understand me?" asked Heckewelder, putting into his voice all the power and intensity of feeling of which he was capable.

An almost imperceptible shadow of understanding shone in her eyes.

"Listen. You have had a terrible shock, and it has affected your mind. You are mistaken in what you think, what you dream of all the time. Do you understand? You are wrong!"

Nell's eyes quickened with a puzzled, questioning doubt. The minister's magnetic, penetrating voice had pierced her dulled brain.

"See, I have brought you Jim!"

Heckewelder stepped aside as Jim fell on his knees by the bed. He took her cold hands in his and bent over her. For the moment his voice failed.

The doubt in Nell's eyes changed to a wondrous gladness. It was like the rekindling of a smoldering fire.

"Jim?" she whispered.

"Yes, Nellie, it's Jim alive and well. It's Jim come back to you."

A soft flush stained her white face. She slipped her arm tenderly around his neck, and held her cheek close to his.

"Jim," she murmured.

"Nellie, don't you know me?" asked Mr. Wells, trembling, excited. This was the first word she had spoken in four days.

"Uncle!" she exclaimed, suddenly loosening her hold on Jim, and sitting up in bed, then she gazed wildly at the others.

"Was it all a horrible dream?"

Mr. Wells took her hand soothingly, but he did not attempt to answer her question. He looked helplessly at Heckewelder, but that missionary was intently studying the expression on Nell's face.

"A part of it was a dream," he answered, impressively.

"Then that horrible man did take us away?"

"Yes."

"Oh-h! but we're free now? This is my room. Oh, tell me?"

"Yes, Nellie, you're safe at home now."

"Tell—tell me," she cried, shudderingly, as she leaned to Jim and raised a white, imploring face to his. "Where is Kate?—Oh! Jim—say, say she wasn't left with Girty?"

"Kate is dead," answered Jim, quickly. He could not endure the horror in her eyes. He deliberately intended to lie, as had Heckewelder.

It was as if the tension of Nell's nerves was suddenly relaxed. The relief from her worst fear was so great that her mind took in only the one impression. Then, presently, a choking cry escaped her, to be followed by a paroxysm of sobs.

Chapter
XX

Early on the following day Heckewelder, astride his horse, appeared at the door of Edwards' cabin.

"How is George?" he inquired of Dave, when the latter had opened the door.

"He had a bad night, but is sleeping now. I think he'll be all right after a time," answered Dave.

"That's well. Nevertheless keep a watch on him for a few days."

"I'll do so."

"Dave, I leave matters here to your good judgment. I'm off to Goshocking to join Zeisberger. Affairs there demand our immediate attention, and we must make haste."

"How long do you intend to be absent?"

"A few days; possibly a week. In case of any unusual disturbance among the Indians, the appearance of Pipe and his tribe, or any of the opposing factions, send a fleet runner at once to warn me. Most of my fears have been allayed by Wingenund's attitude toward us. His freeing Jim in the face of the opposition of his chiefs is a sure sign of friendliness. More than once I have suspected that he was interested in

Christianity. His daughter, Whispering Winds, exhibited the same intense fervor in religion as has been manifested by all our converts. It may be that we have not appealed in vain to Wingenund and his daughter; but their high position in the Delaware tribe makes it impolitic for them to reveal a change of heart. If we could win over those two we'd have every chance to convert the whole tribe. Well, as it is we must be thankful for Wingenund's friendship. We have two powerful allies now. Tarhe, the Wyandot chieftain, remains neutral, to be sure, but that's almost as helpful as his friendship."

"I, too, take a hopeful view of the situation," replied Edwards.

"We'll trust in Providence, and do our best," said Heckewelder, as he turned his horse. "Good-bye."

"Godspeed!" called Edwards, as his chief rode away.

The missionary resumed his work of getting breakfast. He remained indoors all that day, except for the few moments when he ran over to Mr. Wells' cabin to inquire regarding Nell's condition. He was relieved to learn she was so much better that she had declared her intention of moving about the house. Dave kept a close watch on Young. He, himself, was suffering from the same blow which had prostrated his friend, but his physical strength and fortitude were such that he did not weaken. He was overjoyed to see that George rallied, and showed no further indication of breaking down.

True it was, perhaps, that Heckewelder's earnest prayer on behalf of the converted Indians had sunk deeply into George's heart and thus kept it from breaking. No stronger plea could have been made than the allusion to those gentle, dependent Christians. No one but a missionary could realize the sweetness, the simplicity, the faith, the eager hope for a good, true life which had been implanted in the hearts of these Indians. To bear it in mind, to think of what he, as a missionary and teacher, was to them, relieved him of half his burden, and for strength to bear the remainder he went to God. For all worry there is a sovereign cure, for all suffering there is a healing balm: it is religious faith. Happiness had suddenly flashed with a meteorlike radiance into Young's life only to be snuffed out like a candle in a windy gloom, but his work, his duty remained. So in his trial he learned the necessity of resignation. He chafed no more at the mysterious, seemingly brutal methods of nature; he questioned no more. He wondered no more at the apparent indifference of Providence. He had one hope, which was to be true to his faith and teach it to the end.

Nell mastered her grief by an astonishing reserve of strength. Undoubtedly it was that marvelously merciful power which enables a person, for the love of others, to bear up under a cross, or even to fight death himself. As Young had his bright-eyed Indian boys and girls, who had learned Christianity from him, and whose future depended on him, so Nell had her aged and weakening uncle to care for and cherish.

Jim's attentions to her before the deep affliction had not been slight, but now they were so marked as to be unmistakable. In some way Jim seemed changed since he had returned from the Delaware encampment. Although he went back to the work with his old aggressiveness, he was not nearly so successful as he had been before. Whether or not this was his fault, he took his failure deeply to heart. There was that in his tenderness which caused Nell to regard him, in one sense, as she did her uncle. Jim, too, leaned upon her, and she accepted his devotion where once she had repelled it. She had unconsciously betrayed a great deal when she had turned so tenderly to him in the first moments after her recognition, and he remembered. He did not speak of love to her; he let a thousand little acts of kindness, a constant thoughtfulness of her, plead his cause.

The days succeeding Heckewelder's departure were remarkable for several reasons. Although the weather was enticing, the number of visiting Indians gradually decreased. Not a runner from any tribe came into the village, and finally the day dawned when not a single Indian from the outlying towns was present to hear the preaching.

Jim spoke, as usual. After several days had passed and none but converted Indians made up the congregation, the young man began to be uneasy in mind.

Young and Edwards were unable to account for the unusual absence from worship, yet they did not see in it anything to cause especial concern. Often there had been days without visitation to the Village of Peace.

Finally Jim went to consult Glickhican. He found the Delaware at work in the potato patch. The old Indian dropped his hoe and bowed to the missionary. A reverential and stately courtesy always characterized the attitude of the Indians toward the young White Father.

"Glickhican, can you tell me why no Indians have come here lately?"

The old chief shook his head.

"Does their absence signify ill to the Village of Peace?"

"Glickhican saw a blackbird flitting in the shadow of the moon. The bird hovered above the Village of Peace, but sang no song."

The old Delaware vouchsafed no other than this strange reply.

Jim returned to his cabin decidedly worried. He did not at all like Glickhican's answer. The purport of it seemed to be that a cloud was rising on the bright horizon of the Christian village. He confided his fears to Young and Edwards. After discussing the situation, the three missionaries decided to send for Heckewelder. He was the leader of the Mission; he knew more of Indian craft than any of them, and how to meet it. If this calm in the heretofore busy life of the Mission was the lull before the storm, Heckewelder should be there with his experience and influence.

"For nearly ten years Heckewelder has anticipated trouble from hostile savages," said Edwards, "but so far he has always averted it. As you know, he has confined himself mostly to propitiating the Indians, and persuading them to be friendly, and listen to us. We'll send for him."

Accordingly they dispatched a runner to Goshocking. In due time the Indian returned with the startling news that Heckewelder had left the Indian village days before, as had, in fact, all the savages except the few converted ones. The same held true in the case of Sandusky, the adjoining town. Moreover, it had been impossible to obtain any news in regard to Zeisberger.

The missionaries were now thoroughly alarmed and knew not what to do. They concealed the real state of affairs from Nell and her uncle, desiring to keep them from anxiety as long as possible. That night the three teachers went to bed with heavy hearts.

The following morning at daybreak, Jim was awakened from a sound sleep by someone calling at his window. He got up to learn who it was, and, in the gray light, saw Edwards standing outside.

"What's the matter?" questioned Jim, hurriedly.

"Matter enough. Hurry. Get into your clothes," replied Edwards. "As soon as you are dressed, quietly awaken Mr. Wells and Nellie, but do not frighten them."

"But what's the trouble?" queried Jim, as he began to dress.

"The Indians are pouring into the village as thickly as flying leaves in autumn."

Edwards' exaggerated assertion proved to be almost literally true. No sooner had the rising sun dispelled the mist than it shone on long lines of marching braves, mounted warriors, hundreds of packhorses approaching from the forest. The orderly procession was proof of a concerted plan on the part of the invaders.

From their windows the missionaries watched with bated breath; with wonder and fear they saw the long lines of dusky forms. When they were in the clearing the savages busied themselves with their packs. Long rows of teepees sprung up as if by magic. The savages had come to stay! The number of incoming visitors did not lessen until noon, when a few straggling groups marked the end of the invading host. Most significant of all was the fact that neither child, maiden, nor squaw accompanied this army.

Jim appraised the number at six or seven hundred, more than had ever before visited the village at one time. They were mostly Delawares, with many Shawnees, and a few Hurons among them. It was soon evident, however, that for the present, at least, the Indians did not intend any hostile demonstration. They were quiet in manner, and busy about their teepees and campfires, but there was an absence of the curiosity that had characterized the former sojourns of Indians at the peaceful village.

After a brief consultation with his brother missionaries, who all were opposed to his preaching that afternoon, Jim decided he would not deviate from his usual custom. He held the afternoon service and spoke to the largest congregation that had ever sat before him. He was surprised to find that the sermon, which heretofore so strongly impressed the savages, did not now arouse the slightest enthusiasm. It was followed by a brooding silence of a boding, ominous import.

Four white men, dressed in Indian garb, had been the most attentive listeners to Jim's sermon. He recognized three as Simon Girty, Elliott, and Deering, the renegades, and he learned from Edwards that the other was the notorious McKee. These men went through the village stalking into the shops and cabins, and acting as do men who are on a tour of inspection.

So intrusive was their curiosity that Jim hurried back to Mr. Wells' cabin and remained there in seclusion. Of course, by this time Nell and her uncle knew of the presence of the hostile savages. They were frightened, and barely regained their composure when the young man assured them he was certain they had no real cause for fear.

Jim was sitting at the doorstep with Mr. Wells and Edwards when Girty, with his comrades, came toward them. The renegade leader was a tall, athletic man, with a dark, strong face. There was in it none of the brutality and ferocity which marked his brother's visage. Simon Girty appeared keen, forceful, authoritative, as, indeed, he must have been to have attained the power he held in the confederated tribes. His companions presented wide contrasts. Elliott was a small, spare man of cunning, vindictive aspect; McKee looked as might have been supposed from his reputation, and Deering was a fit mate for the absent Girty. Simon appeared to be a man of some intelligence, who had been thrust into a degrading position, but who, once there, used all his power to make that position a great one. The other renegades were desperadoes.

"Where's Heckewelder?" asked Girty, curtly, as he stopped before the missionaries.

"He started out for the Indian towns on the Muskingong," answered Edwards. "But we have had no word from either him or Zeisberger."

"When d'ye expect him?"

"I can't say. Perhaps tomorrow, and then, again, maybe not for a week."

"His is in authority here, ain't he?"

"Yes; but he left me in charge of the Mission. Can I serve you in any way?"

"I reckon not," said the renegade, turning to his companions. They conversed in low tones for a moment. Presently McKee, Elliott, and Deering went toward the newly erected teepees.

"Girty, do you mean us any ill will?" earnestly asked Edwards. He had met the man on more than one occasion, and had no hesitation about questioning him.

"I can't say as I do," answered the renegade, and those who heard him believed him. "But I'm agin this redskin preachin', an' hev been all along. The Injuns are mad clear through, an' I ain't sayin' I've tried to quiet 'em any. This missionary work has got to be stopped, one way or another. Now what I waited here to say is this: I ain't quite forgot I was white once, an' believe you fellers are honest. I'm willin' to go outer my way to help you git away from here."

"Go away?" echoed Edwards.

"That's it," answered Girty, shouldering his rifle.

"But why? We are perfectly harmless; we are only doing good and hurt no one. Why should we go?"

" 'Cause there's liable to be trouble," said the renegade, significantly.

Edwards turned slowly to Mr. Wells and Jim. The old missionary was trembling visibly. Jim was pale; but more with anger than fear.

"Thank you, Girty, but we'll stay," and Jim's voice rang clear.

Chapter
XXI

"Jim, come out here," called Edwards at the window of Mr. Wells' cabin.

The young man arose from the breakfast table, and when outside found Edwards standing by the door with an Indian brave. He was a Wyandot lightly built, lithe and wiry, easily recognizable as an Indian runner. When Jim appeared the man handed him a small packet. He unwound a few folds of some oily skin to find a square piece of birch bark, upon which were scratched the following words:

> *Rev. J. Downs. Greeting.*
> *Your brother is alive and safe. Whispering Winds rescued him by taking him as her husband. Leave the Village of Peace. Pipe and Half King have been influenced by Girty.*
>
> > *ZANE.*

"Now, what do you think of that?" exclaimed Jim, handing the message to Edwards. "Thank Heaven, Joe was saved!"

"Zane? That must be the Zane who married Tarhe's daugh-

ter," answered Edwards, when he had read the note. "I'm re-
joiced to hear of your brother."

"Joe married to that beautiful Indian maiden! Well, of all
wonderful things," mused Jim. "What will Nell say?"

"We're getting warnings enough. Do you appreciate
that?" asked Edwards. " 'Pipe and Half King have been influenced by Girty.' Evidently the writer deemed that brief
sentence of sufficient meaning."

"Edwards, we're preachers. We can't understand such
things. I am learning, at least something every day. Colonel
Zane advised us not to come out here. Wetzel said 'Go back
to Fort Henry.' Girty warned us, and now comes this
peremptory order from Isaac Zane."

"Well?"

"It means that these border men see what we will not
admit. We ministers have such hope and trust in God that we
cannot realize the dangers of this life. I fear that our work
has been in vain."

"Never. We have already saved many souls. Do not be
discouraged."

All this time the runner had stood near at hand straight as
an arrow. Presently Edwards suggested that the Wyandot
was waiting to be questioned, and accordingly he asked the
Indian if he had anything further to communicate.

"Huron—go by—paleface." Here he held up both hands
and shut his fists several times, evidently enumerating how
many white men he had seen. "Here—when—high—sun."

With that he bounded lightly past them and loped off with
an even, swinging stride.

"What did he mean?" asked Jim, almost sure he had not
hear the runner aright.

"He meant that a party of white men are approaching,
and will be here by noon. I never knew an Indian runner to
carry unreliable information. We have joyful news, both in

regard to your brother, and the Village of Peace. Let us go in to tell the others."

The Huron runner's report proved to be correct. Shortly before noon signals from Indian scouts proclaimed the approach of a band of white men. Evidently Girty's forces had knowledge beforehand of the proximity of this band, for the signals created no excitement. The Indians expressed only a lazy curiosity. Soon several Delaware scouts appeared, escorting a large party of frontiersmen.

These men turned out to be Captain Williamson's force, which had been out on an expedition after a marauding tribe of Chippewas. This last-named tribe had recently harried the remote settlers and committed depredations on the outskirts of the white settlements eastward. The company was composed of men who had served in the garrison at Fort Pitt and hunters and backwoodsmen from Yellow Creek and Fort Henry. The captain himself was a typical borderman, rough and bluff, hardened by long years of border life, and, like most pioneers, having no more use for an Indian than for a snake. He had led his party after the marauders, and surprised and slaughtered nearly all of them. Returning eastward he had passed through Goshocking, where he learned of the muttering storm rising over the Village of Peace, and had come more out of curiosity than hope to avert misfortune.

The advent of so many frontiersmen seemed a godsend to the perplexed and worried missionaries. They welcomed the newcomers most heartily. Beds were made in several of the newly erected cabins; the village was given over for the comfort of the frontiersmen. Edwards conducted Captain Williamson through the shops and schools, and the old borderman's weatherbeaten face expressed a comical surprise.

"Wal, I'll be durned If I ever expected to see a redskin work," was his only comment on the industries.

"We are greatly alarmed by the presence of Girty and his followers," said Edwards. "We have been warned to leave, but have not been actually threatened. What do you infer from the appearance here of these hostile savages?"

"It hardly 'pears to me they'll bother you preachers. They're agin the Christian redskins, that's plain."

"Why have we been warned to go?"

"That's natural, seein' they're agin the preachin'."

"What will they do with the converted Indians?"

"Mighty onsartin. They might let them go back to the tribes, but 'pears to me these good Injuns won't go. Another thing, Girty is afeered of the spread of Christianity."

" 'Pears likely."

"And you, also, think we'd do well to leave here."

"I do, sartin. We're startin' for Fort Henry soon. You'd better come along with us."

"Captain Williamson, we're going to stick it out, Girty or no Girty."

"You can't do no good stayin' here. Pipe and Half King won't stand for the singin', prayin' redskins, especially when they've got all these cattle and fields of grain."

"Wetzel said the same."

"Hev you seen Wetzel?"

"Yes; he rescued a girl from Jim Girty, and returned her to us."

"That so? I met Wetzel and Jack Zane back a few miles in the woods. They're layin' for somebody, because when I asked them to come along they refused, sayin' they had work as must be done. They looked like it, too. I never hearn tell of Wetzel advisin' anyone before; but I'll say if he told me to do a thing, by gosh! I'd do it."

"As men, we might very well take the advice given us; but as preachers we must stay here to do all we can for these Christian Indians. One thing more: Will you help us?"

"I reckon I'll stay here to see the thing out," answered Williamson. Edwards made a mental note of the frontiersman's evasive answer.

Jim had, meanwhile, made the acquaintance of a young minister, John Christy by name, who had lost his sweetheart in one of the Chippewa raids, and had accompanied the Williamson expedition in the hope he might rescue her.

"How long have you been out?" asked Jim.

"About four weeks now," answered Christy. "My betrothed was captured five weeks ago yesterday. I joined Williamson's band, which made up at Short Creek to take the trail of the flying Chippewas, in the hope I might find her. But not a trace! The expedition fell upon a band of redskins over on the Walhonding, and killed nearly all of them. I learned from a wounded Indian that a renegade had made off with a white girl about a week previous. Perhaps it was poor Lucy."

Jim related the circumstances of his own capture by Jim Girty, the rescue of Nell, and Kate's sad fate.

"Could Jim Girty have gotten your girl?" inquired Jim, in conclusion.

"It's hardly probable. The description doesn't tally with Girty's. This renegade was short and heavy, and noted especially for his strength. Of course, an Indian would first speak of some such distinguishing feature. There are, however, ten or twelve renegades on the border, and, excepting Jim Girty, one's bad as another."

"Then it's a common occurrence, this abducting girls from the settlements?"

"Yes, and the strange thing is that one never hears of such doings until he gets out on the frontier."

"For that matter, you don't hear much of anything, except of the wonderful richness and promise of the western country."

"You're right. Rumors of fat, fertile lands induce the colonist to become a pioneer. He comes west with his family; two out of every ten lose their scalps, and in some places the average is much greater. The wives, daughters, and children are carried off into captivity. I have been on the border two years, and know that the rescue of any captive, as Wetzel rescued your friend, is a remarkable exception."

"If you have so little hope of recovering your sweetheart what then is your motive for accompanying this band of hunters?"

"Revenge!"

"And you are a preacher?" Jim's voice did not disguise his astonishment.

"I was a preacher, and now I am thirsting for vengeance," answered Christy, his face clouding darkly. "Wait until you learn what frontier life means. You are young here yet; you are flushed with the success of your teaching; you have lived a short time in this quiet village, where until the last few days, all has been serene. You know nothing of the strife, of the necessity of fighting, of the cruelty which makes up this border existence. Only two years have hardened me so that I actually pant for the blood of the renegade who has robbed me. A frontiersman must take his choice of succumbing or cutting his way through flesh and bone. Blood will be spilled; if not yours, then your foe's. The pioneers run from the plow to fight; they halt in the cutting of corn to defend themselves, and in winter must battle against cold and hardship, which would be less cruel if there was time in summer to prepare for winter, for the savages leave them hardly an opportunity to plant crops. How many pioneers have given up and gone back East? Find me any who would not return home tomorrow, if they could. All that brings them out here is the chance for a home, and all that keeps them here is the poor hope of finally attaining their object. Always there is a possibility of future prosperity. But this generation, if it survives, will never see prosperity and happiness. What does this border life engender in a pioneer who holds his own in it? Of all things, not Christianity. He becomes a fighter, keen as the redskin who steals through the coverts."

The serene days of the Village of Peace had passed into history. Soon that depraved vagabond, the French trader, with cheap trinkets and vile whisky, made his appearance. This was all that was needed to inflame the visitors. Where they had been only bold and impudent, they became insulting and abusive. They execrated the Christian Indians for their neutrality; scorned them for worshiping this unknown God, and denounced a religion which made women of strong men.

The slaughtering of cattle commenced; the despoiling of maize fields and robbing of corncribs began with the drunkenness.

All this time it was seen that Girty and Elliott consulted often with Pipe and Half King. The latter was the only Huron chief opposed to neutrality toward the Village of Peace, and he was, if possible, more fierce in his hatred than Pipe. The future of the Christian settlement rested with these two chiefs. Girty and Elliott, evidently, were the designing schemers, and they worked diligently on the passions of these simpleminded, but fierce, warlike chiefs.

Greatly to the relief of the distracted missionaries, Heckewelder returned to the village. Jaded and haggard, he presented a travelworn appearance. He made the astonishing assertions that he had been thrice waylaid and assaulted on his way to Goshocking; then detained by a roving band of Chippewas, and soon after his arrival at their camping ground a renegade had run off with a white woman captive, while the Indians west of the village were in an uproar. Zeisberger, however, was safe in the Moravian town of Salem, some miles west of Goshocking. Heckewelder had expected to find the same condition of affairs as existed in the Village of Peace; but he was bewildered by the great array of hostile Indians. Chiefs who had once extended friendly hands to him now drew back coldly, as they said:

"Washington is dead. The American armies are cut to pieces. The few thousands who had escaped the British are collecting at Fort Pitt to steal the Indian's land."

Heckewelder vigorously denied all these assertions, knowing they had been invented by Girty and Elliott. He exhausted all his skill and patience in the vain endeavor to show Pipe where he was wrong. Half King had been so well coached by the renegades that he refused to listen. The other chiefs maintained a cold reserve that was baffling and exasperating. Wingenund took no active part in the councils; but his presence apparently denoted that he had sided with the others. The outlook was altogether discouraging.

"I'm completely fagged out," declared Heckewelder that night when he returned to Edwards' cabin. He dropped into a chair as one whose strength is entirely spent, whose indomitable spirit has at last been broken.

"Lie down to rest," said Edwards.

"Oh, I can't. Matters look so black."

"You're tired out and discouraged. You'll feel better tomorrow. The situation is not, perhaps, so hopeless. The presence of these frontiersmen should encourage us."

"What will they do? What can they do?" cried Heckewelder, bitterly. "I tell you never before have I encountered such gloomy, stony Indians. It seems to me that they are in no vacillating state. They act like men whose course is already decided upon and who are only waiting."

"For what?" asked Jim, after a long silence.

"God only knows! Perhaps for time; possibly for a final

decision, and it may be for a reason the very thought of which makes me faint."

"Tell us," said Edwards, speaking quietly, for he had ever been the calmest of the missionaries.

"Never mind. Perhaps it's only my nerves. I'm all unstrung, and could suspect anything tonight."

"Heckewelder, tell us?" Jim asked, earnestly.

"My friends, I pray I am wrong. God help us if my fears are correct. I believe the Indians are waiting for Jim Girty."

Chapter
XXII

Simon Girty lolled on a blanket in Half King's teepee. He was alone, awaiting his allies. Rings of white smoke curled lazily from his lips as he puffed on a long Indian pipe and gazed out over the clearing that contained the Village of Peace.

Still water has something in its placid surface significant of deep channels, of hidden depths; the dim outlines of the forest is dark with meaning, suggestive of its wild internal character. So Simon Girty's hard, bronzed face betrayed the man. His degenerate brother's features were revolting; but his own were striking, and fell short of being handsome only because of their craggy hardness. Years of revolt, of bitterness, of consciousness of wasted life, had graven their stern lines on that copper, masklike face. Yet despite the cruelty there, the forbidding shade on it, as if a reflection from a dark soul, it was not wholly a bad countenance. Traces still lingered, faintly, of a man in whom kindlier feelings had once predominated.

In a moment of pique Girty had deserted his military post at Fort Pitt and become an outlaw of his own volition. Previous to that time he had been an able soldier and a good fellow. When he realized that his step was irrevocable, that even his best friends condemned him, he plunged, with anger and despair in his heart, into a war upon his race. Both of his brothers had long been border ruffians, whose only protection from the outraged pioneers lay in the faraway camps of hostile tribes. George Girty had so sunk his individuality into the savage's that he was no longer a white man. Jim Girty stalked over the borderland with a bloody tomahawk, his long arm outstretched to clutch some unfortunate white woman, and with his hideous smile of death. Both of these men were far lower than the worst savages, and it was almost wholly to their deeds of darkness that Simon Girty owed his infamous name.

Today, White Chief, as Girty was called, awaited his men. A slight tremor of the ground caused him to turn his gaze. The Huron chief, Half King, resplendent in his magnificent array, had entered the teepee. He squatted in a corner, rested the bowl of his great pipe on his knee, and smoked in silence. The habitual frown of his black brow, like a shaded, overhanging cliff; the fire flashing from his eyes, as a shining light is reflected from a dark pool; his closely shut, bulging jaw, all bespoke a nature lofty in its Indian pride and arrogance but more cruel than death.

Another chief stalked into the teepee and seated himself. It was Pipe. His countenance denoted none of the intelligence that made Wingenund's face so noble; it was even coarser than Half King's, and his eyes, resembling live coals in the dark; the long, cruel lines of his jaw; the thin, tightly closed lips, which looked as if they could relax only to utter a savage command, expressed fierce cunning and brutality.

"White Chief is idle today," said Half King, speaking in the Indian tongue.

"King, I am waiting. Girty is slow, but sure," answered the renegade.

"The eagle sails slowly round and round, up and up," replied Half King, with majestic gestures, "until his eye sees all, until he knows his time; then he folds his wings and swoops down from the blue sky like the forked fire. So does White Chief. But Half King is impatient."

"Today decides the fate of the Village of Peace," answered Girty, imperturbably.

"Ugh!" grunted Pipe.

Half King vented his approval in the same meaning exclamation.

An hour passed; the renegade smoked in silence; the chiefs did likewise.

A horseman rode up to the door of the teepee, dismounted, and came in. It was Elliott. He had been absent twenty hours. His buckskin suit showed the effect of hard riding through the thickets.

"Hullo, Bill, any sign of Jim?" was Girty's greeting to his lieutenant.

"Nary. He's not been seen near the Delaware camp. He's after that chap who married Winds."

"I thought so. Jim's roundin' up a tenderfoot who will be a bad man to handle if he has half a chance. I saw as much the day he took his horse away from Silver. He finally did fer the Shawnee, an' almost put Jim out. My brother oughtn' to give rein to personal revenge at a time like this." Girty's face did not change, but his tone was one of annoyance.

"Jim said he'd be here today, didn't he?"

"Today is as long as we allowed to wait."

"He'll come. Where's Jake and Mac?"

"They're here somewhere, drinkin' like fish an' raisin' hell."

Two more renegades appeared at the door, and, entering

the teepee, squatted down in Indian fashion. The little wiry man with the wizened face was McKee; the other was the latest acquisition to the renegade force, Jake Deering, deserter, thief, murderer—everything that is bad. In appearance he was of medium height, but very heavily, compactly built, and evidently as strong as an ox. He had a tangled shock of red hair, a broad, bloated face; big, dull eyes, like the openings of empty furnaces, and an expression of beastliness.

Deering and McKee were intoxicated.

"Bad time fer drinkin'," said Girty, with disapproval in his glance.

"What's that ter you?" growled Deering. "I'm here ter do your work, an' I reckon it'll be done better if I'm drunk."

"Don't git careless," replied Girty, with that cool tone and dark look such as dangerous men use. "I'm only sayin' it's a bad time fer you, because if this bunch of frontiersmen happen to git onto you bein' the renegade that was with the Chippewas an' got thet young feller's girl, there's liable to be trouble."

"They ain't agoin' ter find out."

"Where is she?"

"Back there in the woods."

"Mebbe it's as well. Now, don't git so drunk you'll blab all you know. We've lots of work to do without havin' to clean up Williamson's bunch," replied Girty. "Bill, tie up the tent flaps an' we'll git to council."

Elliott arose to carry out the order, and had pulled in the deerhide flaps, when one of them was jerked outward to disclose the befrilled person of Jim Girty. Except for a discoloration over his eye, he appeared as usual.

"Ugh!" grunted Pipe, who was glad to see his renegade friend.

Half King evinced the same feeling.

"Hullo," was Simon Girty's greeting.

" 'Pears I'm on time fer the picnic," said Jim Girty, with his ghastly leer.

Bill Elliott closed the flaps after giving orders to the guard to prevent any Indians from loitering near the teepee.

"Listen," said Simon Girty, speaking low in the Delaware language. "The time is ripe. We have come here to break forever the influence of the white man's religion. Our councils have been held; we shall drive away the missionaries and burn the Village of Peace."

He paused, leaning forward in his exceeding earnestness, with his bronzed face lined by swelling veins, his whole person made rigid by the murderous thought. Then he hissed between his teeth: *"What shall we do with these Christian Indians?"*

Pipe raised his war club, struck it upon the ground, then handed it to Half King.

Half King took the club and repeated the action.

Both chiefs favored the death penalty.

"Feed 'em to the buzzards," croaked Jim Girty.

Simon Girty knitted his brows in thought. The question of what to do with the converted Indians had long perplexed him.

"No," said he; "let us drive away the missionaries, burn the village, and take the Indians back to camp. We'll keep them there; they'll soon forget."

"Pipe does not want them," declared the Delaware.

"Christian Indians shall never sit round Half King's fire," cried the Huron.

Simon Girty knew the crisis had come; that but few moments were left him to decide as to the disposition of the Christians; and he thought seriously. Certainly he did not want the Christians murdered. However cruel his life, and great his misdeeds, he was still a man. If possible, he desired to burn the village and ruin the religious influence, but without shedding blood. Yet, with all his power, he was handicapped, and that by the very chiefs most nearly under his control. He could not subdue this growing Christian influence without the help of Pipe and Half King. To these savages a thing was either right or wrong. He had sown the seed of unrest and jealousy in the savage breasts, and the fruit was the decree of death. As far as these Indians were concerned, this decision was unalterable.

On the other hand, if he did not spread ruin over the Village of Peace, the missionaries would soon get such a grasp on the tribes that their hold would never be broken. He could not allow that, even if he was forced to sacrifice the missionaries along with their converts, for he saw in the growth of this religion his own downfall. The border must be hostile to the whites, or it could no longer be his home. To be sure, he had aided the British in the Revolution, and could find a refuge among them; but this did not suit him.

He became an outcast because of failure to win the military promotion which he had so much coveted. He had failed among his own people. He had won a great position in an alien race, and he loved his power. To sway men—Indians, if not others—to his will, to avenge himself for the fancied wrong done him, to be great had been his unrelenting purpose.

He knew he must sacrifice the Christians, or eventually lose his own power. He had no false ideas about the converted Indians. He knew they were innocent; that they were a thousand times better off than the pagan Indians; that they had never harmed him, nor would they ever do so; but if he allowed them to spread their religion there was an end of Simon Girty.

His decision was characteristic of the man. He would sacrifice anyone, or all, to retain his supremacy. He knew the fulfillment of the decree as laid down by Pipe and Half King would be known as his work. His name, infamous now, would have an additional horror, and ever be remembered by posterity in unspeakable loathing, in unsoftening wrath. He knew this, and deep down in his heart awoke a numbed chord of humanity that twinged with strange pain. What awful work he must sanction to keep his vaunted power! More bitter than all was the knowledge that to retain this hold over the Indians he must commit a deed which, so far as the whites were concerned, would take away his great name and brand him a coward.

He briefly reviewed his stirring life. Singularly fitted for a leader, in a few years he had risen to the most powerful position on the border. He wielded more influence than any chief. He had been opposed to the invasion of the pioneers, and this alone, without his sagacity or his generalship, would have given him control of many tribes. But hatred for his own people, coupled with unerring judgment, a remarkable ability to lead expeditions, and his invariable success, had raised him higher and higher until he stood alone. He was the most powerful man west of the Alleghenies. His fame was such that the British had importuned him to help them, and had actually, in more than one instance, given him command over British subjects.

All of which meant that he had a great, even though an infamous name. No matter what he was blamed for; no matter how many dastardly deeds had been committed by his depraved brothers and laid to his door, he knew he had never done a cowardly act. That which he had committed while he was drunk he considered as having been done by the liquor, and not by the man. He loved his power, and he loved his name.

In all Girty's eventful, ignoble life, neither the alienation from his people, the horror they ascribed to his power, nor the sacrifice of his life to stand high among the savage races, nor any of the cruel deeds committed while at war, hurt him a tithe as much as did this sanctioning the massacre of the Christians.

Although he was a vengeful, unscrupulous, evil man, he had never acted the coward.

Half King waited long for Girty to speak; since he remained silent, the wily Huron suggested they take a vote on the question.

"Let us burn the Village of Peace, drive away the missionaries, and take the Christians back to the Delaware towns—all without spilling blood," said Girty, determined to carry his point, if possible.

"I say the same," added Elliott, refusing the war club held out to him by Half King.

"Me, too," voted McKee, not so drunk but that he understood the lightninglike glance Girty shot at him.

"Kill 'em all; kill everybody," cried Deering in drunken glee. He took the club and pounded with it on the ground.

Pipe repeated his former performance, as also did Half King, after which he handed the black, knotted symbol of death to Jim Girty.

Three had declared for saving the Christians, and three for the death penalty.

Six pairs of burning eyes were fastened on the Deathshead.

Pipe and Half King were coldly relentless; Deering awoke to brutal earnestness; McKee and Elliott watched with bated breath. These men had formed themselves into a tribunal to decide on the life or death of many, and the situation, if not the greatest in their lives, certainly was one of vital importance.

Simon Girty cursed all the fates. He dared not openly oppose the voting, and he could not, before those cruel but just chiefs, try to influence his brother's vote.

As Jim Girty took the war club, Simon read in his brother's face the doom of the converted Indians, and he muttered to himself:

"Now tremble an' shrink, all you Christians!"

Jim was not in a hurry. Slowly he poised the war club. He was playing as a cat plays with a mouse; he was glorying in his power. The silence was that of death. *It signified the silence of death.* The war club descended with violence.

"Feed the Christians to ther buzzards!"

Chapter
XXIII

"I have been here before," said Joe to Whispering Winds. "I remember that vine-covered stone. We crawled over it to get at Girty and Silvertip. There's the little knoll; here's the very spot where I was hit by a flying tomahawk. Yes, and there's the spring. Let me see, what did Wetzel call this spot?"

"Beautiful Spring," answered the Indian girl.

"That's it, and it's well named. What a lovely place!"

Nature had been lavish in the beautifying of this enclosed dell. It was about fifty yards wide and nestled among little wooded knolls and walls of gray, lichen-covered stone. Though the sun shone brightly into the opening, and the rain had free access to the mossy ground, no stormy winds ever entered this well-protected glade.

Joe reveled in the beauty of the scene, even while he was too weak to stand erect. He suffered no pain from his wound, although he had gradually grown dizzy, and felt as if the ground was rising before him. He was glad to lie upon the mossy ground in the little cavern under the cliff.

Upon examination his wound was found to have opened and was bleeding. His hunting coat was saturated with blood.

Whispering Winds washed the cut and dressed it with cooling leaves. Then she rebandaged it tightly with Joe's linsey handkerchiefs, and while he rested comfortably she gathered bundles of ferns, carrying them to the little cavern. When she had a large quantity of these she sat down near Joe and began to weave the long stems into a kind of screen. The fern stalks were four feet long and half a foot wide; these she deftly laced together, making broad screens which would serve to ward off the night dews. The done, she next built a fireplace with flat stones. She found wild apples, plums, and turnips on the knoll above the glade. Then she cooked strips of meat which had been brought with them. Lance grazed on the long grass just within the glade, and Mose caught two rabbits. When darkness settled down Whispering Winds called the dog within the cavern and hung the screens before the opening.

Several days passed. Joe rested quietly, and began to recover strength. Besides the work of preparing their meals, Whispering Winds had nothing to do save sit near the invalid and amuse or interest him so that he would not fret or grow impatient while his wound was healing.

They talked about their future prospects. After visiting the Village of Peace, they would go to Fort Henry, where Joe could find employment. They dwelt upon the cabin they would build and passed many happy moments planning a new home. Joe's love of the wilderness had in no wise diminished; but a blow on his head from a heavy tomahawk and a vicious stab in the back had lessened his zeal so far that he understood it was not wise to sacrifice life for the pleasures of the pathless woods. He could have the last without the danger of being shot at from behind every tree. He reasoned that it would be best for him to take his wife to Fort Henry, there find employment, and devote his leisure time to roaming in the forest.

"Will the palefaces be kind to the Indian who has learned to love them?" Whispering Winds asked wistfully of Joe.

"Indeed they will," answered Joe, and he told her the story of Isaac Zane; how he took his Indian bride home; how her beauty and sweetness soon won all the white people's love. "It will be so with you, my wife."

"Whispering Winds knows so little," she murmured.

"Why, you are learning every day, and even if such was not the case, you know enough for me."

"Whispering Winds will be afraid; she fears a little to go."

"I'll be glad when we can be on the move," said Joe, with his old impatient desire for action. "How soon, Winds, can we set off?"

"As many days," answered the Indian girl, holding up five fingers.

"So long? I want to leave this place."

"Leave Beautiful Spring?"

"Yes, even this sweet place. It was a horror for me. I'll never forget the night I first saw that spring shining in the moonlight. It was right above the rock that I looked into the glade. The moon was reflected in the dark pool, and as I gazed into the shadowy depths of the dark water, I suddenly felt an unaccountable terror; but I oughtn't to have the same feeling now. We are safe, are we not?"

"We are safe," murmured Whispering Winds.

"Yet I have the same chill of fear whenever I look at the beautiful spring, and at night as I awake to hear the soft babble of running water, I freeze until my heart feels like cold lead. Winds, I'm not a coward; but I can't help this feeling. Perhaps, it's only the memory of that awful night with Wetzel."

"An Indian feels so when he passes to his unmarked grave," answered Winds, gazing solemnly at him. "Whispering Winds does not like this fancy of yours. Let us leave Beautiful Spring. You are almost well. Ah! if Whispering Winds should lose you! I love you!"

"And I love you, my beautiful wildflower," answered Joe, stroking the dark head so near his own.

A tender smile shone on his face. He heard a slight noise without the cave, and, looking up, saw that which caused the smile to fade quickly.

"Mose!" he called, sharply. The dog was away chasing rabbits.

Whispering Winds glanced over her shoulder with a startled cry, which ended in a scream.

Not two yards behind her stood Jim Girty.

Hideous was his face in its triumphant ferocity. He held a long knife in his hand, and, snarling like a mad wolf, he made a forward lunge.

Joe raised himself quickly; but almost before he could lift his hand in defense, the long blade was sheathed in his breast.

Slowly he sank back, his gray eyes contracting with the old steely flash. The will to do was there, but the power was gone forever.

"Remember, Girty, murderer! I am Wetzel's friend," he cried, gazing at his slayer with unutterable scorn.

Then the gray eyes softened and sought the blanched face of the stricken maiden.

"Winds," he whispered faintly.

She was as one frozen with horror.

The gray eyes gazed into hers with lingering tenderness; then the film of death came upon them.

The renegade raised his bloody knife and bent over the prostrate form.

Whispering Winds threw herself upon Girty with the blind fury of a maddened lioness. Cursing fiercely, he stabbed her once, twice, three times. She fell across the body of her lover and clasped it, convulsively.

Girty gave one glance at his victims; deliberately wiped the gory knife on Winds' leggings, and, with another glance, hurried and fearful, around the glade, he plunged into the thicket.

An hour passed. A dark stream crept from the quiet figures toward the spring. It dyed the moss and the green violet leaves. Slowly it wound its way to the clear water, dripping between the pale blue flowers. The little fall below the spring was no longer snowy white; blood had tinged it red.

A dog came bounding into the glade. He leaped the brook, hesitated on the bank, and lowered his nose to sniff at the water. He bounded up the bank to the cavern.

A long, mournful howl broke the wilderness's quiet.

Another hour passed. The birds were silent; the insects still. The sun sank behind the trees, and the shades of evening gathered.

The ferns on the other side of the glade trembled. A slight rustle of dead leaves disturbed the stillness. The dog whined, then barked. The tall form of a hunter rose out of the thicket and stepped into the glade with his eyes bent upon moccasin tracks in the soft moss.

The trail he had been following led him to this bloody spring.

"I might hev knowed it," he muttered.

Wetzel, for it was he, leaned upon his long rifle while his keen eyes took in the details of the tragedy. The whining dog, the bloody water, the motionless figures lying in a last embrace, told the sad story.

"Joe an' Winds," he muttered.

Only a moment did he remain lost in sad reflection. A familiar moccasin print in the sand on the bank pointed westward. He examined it carefully.

"Two hours gone," he muttered. "I might overtake him."

Then his motions became swift. With two blows of his tomahawk he secured a long piece of grapevine. He took a heavy stone from the bed of the brook. He carried Joe to the spring, and, returning for Winds, placed her beside her lover. This done, he tied one end of the grapevine around the stone, and wound the other about the dead bodies.

He pushed them off the bank into the spring. As the lovers sank into the deep pool they turned, exposing first Winds' sad face, and then Joe's. Then they sank out of sight. Little waves splashed on the shore of the pool; the ripple disappeared, and the surface of the spring became tranquil.

Wetzel stood one moment over the watery grave of the maiden who had saved him and the boy who had loved him. In the gathering gloom his stalwart form assumed gigantic proportions, and when he raised his long arm and shook his clenched fist toward the west, he resembled a magnificent statue of dark menace.

With a single bound he cleared the pool, and then sped out of the glade. He urged the dog on Girty's trail, and followed the eager beast toward the west. As he disappeared, a long, low sound like a sigh of the night wind swelled and moaned through the gloom.

Chapter
XXIV

When the first ruddy rays of the rising sun crimsoned the eastern sky, Wetzel slowly wound his way down a rugged hill far west of Beautiful Spring. A white dog, weary and footsore, limped at his side. Both man and beast showed evidences of severe exertion.

The hunter stopped in a little cave under a projecting stone, and, laying aside his rifle, began to gather twigs and sticks. He was particular about selecting the wood, and threw aside many pieces which would have burned well; but when he did kindle a flame it blazed hotly, yet made no smoke.

He sharpened a green stick, and, taking some strips of meat from his pocket, roasted them over the hot flame. He fed the dog first. Mose had crouched close on the ground with his head on his paws and his brown eyes fastened upon the hunter.

"He had too big a start fer us," said Wetzel, speaking as if the dog were human. It seemed that Wetzel's words were a protest against the meaning in those large, sad eyes.

Then the hunter put out the fire, and, searching for a more

secluded spot, finally found one on top of the ledge, where he commanded a good view of his surroundings. The weary dog was asleep. Wetzel settled himself to rest, and was soon wrapped in slumber.

About noon he awoke. He arose, stretched his limbs, and then took an easy position on the front of the ledge, where he could look below. Evidently the hunter was waiting for something. The dog slept on. It was the noonday hour, when the stillness of the forest almost matched that of midnight. The birds were more quiet than at any other time during daylight.

Wetzel reclined there with his head against the stone, and his rifle resting across his knees.

He listened now to the sounds of the forest. The soft breeze fluttering among the leaves, the rain call of the tree frog, the caw of crows from distant hilltops, the sweet songs of the thrush and oriole, were blended together naturally, harmoniously.

But suddenly the hunter raised his head. A note, deeper than the others, a little too strong, came from far down the shaded hollow. To Wetzel's trained ear it was a discord. He manifested no more than this attention, for the birdcall was the signal he had been awaiting. He whistled a note in answer that was as deep and clear as the one which had aroused him.

Moments passed. There was no repetition of the sound. The songs of the other birds had ceased. Besides Wetzel there was another intruder in the woods.

Mose lifted his shaggy head and growled. The hunter patted the dog. In a few minutes the figure of a tall man appeared among the laurels down the slope. He stopped while gazing up at the ledge. Then, with noiseless step, he ascended the ridge, climbed the rocky ledge, and turned the corner of the stone to face Wetzel. The newcomer was Jonathan Zane.

"Jack, I expected you afore this," was Wetzel's greeting.

"I couldn't make it sooner," answered Zane. "After we left Williamson and separated, I got turned around by a band of several hundred redskins makin' for the Village of Peace. I went back again, but couldn't find any sign of the trail we're huntin'. Then I makes for this meetin' place. I've been goin' for some ten hours, and am hungry."

"I've got some b'ar ready cooked," said Wetzel, handing Zane several strips of meat.

"What luck did you have?"

"I found Girty's trail, an old one, over here some eighteen or twenty miles, an' follored it until I went almost into the Delaware town. It led to a hut in a deep ravine. I ain't often surprised, but I wus then. I found the dead body of that girl, Kate Wells, we fetched over from Fort Henry. That's sad, but it ain't the surprisin' part. I also found Silvertip, the Shawnee I've been lookin' fer. He was all knocked an' cut up, deader'n a stone. There's been somethin' of a scrap in the hut. I calkilate Girty murdered Kate, but I couldn't think then who did fer Silver, though I allowed the renegade might hev done thet, too. I watched round an' seen Girty come back to the hut. He had ten Injuns with him, an' presently they all made fer the west. I trailed them, but didn't calkilate it'd be wise to tackle the bunch singlehanded, so laid back. A mile or so from the hut I came across hoss tracks minglin' with the moccasin prints. About fifteen mile or so from the Delaware town, Girty left his buckskins, an' they went west, while he stuck to the hoss tracks. I was onto his game in a minute. I cut across country fer Beautiful Spring, but I got there too late. I found the warm bodies of Joe and thet Injun girl, Winds. The snake hed murdered them."

"I allow Joe won over Winds, got away from the Delaware town with her, tried to rescue Kate, and killed Silver in the fight. Girty probably was surprised an' run after he had knifed the girl."

" 'Pears so to me. Joe had two knife cuts, an' one was an old wound."

"You say it was a bad fight?"

"Must hev been. The hut was all knocked in, an' stuff scattered about. Wal, Joe could go some if he onct got started."

"I'll bet he could. He was the likeliest lad I've seen for many a day."

"If he'd lasted, he'd been somethin' of a hunter an' fighter."

"Too bad. But Lord! you couldn't keep him down, no more than you can lots of these wild young chaps that drift out here."

"I'll allow he had the fever bad."

"Did you hev time to bury them?"

"I hedn't time fer much. I sunk them in the spring."

"It's a pretty deep hole," said Zane, reflectively. "Then you and the dog took Girty's trail, but couldn't catch up with him. He's now with the renegade cutthroats and hundreds of riled Indians over there in the Village of Peace."

"I reckon you're right."

A long silence ensued. Jonathan finished his simple repast, drank from the little spring that trickled under the stone, and, sitting down by the dog, smoothed out his long silken hair.

"Lew, we're pretty good friends, ain't we?" he asked, thoughtfully.

"Jack, you an' the colonel are all the friends I ever had, 'ceptin' thet boy lyin' quiet back there in the woods."

"I know you pretty well, and ain't sayin' a word about your runnin' off from me on many a hunt, but I want to speak plain about this fellow Girty."

"Wal?" said Wetzel, as Zane hesitated.

"Twice in the last few years you and I have had it in for the same men, both white-livered traitors. You remember? First it was Miller, who tried to ruin my sister Betty, and next it was Jim Girty, who murdered our old friend, as good an old man as ever wore moccasins. Wal, after Miller ran off from the fort, we trailed him down to the river, and I points across and says, 'You or me?' and you says, 'Me.' You was Betty's friend, and I knew she'd be avenged. Miller is lyin' quiet in the woods, and violets have blossomed twice over his grave, though you never said a word; but I know it's true because I know you."

Zane looked earnestly into the dark face of his friend, hoping perhaps to get some verbal assurance there that his brief was true. But Wetzel did not speak, and he continued:

"Another day not so long ago we both looked down at an old friend, and saw his white hair matted with blood. He'd been murdered for nothin'. Again you and me trailed a coward and found him to be Jim Girty. I knew you'd been huntin' him for years, and so I says, 'Lew, you or me?' and you says, 'Me.' I give in to you, for I knew you're a better man than me, and because I wanted you to have the satisfaction. Wal, the months have gone by, and Jim Girty's still livin' and carryin' on. Now he's over there after them poor preachers. I ain't sayin', Lew, that you haven't more agin' him than me, but I do say, let me in on it with you. He always has a gang of redskins with him; he's afraid to travel alone, else you'd had him long ago. Two of us'll have more chance to git him. Let me go with you. When it comes to a finish, I'll stand aside while you give it to him. I'd enjoy seein' you cut him from shoulder to hip. After he leaves the Village of Peace we'll hit his trail, camp on it, and stick to it until it ends in his grave."

The earnest voice of the backwoodsman ceased. Both men rose and stood facing each other. Zane's bronzed face was hard and tense, expressive of an indomitable will; Wetzel's was coldly dark, with fateful resolve, as if his decree of vengeance, once given, was as immutable as destiny. The big, horny hands gripped in a viselike clasp born of fierce passion, but no word was spoken.

Far to the west somewhere, a befrilled and bedizened renegade pursued the wild tenor of his ways; perhaps, even now steeping his soul in more crime, or staining his hands a deeper red, but sleeping or waking, he dreamed not of this deadly compact that meant his doom.

The two hunters turned their stern faces toward the west, and passed silently down the ridge into the depths of the forest. Darkness found them within rifle shot of the Village of Peace. With the dog creeping between them, they crawled to a position which would, in daylight, command a view of the clearing. Then, while one stood guard, the other slept.

When morning dawned they shifted their position to the top of a low, fern-covered cliff, from which they could see every movement in the village. All the morning they watched with that wonderful patience of men who knew how to wait. The visiting savages were quiet, the missionaries moved about in and out of the shops and cabins; the Christian Indians worked industriously in the fields, while the renegades lolled before a prominent teepee.

"This quiet looks bad," whispered Jonathan to Wetzel. No shouts were heared; not a hostile Indian was seen to move.

"They've come to a decision," whispered Jonathan, and Wetzel answered him:

"If they hev, the Christians don't know it."

An hour later the deep pealing of the church bells broke the silence. The entire band of Christian Indians gathered near the large log structure, and then marched in orderly form toward the maple grove where the service was always held in pleasant weather. This movement brought the Indians within several hundred yards of the cliff where Zane and Wetzel lay concealed.

"There's Heckewelder walking with old man Wells," whispered Jonathan. "There's Young and Edwards, and yes, there's the young missionary, brother of Joe. 'Pears to me they're foolish to hold service in the face of all those riled Injuns."

"Wuss'n foolish," answered Wetzel.

"Look! By gum! As I'm a livin' sinner there comes the whole crowd of hostile redskins. They've got their guns, and—by gum! they're painted. Looks bad, bad! Not much friendliness about that bunch!"

"They ain't intendin' to be peaceable."

"By gum! You're right. There ain't one of them settin' down. 'Pears to me I know some of them redskins. There's Pipe, sure enough, and Kotoxen. By gum! If there ain't Shingiss; he was friendly once."

"None of them's friendly."

"Look! Lew, look! Right behind Pipe. See that long war bonnet. As I'm a born sinner, that's your old friend, Wingenund. 'Pears to me we've rounded up all our acquaintances."

The two bordermen lay close under the tall ferns and watched the proceedings with sharp eyes. They saw the converted Indians seat themselves before the platform. The crowd of hostile Indians surrounded the glade on all sides, except one, which, singularly enough, was next to the woods.

"Look thar!" exclaimed Wetzel, under his breath. He pointed off to the right of the maple glade. Jonathan gazed in the direction indicated, and saw two savages stealthily slipping through the bushes and behind trees. Presently these suspicious acting spies, or scouts, stopped on a little knoll perhaps a hundred yards from the glade.

Wetzel groaned.

"This ain't comfortable," growled Zane, in a low whisper. "Them red devils are up to somethin' bad. They'd better not move round over here."

The hunters, satisfied that the two isolated savages meant mischief, turned their gaze once more toward the maple grove.

"Ah! Simon, you white traitor! See him, Lew, comin' with his precious gang," said Jonathan. "He's got the whole thing fixed, you can plainly see that. Bill Elliott, McKee; and who's that renegade with Jim Girty? I'll allow he must be the feller we heard was with the Chippewas. Tough lookin' customer; a good mate fer Jim Girty! A fine lot of border hawks!"

"Somethin' comin' off," whispered Wetzel, as Zane's low growl grew unintelligible.

Jonathan felt, rather than saw, Wetzel tremble.

"The missionaries are consultin'. Ah, there comes one! Which? I guess it's Edwards. By gum! who's that Injun stalkin' over from the hostile bunch. Big chief, whoever he is. Blest if it ain't Half King!"

The watchers saw the chief wave his arm and speak with evident arrogance to Edwards, who, however, advanced to the platform and raised his hand to address the Christians.

"Crack!"

A shot rang out from the thicket. Clutching wildly at his breast, the missionary reeled back, staggered, and fell.

"One of those skulkin' redskins has killed Edwards," said Zane. "But, no; he's not dead! He's getting up. Mebbe he ain't hurt bad. By gum! there's Young comin' forward. Of all the fools!"

It was indeed true that Young had faced the Indians. Half King addressed him as he had the other; but Young raised his hand and began speaking.

"Crack!"

Another shot rang out. Young threw up his hands and fell heavily. The missionaries rushed toward him. Mr. Wells ran round the group, wringing his hands as if distracted.

"He's hard hit," hissed Zane, between his teeth. "You can tell that by the way he fell."

Wetzel did not answer. He lay silent and motionless, his long body rigid, and his face like marble.

"There comes the other young feller—Joe's brother. He'll get plugged, too," continued Zane, whispering rather to himself than to his companion. "Oh, I hoped they'd show some sense! It's noble for them to die for Christianity, but it won't do no good. By gum! Heckewelder has pulled him back. Now, that's good judgment!"

Half King stepped before the Christians and addressed them. He held in his hand a black war club, which he wielded as he spoke.

Jonathan's attention was now directed from the maple grove to the hunter beside him. He had heard a slight metallic click, as Wetzel cocked his rifle. Then he saw the black barrel slowly rise.

"Listen, Lew. Mebbe it ain't good sense. We're after Girty, you remember; and it's a long shot from here—full three hundred yards."

"You're right, Jack, you're right," answered Wetzel, breathing hard.

"Let's wait, and see what comes off."

"Jack, I can't do it. It'll make our job harder; but I can't help it. I can put a bullet just over the Huron's left eye, an' I'm goin' to do it."

"You can't do it, Lew; you can't! It's too far for any gun. Wait! Wait!" whispered Jonathan, laying his hand on Wetzel's shoulder.

"Wait? Man, can't you see what the unnamable villain is doin'?"

"What?" asked Zane, turning his eyes again to the glade.

The converted Indians sat with bowed heads. Half King raised his war club and threw it on the ground in front of them.

"He's announcin' the death decree!" hissed Wetzel.

"Well! if he ain't!"

Jonathan looked at Wetzel's face. Then he rose to his knees, as had Wetzel, and tightened his belt. He knew that in another instant they would be speeding away through the forest.

"Lew, my rifle's no good fer that distance. But mebbe yours is. You ought to know. It's not sense, because there's Simon Girty, and there's Jim, the men we're after. If you can hit one, you can another. But go ahead, Lew. Plug that cowardly redskin!"

Wetzel knelt on one knee and thrust the black rifle forward through the fern leaves. Slowly the fatal barrel rose to a level, and became as motionless as the immovable stones.

Jonathan fixed his keen gaze on the haughty countenance of Half King as he stood with folded arms and scornful mien in front of the Christians he had just condemned.

Even as the short, stinging crack of Wetzel's rifle broke the silence, Jonathan saw the fierce expression of Half King's dark face change to one of vacant wildness. His arms never relaxed from their folded position. He fell, as falls a monarch of the forest trees, a dead weight.

Chapter
XXV

"Please do not preach today," said Nell, raising her eyes imploringly to Jim's face.

"Nellie, I must conduct the services as usual. I cannot shirk my duty, nor let these renegades see I fear to face them."

"I have such a terrible feeling. I am afraid. I don't want to be left alone. Please do not leave me."

Jim strode nervously up and down the length of the room. Nell's worn face, her beseeching eyes and trembling hands touched his heart. Rather than almost anything else, he desired to please her, to strengthen her; yet how could he shirk his duty?

"Nellie, what is it you fear?" he asked, holding her hands tightly.

"Oh, I don't know what—everything. Uncle is growing weaker every day. Look at Mr. Young; he is only a shadow of his former self, and his anxiety is wearing Mr. Heckewelder out. He is more concerned than he dares admit. You needn't shake your head, for I know it. Then those Indians who are waiting, waiting—for God only knows what? Worse than all to me, I saw that renegade, that fearful beast who made away with poor dear Kate!"

Nell burst into tears, and leaned sobbing on Jim's shoulder.

"Nell, I've kept my courage only because of you," replied Jim, his voice trembling slightly.

She looked up quickly. Something in the pale face which was bent over her told her that now, if ever, was the time for a woman to forget herself, and to cheer, to inspire those around her.

"I am a silly baby, and selfish!" she cried, freeing herself from his hold. "Always thinking of myself." She turned away and wiped the tears from her eyes. "Go, Jim, do your duty; I'll stand by and help you all a woman can."

The missionaries were consulting in Heckewelder's cabin. Zeisberger had returned that morning, and his aggressive, dominating spirit was just what they needed in an hour like this. He raised the downcast spirits of the ministers.

"Hold the service? I should say we will," he declared, waving his hands. "What have we to be afraid of?"

"I do not know," answered Heckewelder, shaking his head doubtfully. "I do not know what to fear. Girty himself told me he bore us no ill will; but I hardly believe him. All this silence, this ominous waiting perplexes, bewilders me."

"Gentlemen, our duty at least is plain," said Jim, impressively. "The faith of these Christian Indians in us is so absolute that they have no fear. They believe in God, and in us. These threatening savages have failed signally to impress our Christians. If we do not hold the service they will think we fear Girty, and that might have a bad influence."

"I am in favor of postponing the preaching for a few days.

I tell you I am afraid of Girty's Indians, not for myself, for these Christians whom we love so well. I am afraid." Heckewelder's face bore testimony to his anxious dread.

"You are our leader; we have but to obey," said Edwards. "Yet I think we owe it to our converts to stick to our work until we are forced by violence to desist."

"Ah! What form will that violence take?" cried Heckewelder, his face white. "You cannot tell what these savages mean. I fear! I fear!"

"Listen, Heckewelder, you must remember we had this to go through once before," put in Zeisberger earnestly. "In '78 Girty came down on us like a wolf on the fold. He had not so many Indians at his beck and call as now; but he harangued for days, trying to scare us and our handful of Christians. He set his drunken fiends to frighten us, and he failed. We stuck it out and won. He's trying the same game. Let us stand against him, and hold our services as usual. We should trust in God!"

"Never give up!" cried Jim.

"Gentlemen, you are right; you shame me, even though I feel that I understand the situation and its dread possibilities better than any one of you. Whatever befalls we'll stick to our post. I thank you for reviving the spirit in my cowardly heart. We will hold the service today as usual, and to make it more impressive, each shall address the congregation in turn."

"And, if need be, we will give our lives for our Christians," said Young, raising his pale face.

The deep mellow peals of the church bell awoke the slumbering echoes. Scarcely had its melody died away in the forest when a line of Indians issued from the church and marched toward the maple grove. Men, women, youths, maidens and children.

Glickhican, the old Delaware chief, headed the line. His step was firm, his head erect, his face calm in its noble austerity. His followers likewise expressed in their countenances the steadfastness of their belief. The maidens' heads were bowed, but with shyness, not fear. The children were happy, their bright faces expressive of the joy they felt in the anticipation of listening to their beloved teachers.

This procession passed between rows of painted savages, standing immovable with folded arms and somber eyes.

No sooner had the Christians reached the maple grove when from all over the clearing appeared hostile Indians, who took positions near the knoll where the missionaries stood.

Heckewelder's faithful little band awaited him on the platform. The converted Indians seated themselves as usual at the foot of the knoll. The other savages crowded closely on both sides. They carried their weapons and maintained the same silence that had so singularly marked their mood of the last twenty-hour hours. No human skill could have divined their intention. This coldness might be only habitual reserve, and it might be anything else.

Heckewelder approached at the same time that Simon Girty and his band of renegades appeared. With the renegades were Pipe and Half King. These two came slowly across the clearing, passed through the opening in the crowd, and stopped close to the platform.

Heckewelder went hurriedly up to his missionaries. He seemed beside himself with excitement, and spoke with difficulty.

"Do not preach today. I have been warned again," he said, in a low voice.

"Do you forbid it?" inquired Edwards.

"No, no. I have not that authority, but I implore it. Wait, wait until the Indians are in better mood."

Edwards left the group, and, stepping upon the platform, faced the Christians.

At the same moment Half King stalked majestically from before his party. He carried no weapon save a black, knotted war club. A surging forward of the crowd of savages behind him showed the intense interest which his action had aroused. He walked forward until he stood halfway between the platform and the converts. He ran his evil glance slowly over the Christians, and then rested it upon Edwards.

"Half King's orders are to be obeyed. Let the paleface keep his mouth closed," he cried in the Indian tongue. The imperious command came as a thunderbolt from a clear sky. The missionaries behind Edwards stood bewildered, awaiting the outcome.

But Edwards, without a moment's hesitation, calmly lifted his hand and spoke.

"Beloved Christians, we meet today as we have met before, as we hope to meet in—"

"Spang!"

The whistling of a bullet over the heads of the Christians, accompanied the loud report of a rifle. All present plainly heard the leaden missile strike. Edwards wheeled, clutching his side, breathed hard, and then fell heavily without uttering a cry. He had been shot by an Indian concealed in the thicket.

For a moment no one moved, nor spoke. The missionaries were stricken with horror; the converts seemed turned to stone, and the hostile throng waited silently, as they had for hours.

"He's shot! He's shot! Oh, I feared this!" cried Heck-

ewelder, running forward. Thg missionaries followed him.
Edwards was lying on his back, with a bloody hand pressed
to his side.

"Dave, Dave, how is it with you?" asked Heckewelder, in
a voice low with fear.

"Not bad. It's too far out to be bad, but it knocked me
over," answered Edwards, weakly. "Give me—water."

They carried him from the platform and laid him on the
grass under a tree.

Young pressed Edwards's hand; he murmured something
that sounded like a prayer and then walked straight upon the
platform, as he raised his face, which was sublime with a
white light.

"Paleface! Back!" roared Half King, as he waved his war
club.

"You Indian dog! Be silent!"

Young's clear voice rolled out on the quiet air so imperi-
ously, so powerful in its wonderful scorn and passion, that
the hostile savages were overcome by awe, and the Christians thrilled anew with reverential love.

Young spoke again in a voice which had lost its passion,
and was singularly sweet in its richness.

"Beloved Christians, if it is God's will that we must die to
prove our faith, then as we have taught you how to live, so
we can show you how to die—"

"Spang!"

Again a whistling sound came with the bellow of an over-
charged rifle; again the sickening thud of a bullet striking
flesh.

Young fell backwards from the platform.

The missionaries laid him beside Edwards, and then stood
in shuddering silence. A smile shone on Young's pale face; a
stream of dark blood welled from his breast. His lips moved;
he whispered:

"I ask no more—God's will."

Jim looked down once at his brother missionaries; then with blanched face, but resolute and stern, he marched toward the platform.

Heckewelder ran after him and dragged him back.

"No! no! no! My God! Would you be killed? Oh! I tried to prevent this!" cried Heckewelder, wringing his hands.

One long, fierce, exultant yell pealed throughout the grove. It came from those silent breasts in which was pent up hatred; it greeted this action which proclaimed victory over the missionaries.

All eyes turned on Half King. With measured stride he paced to and fro before the Christian Indians.

Neither cowering nor shrinking marked their manner; to a man, to a child, they rose with proud mien, heads erect and eyes flashing. This mighty chief with his bloodthirsty crew could burn the Village of Peace, could annihilate the Christians, but he could never change their hope and trust in God.

"Blinded fools" cried Half King. "The Huron is wise; he tells no lies. Many moons ago he told the Christians they were sitting halfway between two angry gods, who stood with mouths open wide and looking ferociously at each other. If they did not move back out of the road they would be ground to powder by the teeth of one or the other, or both. Half King urged them to leave the peaceful village, to forget the paleface God; to take their horses, and flocks, and return to their homes. The Christians scorned the Huron King's counsel. The sun has set for the Village of Peace. The time has come. Pipe and the Huron are powerful. They will not listen to the paleface God. They will burn the Village of Peace. Death to the Christians!"

Half King threw the black war club with a passionate energy on the grass before the Indians.

They heard this decree of death with unflinching front.

Even the children were quiet. Not a face paled, not an eye was lowered.

Half King cast their doom in their teeth. The Christians eyed him with unspoken scorn.

"My God! My God! It is worse than I thought!" moaned Heckewelder. "Utter ruin! Murder! Murder!"

In the momentary silence which followed his outburst, a tiny cloud of blue-white smoke came from the ferns overhanging a cliff.

"Crack!"

All heard the shot of a rifle; all noticed the difference between its clear, ringing intonation and the loud reports of the other two. All distinctly heard the zip of a bullet as it whistled over their heads.

All? No, not all. One did not hear that speeding bullet. He who was the central figure if this tragic scene, he who had doomed the Christians might have seen that tiny puff of smoke which heralded his own doom, but before the ringing report could reach his ears a small blue hole appeared as if by magic, over his left eye, and pulse, and sense, and life had fled forever.

Half King, great, cruel chieftain, stood still for an instant as if he had been an image of stone; his haughty head lost its erect poise, the fierceness seemed to fade from his dark face, his proud plume waved gracefully as he swayed to and fro, and then fell before the Christians, inert and lifeless.

No one moved; it was as if no one breathed. The superstitious savages awaited fearfully another rifle shot, another lightning stroke, another visitation from the palefaces' God.

But Jim Girty, with a cunning born of his terrible fear, had recognized the ring of that rifle. He had felt the zip of a bullet which could just as readily have found his brain as Half King's. He had stood there as fair a mark as the cruel

Huron, yet the Avenger had not chosen him. Was he reserved for a different fate? Was not such a death too merciful for the frontier Deathshead? He yelled in his craven fear:

"Le vent de la Mort!"

The well-known, dreaded appellation aroused the savages from a fearful stupor into a fierce manifestation of hatred. A tremendous yell rent the air. Instantly the scene changed.

Chapter
XXVI

In the confusion the missionaries carried Young and Edwards into Mr. Wells' cabin. Nell's calm, white face showed that she had expected some such catastrophe as this, but she of all was the least excited. Heckewelder left them at the cabin and hurried away to consult Captain Williamson. While Zeisberger, who was skilled in surgery, attended to the wounded men, Jim barred the heavy door, shut the rude, swinging windows, and made the cabin temporarily a refuge from prowling savages.

Outside the clamor increased. Shrill yells rent the air, long, rolling war cries sounded above all the din. The measured stamp of moccasined feet, the rush of Indians past the cabin, the dull thud of hatchets struck hard into the trees— all attested to the excitement of the savages, and the imminence of terrible danger.

In the front room of Mr. Wells' cabin Edwards lay on a bed, his face turned to the wall, and his side exposed. There was a bloody hole in his white skin. Zeisberger was probing for the bullet. He had no instruments, save those of his own manufacture, and they were darning needles with bent points and a long knife blade ground thin.

"There, I have it," said Zeisberger. "Hold still, Dave. There!" As Edwards moaned Zeisberger drew forth the bloody bullet. "Jim, wash and dress this wound. It isn't bad. Dave will be all right in a couple of days. Now I'll look at George."

Zeisberger hurried into the other room. Young lay with quiet face and closed eyes, breathing faintly. Zeisberger opened the wounded man's shirt and exposed the wound, which was on the right side, rather high up. Nell, who had followed Zeisberger that she might be of some assistance if needed, saw him look at the wound and then turn a pale face away for a second. That hurried shuddering movement of the sober, practical missionary was most significant. Then he bent over Young and inserted one of the probes into the wound. He pushed the steel an inch, two, three, four inches into Young's breast, but the latter neither moved nor moaned. Zeisberger shook his head and finally removed the instrument. He raised the sufferer's shoulder to find the bed saturated with blood. The bullet wound extended completely through the missionary's body, and was bleeding from the back. Zeisberger folded strips of linsey cloth into small pads and bound them tightly over both apertures of the wound.

"How is he?" asked Jim, when the amateur surgeon returned to the other room, and proceeded to wash the blood from his hands.

Zeisberger shook his head gloomily.

"How is George?" whispered Edwards, who had heard Jim's question.

"Shot through the right lung. Human skill cannot aid him! Only God can save."

"Didn't I hear a third shot?" whispered Dave, gazing round with sad, questioning eyes. "Heckewelder?"

"Is safe. He has gone to see Williamson. You did hear a third shot. Half King fell dead with a bullet over his left eye. He had just folded his arms in a grand pose after his death decree to the Christians."

"A judgment of God!"

"It does seem so, but it came in the form of leaden death from Wetzel's unerring rifle. Do you hear all that yelling? Half King's death has set the Indians wild."

There was a gentle knock at the door, and then the word, "Open," in Heckewelder's voice.

Jim unbarred the door. Heckewelder came in carrying over his shoulder what apparently was a sack of meal. He was accompanied by young Christy. Heckewelder put the bag down, opened it, and lifted out a little Indian boy. The child gazed round with fearful eyes.

"Save Benny! Save Benny!" he cried, running to Nell, and she clasped him closely in her arms.

Heckewelder's face was like marble as he asked concerning Edward's condition.

"I'm not badly off," said the missionary with a smile.

"How's George?" whispered Heckewelder.

No one answered him. Zeisberger raised his hands. All followed Heckewelder into the other room, where Young lay in the same position as when first brought in. Heckewelder stood gazing down into the wan face with its terribly significant smile.

"I brought him out here. I persuaded him to come!" whispered Heckewelder. "Oh, Almighty God!" he cried. His voice broke, and his prayer ended with the mute eloquence of clasped hands and uplifted, appealing face.

"Come out," said Zeisberger, leading him into the larger room. The others followed, and Jim closed the door.

"What's to be done?" said Zeisberger, with his practical

common sense. "What did Williamson say? Tell us what you learned?"

"Wait—directly," answered Heckewelder, sitting down and covering his face with his hands. There was a long silence. At length he raised his white face and spoke calmly:

"Gentlemen, the Village of Peace is doomed. I entreated Captain Williamson to help us, but he refused. Said he dared not interfere. I prayed that he would speak at least a word to Girty, but he denied my request."

"Where are the converts?"

"Imprisoned in the church, every one of them except Benny. Mr. Christy and I hid the child in the meal sack and were thus able to get him here. We must save him."

"Save him?" asked Nell, looking from Heckewelder to the trembling Indian boy.

"Nellie, the savages have driven all our Christians into the church, and shut them up there, until Girty and his men shall give the word to complete their fiendish design. The converts asked but one favor—an hour in which to pray. It was granted. The savages intend to murder them all."

"Oh! Horrible! Monstrous!" cried Nell. "How can they be so inhuman?" She lifted Benny up in her arms. "They'll never get you, my boy. We'll save you—I'll save you!" The child moaned and clung to her neck.

"They are scouring the clearing now for Christians, and will search all the cabins. I'm positive."

"Will they come here?" asked Nell, turning her blazing eyes on Heckewelder.

"Undoubtedly. We must try to hide Benny. Let me think; where would be a good place? We'll try a dark corner of the loft."

"No, no," cried Nell.

"Put Benny in Young's bed," suggested Jim.

"No, no," cried Nell.

"Put him in a bucket and let him down in the well," whispered Edwards, who had listened intently to the conversation.

"That's a capital place," said Heckewelder. "But might he not fall out and drown?"

"Tie him in the bucket," said Jim.

"No, no, no," cried Nell.

"But Nellie, we must decide upon a hiding place, and in a hurry."

"I'll save Benny."

"You? Will you stay here to face those men? Jim Girty and Deering are searching the cabins. Could you bear it to see them? You couldn't."

"Oh! No, I believe it would kill me! That man; that beast! will he come here?" Nell grew ghastly pale, and looked as if about to faint. She shrunk in horror at the thought of again facing Girty. "For God's sake, Heckewelder, don't let him see me! Don't let him come in! Don't!"

Even as the imploring voice ceased a heavy thump sounded on the door.

"Who's there?" demanded Heckewelder.

Thump! Thump!

The heavy blows shook the cabin. The pans rattled on the shelves. No answer came from without.

"Quick! Hide Benny! It's as much as our lives are worth to have him found here," cried Heckewelder in a fierce whisper as he darted toward the door.

"All right, all right, in a moment," he called out, fumbling over the bar.

He opened the door a moment later and when Jim Girty and Deering entered he turned to his friends with a dread uncertainty in his haggard face.

Edwards lay on the bed with wide-open eyes staring at

the intruders. Mr. Wells sat with bowed head. Zeisberger calmly whittled a stick, and Jim stood bolt upright, with a hard light in his eyes.

Nell leaned against the side of a heavy table. Wonderful was the change that had transformed her from a timid, appealing, fear-agonized girl to a woman whose only evidences of unusual excitement were the flame in her eyes and the peculiar whiteness of her face.

Benny was gone!

Heckewelder's glance returned to the visitors. He thought he had never seen such brutal, hideous men.

"Wal, I reckon a preacher ain't agoin' to lie. Hev you seen any Injun Christians round here?" asked Girty, waving a heavy sledgehammer.

"Girty, we have hidden no Indians here," answered Heckewelder, calmly.

"Wal, we'll hev a look, anyway," answered the renegade.

Girty surveyed the room with wolfish eyes. Deering was so drunk that he staggered. Both men, in fact, reeked with the vile fumes of rum. Without another word they proceeded to examine the room, by looking into every box, behind a stone oven, and in the cupboard. They drew the bedclothes from the bed, and with a kick demolished a pile of stove wood. Then the ruffians passed into the other apartments, where they could be heard making thorough search. At length both returned to the large room, when Girty directed Deering to climb the ladder leading to the loft, but because Deering was too much under the influence of liquor to do so, he had to go himself. He rummaged around up there for a few minutes, and then came down.

"Wal, I reckon you wasn't lyin' about it," said Girty, with his ghastly leer.

He and his companion started to go out. Deering had stood with bloodshot eyes fixed on Nell while Girty searched the loft, and as they passed the girl on their way to the open air, the renegade looked at Girty as he motioned with his head toward her. His besotted face expressed some terrible meaning.

Girty had looked at Nell when he first entered, but had not glanced twice at her. As he turned now, before going out of the door, he fixed on her his baleful glance. His aspect was more full of meaning than could have been any words. A horrible power, of which he was boastfully conscious, shone from his little, pointed eyes. His mere presence was deadly. Plainly as if he had spoken was the significance of his long gaze. Anyone could have translated that look.

Once before Nell had faced it, and fainted when its dread meaning grew clear to her. But now she returned his gaze with one in which flashed lightning scorn, and repulsion, in which glowed a wonderful defiance.

The cruel face of this man, the boastful barbarity of his manner, the long, dark, bloody history which his presence recalled, was, indeed, terrifying without the added horror of his intent toward her, but now the self-forgetfulness of a true woman sustained her.

Girty and Deering backed out of the door. Heckewelder closed it and dropped the bar in place.

Nell fell over the table with a long, low gasp. Then with one hand she lifted her skirt. Benny walked from under it. His big eyes were bright. The young woman clasped him again in her arms. Then she released him, and, laboring under intense excitement, ran to the window.

"There he goes! Oh, the horrible beast! If I only had a gun and could shoot! Oh, if only I were a man! I'd kill him. To think of poor Kate! Ah! he intends the same for me!"

Suddenly she fell upon the floor in a faint. Mr. Wells and Jim lifted her on the bed beside Edwards, where they endeavored to revive her. It was some moments before she opened her eyes.

Jim sat holding Nell's hand. Mr. Wells again bowed his head. Zeisberger continued to whittle a stick, and Heckewelder paced the floor. Christy stood by with every evidence of sympathy for this distracted group. Outside the clamor increased.

"Just listen!" cried Heckewelder. "Did you ever hear the like? All drunk, crazy, fiendish! They drank every drop of liquor the French traders had. Curses on the vagabond dealers! Rum has made these renegades and savages wild. Oh! my poor, innocent Christians!"

Heckewelder leaned his head against the mantel shelf. He had broken down at last. Racking sobs shook his frame.

"Are you all right again?" asked Jim of Nell.

"Yes."

"I am going out, first to see Williamson, and then the Christians," he said, rising very pale, but calm.

"Don't go!" cried Heckewelder. "I have tried everything. It was all of no use."

"I will go," answered Jim.

"Yes, Jim, go," whispered Nell, looking up into his eyes. It was an earnest gaze in which a faint hope shone.

Jim unbarred the door and went out.

"Wait, I'll go along," cried Zeisberger, suddenly dropping his knife and stick.

As the two men went out a fearful spectacle met their eyes. The clearing was alive with Indians. But such Indians! They were painted demons, maddened by rum. Yesterday they had been silent; if they moved at all it had been with deliberation and dignity. Today they were a yelling, running, bloodseeking mob.

"Awful! Did you ever see human beings like these?" asked Zeisberger.

"No, no!"

"I saw such a frenzy once before, but, of course, only in a small band of savages. Many times have I seen Indians preparing for the warpath, in search of both white men and redskins. They were fierce then, but nothing like this. Every one of these frenzied fiends is honest. Think of that! Every man feels it his duty to murder these Christians. Girty has led up to this by cunning, and now the time is come to let them loose."

"It means death for all."

"I have given up any thought of escaping," said Zeisberger, with the calmness that had characterized his manner since he returned to the village. "I shall try to get into the church."

"I'll join you there as soon as I see Williamson."

Jim walked rapidly across the clearing to the cabin where Captain Williamson had quarters. The frontiersmen stood in groups, watching the savages with an interest which showed little or no concern.

"I want to see Captain Williamson," said Jim to a frontiersman on guard at the cabin door.

"Wal, he's inside," drawled the man.

Jim thought the voice familiar, and he turned sharply to see the sun-burnt features of Jeff Lynn, the old riverman who had taken Mr. Wells' party to Fort Henry.

"Why, Lynn! I'm glad to see you," exclaimed Jim.

"Purty fair to middlin'," answered Jeff, extending his big hand. "Say, how's the other one, your brother as wus called Joe?"

"I don't know. He ran off with Wetzel, was captured by Indians, and when I last heard of him he had married Wingenund's daughter."

"Wal, I'll be doggoned!" Jeff shook his grizzled head and slapped his leg. "I jest knowed he'd raise somethin'!"

"I'm in a hurry. Do you think Captain Williamson will stand still and let all this go on?"

"I'm afeerd so."

Evidently the captain heard the conversation, for he appeared at the cabin door, smoking a long pipe.

"Captain Williamson, I have come to entreat you to save the Christians from this impending massacre."

"I can't do nuthin'," answered Williamson, removing his pipe to puff forth a great cloud of smoke.

"You have eighty men here!"

"If we interfered Pipe would eat us alive in three minutes. You preacher fellows don't understand this thing. You've got Pipe and Girty to deal with. If you don't know them, you'll be better acquainted by sundown."

"I don't care who they are. Drunken ruffians and savages! That's enough. Will you help us? We are men of your own race, and we come to you for help. Can you withhold it?"

"I won't hev nuthin' to do with this bizness. The chiefs hev condemned the village, an' it'll hev to go. If you fellers hed been careful, no white blood would hev been spilled. I advise you all to lay low till it's over."

"Will you let me speak to your men, to try and get them to follow me?"

"Heckewelder asked the same thing. He was persistent, and I took a vote fer him just to show how my men stood. Eighteen of them said they'd follow him; the rest wouldn't interfere."

"Eighteen! My God!" cried Jim, voicing the passion which consumed him. "You are white men, yet you will stand by and see these innocent people murdered! Man, where's your humanity? Your manhood? These converted Indians are savages no longer, they are Christians. Their children are as good, pure, innocent as your own. Can you remain idle and see these little ones murdered?"

Williamson made no answer; the men who had crowded round were equally silent. Not one lowered his head. Many looked at the impassioned missionary; others gazed at the savages who were circling around the trees brandishing their weapons. If any pitied the unfortunate Christians, none showed it. They were indifferent, with the indifference of men hardened to cruel scenes.

Jim understood, at last, as he turned from face to face to find everywhere that same imperturbability. These bordermen were like Wetzel and Jonathan Zane. The only good Indian was a dead Indian. Years of war and bloodshed, of merciless cruelty at the hands of redmen, of the hard, border life had rendered these frontiersmen incapable of compassion for any savage.

Jim no longer restrained himself.

"Bordermen you may be, but from my standpoint, from any man's, from God's, you are a lot of coldly indifferent cowards!" exclaimed Jim, with white, quivering lips. "I understand now. Few of you will risk anything for Indians. You will not believe a savage can be a Christian. You don't care if they are all murdered. Any man among you—any man, I say—would step out before those howling fiends and boldly demand that there be no bloodshed. A courageous leader with a band of determined followers could avert this tragedy. You might readily intimidate yonder horde of drunken demons. Captain Williamson, I am only a minister, far removed from a man of war and leader, as you claim to be, but, sir, I curse you as a miserable coward. If I ever get back to civilization I'll brand this inhuman coldness of yours, as the most infamous and dastardly cowardice that ever disgraced a white man. You are worse than Girty!"

Williamson turned a sickly yellow; he fumbled a second with the handle of his tomahawk, but made no answer. The other bordermen maintained the same careless composure. What to them was the raving of a mad preacher?

Jim saw it and turned, baffled, fiercely angry, and hopeless. As he walked away Jeff Lynn took his arm, and after they were clear of the crowd of frontiersmen he said:

"Young feller, you give him pepper, an' no mistake. An' mebbe you're right from your side of the fence. But you can't see the Injuns from our side. We hunters hevn't much humanity—I reckon that's what you called it—but we've lost so many friends an' relatives, an' heard of so many murders by the reddys that we look on all of 'em as wild varmints that should be killed on sight. Now, mebbe it'll interest you to know I was the feller who took the vote Williamson told you about, an' I did it 'cause I had an interest in you. I wus watchin' you when Edwards and the other missionary got shot. I like grit in a man, an' I seen you had it clear through. So when Heckewelder comes over I talked to the fellers, an' all I could git interested was eighteen, but they wanted to fight simply fer fightin' sake. Now, old Jeff Lynn is your friend. You just lay low until this is over."

Jim thanked the old riverman and left him. He hardly knew which way to turn. He would make one more effort. He crossed the clearing to where the renegades' teepee stood. McKee and Elliott were sitting on a log. Simon Girty stood beside them, his hard, keen, roving eyes on the scene. The missionary was impressed by the white leader. There was a difference in his aspect, a wilder look than the others wore, as if the man had suddenly awakened to the fury of his Indians. Nevertheless the young man went straight toward him.

"Girty, I come—"

"Git out! You meddlin' preacher!" yelled the renegade, shaking his fist at Jim.

Simon Girty was drunk.

Jim turned from the white fiends. He knew his life to them was not worth a pinch of powder.

"Lost! Lost! All lost!" he exclaimed in despair.

As he went toward the church he saw hundreds of savages bounding over the grass, brandishing weapons and whooping fiendishly. They were concentrating around Girty's teepee, where already a great throng had congregated. Of all the Indians to be seen not one walked. They leaped by Jim, and ran over the grass nimble as deer.

He saw the eager, venomous fire in their dusky eyes, and the cruelly clenched teeth like those of wolves when they snarl. He felt the hissing breath of many savages as they raced by him. More than one whirled a tomahawk close by Jim's head and uttered horrible yells in his ear. They were like tigers lusting for blood.

Jim hurried to the church. Not an Indian was visible near the log structure. Even the savage guards had gone. He entered the open door to be instantly struck with reverence and awe.

The Christians were singing.

Miserable and full of sickening dread though Jim was, he could not but realize that the scene before him was one of extraordinary beauty and pathos. The doomed Indians lifted up their voices in song. Never had they sung so feelingly, so harmoniously.

When the song ended Zeisberger, who stood upon a platform, opened his Bible and read:

"In a little wrath I hid my face from thee for a moment, but with everlasting kindness will I have mercy on thee, saith the Lord, thy Redeemer."

In a voice low and tremulous the venerable missionary began his sermon.

The shadow of death hovered over these Christian martyrs; it was reflected in their somber eyes, yet not one was sullen or sad. The children who were too young to understand, but instinctively feeling the tragedy soon to be enacted there, cowered close to their mothers.

Zeisberger preached a touching and impressive, though short, sermon. At its conclusion the whole congregation rose and surrounded the missionary. The men shook his hands, the women kissed them, the children clung to his legs. It was a wonderful manifestation of affection.

Suddenly Glickhican, the old Delaware chief, stepped on the platform, raised his hand, and shouted one Indian word.

A long, low wail went up from the children and youths; the women slowly, meekly bowed their heads. The men, true to the stoicism of their nature and the Christianity they had learned, stood proudly erect awaiting the death that had been decreed.

Glickhican pulled the bell rope.

A deep, mellow tone pealed out.

The sound transfixed all the Christians. No one moved.

Glickhican had given the signal which told the murderers the Christians were ready.

"Come, man, my God! We can't stay here!" cried Jim to Zeisberger.

As they went out both men turned to look their last on the martyrs. The death knell which had rung in the ears of the Christians was to them the voice of God. Stern, dark visages of men and the sweet, submissive faces of women were uplifted with rapt attention. A light seemed to shine from these faces as if the contemplation of God had illumined them.

As Zeisberger and Jim left the church and hurried toward the cabins, they saw the crowd of savages in a black mass round Girty's teepee. The yelling and leaping had ceased.

Heckewelder opened the door. Evidently he had watched for them.

"Jim! Jim!" cried Nell, when he entered the cabin. "Oh-h! I was afraid. Oh! I am glad you're back safe. See, this noble Indian has come to help us."

Wingenund stood calm and erect by the door.

"Chief, what will you do?"

"Wingenund will show you the way to the big river," answered the chieftain, in his deep bass.

"Run away? No, never! That would be cowardly. Heckewelder, you would not go? Nor you, Zeisberger? We may yet be of use; we may yet save some of the Christians."

"Save the yellow-hair," sternly said Wingenund.

"Oh, Jim, you don't understand. The chief has come to warn me of Girty. He intends to take me as he has others, as he did poor Kate. Did you not see the meaning in his eyes today? How they scorched me! Oh! Jim, take me away! Save me! Do not leave me here to that horrible fate! Oh! Jim, take me away!"

"Nell, I will take you," cried Jim, grasping her hands.

"Hurry! There's a blanket full of things I packed for you," said Heckewelder. "Lose no time. Ah! hear that! My heavens! what a yell!" Heckewelder rushed to the door and looked out. "There they go, a black mob of imps; a pack of hungry wolves! Jim Girty is in the lead. How he leaps! How he waves his sledge! He leads the savages toward the church. Oh, it's the end!"

"Benny, where's Benny?" cried Jim hurriedly, lacing the hunting coat he had flung about him.

"Benny's safe. I've hidden him. I'll get him away from here," answered young Christy. "Go! Now's your time. God-speed you!"

"I'm ready," declared Mr. Wells. "I—have—finished!"

"There goes Wingenund! He's running. Follow him, quick! Good-bye! Good-bye! God be with you!" cried Heckewelder.

"Good-bye! Good-bye!"

Jim hurried Nell toward the bushes where Wingenund's tall form could dimly be seen. Mr. Wells followed them. On the edge of the clearing Jim and Nell turned to look back.

They saw a black mass of yelling, struggling, fighting savages crowding around the church.

"Oh Jim, look back! Look back!" cried Nell, holding hard to his hand. "Look back! See if Girty is coming!"

Chapter
XXVII

At last the fugitives breathed free under the gold and red cover of the woods. Never speaking, never looking back, the guide hurried eastward with long strides. His followers were almost forced to run in order to keep him in sight. He had waited at the edge of the clearing for them, and, relieving Jim of the heavy pack, which he swung lightly over his shoulder, he set a pace that was most difficult to maintain. The young missionary half led, half carried Nell over the stones and rough places. Mr. Wells labored in the rear.

"Oh! Jim! Look back! Look back! See if we are pursued!" cried Nell frequently, with many a fearful glance into the dense thickets.

The Indian took a straight course through the woods. He leaped the brooks, climbed the rough ridges, and swiftly trod the glades that were free of windfalls. His hurry and utter disregard for the plain trail left behind, proved his belief in the necessity of placing many miles between the fugitives and the Village of Peace. Evidently they would be followed, and it would be a waste of valuable time to try to conceal their trail. Gradually the ground began to rise, the way became more difficult, but Wingenund never slackened his pace. Nell was strong, supple, and light of foot. She held her own with Jim, but time and time again they were obliged to wait for her uncle. Once he was far behind. Wingenund halted for them at the height of a ridge where the forest was open.

"Ugh!" exclaimed the chieftain, as they finished the ascent. He stretched a long arm toward the sun; his falcon eye gleamed.

Far in the west a great black and yellow cloud of smoke rolled heavenward. It seemed to rise out of the forest and to hang low over the trees; then it soared aloft and grew thinner until it lost its distinct line far in the clouds. The setting sun stood yet an hour high over a distant hill, and burned dark red through the great pall of smoke.

"Fire, of course, but—" Jim did not voice his fear; he looked closely at Wingenund.

The chieftain stood silent a moment as was his wont when addressed. The dull glow of the sun was reflected in the dark eyes that gazed far away over the forest and field.

"Fire," said Wingenund, and it seemed that as he spoke a sterner shadow flitted across his bronzed face. "The sun sets tonight over the ashes of the Village of Peace."

He resumed his rapid march eastward. With never a backward glance the saddened party followed. Nell kept close beside Jim, and the old man tramped after them with bowed head. The sun set, but Wingenund never slackened his stride. Twilight deepened, yet he kept on.

"Indian, we can go no farther tonight, we must rest," cried Jim, as Nell stumbled against him and Mr. Wells panted wearily in the rear.

"Rest soon," replied the chief, and kept on.

Darkness had settled down when Wingenund at last halted. The fugitives could see little in the gloom, but they heard the music of running water and felt soft moss beneath their feet.

They sank wearily down upon a projecting stone. The moss was restful to their tired limbs. Opening the pack they found food with which to satisfy the demands of hunger. Then, close under the stone, the fugitives sank into slumber while the watchful Indian stood silent and motionless.

Jim thought he had just closed his eyes when he felt a gentle pressure on his arm.

"Day is here," said the Indian.

Jim opened his eyes to see the bright red sun crimsoning the eastern hills and streaming gloriously over the colored forests. He raised himself on his elbow to look around. Nell was still asleep. The blanket was tucked close to her chin. Her chestnut hair was tumbled like a schoolgirl's; she looked as fresh and sweet as the morning.

"Nell, Nell, wake up," said Jim, thinking the while how he would love to kiss those white eyelids.

Nell's eyes opened wide; a smile lay deep in their hazel shadows.

"Where am I? Oh, I remember," she cried, sitting up. "Oh, Jim, I had such a sweet dream. I was at home with Mother and Kate. Oh, to wake to find it all a dream, I am fleeing for life. But, Jim we are safe, are we not?"

"Another day, and we'll be safe."

"Let us fly," she cried, leaping up and shaking out her crumpled skirt. "Uncle, come!"

Mr. Wells lay quietly with his mild blue eyes smiling up at her. He neither moved nor spoke.

"Eat, drink," said the chief, opening the pack.

"What a beautiful place!" exclaimed Nell, taking the bread and meat handed to her. "This is a lovely little glade. Look at those golden flowers, the red and purple leaves, the brown shining moss, and those lichen-covered stones. Why! someone had camped here. See the little cave, the screens of plaited ferns, and the stone fireplace."

"It seems to me this dark spring and those gracefully spreading branches are familiar," said Jim.

"Beautiful Spring," interposed Wingenund.

"Yes, I know this place," cried Nell excitedly. "I remember this glade though it was moonlight when I saw it. Here Wetzel rescued me from Girty."

"Nell, you're right," replied Jim. "How strange we should run across this place again."

Strange fate, indeed, which had brought them again to Beautiful Spring! It was destined that the great scenes of their lives were to be enacted in this mossy glade.

"Come, Uncle, you are lazy," cried Nell, a touch of her old roguishness making playful her voice.

Mr. Wells lay still, and smiled up at them.

"You are not ill?" cried Nell, seeing for the first time how pallid was his face.

"Dear Nellie, I am not ill. I do not suffer, but I am dying," he answered, again with that strange, sweet smile.

"Oh-h-h!" breathed Nell, falling on her knees.

"No, no, Mr. Wells, you are only weak; you will be all right again soon," cried Jim.

"Jim, Nellie, I have known all night. I have lain here wakeful. My heart never was strong. It gave out yesterday, and now it is slowly growing weaker. Put your hand on my breast. Feel. Ah! you see! My life is flickering. God's will be done. I am content. My work is finished. My only regret is that I brought you out to this terrible borderland. But I did not know. If only I could see you safe from the peril of this wilderness, at home, happy, married."

Nell bent over him blinded by her tears, unable to see or speak, crushed by this last overwhelming blow. Jim sat on the other side of the old missionary, holding his hand. For many moments neither spoke. They glanced at the pale face, watching with eager, wistful eyes for a smile, or listening for a word.

"Come," said the Indian.

Nell silently pointed toward her uncle.

"He is dying," whispered Jim to the Indian.

"Go, leave me," murmured Mr. Wells. "You are still in danger."

"We'll not leave you," cried Jim.

"No, no, no," sobbed Nell, bending over to kiss him.

"Nellie, may I marry you to Jim?" whispered Mr. Wells into her ear. "He has told me how it is with him. He loves you, Nellie. I'd die happier knowing I'd left you with him."

Even at that moment, with her heart almost breaking, Nell's fair face flushed.

"Nell, will you marry me?" asked Jim, softly. Low though it was, he had heard Mr. Wells' whisper.

Nell stretched a little trembling hand over her uncle to Jim, who enclosed it in his own. Her eyes met his. Through her tears shone faintly a light, which, but for the agony that made it dim, would have beamed radiant.

"Find the place," said Mr. Wells, handing Jim a Bible. It was the one he always carried in his pocket.

With trembling hand Jim turned the leaves. At last he found the lines and handed the book back to the old man.

Simple, sweet, and sad was that marriage service. Nell and Jim knelt with hands clasped over Mr. Wells. The old missionary's voice was faint; Nell's responses were low, and Jim answered with deep and tender feeling. Beside them stood Wingenund, a dark, magnificent figure.

"There! May God bless you!" murmured Mr. Wells with a happy smile, closing the Bible.

"Nell, my wife!" whispered Jim, kissing her hand.

"Come!" broke in Wingenund's voice, deep, strong, like that of a bell.

Not one of them had observed the chief as he stood erect, motionless, poised like a stag scenting the air. His dark eyes seemed to pierce the purple-golden forest, his keen ear seemed to drink in the singing of the birds and the gentle rustling of leaves. Native to these haunts as were the wild creatures, they were no quicker than the Indian to feel the approach of foes. The breeze had borne faint, suspicious sounds.

"Keep—the Bible," said Mr. Wells, "remember—its—words." His hand closely clasped Nell's, and then suddenly loosened. His pallid face was lighted by a meaning, tender smile which slowly faded—faded, and was gone. The venerable head fell back. The old missionary was dead.

Nell kissed the pale, cold brow, and then rose, half dazed and shuddering. Jim was vainly trying to close the dead man's eyes. She could no longer look. On rising she found herself near the Indian chief. He took her fingers in his great hand, and held them with a strong, warm pressure. Strangely thrilled, she looked up at Wingenund. His somber eyes, fixed piercingly on the forest, and his dark stern face, were, as always, inscrutable. No compassion shone there; no emotion unbefitting a chieftain would ever find expression in that cold face, but Nell felt a certain tenderness in this Indian, a response in his great heart. Felt it so surely, so powerfully that she leaned her head against him. She knew he was her friend.

"Come," said the chief once more. He gently put Nell aside before Jim arose from his sad task.

"We cannot leave him unburied," expostulated Jim.

Wingenund dragged aside a large stone which formed one wall of the cavern. Then he grasped a log which was half covered by dirt, and, exerting his great strength, pulled it from its place. There was a crash, a rumble, the jar of a heavy weight striking the earth, then the rattling of gravel, and, before Nell and Jim realized what had happened, the great rock forming the roof of the cavern slipped down the bank followed by a small avalanche. The cavern was completely covered. Mr. Wells was buried. A mossy stone marked the old missionary's grave.

Nell and Jim were lost in wonder and awe.

"Ugh!" cried the chief, looking toward the opening in the glade.

Fearfully Nell and Jim turned, to be appalled by four naked, painted savages standing with levelled rifles. Behind them stood Deering and Jim Girty.

"Oh, God! We are lost! Lost! Lost!" exclaimed Jim, unable to command himself. Hope died in his heart.

No cry issued from Nell's white lips. She was dazed by this final blow. Having endured so much, this last misfortune, apparently the ruin of her life, brought no added suffering, only a strange, numb feeling.

"Ah-huh! Thought you'd give me the slip, eh?" croaked Girty, striding forward, and as he looked at Wingenund his little yellow eyes flared like flint. "Does a wolf befriend Girty's captives? Chief, you hev led me a hard chase."

Wingenund deigned no reply. He stood as he did so often, still and silent, with folded arms, and a look that was haughty, unresponsive.

The Indians came forward into the glade, and one of them quickly bound Jim's hands behind his back. The savages wore a wild, brutish look. A feverish ferocity, very near akin to insanity, possessed them. They were not quiet a moment, but ran here and there, for no apparent reason, except, possibly, to keep in action with the raging fire in their hearts. The cleanliness which characterized the normal Indian was absent in them; their scant buckskin dress was bedragged and stained. They were still drunk with rum and the lust for blood. Murder gleamed from the glance of their eyes.

"Jake, come over here," said Girty to his renegade friend. "Ain't she a prize?"

Girty and Deering stood before the poor, stricken girl and gloated over her fair beauty. She stood as when first transfixed by the horror from which she had been fleeing. Her pale face was lowered, her hands clenched tightly in the folds of her skirt.

Never before had two such coarse, cruel fiends as Deering and Girty encumbered the earth. Even on the border, where the best men were bad, they were the worst. Deering was yet drunk, but Girty had recovered somewhat from the effects of the rum he had absorbed. The former rolled his big eyes and nodded his shaggy head. He was passing judgment, from his point of view, on the fine points of the girl.

"She cer'aintly is," he declared, with a grin. "She's a little beauty. Beats any I ever seen!"

Jim Girty stroked his sharp chin with dirty fingers. His yellow eyes, his burnt saffron skin, his hooked nose, his thin lips—all his evil face seemed to shine with an evil triumph. To look at him was painful. To have him gaze at her was enough to drive any woman mad.

Dark stains spotted the bright frills of his gaudy dress, his buckskin coat and leggings, and dotted his white eagle plumes. Dark stains, horribly suggestive, covered him from head to foot. Bloodstains! The innocent blood of Christians crimsoned his renegade's body, and every dark red blotch cried murder.

"Girl, I burned the Village of Peace to git you," growled Girty. "Come here!"

With a rude grasp that tore open her dress, exposing her beautiful white shoulder and bosom, the ruffian pulled her toward him. His face was transfixed with a fierce joy, a brutal passion.

Deering looked on with a drunken grin while his renegade friend hugged the almost dying girl. The Indians paced the glade with short strides like leashed tigers. The young missionary lay on the moss with closed eyes. He could not endure the sight of Nell in Girty's arms.

No one noticed Wingenund. He stood back a little, half screened by drooping branches. Once again the chief's dark eyes gleamed, his head turned a trifle aside, and, standing in the statuesque position habitual with him when resting, he listened, as one who hears mysterious sounds. Suddenly his keen glance was riveted on the ferns above the low cliff. He had seen their graceful heads quivering. The two blinding sheets of flame burst from the ferns.

Spang! Spang!

Two rifle reports thundered through the glade. Two Indians staggered and fell in their tracks—dead without a cry.

A huge yellow body, spread out like a panther in his spring, descended with a crash upon Deering and Girty.

The girl fell away from the renegade as he went down with a shrill screech, dragging Deering with him. Instantly began a terrific, whirling, wrestling struggle.

A few feet farther down the cliff another yellow body came crashing down to alight with a thud, to bound erect, to rush forward swift as a leaping deer.

The two remaining Indians had only time to draw their weapons before this lithe, threatening form whirled upon them. Shrill cries, hoarse yells, the clash of steel and dull blows mingled together. One savage went down, twisted over, writhed, and lay still. The other staggered, warded off lightninglike blows until one passed under his guard and crashed dully on his head. Then he reeled and rose again, but only to have his skull cloven by a bloody tomahawk.

The victor darted toward the whirling mass.

"Lew, shake him loose! Let him go!" yelled Jonathan Zane, swinging his bloody weapon.

High above Zane's cry, Deering's shouts and curses, Girty's shrieks of fear and fury, above the noise of wrestling bodies and dull blows, rose a deep, booming roar.

It was Wetzel's awful cry of vengeance.

"Shake him loose!" yelled Jonathan.

Baffled, he ran wildly around the wrestlers. Time and time again his gory tomahawk was raised only to be lowered. He found no opportunity to strike. Girty's ghastly countenance gleamed at him from the whirl of legs and arms and bodies. Then Wetzel's dark face, lighted by merciless eyes, took its place, and that gave way to Deering's broad features. The men being clad alike in buckskin, and their motions so rapid, prevented Zane from lending a helping hand.

Suddenly Deering was propelled from the mass as if by a catapult. His body straightened as it came down with a heavy thud. Zane pounced upon it with catlike quickness. Once more he swung aloft the bloody hatchet; then once more he lowered it, for there was no need to strike. The renegade's side was torn open from shoulder to hip. A deluge of blood poured out upon the moss. Deering choked, a bloody froth formed on his lips. His fingers clutched at nothing. His eyes rolled violently and then were fixed in an awful stare.

The girl lying so quiet in the woods near the old hut was avenged!

Jonathan turned again to Wetzel and Girty, not with any intention to aid the hunter, but simply to witness the end of the struggle.

Without the help of the powerful Deering, how pitifully weak was the Deathshead of the frontier in the hands of the Avenger!

Jim Girty's tomahawk was thrown in one direction and

his knife in another. He struggled vainly in the iron grip that held him.

Wetzel rose to his feet clutching the renegade. With his left arm, which had been bared in the fight, he held Girty by the front of his buckskin shirt, and dragged him to that tree which stood alone in the glade. He pushed him against it and held him there.

The white dog leaped and snarled around the prisoner.

Girty's hands pulled and tore at the powerful arm which forced him hard against the beech. It was a brown arm, and huge with its bulging, knotted, rigid muscles. A mighty arm, strong as the justice which ruled it.

"Girty, thy race is run!" Wetzel's voice cut the silence like a steel whip.

The terrible, ruthless smile, the glittering eyes of doom seemed literally to petrify the renegade.

The hunter's right arm rose slowly. The knife in his hand quivered as if with eagerness. The long blade, dripping with Deering's blood, pointed toward the hilltop.

"Look thar! See 'em! Thar's yer friends!" cried Wetzel.

On the dead branches of trees standing far above the hilltops, were many great, dark birds. They sat motionless as if waiting.

"Buzzards! Buzzards!" hissed Wetzel.

Girty's ghastly face became an awful thing to look upon. No living countenance ever before expressed such fear, such horror, such agony. He foamed at the mouth, he struggled, he writhed. With a terrible fascination he watched that quivering, dripping blade, now poised high.

Wetzel's arm swung with the speed of a shooting star. He drove the blade into Girty's groin, through flesh and bone, hard and fast into the tree. He nailed the renegade to the beech, there to await his lingering doom.

"Ah-h! Ah-h! Ah-h!" shrieked Girty, in cries of agony. He fumbled and pulled at the heft of the knife, but could not loosen it. He beat his breast, he tore his hair. His screams were echoed from the hilltop as if in mockery.

The white dog stood near, his hair bristling, his teeth snapping.

The dark birds sat on the dead branches above the hilltop, as if waiting for their feast.

Chapter
XXVIII

Zane turned and cut the young missionary's bonds. Jim ran to where Nell was lying on the ground and tenderly raised her head, calling to her that they were saved. Zane bathed the girl's pale face. Presently she sighed and opened her eyes.

Then Zane looked from the statuelike form of Wingenund to the motionless figure of Wetzel. The chief stood erect with his eyes on the distant hills. Wetzel remained with folded arms, his cold eyes fixed upon the writhing, moaning renegade.

"Lew, look here," said Zane, unhesitatingly, and pointed toward the chief.

Wetzel quivered as if sharply stung; the cold glitter in his eyes changed to lurid fire. With upraised tomahawk he bounded across the brook.

"Lew, wait a minute!" yelled Zane.

"Wetzel! wait, wait!" cried Jim, grasping the hunter's arm; but the latter flung him off, as the wind tosses a straw.

"Wetzel, wait, for God's sake, wait!" screamed Nell. She had risen at Zane's call, and now saw the deadly resolve in the hunter's eyes. Fearlessly she flung herself in front of him;

bravely she risked her life before his mad rush; frantically she threw her arms around him and clung to his hands desperately.

Wetzel halted; frenzied as he was at sight of his foe, he could not hurt a woman.

"Girl, let go!" he panted, and his broad breast heaved.

"No, no, no! Listen, Wetzel, you must not kill the chief. He is a friend."

"He is my great foe!"

"Listen, oh! please listen!" pleaded Nell. "He warned me to flee from Girty; he offered to guide us to Fort Henry. He has saved my life. For my sake, Wetzel, do not kill him! Don't let me be the cause of his murder! Wetzel, Wetzel, lower your arm, drop your hatchet. For pity's sake do not spill more blood. Wingenund is a Christian!"

Wetzel stepped back breathing heavily. His white face resembled chiseled marble. With those little hands at his breast he hesitated in front of the chief he had hunted for so many long years.

"Would you kill a Christian?" pleaded Nell, her voice sweet and earnest.

"I reckon not, but this Injun ain't one," replied Wetzel slowly.

"Put away your hatchet. Let me have it. Listen, and I will tell you, after thanking you for this rescue. Do you know of my marriage? Come, please listen! forget for a moment your enmity. Oh! you must be merciful! Brave men are always merciful!"

"Injun, are you a Christian?" hissed Wetzel.

"Oh! I know he is! I know he is!" cried Nell, still standing between Wetzel and the chief.

Wingenund spoke no word. He did not move. His falcon eyes gazed tranquilly at his white foe. Christian or pagan, he would not speak one word to save his life.

"Oh! tell him you are a Christian," cried Nell, running to the chief.

"Yellow-hair, the Delaware is true to his race."

As he spoke gently to Nell a noble dignity shone upon his dark face.

"Injun, my back bears the scars of your braves' whips," hissed Wetzel, once more advancing.

"Deathwind, your scars are deep, but the Delaware's are deeper," came the calm reply. "Wingenund's heart bears two scars. His son lies under the moss and ferns; Deathwind killed him; Deathwind alone knows his grave. Wingenund's daughter, the delight of his waning years, freed the Delaware's great foe, and betrayed her father. Can the Christian God tell Wingenund of his child?"

Wetzel shook like a tree in a storm. Justice cried out in the Indian's deep voice. Wetzel fought for mastery of himself.

"Delaware, your daughter lays there, with her lover," said Wetzel firmly, and pointed into the spring.

"Ugh!" exclaimed the Indian, bending over the dark pool. He looked long into its murky depths. Then he thrust his arm down into the brown water.

"Deathwind tells no lie," said the chief, calmly, and pointed toward Girty. The renegade had ceased struggling, his head was bowed upon his breast. "The white serpent has stung the Delaware."

"What does it mean?" cried Jim.

"Your brother Joe and Whispering Winds lie in the spring," answered Jonathan Zane. "Girty murdered them, and Wetzel buried the two there."

"Oh, is it true?" cried Nell.

"True, lass," whispered Jim, brokenly, holding out his arms to her. Indeed, he needed her strength as much as she needed his. The girl gave one shuddering glance at the spring, and then hid her face on her husband's shoulder.

"Delaware, we are sworn foes," cried Wetzel.

"Wingenund asks no mercy."

"Are you a Christian?"

"Wingenund is true to his race."

"Delaware, begone! Take these weapons an' go. When your shadow falls shortest on the ground, Deathwind starts on your trail."

"Deathwind is the great white chief; he is the great Indian foe; he is as sure as the panther in his leap; as swift as the wild goose in his northern flight. Wingenund never felt fear." The chieftain's sonorous reply rolled through the quiet glade. "If Deathwind thirsts for Wingenund's blood, let him spill it now, for when the Delaware goes into the forest his trail will fade."

"Begone!" roared Wetzel. The fever for blood was once more rising within him.

The chief picked up some weapons of the dead Indians and with a haughty stride stalked from the glade.

"Oh, Wetzel, thank you, I knew—" Nell's voice broke as she faced the hunter. She recoiled from this changed man.

"Come, we'll go," said Jonathan Zane. "I'll guide you to Fort Henry." He lifted the pack, and led Nell and Jim out of the glade.

They looked back once to picture forever in their minds the lovely spot with its ghastly quiet bodies, the dark, haunting spring, the renegade nailed to the tree, and the tall figure of Wetzel as he watched his shadow on the ground.

When Wetzel also had gone, only two living creatures remained in the glade—the doomed renegade and the white dog. The gaunt beast watched the man with hungry, mad eyes.

A long moan wailed through the forest. It swelled mournfully on the air and died away. The doomed man heard it. He raised his ghastly face; his dulled senses seemed to revive. He gazed at the stiffening bodies of the Indians, at the gory corpse of Deering, at the savage eyes of the dog.

Suddenly life seemed to surge strong within him.

"Hell's fire! I'm not done fer yet," he gasped. "This damned knife can't kill me; I'll pull it out."

He worked at the heavy knife hilt. Awful curses passed his lips, but the blade did not move. Retribution had spoken his doom.

Suddenly he saw a dark shadow moving along the sunlit ground. It swept past him. He looked up to see a great bird with wide wings sailing far above. He saw another still higher, and then a third. He looked at the hilltop. The quiet, black birds had taken wing. They were floating slowly, majestically upward. He watched their graceful flight. How easily they swooped in wide circles. He remembered that they had fascinated him when a boy, long, long ago, when he had a home. Where was that home? He had one once. Ah, the long, cruel years have rolled back. A youth blotted out by evil returned. He saw a little cottage, he saw the old Virginia homestead, he saw his brothers and his mother.

"Ah-h!" A cruel agony tore his heart. He leaned hard against the knife. With the pain the present returned, but the past remained. All his youth, all his manhood flashed before him. The long, bloody, merciless years faced him, and his crimes crushed upon him with awful might.

Suddenly a rushing sound startled him. He saw a great bird swoop down and graze the treetops. Another followed, and another, and then a flock of them. He saw their gray, spotted breasts and hooked beaks.

"Buzzards," he muttered, darkly eyeing the dead savages. The carrion birds were swooping to their feast.

"By God! He's nailed me fast for buzzards!" he screamed in sudden, awful frenzy. "Nailed fast! Ah-h! Ah-h! Ah-h! Eaten alive by buzzards! Ah-h! Ah-h! Ah-h!"

He shrieked until his voice failed, and then he gasped.

Again the buzzards swooped overhead, this time brushing the leaves. One, a great grizzled bird, settled upon a limb of the giant oak and stretched its long neck. Another alighted beside him. Others sailed round and round the dead tree top.

The leader arched his wings, and with a dive swooped into the glade. He alighted near Deering's dead body. He was a dark, uncanny bird, with long, scraggy, bare neck, a wreath of white, grizzled feathers, a cruel, hooked beak, and cold eyes.

The carrion bird looked around the glade and put a great claw on the dead man's breast.

"Ah-h! Ah-h!" shrieked Girty. His agonized yell of terror and horror echoed mockingly from the wooded bluff.

The huge buzzard flapped his wings and flew away, but soon returned to his gruesome feast. His followers, made bold by their leader, floated down into the glade. Their black feathers shone in the sun. They hopped over the moss; they stretched their grizzled necks and turned their heads sideways.

Girty was sweating blood. It trickled from his ghastly face. All the suffering and horror he had caused in all his long career was as nothing to that which then rended him. He, the renegade, the white Indian, the Deathshead of the frontier, panted and prayed for a merciful breath. He was exquisitely alive. He was human.

Presently the huge buzzard, the leader, raised his hoary head. He saw the man nailed to the tree. The bird bent his head wisely to one side and then lightly lifted himself into the air. He sailed round the glade, over the fighting buzzards, over the spring, and over the doomed renegade. He flew out of the glade, and in again. He swooped close to Girty. His broad wings scarcely moved as he sailed along.

Girty tried to strike the buzzard as he sailed close by, but his arm fell useless. He tried to scream, but his voice failed.

Slowly the buzzard king sailed by and returned. Every time he swooped a little nearer and bent his long, scraggy neck.

Suddenly he swooped down, light and swift as a hawk: his wide wings fanned the air; he poised under the tree and then fastened sharp talons in the doomed man's breast.

Chapter
XXIX

The fleeting human instinct of Wetzel had given way to the habit of years. His merciless quest for many days had been to kill the frontier fiend. Now that it had been accomplished, he turned his vengeance into its accustomed channel, and once more become the ruthless Indian slayer.

A fierce, tingling joy surged through him as he struck the Delaware's trail. Wingenund had made little or no effort to conceal his tracks; he had gone northwest, straight as a crow flies, toward the Indian encampment. He had a start of sixty minutes, and it would require six hours of rapid traveling to gain the Delaware town.

"Reckon he'll make fer home," muttered Wetzel, following the trail with all possible speed.

The hunter's method of trailing an Indian was singular. Intuition played as great a part as sight. He seemed always to divine his victim's intention. Once on the trail he was as hard to shake off as a bloodhound. Yet he did not, by any means, always stick to the Indian's footsteps. With Wetzel the direction was of the greatest importance.

For half a mile he closely followed the Delaware's plainly

marked trail. Then he stopped to take a quick survey of the forest before him. He abruptly left the trail, and, breaking into a run, went through the woods as fleetly and noiselessly as a deer, running for a quarter of a mile, when he stopped to listen. All seemed well, for he lowered his head, and walked slowly along examining the moss and leaves. Presently he came up a little open space where the soil was a sandy loam. He bent over, then rose quickly. He had come upon the Indian's trail. Cautiously he moved forward, stopping every moment to listen. In all the close pursuits of his maturer years he had never been a victim of that most cunning of Indian tricks, an ambush. He relied solely on his ear to learn if foes were close by. The wild creatures of the forest were his informants. As soon as he heard any change in their twittering, humming or playing—whichever way they manifested their joy or fear of life—he became as hard to see, as difficult to hear as a creeping snake.

The Delaware's trail led to a rocky ridge and there disappeared. Wetzel made no effort to find the chief's footprints on the flinty ground, but halted a moment and studied the ridge, the lay of the land around, a ravine on one side, and a dark impenetrable forest on the other. He was calculating his chances of finding the Delaware's trail far on the other side. Indian woodcraft, subtle, wonderful as it may be, is limited to each Indian's ability. Savages, as well as other men, were born unequal. One might leave a faint trail through the forest, while another could be readily traced, and a third, more cunning and skillful than his fellows, have flown under the shady trees, for all the trail he left. But redmen followed the same methods of woodcraft from tradition, as Wetzel had learned after long years of study and experience.

And now, satisfied that he had divined the Delaware's intention, he slipped down the bank of the ravine, and once more broke into a run. He leaped lightly, sure-footed as a goat, from stone to stone, over fallen logs, and the brawling brook. At every turn of the ravine, at every open place, he stopped to listen.

Arriving on the other side of the ridge, he left the ravine and passed along the edge of the rising ground. He listened to the birds, and searched the grass and leaves. He found not the slightest indication of a trail where he had expected to find one. He retraced his steps patiently, carefully scrutinized every inch of the ground. But it was all in vain. Wingenund had begun to show his savage cunning. In his warrior days for long years no chief could rival him. His boast had always been that, when Wingenund sought to elude his pursuers, his trail faded among the moss and the ferns.

Wetzel, calm, patient, resourceful, deliberated a moment. The Delaware had not crossed this rock ridge. He had been cunning enough to make his pursuer think such was his intention. The hunter hurried to the eastern end of the ridge for no other reason than apparently that course was the one the savage had the least reason to take. He advanced hurriedly because every moment was precious. Not a crushed blade of grass, a brushed leaf, an overturned pebble nor a snapped twig did he find. He saw that he was getting near to the side of the ridge where the Delaware's trail had abruptly ended. Ah! what was there? A twisted bit of fern, with the drops of dew brushed off. Bending beside the fern, Wetzel examined the grass; it was not crushed. A small plant with triangular leaves of dark green lay under the fern. Breaking off one of these leaves, he exposed its lower side to the light. The fine, silvery hair or fuzz that grew upon the leaf had been crushed. Wetzel knew that an Indian could tread so softly as not to break the springy grass blades, but the underside of one of these leaves, if a man steps on it, always betrays his passage through the woods. To keen eyes this leaf showed that it had been bruised by a soft moccasin. Wetzel had located the trail but was still ignorant of its direction. Slowly he traced the shaken ferns and bruised leaves down over the side of the ridge, and at last, near a stone, he found a moccasin print in the moss. It pointed east. The Delaware was traveling in exactly the opposite direction to that which he should be going. He was, moreover, exercising wonderful sagacity in hiding his trail. This, however, did not trouble Wetzel, for if it took him a long time to find the trail, certainly the Delaware had expended as much, or more, in choosing hard ground, logs or rocks on which to tread.

Wetzel soon realized that his own cunning was matched. He trusted no more to his intuitive knowledge, but stuck close to the trail, as a hungry wolf holds to the scent of his quarry.

The Delaware's trail led over logs, stones and hardbaked ground, up stony ravines and over cliffs. The wily chief used all of his old skill; he walked backward over moss and sand where his footprints showed plainly; he leaped wide fissures in stony ravines, and then jumped back again; he let himself down over ledges by branches; he crossed creeks and gorges by swinging himself into trees and climbing from one to another; he waded brooks where he found hard bottom, and avoided swampy, soft ground.

With dogged persistence and tenacity of purpose Wetzel stuck to this gradually fading trail. Every additional rod he was forced to go more slowly, and take more time in order to find any sign of his enemy's passage through the forests. One thing struck him forcibly. Wingenund was gradually circling to the southwest, a course that took him farther and farther from the Delaware encampment.

Slowly it dawned upon Wetzel that the chief could hardly have any reason for taking this circling course save that of pride and savage joy in misleading, in fooling the foe of the

Delawares, in deliberately showing Deathwind that there was one Indian who could laugh at and lose him in the forests. To Wetzel this was bitter as gall. To be led a wild-goose chase! His fierce heart boiled with fury. His dark, keen eyes sought the grass and moss with terrible earnestness. Yet in spite of the anger that increased to the white heat of passion, he became aware of some strange sensation creeping upon him. He remembered that the Delaware had offered his life. Slowly, like a shadow, Wetzel passed up and down the ridges, through the brown and yellow aisles of the forest, over the babbling brooks, out upon the golden-flecked fields—always close on the trail.

At last in an open part of the forest, where a fire had once swept away the brush and smaller timber, Wetzel came upon the spot where the Delaware's trail ended.

There in the soft, black ground was a moccasin print. The forest was not dense; there was plenty of light; no logs, stones or trees were near, and yet over all that glade no further evidence of the Indian's trail was visible.

It faded there as the great chief had boasted it would.

Wetzel searched the burnt ground; he crawled on his hands and knees; again and again he went over the surroundings. The fact that one moccasin print pointed west and the other east, showing that the Delaware had turned in his tracks, was the most baffling thing that had ever crossed the hunter in all his wild wanderings.

For the first time in many years he had failed. He took his defeat hard, because he had been successful for so long he thought himself almost infallible, and because the failure lost him the opportunity to kill his great foe. In his passion he cursed himself for being so weak as to let the prayer of a woman turn him from his life's purpose.

With bowed head and slow, dragging steps he made his way westward. The land was strange to him, but he knew he was going toward familiar ground. For a time he walked quietly, all the time the fierce fever in his veins slowly abating. Calm he always was, except when that unnatural lust for Indians' blood overcame him.

On the summit of a high ridge he looked around to ascertain his bearings. He was surprised to find he had traveled in a circle. A mile or so below him arose the great oak tree which he recognized as the landmark of Beautiful Spring. He found himself standing on the hill, under the very dead tree to which he had directed Girty's attention a few hours previous.

With the idea that he would return to the spring to scalp the dead Indians, he went directly toward the big oak tree. Once out of the forest a wide plain lay between him and the wooded knoll which marked the glade of Beautiful Spring. He crossed this stretch of verdant meadowland, and entered the copse.

Suddenly he halted. His keen sense of the usual harmony of the forest, with its innumerable quiet sounds, had received a severe shock. He sank into the tall weeds and listened. Then he crawled a little further. Doubt became certain. A single note of an oriole warned him, and it needed not the quick notes of a catbird to tell him that near at hand, somewhere, was human life.

Once more Wetzel became a tiger. The hot blood leaped from his heart, firing all his veins and nerves. But calmly noiselessly, certain, cold, deadly as a snake he began the familiar crawling method of stalking his game.

On, on under the briars and thickets, across the hollows full of yellow leaves, up over stony patches of ground to the fern-covered cliff overhanging the glade he glided—lithe, sinuous, a tiger in movement and in heart.

He parted the long, graceful ferns and gazed with glittering eyes down into the beautiful glade.

He saw not the shining spring nor the purple moss, nor the ghastly white bones all that buzzards had left of the dead—nor anything, save a solitary Indian standing erect in the glade.

There, within range of his rifle, was his great Indian foe, Wingenund.

Wetzel sank back into the ferns to still the furious exultations which almost consumed him during the moment when he marked his victim. He lay there breathing hard, gripping tightly his rifle, slowly mastering the passion that alone of all things might render his aim futile.

For him it was the third great moment of his life, the last of three moments in which the Indian's life had belonged to him. Once before he had seen that dark, powerful face over the sights of his rifle, and he could not shoot because his one shot must be for another. Again had that lofty, haughty figure stood before him, calm, disdainful, arrogant, and he yielded to a woman's prayer.

The Delaware's life was his to take, and he swore he would have it! He trembled in the ecstasy of his triumphant passion; his great muscles rippled and quivered, for the moment entirely beyond his control. Then his passion calmed, Such power for vengeance had he that he could almost still the very beats of his heart to make sure and deadly his fatal aim. Slowly he raised himself; his eyes of cold fire glittered; slowly he raised the black rifle.

Wingenund stood erect in his old, grand pose, with folded arms, but his eyes, instead of being fixed on the distant hills, were lowered to the ground.

An Indian girl, cold as marble, lay at his feet. Her garments were wet, and clung to her slender form. Her sad face was frozen into an eternal rigidity.

By her side was a newly dug grave.

The bead on the front sight of the rifle had hardly covered

the chief's dark face when Wetzel's eye took in these other details. He had been so absorbed in his purpose that he did not dream of the Delaware's reason for returning to the Beautiful Spring.

Slowly Wetzel's forefinger stiffened; slowly he lowered the black rifle.

Wingenund had returned to bury Whispering Winds.

Wetzel's teeth clenched, an awful struggle tore his heart. Slowly the rifle rose, wavered and fell. It rose again, wavered and fell. Something terrible was wrong with him; something awful was awakening in his soul.

Wingenund had not made a fool of him. The Delaware had led him a long chase, had given him the slip in the forest, not to boast of it, but to hurry back to give his daughter Christian burial.

Wingenund was a Christian!

Had he not been, once having cast his daughter from him, he would never have looked upon her face again.

Wingenund was true to his race, but he was a Christian.

Suddenly Wetzel's terrible temptation, his heart-racking struggle ceased. He lowered the long, black rifle. He took one last look at the chieftain's dark, powerful face.

Then the Avenger fled like a shadow through the forest.

Chapter
XXX

It was late afternoon at Fort Henry. The ruddy sun had already sunk behind the wooded hill, and the long shadows of the trees lengthened on the green square in front of the fort.

Colonel Zane stood in his doorway watching the river with eager eyes. A few minutes before a man had appeared on the bank of the island and hailed. The colonel had sent his brother Jonathan to learn what was wanted. The latter had already reached the other shore in his flatboat, and presently the little boat put out again with the stranger seated at the stern.

"I thought, perhaps, it might be Wetzel." mused the colonel, "though I never knew of Lew's wanting a boat."

Jonathan brought the man across the river, and up the winding path to where Colonel Zane was waiting.

"Hello! It's young Christy!" exclaimed the colonel, jumping off the steps, and cordially extending his hand. "Glad to see you! Where's Williamson. How did you happen over here?"

"Captain Williamson and his men will make the river eight or ten miles above," answered Christy. "I came across to inquire about the young people who left the Village of Peace. Was glad to learn from Jonathan they got out all right."

"Yes, indeed, we're all glad. Come and sit down. Of course you'll stay overnight. You look tired and worn. Well, no wonder, when you saw all that Moravian massacre. You must tell me about it. I saw Sam Brady yesterday, and he spoke of seeing you over there. Sam told me a good deal. Ah! here's Jim now."

The young missionary came out of the open door, and the two young men greeted each other warmly.

"How is she?" asked Christy, when the first greetings had been exchanged.

"Nell's just beginning to get over the shock. She'll be glad to see you."

"Jonathan tells me you got married just before Girty came up with you at Beautiful Spring."

"Yes; it is true. In fact, the whole wonderful story is true, yet I cannot believe as yet. You look thin and haggard. When we last met you were well."

"That awful time pulled me down. I was an unwilling spectator of all that horrible massacre, and shall never get over it. I can still see the fiendish savages running about with the reeking scalps of their own people. I actually counted the bodies of forty-nine grown Christians and twenty-seven children. An hour after you left us the church was in ashes, and the next day I saw the burned bodies. Oh! the sickening horror of the scene! It haunts me! That monster Jim Girty killed fourteen Christians with his sledgehammer."

"Did you hear of his death?" asked Colonel Zane.

"Yes, and a fitting end it was to the frontier 'Skull and Crossbones'."

"It was like Wetzel to think of such a vengeance."

"Has Wetzel came in since?"

"No. Jonathan says he went after Wingenund, and there's no telling when he'll return."

"I hoped he would spare the Delaware."

"Wetzel spare an Indian!"

"But the chief was a friend. He surely saved the girl."

"I am sorry, too, because Wingenund was a fine Indian. But Wetzel is implacable."

"Here's Nell, and Mrs. Clarke too. Come out, both of you," cried Jim.

Nell appeared in the doorway with Colonel Zane's sister. The two girls came down the steps and greeted the young man. The bride's sweet face was white and thin, and there was a shadow in her eyes.

"I am so glad you got safely away from—from there," said Christy, earnestly.

"Tell me of Benny?" asked Nell, speaking softly.

"Oh, yes, I forgot. Why, Benny is safe and well. He was the only Christian Indian to escape the Christian massacre. Heckewelder hid him until it was all over. He is going to have the lad educated."

"Thank Heaven!" murmured Nell.

"And the missionaries?" inquired Jim, earnestly.

"Were all well when I left, except of course, Young. He was dying. The others will remain out there, and try to get another hold, but I fear it's impossible."

"It is impossible, not because the Indian does not want Christianity, but because such white men as the Girtys rule. The beautiful Village of Peace owes its ruin to the renegades," said Colonel Zane impressively.

"Captain Williamson could have prevented the massacre," remarked Jim.

"Possibly. It was a bad place for him, and I think he was wrong not to try," declared the colonel.

"Hullo!" cried Jonathan Zane, getting up from the steps where he sat listening to the conversation.

A familiar soft-moccasined footfall sounded on the path. All turned to see Wetzel come slowly toward them. His buckskin hunting costume was ragged and worn. He looked tired and weary, but the dark eyes were calm.

It was the Wetzel whom they all loved.

They greeted him warmly. Nell gave him her hands, and smiled up at him.

"I'm so glad you've come home safe," she said.

"Safe an' sound, lass, an' glad to find you well," answered the hunter, as he leaned on his long rifle, looking from Nell to Colonel Zane's sister. "Betty, I allus gave you first place among border lasses, but here's one as could run you most any kind of a race," he said, with the rare smile which so warmly lighted his dark, stern face.

"Lew Wetzel making compliments! Well, of all things!" exclaimed the colonel's sister.

Jonathan Zane stood closely scanning Wetzel's features. Colonel Zane, observing his brother's close scrutiny of the hunter, guessed the cause, and said:

"Lew, tell us, did you see Wingenund over the sights of your rifle?"

"Yes," answered the hunter simply.

A chill seemed to strike the hearts of the listeners. That simple answer, coming from Wetzel, meant so much. Nell bowed her head sadly. Jim turned away biting his lip. Christy looked across the valley. Colonel Zane bent over and picked up some pebbles which he threw hard at the cabin wall. Jonathan Zane abruptly left the group, and went into the house.

But the colonel's sister fixed her large, black eyes on Wetzel's face.

"Well?" she asked, and her voice rang.

Wetzel was silent for a moment. He met her eyes with that old, inscrutable smile in his own. A slight shade flitted across his face.

"Betty, I missed him," he said, calmly, and, shouldering his long rifle, he strode away.

Nell and Jim walked along the bluff above the river. Twilight was deepening. The red glow in the west was slowly darkening behind the boldly defined hills.

"So it's all settled, Jim, that we stay here," said Nell.

"Yes, dear. Colonel Zane has offered me work, and a church besides. We are very fortunate, and should be contented. I am happy because you're my wife, and yet I am sad when I think of—him. Poor Joe!"

"Don't you ever think we—we wronged him?" whispered Nell.

"No, he wished it. I think he knew how he would end. No, we did not wrong him; we loved him."

"Yes, I loved him—I loved you both," said Nell softly.

"Then let us always think of him as he would have wished."

"Think of him? Think of Joe? I shall never forget. In winter, spring and summer I shall remember him, but always most in autumn. For I shall see that beautiful glade with its gorgeous color and the dark, shaded spring where he lies asleep."

The years rolled by with their changing seasons; every autumn the golden flowers bloomed richly, and the colored leaves fell softly upon the amber moss in the glade of Beautiful Spring.

The Indians camped there no more; they shunned the glade

and called it the Haunted Spring. They said the spirit of a white dog ran there at night, and the Wind-of-Death mourned over the lonely spot.

At long intervals an Indian chief of lofty frame and dark, powerful face stalked into the glade to stand for many moments silent and motionless.

And sometimes at twilight when the red glow of the sun had faded to gray, a stalwart hunter slipped like a shadow out of the thicket, and leaned upon a long, black rifle while he gazed sadly into the dark spring, and listened to the sad murmur of the waterfall. The twilight deepened while he stood motionless. The leaves fell into the water with a soft splash, a whip-poor-will caroled his melancholy song.

From the gloom of the forest came a low sigh which swelled thrillingly upon the quiet air, and then died away like the wailing of the night wind.

Quiet reigned once more over the dark, murky grave of the boy who gave his love and his life to the wilderness.

GREAT BOOKS,
GREAT SAVINGS!

When You Visit Our Website:
www.kensingtonbooks.com

You Can Save Money Off The Retail Price
Of Any Book You Purchase!

- **All Your Favorite Kensington Authors**
- **New Releases & Timeless Classics**
- **Overnight Shipping Available**
- **eBooks Available For Many Titles**
- **All Major Credit Cards Accepted**

Visit Us Today To Start Saving!
www.kensingtonbooks.com

All Orders Are Subject To Availability.
Shipping and Handling Charges Apply.
Offers and Prices Subject To Change Without Notice.